Mari Hannah is a multi-award-winning, bestselling author/screenwriter. She writes across three crime series: DCI Kate Daniels (in development for TV with Sprout Pictures & Atlantic Nomad), Stone & Oliver and Ryan & O'Neil. Among her numerous awards is a Crime Writers' Association Dagger in the Library 2017. In 2019, Mari was the programming chair of Theakston's Old Peculier Crime Writing Festival. In 2020, she was the recipient of Capital Crime International Crime Writing Festival's Crime Book of the Year. She lives in rural Northumberland with her partner, an ex-murder detective.

CW01497581

HER SISTER'S KILLER

A STONE AND OLIVER NOVEL

MARI HANNAH

ORION

An Orion Paperback
First published in Great Britain in 2025 by Orion Fiction,
an imprint of The Orion Publishing Group Ltd.
Carmelite House, 50 Victoria Embankment
London EC4Y 0DZ

An Hachette UK Company

The authorised representative in the EEA is Hachette Ireland, 8 Castlecourt
Centre, Dublin 15, D15 XTP3, Ireland (email: info@hbgi.ie)

1 3 5 7 9 10 8 6 4 2

A CIP catalogue record for this book is
available from the British Library.

ISBN (Mass Market Paperback) 9781 3987 1598 1
ISBN (Ebook) 9781 3987 1599 8
ISBN (Audio) 9781 3987 1600 1

Typeset by Input Data Services Ltd, Bridgwater, Somerset

Printed in Great Britain by Clays Ltd, Elcograf, S.p.A.

MIX
Paper | Supporting
responsible forestry
FSC® C104740

www.orionbooks.co.uk

For Max, Frances, Daisy and Finn.
I'm so proud of you.

Prologue

You can always tell a cop who's new to death. You get the bare facts. They don't look you in the eye. They can't see past the image in their heads. They can't get away quick enough, desperate to process what no training course has prepared them for – the grim reality of policing. When it finally lands, some don't stick around . . .

Who can blame them?

The on-call detective inspector had been summoned to Wearside shortly after 11 p.m. He'd arrived in Southwick, Sunderland, with no more sense of foreboding on that night than on any other, pulling up behind other police vehicles, their blue lights flashing, all adjacent roads blocked off, police tape restricting public access. A young PC stood at the entrance to the park as he drove in, his face laced with tension.

'Good job,' the DI said as he climbed from his car.

'Thank you, sir.'

'What's your name?'

'Stu. Stuart Wright.'

'First on scene?'

A nod.

Wright had already learned vital lessons: you never got used to it. This was the end for the victim, but also the beginning of a nightmare for her friends and family, who at that moment were blissfully unaware of anything untoward. And for the MIT, the buzz of a murder investigation beginning to bite.

Turning his back on the rookie, the DI scanned the faces at the windows on the quiet street, a community in shock, residents wondering what was going on, imagining the worst, frantically calling to check on loved ones who'd gone out and not come home.

He swung round. 'You checked for signs of life?'

A nod. 'She's just a kid, guv.'

'Show me.'

The DI followed him along the footpath, intending to check for himself. He'd once been at a mortuary when a victim was found to be alive. As they closed on the scene, Wright stepped aside. The detective stopped walking, paralysed by what he could see.

He dry-heaved, his world in pause mode.

She wasn't 'just a kid', she was *his* kid.

A fifteen-year-old going on twenty.

Vibrant, cheeky and smart.

So full of fun.

She lay face up on the ground, body rigid, eyes open, lips parted slightly, a dark patch of blood on her clothing. It looked like a stab wound. Praying that Wright had been mistaken, the detective's breath came in short, sharp gasps as he placed two fingers on his daughter's neck, searching for a pulse.

A pitiful wail left him as he found none.

She was cold.

It took a moment to register that he was on his knees, mind and body shutting down, other cops running towards him. They hauled him off the ground, dragging his dead weight away so as not to contaminate the scene, aware that he knew the victim, though not in what capacity. He couldn't move, couldn't stop shaking, a cold sweat seeping across his body, an unbearable pain in his chest.

Joanna must've been terrified and helpless. He covered his ears, blocking out her imaginary screams, sobbing uncontrollably. He had no sense of time, though before he left for work they'd had words. Joanna had given her mother some lip. He grounded her. She begged him to change his mind and let her meet with friends in Newcastle. He relented, on condition that she was home early, a curfew she swore she'd stick to.

She'd called him earlier.

He hadn't taken the call.

It wasn't that he was busy with another violent death in the city's West End, though that was true. Julie, his wife, had alerted him to the fact that Joanna hadn't kept her promise. She was late.

He was angry, with their daughter and himself.

Guilt consumed him. He'd ignored her call. The fact that she was no longer breathing was down to him. If he lived to a very old age, he'd never forgive himself. It was the 164th day of 1992, a leap year. The date was now ingrained in his head: 12 June. His name was Frank Oliver.

His life was over.

1

The first domino had fallen. Others followed, knocking down the next and the next until the last one fell, a solid wall collapsing inside Detective Chief Inspector David Stone's head – a metaphor of what was to come. If his suspicions were correct, the Murder Investigation Team and those working within it would crash and burn . . .

Frankie Oliver along with them.

David had been about to slip out of the police club, when he overheard a comment that blew him away. Adam Hall had come to the party with another man he didn't recognise. He guessed they had gatecrashed, taking advantage of a free bar. As he continued to observe them, harsh words spilled from Hall's mouth.

Words designed to injure.

Anna Jónsdóttir, an Icelandic DCI who'd flown in as Frankie's special guest, was standing nearby in a figure-hugging cocktail dress, in stark contrast to those who'd got the memo that the party theme was glam rock. Uncomfortable with the exchange going on next to her, she moved away.

Egged on by his pal, Hall persisted –ignored by those around him . . .

Except one.

If David had to describe the expression on the face of their target, he'd have said it was a mixture of fear and rage. So strong was the reaction, it triggered one in him too. The hair on his head stood on end, as if a blast of cold air had swept in from the Arctic, bringing with it a ghost he knew by name only. Even if he'd been able to dismiss what had been said, he'd never forget that look.

He was never meant to see it.

Surrounded by family and friends – newly promoted Inspector Frankie Oliver was feeling ambivalent. She wanted and deserved the next rank. She'd earned it. That said, her departure from the MIT was tinged with sadness. Temporarily, she was destined for a new post in Berwick, regulations dictating that she must return for a stint in uniform before re-joining the murder squad. David had reassured her that it wouldn't be for long. In theory, that sounded great, but in police work there were no guarantees.

That gut-wrenching thought worried her.

All around, beneath congratulatory balloons and streamers, detectives were having the time of their lives. After a complex, often divisive investigation where opinions had been split both in the UK and abroad, the in-fighting was over. Frankie's colleagues were kicking back, making up for lost time.

Deep in the pit of her stomach, she felt an ache.

Everyone important to her was in the police club, bar one.

For a split second, she imagined Joanna among the crowd, always happy – smart as well as funny. It wasn't unusual for her to appear during family celebrations . . . but only as a figment of Frankie's forlorn imagination.

With every fibre of his being, David felt compelled to step in and punch the recipient of the malicious comment, rather than the instigator. Resisting the temptation to take him by the scruff of the neck and haul him outside, he steadied himself. Surrounded by music, couples dancing, cops eating, drinking, having fun, for a moment he convinced himself that he'd misheard.

The thought left him as soon as it arrived.

Something weird was happening.

It was as if someone had flicked a switch, or spiked his drink, plunging him into the centre of an LSD trip. Spandex and glitter worn by partygoers morphed into a kaleidoscope of colour, swaying with the music. The sound was cut. Everyone faded from view, sucked to the edges of the room. A game of statues. No one moving, leaving Hall playing blink first with the officer he'd been winding up.

David shook his head.

The image stuttered, his heart rate dropping to a level nowhere close to normal. He studied the troublemaker closely, having second thoughts. If he was wrong, he'd be entering unknown terrain and may never find his way back. He knew then that challenging Hall wasn't an option. Not here. Not now. Lobbing a grenade onto the dance floor would take out people he cared for. There would be multiple casualties.

Hall supped off his beer and was on the move.

David's laser eyes followed him.

Time to leave?

So soon?

Shadowed by his pal, Hall weaved his way through a sea of bodies, extending an upward nod or handshake with one or two detectives on the way out, a peck on the cheek to wives and girlfriends. There was an arrogance in the way he moved. Too old to strut, he made a fist of it all the same. His jaw was rigid, bloodshot eyes reflecting a small victory as he brushed shoulders with David on the short distance to the exit, like he'd put someone down he didn't rate and enjoyed doing it. That someone wouldn't dare knock him on his arse with witnesses present.

2

'What's up, Frank?' Her father's arm slipped around her shoulders. He was taking the party theme seriously, wearing a ripped vest under a silver satin jacket and purple flares. He had big hair, jet-black eye make-up and a huge smile on his face. He lifted his mobile, taking a selfie of the two of them with Frankie's grandma photobombing in the background, then pulled his daughter into a tight hug, leaning in, dropping his voice to a whisper as the music died. 'If you don't cheer up, rent-a-crowd will bale.'

'I'm fine,' Frankie said.

'Your face disagrees. It's more glum than glam. Just sayin'.'

'I'm just hoping my new posting will be short . . .'

She took in the room. PC Indira Sharma was leaning against the bar deep in conversation with Ben, David's nephew. Behind the counter, Charlie, the MIT's red-faced office manager, was struggling to lend a hand. He was being hassled by DS Dick Abbott to up his game, goaded by journalist Belinda Wells and Bright, the most senior detective on the force.

It was bloody mayhem.

Now, Frankie smiled at her father. 'I'm going miss this lot.'

'Anyone in particular?'

'Dick mostly,' was the first thing that came into her head. That was the truth – she couldn't imagine life without him – though she hoped that throwing her father a crumb would stop him from prying into who she was really going to miss. He too had a soft spot for David, though if he thought she'd slip up while her guard was down he could think again.

'He's no longer sulking?' her dad said.

'Dick?' she scoffed. 'Hell no, we kissed and made up.'

After a kick up the arse from David, Dick had finally accepted that she now outranked him, even though he'd lucked out in the same promotion board despite having been in the job a lot longer.

For a split second, she thought her ploy to steer her father elsewhere had worked.

It hadn't.

'Kiss anyone else tonight?'

'Loads of people . . .' She wondered what he'd seen. 'Including you, as I recall—'

'I meant anyone special—'

'You're special.'

'Not even tempted?'

'Dad!'

He stopped teasing.

Frankie had no intention of putting him in the picture. David wasn't the only reason she wanted to return to the MIT, but he was the main one. She scanned the room, hoping to catch his eye, panic setting in when she didn't spot him. An intense moment between them earlier had been rudely interrupted by her old man dragging her onto the dance floor.

In the men's room, David splashed his face with cold water. Lifting his head, he caught his reflection in the mirror. The image didn't please him. His five o'clock shadow was less designer stubble, more a scruffy individual who hadn't bothered to shave. A big part of him regretted asking another DCI to cover his on-call duty.

He dried his face.

The last time he'd seen Frankie, she was in hysterics – as happy as he'd seen her. Whatever had gone down between them tonight, or might happen in the future, he couldn't spoil her evening by telling her what he'd overheard. A potential break-through in a cold case was no longer her problem.

Besides, he wasn't ready to face her, let alone her family. The Olivers spanned three generations of police officers from as far back as the mid-sixties. Her father and grandfather, also called Frank Oliver, would clock his anxiety for sure.

He wasn't having that.

They had become a big part of his life since he'd arrived back in Northumberland where he grew up – the best decision he'd ever made . . . until now. If there was any truth in what Hall had said tonight, David had a duty to investigate. As it was, he was confident that he had enough ammunition to revisit an open un-solved case he'd known about for some time. He'd been waiting for the opportunity, for a piece of evidence to emerge that would justify his involvement.

He had a starting point.

No more, no less.

Pre-judging the credibility of what Hall had said or second-guessing the outcome wasn't in David's nature. To review a case that had lain on file for decades required time to plan, even longer to execute. The best he could do for Frankie was leave.

Frankie was having doubts. Had she read David wrong when they spoke earlier? Had the wine gone to her head? She was beginning to think she'd made the whole thing up. No one had ever looked at her the way he did. Mutual attraction was one thing. Sexual chemistry was undeniable. You could cut it with a knife.

Frankie could think of nothing else.

A soft voice with a foreign accent came from over her shoulder. She turned to face Anna with a smile so thin and so brief her Icelandic guest almost missed it.

'You have quite a crew,' she said.

'I do.'

'So why do they seem happier than you?' No slouch, Anna had spotted Frankie's melancholy from across the room. 'Isn't the next rank what you want? What you've always dreamed of? You seem oddly distracted, if you don't mind me saying so . . .' She looked away, eyes scanning the room briefly before fixing on Frankie. 'Looking for someone?'

Frankie felt herself blush.

Anna caught the tell. 'I haven't seen him.'

'You read minds now?'

'Maybe . . . I believe in elves, remember?'

Frankie laughed.

Anna raised a suspicious eyebrow, letting her know that her sleeve had grown a heart. 'He was with your grandfather a moment ago. Perhaps they stepped outside for some air.'

'Possibly. Granddad doesn't do noise.'

Anna eyed her empty glass. 'Can I get you a top-up?'

'I've probably had enough.'

'Nonsense. I came a thousand miles. You owe me.'

'A small one then. I'll get it. You're my guest—'

'Which means I'll get served quicker.' Anna took Frankie's glass, a cheeky smile.

Frankie observed her as she walked towards the bar, bodies parting to let in the enigmatic stranger, detectives young and old smitten with their foreign visitor.

When Frankie turned, David was studying her intently from the other side of the room, an odd look on his face. He remained where he was, making no attempt to approach her, yet holding her gaze intently. Instantly, she knew there was something wrong. Unable to fathom the change in his mood, she frowned: *What's up?*

He stared back at her.

Even from a distance, she detected a radical change in his mood, as if he'd done an about-face. Was he trying to tell her something? Or not tell her? She resisted the urge to charge across the room to stake her claim, reminding him that their earlier conversation amounted to a bittersweet goodbye professionally, but a bloody big hint of a personal hello. If he was having reservations about seeing her outside of work, he could think again. Had she not been the centre of attention, she'd grab him by the hand and get the hell out of there.

Instead, she crossed the room slowly. 'What's up?'

'Nothing.'

'Doesn't look like nothing—'

'It's been a long day.'

'Lightweight.' She tried to take him to one side.

He pulled away, turned his back on her and left.

3

The heavens opened as David left the police club, heavy rain bouncing off the ground, pooling in places as he took the road north. It was after 1 a.m. when he arrived at his single-storey seventeenth-century cottage in Pauperhaugh – a tiny Northumberland hamlet with fewer than sixty inhabitants – a place of safety and security since he was a lad. Along with his brother, Luke, David had been raised there by their grandmother when his parents failed to return from a Glen Coe climbing expedition when he was six years old.

No rain here, just an empty village that hadn't changed in centuries.

Not a soul about as he stepped from his car. An owl hooted in the distance – a consolatory, haunting, welcome home. David sat down on a drystone wall where he did his best thinking, breathing in the cool night air. A fox padded across the road, a small mammal in its mouth. As it reached the other side, it turned, completely motionless, wary of its audience, ears erect, wild eyes.

It skulked away as David had done from Frankie's party.

You could say that trauma had brought them closer. He had his problems. Frankie had hers. The only difference was that he'd come clean, emerging little by little from the darkness. That was down to her, but when he tried to reciprocate, broaching the subject of what was bothering her, it was like talking to the wall. She was stuck in the past, unable to share her most intimate secrets, even with him.

And now as he sat quietly in the darkness, her voice echoed in his head . . . *I can't talk about it, David. I'm sorry*. It was an admission that there was something. An experience too painful to share. He may not have discovered what it was until much later, but that day he'd recognised the signs.

Frankie was a mirror image of him.

They'd been to hell and back.

Her weird behaviour manifested itself on a four-hander investigation, one of the worst in the history of the force. Four professional female victims, the last of whom happened to be called Joanna. And though it had taken David ages to get to the bottom of what was troubling her, she'd confessed that the case had got to her.

Inside his tiny cottage, he grabbed a beer from the fridge, prising off the top before entering the living room. He sat down in his grandmother's rocking chair, deep in thought, wondering how Frankie had reacted when he left so abruptly. With no clue how he'd manage to explain it, he considered his options. He could and should consult with his guv'nor. The difficulty was, Bright would demand answers he didn't yet have.

What he'd overheard was hearsay.

He decided to hold the line and gather intel before kicking it upstairs.

Whichever way he jumped, the investigation would be handled correctly, with as little collateral damage to the Oliver family as he could manage. The ramifications for them and for the MIT were enormous.

For Frankie's sake, he couldn't afford to put a foot wrong.

He'd been tempted to pull his guv'nor to one side at the party. In the end, he'd decided to get his head straight before making his move. He was stone-cold sober. Bright was far from it. Frankie had once told David that her sister's violent death had hit Bright almost as hard as it had the family, dominating their lives and hers since she was eleven. David had seen at first-hand how losing a sister at such a young age had affected her.

He hauled himself out of his chair.

From his desk drawer, he pulled out a statement Dick had once brought to his attention to explain away Frankie's reaction to a detective who'd been having a go. Had Dick not moved to protect her, she'd have been facing a disciplinary and possibly a demotion. She'd decked the officer who, like Adam Hall tonight, had spoken out of turn, causing her untold grief, disrespecting her father's inability to bring her sister's murderer to justice before he handed in his warrant card.

David had read the statement several times.

When he turned around, the rocking chair was moving.

Had he believed in ghosts, it would have added to his sense of dread. He knew it was a downdraught in the chimney, a frequent occurrence in his home. And yet it felt symbolic. For a moment, he imagined his late grandmother sitting there, with wise words and sympathy, telling him not to fret until he had something to fret about.

His nan was a gem.

David eyed the Odin stone she'd given him to ward off childhood nightmares after his parents died. Superstitious nonsense, Frankie called it. He'd kept it all the same, hanging it on the side of the fireplace closest to the front door. Not to ward off evil that might enter through it, but as a comforting reminder of the woman who'd sacrificed the end of her life for the potential of his.

Below, the fire in the grate was neatly set. David put a match to it. There was no way he'd sleep with this case weighing on his mind. Unfolding the statement, he sat down and began to read . . .

I am Detective Inspector Frank Oliver, Northumbria Police. At 23:05, on Friday, 12 June 1992 I was the on-call DI for the force area. I was called to an incident at Park Terrace, Southwick, Sunderland, described as a fatal stabbing of a young woman. On arrival at the scene, I was shown to the body by PC Stuart Wright. On further examination, I found that the young woman was my fifteen-year-old daughter, Joanna Oliver . . .

A shiver ran the length of David's spine. He didn't read on. He'd read it before, so many times he'd lost count. Having made formal identification, Frank Oliver II had left the scene and contacted senior supervision. He was informed that he could take no further part in the investigation and withdrew, the fact that he had to be ruled in or out as a suspect adding insult to injury.

It was a painful read the first time . . .

Tonight, it was ten times worse; not only because David now knew Frankie's father personally, but also because she hadn't shared the fact that her dad was the first detective to reach the crime scene. Had he not been told, to save her from a disciplinary hearing, a potential assault charge, David may never have known about it.

The document in his hand was a cold hard statement of the facts. A contemporaneous note of how and why Frank Oliver had come to attend the scene and what he discovered when he got there. The short record only told half the story. Hiding between the sterile language was emptiness: helplessness, heartbreak, anger, guilt, and denial of a father in distress. David couldn't begin to imagine what had really gone down that night. How any parent found the strength to get over such an occurrence was beyond his comprehension, but . . .

Frank Oliver II was an extraordinary man.

4

Did that really happen? That was the question Frankie was asking herself. Living at the coast, forty-five minutes away from Newcastle city centre, she'd arranged to stay with her parents, saving the price of a cab. Now she was having second thoughts. Moping was best done at home . . .

Alone.

In a crowded taxi Frankie felt disconnected from those around her, lost in her own thoughts. Questions were piling up. Were two pips on her shoulder worth leaving the MIT? Undoubtedly. Would she miss her mates? Of course, but she'd make new ones. The old ones would still be there when she returned.

Would she miss David?

Hours ago, she'd have said yes.

Now, she had to think about it.

She'd put her life on hold for someone to come along who'd care for her in a way that no one else had. Until now, the love of a close family had always been enough. More than enough. Frankie considered herself lucky. Despite a shared loss that had cast a shadow over them, her family had remained solid. But, as the miles flew by, Frankie realised that life had more to offer all of them than chasing ghosts.

She glanced sideways.

Her mum and dad were holding hands. They had each other. The same could be said of her grandparents . . . and of her sister Rae, who was in a civil partnership with Andrea, a Traffic cop, one of Frankie's closest friends.

What did she have?

For years, she and David had stared death in the face, personally and professionally, a shared grief drawing them ever closer. Tonight, he'd given her hope that they were meant to be. She'd begun to believe that they'd be good together, always, and for ever. She felt safe in his company. Now she felt vulnerable, a lingering doubt that she could ever trust anyone enough to fall in love and be happy.

From the day he blew in from the Met where he'd spent the first fifteen years of his police career, she'd been attracted to him, though hadn't acted on it. In fact, she'd ruled it out. The guy had more baggage than British Airways. She didn't want to complicate his life, or hers. So, pushing a potential relationship away as unattainable seemed like the thing to do, until she was handed her new posting. Then it became not only possible, but essential – a case of not knowing what you've got till it's gone.

And now it was gone.

His loss.

He'd pissed off without a word. No good luck wishes or see you around. No thanks for everything or call me invitation. Why? Had he got cold feet? Did he not think she was anxious too? Wasn't that half the fun of transitioning from friendship to a relationship? It was hard to describe how she was feeling now. He'd spoiled what had otherwise been a cracking night, a new beginning – in more ways than one.

'You OK, Fr . . .' Mitch hesitated. 'Boss, I meant boss.'

Frankie felt a stab of pride.

Although she outranked her mentee, he'd never called her that before. Probably never would again if she didn't make it back to the MIT. He'd cadged a lift home, hopping in the front of the cab, Frankie behind the driver, her mum on the far side in the rear, her dad squashed in between.

'You may as well talk to the wall,' he said to Mitch. 'Her mum's sending the zeds up.'

'Wrong. I'm resting!' Julie said. 'It's been an emotional day. A happy day.'

'Go to sleep, love. If I didn't know better, I'd have said Frankie was already there. Only her eyes are wide open and currently fixed on me. Full of hell might be an apt description, like someone stole her chips.'

'Sorry, I was miles away.' Frankie's apology was for Mitch, not her father.

'In which direction?' her dad pushed.

He knew.

He'd always been able to read her.

The cab pulled over, a chance to ignore him taking her somewhere she didn't want to go. Mitch jumped out of the car, turning to face her through the glass. Seeing his rueful expression, Frankie wound down the window. 'Hey!' She summoned a smile. 'Keep my seat warm. I'll be back before you know it.'

'Thanks, boss.'

'For what?'

'Everything.'

He fell over himself to wish her well. Briefly, it made her think of David, which would have brought a tear to her eye had she been less angry. He'd trusted her instinct, bringing Mitch into the MIT as a rookie. Under her guidance, he'd more than earned his place.

She raised the window as the cab sped off.

Her father put his arm around her shoulder, giving it a gentle squeeze. 'Any idea why David shot off?'

'Did he?' Frankie kept her eyes front. 'I didn't notice.'

'Your pet lip says you did.'

She didn't answer.

'You were about four years old when you told your first lie,' he teased. 'You're no better at it now than you were then.'

'Speaks the guy who knows the difference between lying and sidestepping a stupid question,' Julie said in Frankie's defence. 'And doesn't know when to mind his own business.'

Frankie looked out of the window, stifling a grin.

Her dad continued. 'Want to talk about it?'

'There's nowt to say.'

'I'm a good listener.'

'Is that a euphemism for nosy?' Frankie turned to look at him. 'Didn't you once tell me that some things are better left unsaid?'

'I didn't mean me, did I? I'm your old man. You can tell me anything—'

'Especially if you want it broadcast.' Julie giggled, opening her eyes, turning to face her daughter. 'Keep schtum, Frances. He'll get the message . . . eventually. If he doesn't, he can get out and walk.'

Grinning at his daughter, Frank changed the subject. 'You enjoyed the party, didn't you?'

How could she not? Her family had insisted on shelling out for the lot, Rae taking care of the music, Andrea the guests, her mum and grandma sorting the catering, her old man picking up the bar bill – no mean feat, given the appetite of a team of hungry, thirsty detectives making the most of their freedom while seeing her off with a bang.

Frankie beamed at him. 'It was really cool.'

'Did David think so?'

'Stop digging, Dad.'

'Only asking.'

'Sounds like an interrogation to me.' Julie gave him a playful nudge with her elbow. 'Zip it or sling your hook. I'm serious, Frank. Your choice.'

He made a face at Frankie.

She laughed, her mood improving.

She could never stay mad at him for long.

There was no one in the world she loved more.

She laid her head on his shoulder, as she used to as a kid with a problem only he could solve. Somehow, he always managed to lift her. He stroked her hair, soothing her, letting her know that when she was ready, whatever was bothering her, he'd be there to help her through it.

Now, her mum was really sending the zeds up.

Her father had clocked it too. He dropped his voice so as not to wake her. 'You'll work it out, Frank. You always do. And since when does my girl sulk over boys? David is the on-call SIO—'

'No, he's not. He'd arranged cover . . .'

'Doesn't mean he wasn't required.'

'True. Why are you making excuses for him?'

'What other explanation could there be?'

'You know David . . .' She tilted her head, a wry smile developing as she met his gaze. 'It was probably time for his cocoa.'

5

David was facing the investigation of his life. He'd given Frankie his word that he'd catch her sister's killer, laying the case to rest, Joanna along with it . . . finally, a promise he intended to keep. One that would end her father's obsession with her hideous death. Given the time-lapse, reopening the enquiry wasn't straightforward. Joanna had died before many of the MIT's records were digitised. The investigation would involve a painstaking study of hard-copy documentation. Time was no barrier to justice, but no fresh evidence had presented itself . . .

Until now.

David took another swig of his beer. The dilemma he faced was significant. Keeping his suspicions from Frankie would be viewed as a violation of trust in a relationship that was otherwise open and honest. The omission – he had no intention to deceive – didn't sit well with him. Even though he'd be acting for her own good, there wasn't a snowball's chance in hell she'd see it that way.

If she got wind of it . . .

David wouldn't go there.

The best he could hope for was that her new posting would keep her occupied. He had no doubt that she'd give it her all. The cases she came across would consume her, as they always did. By luck, not by accident, her new beat was perfect. Berwick was the most northerly Northumbria Police outpost, a long way from Middle Earth – the squad's nickname for Northern Area Command owing to its location on Middle Engine Lane. Consequently, she'd be out of his way during her shifts, geographically speaking, breathing space while he got his head straight.

He was grateful for that, though the thought lingered.

Outside of her shift pattern was a different story. She'd be around, keeping in contact with ex-colleagues, possibly in and out of her former base, less than a thirty-minute drive from her apartment at Coble Quay in Amble, a stopping-off point, halfway between her home and that of her parents. There was nothing he could do about that, except pray.

What he had in mind to do she couldn't be involved in, or even party to, but therein lay the rub. She was one of the smartest detectives he knew. Unless he was 100 per cent discreet, he wouldn't keep it from her for long.

He stared into the flickering fire, then checked his phone for messages, relieved to see that Frankie hadn't been in touch. He was about to pocket the device, when it rang in his hand, killing the silence in his tiny living room.

Panic subsided when he saw that the caller was in fact Ben, the nephew-cum-surrogate-son he'd inherited when his father – David's brother, Luke – died in a car crash on his way to collect him from the hospital.

At the time, David hadn't reacted well.

He was angry and grieving, unwilling to take the lad in.

It struck David how much his life had changed since then. That was down to Frankie. Family was everything to her. Without her intervention, he'd have none. What would she think of him if she knew he'd promised Ben a lift home, then abandoned the party, leaving his nephew high and dry. Swearing under his breath, David pressed to answer, steeling himself for a blasting he deserved, while trying to sound upbeat.

'Hey, Ben—'

'You left me stranded.' His speech was slurred.

'No, I didn't,' David lied. 'I'm busy.'

'Where the fuck are you?'

He sidestepped the question. 'I'm the on-call SIO—'

'I asked where you are, not who you are.'

'Need to know, mate.'

Ben mimicked David. 'Busted is what you are, *mate*. I can hear great-grandma's clock ticking away in the background, so tell the truth. You forgot me and went home . . . again.'

The kid never missed a trick. 'Where are you?'

'Outside the police club like Billy No-Mates with no wheels. Are you coming back for me?'

David eyed his empty beer bottles. 'Not possible. I've had a drink. Grab a hotel and get your head down.'

'On my wages?' Ben scoffed. 'You're 'avin' a laugh.'

'Can't you stay with Belinda?'

'Would you choose to kip at her place without a lock on the door?'

Despite his preoccupation with the night's events, David laughed. The journalist, Ben's boss and mentor at *North East Times*, was a man-eating, daiquiri-swilling, sex-crazed woman who'd once told him that the word age should only ever be used if it followed bond. The scary lady was a close friend who'd nick-named his nephew the Boy Wonder.

'I'll shout you then,' David said.

'Really?'

'Anything to shut you up.'

'Cool. Meliá?'

'Premier Inn. And if that's not good enough, try a park bench.'

David hung up, a smile on his face after their friendly banter.

His life was enriched by having Ben around, even if he didn't always get fatherhood right. When David's brother died, Ben was rude and hostile, an orphaned university dropout permanently off his face on weed, but Frankie's interpretation was sympathetic. She saw the lad as a lost soul, begging to be found.

They had fallen out over it.

Past fights were long forgotten, harsh words not so much. David remembered one heated argument with Frankie. His raised voice echoed in his head . . .

Since when did my family become your business?

Despite his intransigence, Frankie wouldn't let go.

23

She'd single-handedly healed the rift between man and boy, shaken sense into the two of them, convincing David that he'd live to regret rejecting his brother's only child, that the accident was not Ben's fault. Pulling Ben up when he was spiralling out of control, giving him a place to live while David got his shit together. And now, several years on, *her* family had become his business, the roles reversed, a chance to reciprocate.

6

Berwick's nick was on Church Street in the centre of the town. The architectural design of the building was impressive, with mullioned windows and a stair tower at one end, an arched hood at the other. Dating back to the late nineteenth century, it was deserving of its Grade II listing, purpose-built as a law court and police station, centrally located for the community it served.

The upside presented itself as soon as Frankie arrived. For the first time, she had a designated parking spot. That pleased her no end. No jockeying for one, like at Middle Earth. She'd arrived early to meet the team and get to grips with local priorities. She relished the opportunity to get stuck in, though her uniform felt odd after spending years in plain clothes.

Her new office was large, the desk free of paperwork, no murder wall to consult on the way in, no colleagues asking for this or that before her coat was off. The downside hit her the minute she walked through the door. She missed the buzz of human activity, the adrenalin rush of an overnight breakthrough. The peace in a station that was only open on a part-time basis felt decidedly alien.

Having closed the door, she sat down, the isolation hitting her like a brick. In the MIR, her desk was never free. Murder investigations were, by their very nature, complex and time sensitive. Often, they involved a manhunt for a killer on the loose. The first few hours were critical in finding evidence and witnesses. These cases generated hundreds of enquiries. Developments were ongoing, priorities changing on a daily, sometimes hourly, basis – an important and crucial role that kept her busy.

Uniform posts were different.

Everything she did from now on would be reactive: incidents that triggered an immediate response, decision-making on the spot, split-second timing involving life or death, sending troops out to deal, then it would be over. There would be no taking shit home because there weren't enough hours in the day. It was purely and simply getting over a problem or issue, a situation or offence. Dealing with it, then handing it to the next shift inspector. Forgetting it. That was hard for anyone with major enquiry experience.

Frankie was now a team leader.

She could do this.

Last night, David had fallen asleep in his rocking chair through sheer exhaustion, waking at 5 a.m., freezing cold, the fire having died in the grate. In the shower, he'd cobbled together a strategy, convincing himself that in not sharing with Frankie, he'd be protecting a friend, as well as an asset, should she choose to return to the MIT. On the other hand, he'd be committing professional suicide if he attempted to keep it a secret from his guv'nor.

Bright was not a man to mess with.

Incurring his wrath was never wise.

Given his close connection to the Oliver family, Bright would expect total transparency. So, at the end of a very long day, when he'd finished crossing t's and dotting i's on his current murder file to the satisfaction of the Crown Prosecution Service, he made his way to Bright's office ready to make his play.

The corridor seemed longer, the nameplate on the door shinier: *Detective Chief Supt Phillip Reginald Bright*, a reminder of his seniority.

David knocked and waited.

'Come!' Bright looked up as the door swung inward.

David thought he looked tired. 'Sir, apologies for the timing of my visit. I'd like a moment, if I may.' He hesitated. 'It's an odd one. I'm afraid it can't wait.'

Bright put down his fountain pen. 'You'd better sit then.'

'Thank you.'

David pulled up a chair, hiking up the knees of his trousers as he sat down, resting his right foot on his left knee, arms relaxed . . . even if he wasn't. Regretting the fact that he hadn't fully rehearsed his delivery, he cleared his throat. 'I'd like your agreement to run a covert operation in connection with a cold case, guv. I'd rather not say which one at this stage.'

Bright narrowed his eyes. 'Because?'

'What I have in mind requires a very close team, sir. Myself and one other—'

'And who might that be?'

'Indira Sharma. It's sensitive—'

'Then it requires someone with skill and integrity.'

The receiver's voice arrived in David's head: *Indi is good, reliable too, but Frankie can knock spots off her.* Pam Bond was right, but in this instance, Frankie was out of the equation.

David was skating on thin ice. 'Sir, I sincerely believe Indira is that person—'

'Are you out of your mind?' Taking off his reading specs, Bright threw them carelessly on his desk. 'As nice as she is, as professional as she appears to be, Sharma is an aide, not a detective.'

'Not for long, if I have anything to do with it.' David meant it. 'Besides, it suits me that she's not part of the team. If that doesn't suit you, you have the power to change her status.'

'Why her?'

'She's ex-Professional Standards, ex-HR, with the necessary authority to access records and any other systems we require to carry out enquiries that may lead to a full-blown review and hopefully a result. It's up to you if you make her a substantive detective or not. I'm not bothered, either way. And no one will question it if she makes a detective grade. She's earned it.'

'I hear you . . .' Bright's tone was laced with suspicion. 'What interests me is what's not coming out of your mouth.'

'I want the operation off-book, guv. If my request is granted, Indi will be temporarily seconded to an admin role, working for me – or should I say, us. During the last case she surpassed herself, proving invaluable to an investigation that also involved historical elements. She's a shoo-in.'

'Is she?' Bright sat forward, spreading his upper body, one hand on his hip, the other propping up his chin.

'With respect, I know her better than you do,' David added. 'I trust her. What she lacks in experience she makes up for in commitment. She has the skills and abilities and will be working under my guidance. To begin with, only three people will know about it: you . . . and the two of us. It's imperative that no one outside of that small circle is in the know.'

7

Having introduced herself to those on duty within the curtilage of her new home, Frankie had a word with the station sergeant to see who was doing what. County lines incidents seemed to be a big priority, the exploitation of vulnerable young people a major concern. With a handle on what she might expect going forward, she called in an area car, hoping to meet those who were out and about dealing with the public.

She spent the rest of the day with Sergeant Graham Ross, a Scot of around her age: fit, dark-haired, a small beard, with the look of Glasgow-born James McAvoy. They shared the same dry sense of humour and he'd been good company. Moreover, he had a calmness about him. When he spoke, people listened. Some of the stuff they dealt with had taken hours, others just minutes. Nothing too serious . . .

That was about to change.

They had just reached the outskirts of Berwick, ready for a break, when the call came in. Now they were heading south at high speed through rural countryside, blue lights engaged, racing to a live incident: a serious RTA, a four-car pile-up on the A1, the main arterial route in and out of the region. Other emergency service personnel were also en route, including GNAAS, the Great North Air Ambulance Service.

Already, Frankie was learning.

She missed the familiarity of her old stomping ground, and everything that went with it, but being back in uniform was a reminder of why she'd entered policing – to preserve life. Some officers spent their whole careers out in the sticks with little or no backup. In Newcastle city centre and its surrounding suburbs, you were never far from help, even if it wasn't a cop, whereas the isolation of North Northumberland was a very different world.

The light was fading. Rain began to spot the windscreen – an added complication.

Anxious to get to the scene, Frankie glanced into the driver's side, realising that if she hadn't been there Graham would be single-crewed, facing God knows what, with finite resources beyond a high-viz jacket and a bit of nous. At night, that was a lonely, scary, sometimes highly dangerous place to be.

The man sitting beside her showed no signs of being fazed by the situation.

The radio burst into life, an update from Control. 'All units. We've had confirmation of one fatality from an off-duty doctor. Ambulance not yet on scene.'

Frankie responded: '7151, we're ten minutes out. Are Traffic responding?'

'En route from the south. ETA, same as yours, Inspector.'

'OK, keep us posted.'

'Shit! This could tie us up for hours.' Graham glanced at Frankie. 'You want out?'

She turned to face him. 'I'm surplus to requirements?'

'Just asking. I can radio for a vehicle to pick you up if you'd prefer—'

'Not a chance. The more bodies, the better. Ours, I mean, not theirs.'

Up ahead, cars were pulling over to let them by. Others were not. Graham engaged his siren, an audible shove. Now, other road users were responding. Like David, Graham was an advanced police driver, shifting through the gears smoothy, his sole focus to get to the scene safely, as soon as humanly possible.

Frankie was impressed.

'Coming from the MIT, this is a bit of a step down for you, isn't it?' he said.

'The price you pay for the next rank, Graham.'

'We have our moments up here too.'

'I can tell . . .' Frankie did her best to mask her unease. Dead bodies she'd learned to cope with. Dying ones, bleeding out in a mass of mangled metal until machinery arrived to release them, was a new kind of hell. 'You have my commitment for as long as I'm here. I'm hoping we might learn from one another.'

'Sounds like a plan.' Graham threw her a half-smile.

Frankie liked him already. 'You show me your moves, I'll show you mine.'

Spotting a gap in the traffic, he floored the accelerator.

8

Clever detectives kept their powder dry, but Bright was having none of that. There was more to what Stone was saying. The Chief Super had no intention of leaving for the day without getting to the bottom of it. Using his intercom, he asked Ellen, who happened to be his second wife as well as his civilian PA, if she'd bring in a pot of coffee, making it clear that there were to be no interruptions beyond that. She arrived a couple of minutes later, a big smile for David as she set the drinks down on Bright's desk.

'Are you going to be late finishing?' she asked him.

'Yes,' he said. 'It might take a while. Take the car. If the DCI needs my ear that badly, he can give me a lift home.' He waited for her to leave before inviting Stone to carry on.

David reiterated the need to keep his investigation under the radar for the time being. 'Let me be clear, sir. No resources or finances are to be assigned or linked. You know what it's like. As soon as we have a budget, it becomes a thing. Everyone in the force will know about it.'

'Except me, apparently. Stop talking bollocks. I want precise details. Which cold case are we talking about?'

'I'll update you in a day or two, guv.'

Bright's temper flared. 'You'll update me now.'

As Graham and Frankie closed on their destination, it began to pour, making driving more hazardous. The road turned red as a stream of brake lights illuminated the wet tarmac, drivers responding to satnav alerts that the road ahead was blocked. Control were reporting that Traffic cars had closed the road south of their position, preventing northbound traffic, setting up a diversion, rerouting drivers away from the crash scene, everyone doing their bit. On minor roads, other units were stationary, preventing entry onto the A1 southbound.

As vehicles moved out of the way to let the area car through, an articulated vehicle put on his hazard lights and came to a stop. Approximately half a mile ahead, strobe lights could be seen, lighting up the night sky. Graham jumped out, asking the HGV driver to create a barrier the width of the carriageway, enabling him and his inspector to proceed safely to the scene of the RTA.

The DCI's half-arsed plan hadn't failed yet. It would if he pushed Bright any further without levelling with him. Taking a deep breath, David repeated most of what he'd overheard from Adam Hall less than twenty-four hours ago at Frankie's party. Having laid it out in more detail than he'd originally intended, there was zero chance that Bright hadn't worked out exactly which investigation he was asking to reopen, though he didn't confirm or deny it.

'What is it you think you know?' he said.

'I'm not entirely sure,' David replied honestly. 'I wasn't close enough to catch it all. Hall was mouthing off about an unsolved case where a white van was never traced and a missing jacket, both of which flagged up a case too close to home. Guv, I checked, there is only one murder investigation he could have been referring to.'

'Joanna Oliver.'

'Correct. I couldn't believe what I was hearing, especially with the family there. I'm surprised one of my crew didn't deck him. He seemed to know a lot about the case. I'm going to check if he worked on it.'

'I can save you the trouble.'

'He didn't?'

Bright shook his head. 'I headhunted the team myself. For obvious reasons I couldn't use Frank Oliver, just as you can't use Frankie now. In fact, if I agree to this, neither needs to know squat until I say otherwise.'

'Understood.'

'How good is your information?'

'Not as good as my gut feeling, guv.'

'Then let me tell you how this is going to go. Frank Oliver was a legend in his time. Still is in my book. He suffered every parent's worst nightmare, but he's a survivor. From chaos, he somehow carved out a level of normality for his parents, his grief-stricken wife and his surviving children. As you are aware, they adore him. What you don't know is, I am . . . I was, Joanna's godfather.'

'I'm so sorry. I didn't—'

'Save it.'

'Sir, what I now suspect but cannot yet prove might uncover the truth of what happened to Joanna. I appreciate that "might" is a modest word for such a colossal responsibility, but you have my word, I'll give it my best shot.'

Bright considered that for a moment. 'If my hand-picked team weren't able to find the perpetrator, what chance is there that you will be able to do it with a rookie wannabe detective and a fucking computer screen?'

'By making connections in a way that wasn't available to detectives at the time. All I can promise you is a thorough examination—'

'Not good enough. Every one of your crew knows that Joanna met a horrible end. They're not just good at what they do, they're excellent. And yet you have no plan to take them into your confidence?'

'With respect, it wouldn't take a genius to work out why that is, would it, sir?' The heavy hint made Bright's jaw bunch, his eyes flare. Before he could respond, David moved on. 'Guv, all I can see is a red flag. This is your call, not mine.'

For a moment, there was silence.

Bright finally broke the impasse. 'You had better be right about this, Stone. Because if you cause the Oliver family a nanosecond of angst over this, and it turns out to be nothing more than some loudmouth talking out of his arse, I will see to it that you piss off back to London and stay there.'

9

At the epicentre of the accident, Frankie grabbed her hat off the rear seat and jumped out first. Leaving his blue lights flashing, Graham followed, pulling on his high-viz jacket, handing her a spare he fished from the boot of the vehicle. It was filthy and four sizes too big. She shrugged it on, her eyes widening as she took in the mayhem going on around her, the strong smell of diesel and petrol fumes hitting her senses, filling her with dread. One car was on fire, a couple of civilians attempting to extinguish the flames, at great risk to themselves.

'Where the hell are the dash and splash when you need them?' she said.

Graham shrugged. 'Welcome to rural Northumberland.'

Frankie did up her coat, scanning the scene.

Bits of metal she didn't recognise were strewn across the road. Behind the crashed vehicles, others whose drivers had managed to brake in time to avoid the collision could not be moved because they were empty, their headlights illuminating the devastation. Fearing a rear-end shunt, doors had been flung open, drivers and passengers fleeing to higher ground. They now stood on the embankment, drenched and shivering, some wearing no outer clothing, one with small children, another with a baby in arms, with no shelter from the driving rain.

Frankie wondered how her sister-in-law dealt with scenes of such devastation daily. Andrea had once told Frankie that when tending casualties, she was on autopilot, stemming the bleeding until medical help arrived, talking to the injured, holding hands, offering reassurance, keeping calm herself.

Easier said than done.

Frankie's chest was pounding.

The only two officers in attendance weren't from Andrea's unit, they were from Frankie's new station, both male.

Graham moved towards them.

She followed.

As they approached, the tallest of the two, a mountain of a man with rugged features and a worried look, addressed her directly. Introducing himself as PC Richard MacArthur, his colleague as PC Asim Haq, he updated her. 'There were two casualties in the Toyota, Inspector.' He'd heard her on the radio. 'One dead, one badly injured. We managed to get her out. It doesn't look good.'

'She has a pulse?'

'She did when we arrived.'

Frankie looked towards what was left of the Toyota. It was facing the wrong way. A woman was lying on the ground next to it, a torniquet pulled tight around her thigh to prevent blood loss. A younger female she assumed was the off-duty doctor on her knees, working frantically, administering CPR.

'She's the doctor?' Frankie had to be sure.

MacArthur nodded. 'Dr Gaynor Charlton. Lucky for us, she's an A&E consultant, Royal Infirmary of Edinburgh. She's got no chance.'

Frankie shot him a look requiring no explanation. 'She's doing her best, which is more than I can say for you.'

She left it there.

MacArthur was showing signs of anxiety. He wasn't the only one. Everyone in her eyeline had that same gaunt look, visibly distressed, ashen-faced, some civilians unable to hold onto their tears. The stress of a high-speed collision had taken its toll on witnesses and service personnel alike.

It can't have been easy for first responders.

Ordinarily, the doctor would have been Frankie's first port of call, but she was working frantically to restart the casualty's heart.

Another two officers arrived.

Within seconds, Frankie was directing operations. 'I want photos, reg numbers, IDs if there are any to be found. Then one of you get yourself over there' – she nodded towards the crowd of onlookers – 'we need names, addresses, statements from everyone.' She turned to face the man she'd spent the day with. 'Graham, have I forgotten anything?'

'No, we stay put until the accident investigator arrives.'

They all looked up, shielding their eyes as the air ambulance appeared from behind the trees, shining a spotlight on the scene, its rotor blades slicing through the rain, a deafening sound above their heads. They would be videoing the lot, deciding where it was safe to put down.

'What do you want me to do?' Haq asked.

Graham gestured towards the doctor. 'Go and give her a hand.'

He hesitated. 'I've never done it before, Sarge.'

'Well now's your chance,' Frankie said. 'You'll be fine, Asim . . . just take your lead from the doc. She looks like she needs a breather.' When Haq had gone, she turned to MacArthur. 'Have you checked every vehicle, Richard?'

'Apart from that one.' He pointed at a dark Mercedes van. 'We just got here.'

'OK, lend Graham a hand, I'll go.'

10

With Bright's warning ringing in his ears, David left Middle Earth. He'd got his point across, but his guv'nor could and would end his career if he upset Frankie or her family after all they had been through.

David wondered how her first day had gone. He hadn't heard from her and didn't expect to.

Having been in the CID for much of her career, she'd told him that throwing on a uniform felt like a backward step. She had a point, reminding him that HMIC – HM Inspectorate of Constabulary – had described the lack of trained detectives as a national crisis, some forces having taken on civilian investigators and retired officers to fill the gap.

There were two sides to every coin.

David couldn't deny that he shared her opinion. Sending her to the back of beyond was nonsensical. She was too valuable. The MIT needed detectives of her calibre, her diligence and experience. However, in his current predicament, it served his purpose that she was working in Berwick, if only in the short term.

Exchanging her police-issue gloves for a forensic pair, Frankie reached into the Mercedes and killed the engine, getting an eyeful of the occupants, two middle-aged guys. Neither was moving. The driver was slumped over, his shaved head resting on the steering wheel, his passenger tilted sideways, his upper body half in and half out of the smashed nearside window, his neck bent at an odd angle that looked impossible to fix.

Both men were covered in blood.

Frankie swallowed the bile in her throat. Without moving the driver, she felt for a pulse. Nothing. Shifting to the passenger side, she did the same. This guy was warm to the touch – but also beyond help.

A cry from nearby drew her focus.

She swung round, unable to see anyone alive bar Graham, MacArthur, Haq and the female doctor. Dropping to the ground, Frankie shone her flashlight under the van in case someone had been flung from another vehicle, ending up beneath it.

She strained to listen.

Still nothing.

She stood.

No one on the embankment seemed to be in distress, searching for a lost loved one who'd wandered away in the dark. Dismissing the cry as a figment of an inflated imagination, Frankie was about to walk away, when she heard it again, barely a whimper this time. Now she was sure it was real.

There was another casualty nearby.

This one she might save.

David was listening to a report on his car radio about a serious RTA that the police were dealing with on the A1, the road closed in both directions. Simultaneously, a traffic hazard popped up on the digital cockpit in his car, a thick red line showing a substantial blockage for some distance north and southbound. He slowed, grateful that it wouldn't affect him. Already he was indicating his intention to take the slip road onto what locals referred to as the Coldstream Road. However, it hadn't passed him by that the A1 was the very road Frankie would be using to get home.

That worried him.

The thought lingered in the back of his mind until he could bear it no longer. He'd already had one sleepless night. Unable to contemplate another, he got in touch with Control, asking what was going on.

'Multiple RTA,' the controller said.

'Yeah, I worked that out all by myself.'

'It's a nasty one, by all accounts.'

'Casualties?' David had to ask.

'The bodies are piling up, guv.'

Stepping sideways, Frankie picked her way through metal frag-ments, torn-off windscreen wipers, smashed glass and personal belongings to reach the rear of the van. Expecting to find it locked, she wondered if Graham had a jemmy she might use to smash her way in and check for signs of life.

That distressed cry was loud in her head.

Training her torch on the ground, she found nothing. Raising the beam, she swept it across the badly damaged rear end and was immediately concerned. The door was slightly ajar, with evidence that it had been forced open from the inside.

Someone had legged it out the back.

Fleetingly, she wondered who might have saved themselves, ignoring the plight of the dead guys in the front and the person whose cry she'd heard a moment ago. Finding this suspicious, she turned to face the crowd of onlookers, wondering if the person who'd fled the vehicle was watching her, watching them. No one struck her as a potential third man – and none of the women looked like they had the strength to blow out a candle, let alone escape from the wreckage of the van without specialist help.

Intrigued, she refocused on the vehicle.

Pulling open the door, the familiar stench of urine, alcohol and stale smoke made her nauseous. Hauling herself up and inside, she scanned the space with her flashlight, first the roof, then the sides, finding nothing but an empty shell, no tools, stickers or documentation that might identify its use. Training the torch downward to the wet corrugated steel floor, she discov-ered shards of a vodka bottle she presumed had been smashed on impact, cigarette butts and food packaging with a recent sell-by date. Instinctively, her detective brain kicked in, her father's advice arriving in her head.

Details matter, Frankie . . .

Everything you see is a signpost.

Wherever she was, whatever she was observing, Frankie did so with patience and a sharp eye. On the other side of the loading area was a filthy sleeping bag, its zip open. Someone had been crashing there recently. Wondering who and why, Frankie moved the torch, finding a lumpy blanket riddled with holes and something else she was all too familiar with. Blood spatter. As she bent down to pull at the woollen material, it moved.

11

David had called Frankie several times during the night. She hadn't picked up. At his wits' end, he'd even tried her landline, as people used to in the last century, almost unheard of now, unless you were into cold-calling. Unsurprisingly, Frankie didn't pick that up either. He texted. Still no reply.

He'd tried to get his head down.

He couldn't.

Frustrated by not knowing where she was, or in what condition, he tossed and turned, occasionally checking the time. At 5 a.m. he gave up. He showered, dressed, scribbled a note for Ben to find when he got home, then left the house, driving at breakneck speed to Middle Earth, where he knew he'd get answers.

The car park was relatively empty when he arrived.

With a sense of dread, he rushed inside, taking the stairs two at a time.

In his office, without removing his coat, he sat down at his desk. Using his warrant card to log on to his computer, he brought up the force-wide incident log, tapping his fingers impatiently as the RTA began to load. *Four fatalities* were the first words he saw. Then his hand flew to his mouth, a sharp intake of breath . . .

Frankie's name jumped out at him.

She was not among the dead but listed as the OIC at the scene, which explained why his calls had been ignored. It sounded horrendous, a baptism of fire on her first day in a new post. Scooping his mobile off the desk, he put it down again, then thought he'd try once more. He could never, would never, give up on Frankie.

*

Frankie was semi-conscious, drifting between sleep and wakefulness, disturbing images of the RTA flashing before her eyes. A text alert arrived. Several had come in during the night, none of which she'd accessed until around 4 a.m. David sounded more and more concerned in each one. That made her feel guilty. Her lack of response had nothing to do with his disappearance from her party and everything to do with the fact that if they had spoken last night, if she'd heard his voice, she'd have lost her shit in public.

Of all the people she wanted to talk to, it was him.

Slipping her mobile from her pocket, she tapped on his text.

He'd kept it short: Tough shift?

She keyed a reply: You could say.

The delivery tick appeared, followed by a blinking ellipsis . . .

You're OK though, right?

Yeah. Tied up. Call you later.

David wasn't fooled. Frankie was not OK – and probably wouldn't call him. Still, if she was talking, she was breathing. That's all that mattered. In a better frame of mind, he got up and made his way along the corridor towards Bright's office, greeting some of the MIT as they arrived for work, though not stopping to chat. Indira, the person he was desperate to see, was not among them.

He called her mobile.

She picked up immediately. 'Morning, guv.'

'You around?'

'Five minutes away.'

'Perfect. Meet me in Bright's anteroom. And if you see anyone on the way in, don't mention it.'

Indi hesitated. 'Am I in trouble?'

'No. I want you to do something for me.'

Frankie was dying inside. The angelic child, asleep on his back in his hospital bed, stirred – a mass of dark curly hair stuck to his forehead, the longest eyelashes she'd ever seen, his beautiful bow lips dry and cracked. After the events of last night, the poor bairn was shattered, physically and psychologically. She'd found him cowering in the corner of the van, behind a cardboard box, his skinny little legs the only part of him covered by the blanket she'd found.

His injuries were extensive.

Standing beside his bed, she took in the cuts to his face and hands. Bone fractures were now in plaster, with superhero stickers attached, none of which made him react when applied. With no idea of his identity, and no reports locally or nationally of a missing child on the PNC, she'd stuck around so that the first face he'd see when he woke would be one he'd seen before. With any luck, he'd remember the friendly officer who'd rescued him from the van, holding his hand en route to Northumbria's Specialist Emergency Care Hospital at Cramlington, a ride in a helicopter he might never remember, having been sedated.

That was all she could hope for.

12

Responding to a knock at the door, David looked up. Indira poked her head in, making sure she was in the right place. This was her first visit to the office adjoining Bright's. It was pristine, a board table in the centre with eight chairs, large enough to accommodate the equipment they required to run an off-book investigation she didn't yet know about. With a separate entrance from the corridor, it was the perfect hideaway, if too close to their guv'nor's territory within the precinct that was Middle Earth.

Bright had insisted that David work from there, updating him on any developments as and when they occurred. He waited for the door to close and for Indira to approach, inviting her to sit. She was a diminutive figure, with fine features and dark eyes that reflected her curiosity. She removed her jacket, pulled up a seat and sat down.

'You're probably wondering why we're meeting here and not in my office,' David began.

'That's an understatement, guv.'

'The job I have for you is off-book.'

'Why me, if you don't mind me asking?'

He threw her a smile of encouragement. 'I recognise potential when I see it, is the short answer. And because you came to us from personnel.'

'Well, I probably shouldn't say this, but it doesn't make me an expert.'

'It does in my book.'

'Bet you wish Frankie hadn't left, all the same.'

David liked Indira. She had no ego. It was not in her nature to big herself up in the eyes of others, to try to look better, smarter or more in the know. She was all of that and more, though she felt no need to prove it. That gave her the edge over some of her contemporaries. It was one of the reasons he'd chosen her. 'In this instance I need you, not her . . .'

'Don't get me wrong, I'm proud to have been selected, but I haven't been here long.'

'No, but in that short time you've been involved in under-the-counter ops. You've demonstrated the ability to grasp complex issues. More importantly, to take instruction and keep your mouth shut. You also have the necessary access to interrogate the admin system. This is your opportunity to show us what you're made of.'

If Indira had reservations, she didn't show it. 'What is it you want me to do?'

'I need you to carry out a deep background check.'

'Anyone I know?'

'I don't think so.'

There would be no ransom demand for the child with no name. He was sleeping soundly, despite nurses coming and going through the night to carry out observations and monitoring of their paediatric patient, checking SATS with a non-invasive device attached to his finger, his temperature with an ear thermometer, allowing the kid to rest and recuperate from his injuries, not to mention the trauma of being secured by cable ties to anchor points in the van's load area.

The dayshift nurse washed her hands and left the room, pausing to reassure Frankie that the boy would recover. She meant physically. Psychologically could take many years, if not the rest of his life.

A tap on the internal window took Frankie by surprise.

She turned, half expecting David.

Her sister-in-law, Andrea, was standing in the corridor beyond. Last night, as the child was being checked over by air ambulance medics and made as comfortable as possible for onward transfer to A&E, Frankie had handed her the scene. A serious crash, especially one involving multiple fatalities, was a major incident, a case for the Accident Investigation Unit. Andrea was the most experienced motor patrols accident investigator in the force.

From the rear of that stinking van, Frankie had watched Andrea swing into action on arriving, her crew ensuring that the car on fire had been fully extinguished, in case it should suddenly burst into flames, a clear and obvious danger to civilians and emergency personnel.

Safety first.

Frankie got up, leaving the bedside for the first time since she'd entered the room. It wasn't often that she and Andrea worked together. In this instance, their respective departments had information to share. They were the same rank, though Andrea would take overall charge.

As Frankie arrived by her side, closing the door quietly behind her, Andrea's focus remained on the sleeping child, her voice catching in her throat when she spoke.

'How is he?'

'Wish I knew.'

'Kids are resilient . . .' Andrea reached for Frankie's hand, giving it a squeeze. 'Did he tell you his name?'

Frankie shook her head. 'He's not said a word since we arrived, nor when he was admitted. I insisted that they put him in a single room. There's no telling what he's been through. He becomes instantly agitated when approached by men. This isn't a fear of strangers lots of kids have. I'm no psychologist, but it goes deeper than that. He's terrified, Andy.'

Andrea looked away, then at Frankie, both choked with emotion to the extent that they couldn't speak. They had been up all night, in Frankie's case since the crack of dawn the day before – and after pulling a full shift with Graham. On the same wavelength, it was Andrea who broke the silence. Changing the subject so as not to get too maudlin, she told Frankie that Graham had been very helpful after she'd left in the air ambulance.

'He's a good bloke,' Frankie said.

Andrea was nodding. 'He even offered to notify the relatives of those we managed to ID at the scene. My lot would rather run a mile than give the death message.'

Frankie looked through the internal window of the rainbow-coloured room, designed with fairy-tale figures kids would identify with. Despite the effort they had put in to make his stay more pleasant, Frankie couldn't wait to get him out of there.

'Right now, it's the living I'm concerned about,' she said.

'Do they think he's mute or in shock?'

'They don't know. He seemed OK in the air, but very anxious once we landed. They had to sedate him.'

Andrea's co-driver arrived with coffee for them both.

They thanked him and he walked away, Andrea telling him not to go far. She informed Frankie that during the night, and again as soon as it was light, the scene had been photographed from every angle, measurements taken before crashed vehicles could be uploaded and transported to the police lock-up, debris collected for forensic examination.

'What did the eyewitnesses say?' Frankie asked.

'They all agreed that the van entered the A1, turning right onto the wrong side of the road, against the traffic, in the fast lane. The woman Dr Charlton was treating at the scene had no-where to go. She hit it head-on.'

'Did she make it?'

Andrea shook her head, turning to face the little boy on the other side of the glass. 'It's a miracle he did.'

13

Before David told Indira who the focus of their attention was going to be, it was important to share the rationale behind his decision to investigate the person concerned. 'Last night, I overheard part of a row that may lead us to a conviction. I don't know the individual personally, so our first objective is to establish what kind of person he is. He could be an informant, accidentally or on purpose, an honest individual or a malicious troublemaker. It's our responsibility, our *duty*,' he stressed, 'to work out if what he said was true – which is what I'm about to ask you to do. First, I want your agreement that you're happy to do this.'

Indira frowned. 'Is there a reason I wouldn't be?'

'The officer concerned is still serving.'

'I see . . .' With experience in Professional Standards as well as HR, albeit at a low level, Indira was aware that it made a difference. 'And you're wondering if I have what it takes to investigate a colleague—'

'Let's just say, I like my team to know what they are up against. You might encounter pressure from colleagues and/or senior supervision to divulge what it is you're doing. If that turns out to be the case, you tell them you're creating a system for the boss and it's mind-numbingly boring.'

'Got it. And if that doesn't satisfy them?'

'Stick to your legend. If they're still unhappy, decline to answer further questions. You shut up shop and refer the matter to me—'

'What if you're not here?'

'You speak directly to the guv'nor. You now have the highest level of authorisation within the personnel system. It comes

49

directly from him. It will mean that you will know everything there is to know about any officer we need to look at. That's a hell of a responsibility. Treat it with integrity.'

Indira nodded her understanding.

'You will see the *real* file, not the one we'd show an officer asking for disclosure. There could be some very dark history there – including mine and Frankie's, not forgetting her father, her grandfather and any of your current colleagues. We all have our secrets. Some are worse than others. Consequently, people will lie and cheat and pretend they're in the know to obtain information you'll be party to. Only three people are aware of what we're up to. The two of us and the guv'nor. It's imperative it stays that way.'

David wanted to tell her that they'd be shown the door if she didn't hold the line. He refrained from doing so. The last thing he wanted to do was rattle her. On the other hand, he had to know what side of the snitch fence she was on. 'I cannot impress on you how important this case is. At the risk of sounding like a spook, what I'm asking you to do is top secret.' He wasn't laughing.

'You don't have to worry about me, guv.'

'Good. Lastly, should anyone try to coax intel out of you, I'd like their names. What I overheard was enough to pique my interest in a cold case, so this job will be your only priority until I say otherwise. Stay out of the MIR.'

'I assume we're talking about someone at Frankie's leaving do?' Indira took in his nod, asking: 'Who are we looking at?'

'DS Adam Hall.'

'I don't know him.'

'You will, soon enough.'

'I assume I'll be using encrypted computerised records?'

'Yes. Where they're not available, you go personally to headquarters and dig out what you need from paper records. We're adopting a zero-trust approach. Nobody there needs to know what you're up to, what year you're looking into, which intake of officers. If anyone at HQ expresses an interest in what you're doing, you shut the file and bring it with you. And if anyone complains about that, you ring me instantly. I don't want to put you in any danger.'

'Is this about Frankie's sister's murder?'

'I'd rather you didn't speculate—'

'You're the SIO of a murder squad, guv. I'd rather know if it affects people we care about.'

'We get to the heart of the story first, but yes. We're nowhere near ready to look at Hall's links with the Oliver family. When we are, you'll be the first to know. I want your focus on him and nothing else. Is that clear?'

'Yes, guv. I see now why Frankie can take no part in the investigation.'

David could see that Indira was uncomfortable. 'For what it's worth, I'm as unhappy about the secrecy as you are. I hate working behind her back, but those are our orders. We do this without alerting her to what is going on. I know it feels like a betrayal. It's not. It's in her best interests. She knows nowt and that's the way it must stay until, or should I say if, we get a result.'

Indira gave a nod. 'You have my word.'

'Bright is running the show, not me. If you didn't have my approval and his, you wouldn't be sitting here. There can be no mistakes. We have new email addresses to use, exclusively to talk to each other. Ditto, mobile phones. This place is secure.' He gestured to a point over her shoulder. 'Inside that cupboard is a safe. At the end of the day, everything goes in it. The door is locked, blinds down, lights on. We have a covert security camera. If anyone breaches this office, we'll know.'

14

The hospital corridor was quiet enough for Frankie and Andrea to have a serious conversation without being overheard. The last nurse to enter the room Frankie had just vacated didn't seem concerned that her patient hadn't woken or been given anything to eat. The nurse explained that sedation, even the mild type, effected each child differently. The boy was well nourished. He'd be OK without food for a few hours.

Consoled by that, Frankie refocused on Andrea. Before the nurse interrupted, she'd been sharing what she'd found out since Frankie left the scene. Despite visible clues of how spent her sister-in-law was, even after the shift they had both put in, Frankie wanted more information. There was no way she'd let Andy escape to bed without sharing everything.

All of it.

'There was no ID on the men who died in the van,' Andy told her. 'The plates were dodgy. The vehicle identification number was a dead giveaway. It's registered to a Brighton address.'

'Sloppy.'

'Very. The van's owner reported it stolen a week ago. Sussex police gave him a knock last night. He's sixty, alive and kicking, though quietly quitting his job as a builder. Can't take it anymore apparently.' Andrea rolled her eyes. 'I know the feeling.'

They both did.

Frankie rubbed at her forehead, her mind in turmoil, thinking through all possibilities. 'So why keep it?' she said.

Andrea was at a loss. 'What?'

'Why keep the van if he no longer needs it?'

'He subcontracts here and there on small jobs when he's short of—'

'Cash?' Frankie raised a sceptical eyebrow. 'Why lift a finger when you can loan a van out to make money?'

'Sussex say he's clean.'

'What do they know?' Frankie didn't try to hide her cynicism.

'Not so much as a parking ticket, they said. Besides, why report it stolen if—'

'Come off it,' Frankie said. 'Since when do we have the resources to deal with vehicle theft anymore? The van owner may have been covering his back. If the guys who paid him got captured, he's in the clear. A classic avoidance tactic.' Frankie paused. 'Did any of the eyewitnesses see who legged it from the rear of the vehicle?'

'Two did. One male escapee, though in the mayhem neither witness could say if he hung around or scarpered.' Andrea turned her back to the glass, a wretched expression. 'They were taking photos. I've asked them to pass on any images they have. With any luck, they might include the runaway.'

'Good call.'

Andrea had more to say. 'The dead guys in the front both had new burners, Frank.'

'Now there's a surprise.'

'It's not all bad—'

'You reckon?' Frankie gave her hard eyes.

'They may not be traceable, but there were voicemails on one of the devices in a foreign language I couldn't get my head around. I'm trying to establish which one. Slavic, is my best guess.'

'Russian?'

'No, something else. I need to trace their next of kin.'

'Sod that. They tied that kid and probably more in the rear.'

'Frank, I see where you're going with this, but if the man who ran away was being trafficked, there would have been more restraints, or signs of them in the van—'

'Not necessarily. He may have taken them with him when he legged it, to hide the fact that he'd been there. Or they could have snapped in the collision and are still attached to his wrists. If he'd entered the country illegally – victim or trafficker – he'd want to avoid law enforcement. My guess is, he's part of it, put in the rear to watch the kid and keep him quiet should they be pulled over. This whole thing has child exploitation written all over it.'

'That's quite a stretch.'

'Is it?' Frankie snapped. 'How much proof do you need? They were in a stolen vehicle. They didn't know the rules of the road. They had burners with foreign chat on them. And he' – Frankie pointed into the child's room – 'was trussed up in the back and flinches whenever men approach him, as if he's expecting a slap. According to A&E staff, some of the bruises on his face are days and weeks old. It fits the profile.' Frankie asked, 'Where are the phones now?'

'With technical support. If the third man is someone the dead guys were regularly in touch with, we'll get a handle on him soon enough.'

'Where does that take us, now they're dead?' Frankie stared at the little boy, her emotions threatening to spill over in the company of someone she loved. Scenarios kept presenting themselves, none of them good. 'As I said, there may have been more than one child in the van, dropped off at various locations before the accident. It's enough to make you vomit.'

'I hope you're wrong.'

'My guts disagree, Andy. I just know that whatever they were planning to do with that child was going to be evil. He's not at an age where he can work, drive or peddle drugs. He's not old enough to be out alone without being noticed. This has all the hallmarks of a paedophile ring. The accident probably saved that little boy from a fate much worse than death.'

15

As David's second in command in Frankie's absence, Dick Abbott had taken charge of the Murder Investigation Team while the boss was tied up elsewhere. He had his instructions and had been given reassurance that David would pop in and out of the incident room in case he was needed. Dick wasn't told what he was doing. He didn't seem to care. Having failed to make the cut in the last round of promotions, he clearly relished the opportunity to step up.

David smiled to himself as he entered Bright's outer office.

In the past hour, it had been transformed into a major incident room of his own, minus a murder wall, which would give away what was going on in there should the room be breached. The board table and chairs had been pushed to one side, two desks facing one another taking centre stage, mainframe computers waiting to be fired up.

Indira was taking her role play seriously.

In a bookcase, she'd placed some administration manuals, alongside newly issued personnel guidelines, and a few of her own magazines should anyone be brave enough to look inside. They were ready to rock and roll.

With Bright out of the building, Indira grabbed coffees from his room, handing David one as she returned to her seat. Cradling his cup, he felt the adrenalin rush of an unsolved case review underway. As personal as this one was, if he could detect it, it was the greatest gift he could ever give Frankie.

Indi's voice bled into his thoughts. 'What exactly did you hear, guv?'

Almost word for word, he repeated what he'd told Bright, including the fact that its usefulness was uncertain. 'We can't afford to ignore it. It's the only potential evidence to emerge in over a decade. We seize it, run with it, dial it up, starting with a full antecedent history of Adam Hall . . .' He waited for her to finish her shorthand, a skill he wished he possessed. 'For now, we focus on intelligence gathering, getting the lowdown on his police career, including recruitment, postings, times and dates, any in-house disciplinaries and/or complaints, particularly of a sexual nature.'

Indira peered across their desks. 'Were there any?'

'That's for you to find out.'

'Well, it won't take long . . .' Unperturbed by the task, Indira logged on. As she waited for Hall's personnel record to load, she spoke again. 'I assume you also want to know how, or should I say *if* his history, in and out of the police, overlapped with either Frankie's father or grandfather.'

'Exactly that.'

'Will I be interviewing senior supervision?'

'Yes, though it's not a task I expect you to do alone.'

Indi's brow creased. 'Won't he get to hear of it?'

'If he does, we'll know where it came from. It's a chance we'll have to take. Anyone we question will be warned. Bright will wield a heavy stick if they don't toe the line.'

David took a moment to explain why Hall's female colleagues were of interest. The culture within their organisation wasn't great now. It was worse when Joanna was murdered. When told something distasteful about a colleague, male officers made a joke of it. Any female officers who got wind of it would have been warned to keep their gobs shut or face isolation. Not a good place to be for a copper.

'I'd like to think that we've moved on,' he said.

Indi's silence spoke volumes.

He was kidding himself.

In recent decades, evidence of gross misconduct had gone un-punished. Serving officers had been accused of sexual offences

56

while in office, some against colleagues too frightened to blow the whistle, fearing that they wouldn't be believed. And then there were the women they had come across in the course of their jobs, many of them vulnerable, and yet no action had been taken to close the guilty down. Sickening was not too strong a word to describe the systematic misogyny within policing that had allowed men's behaviour to go unchecked.

There was a time when a robust selection process would have eliminated unsuitable candidates. Nowadays, it seemed that any moron could join, safe in the knowledge that inexcusable inaction from above would allow them to continue in their roles, even if identified as a danger to women and girls, collecting victims along the way.

It was a disgrace.

And, like every decent officer, David felt tainted by it. 'Just because they weren't privy to locker-room banter doesn't mean they had no inkling,' he added. 'Female insight is vitally important to us.' He took a sip of coffee, meeting Indira's gaze over the rim of his cup, then placed it down on his desk. 'Did you ever see the film *Runaway Jury*?'

'I don't think so.'

'It's one of my favourites, based on a John Grisham legal thriller. It's about jury selection, a simple process in the UK, but taken to another level in the US. Lawyers over there employ professional investigators and trial consultants to get close to prospective candidates from a jury pool, predicting personality types, making deliberate selections based on what they find.'

'Stereotyping, you mean, in order to rule them in or out?'

'They prefer to call it profiling.'

'Fraught with danger, I suspect.'

'Due diligence is the way they see it.' Indira was exceptionally bright, a woman with an enquiring mind and a strong moral code. David needed her onside. 'Doing a job on Hall is for his sake as well as our own. We'll be looking at witnesses close to him, personally and professionally, until we know what makes him tick. We need to know how he reacts if told something in confidence. Does he share it? Does he brag? Doing our homework on him, we find out what he's really like. Because finding out what he's like now could be an indicator of what he was like when Joanna was killed.'

'You took the words out of my mouth, guv.'

'We're going to take him apart, discreetly. Only if we can eliminate him for Joanna's murder will we interview him in person.'

Indira's stare was intense. 'You don't think he did it, do you?'

'Trust me, you'll understand my rationale when we get into it.'

An email alert interrupted their conversation. It had come from Bright, something David had been expecting and couldn't wait to share.

Another thing Indi spotted. 'Good news?'

'You could say that.' He smiled at her. 'As of now, you are the MIT's newest card-carrying detective. Welcome to the madhouse, DC Sharma.'

Indira's jaw dropped. 'Are you serious?'

'Take a look.' David handed her his mobile. 'It's there in black and white.'

She read the email, then looked up. 'Guv, I don't know what to say.'

'Congratulations. No one in this building deserves it more.'

16

The ward was busy. Frankie stuck around until the child woke up, helping him to eat something. He was famished. Couldn't shovel it in quick enough. When he'd finished, she plumped up his pillows, making him comfortable. Speaking gently, she lifted the side rails to stop him from falling out, hoping for a verbal response. The only one she got was physical, his tiny hand reaching out when she turned to leave, a demonstration that he didn't want her to go.

Heart-wrenching.

She had to leave sometime.

She summoned a nurse to stay with him, then moved off the ward to buy the toddler some items from the hospital shop, with no clue of what was appropriate for a child of his age. What was his age? Three, four? Maybe a little older. She scanned the counter, then stood aside, allowing a mother with a pushchair to jump the queue, hoping for inspiration. Her little human looked around the same age as the boy whose bedside Frankie had just left. The mother was no help whatsoever. She bought a magazine and left.

Hmm, Frankie thought, chocolate buttons, Maltesers?

She settled for the latter: more fun. A kid with teeth could do more than suck, couldn't they? Returning to the child's bedside, she placed a small fawn-coloured teddy bear in the crook of his broken arm. He looked at it, then at her, a vacant expression in his beautiful big brown eyes, before drawing the cuddly toy towards his chest, in case she took it away. He may as well have said: *mine*.

Frankie wanted to bawl.

Opening the packet of Maltesers, she allowed three of the chocolate balls to dribble out onto the tray across the bed. The boy stared at them. Did he even know what they were? Testing a hypothesis, she flicked one towards him. He watched it roll to a stop, making no attempt to pick it up. Frankie took another from the packet, popping it into her mouth, making a funny face.

He almost smiled . . . almost.

It never failed to surprise David how much could be achieved in a private office with phones off and concentration very much on. Indi hadn't lifted her head for hours. She'd amassed a huge amount of paperwork already. Impressed with her work ethic, wanting to hear more – and mark her transition to detective grade in some small way – David shouted her to a working lunch.

He chose Riley's Fish Shack, a restaurant with an uninterrupted view of the North Sea shoreline and a menu to die for. Nestled on the beach at King Edward's Bay, it was surrounded by steep cliffs. High above them, the ruins of Tynemouth's medieval priory stood loud and proud, dominating the headland.

They ordered, then got down to business.

By the time their food arrived Indira had drifted off the subject, finding it hard to ignore sailing boats on the spectacular horizon, the surfers in the foreground, the beachcombers strolling in the sun.

David gave her a nudge. 'What else have you got for me?'

'Quite a bit . . .' Indira put down her cutlery and flipped a page in her notebook. 'Hall joined up straight from university. His degree was in Drama and Theatre Studies, so unrelated to law or policing. For obvious reasons, his shift referred to him as "The Drama Queen". He enjoyed the work he was doing, was highly thought of by most, promoted early on, gaining three stripes by the age of twenty-five.'

'Any complaints?'

'A couple when he was in uniform. Nothing particularly related to what we're looking into; offenders claiming he was heavy-handed during the arrest process. The complaints were written off as NFA.' She meant no further action. 'Then his career stalled.'

David took his glass away from his mouth. 'Why?'

Indira dipped a fat chip into mayonnaise before answering. 'I thought you might ask—'

'Do you know?'

'I wouldn't be a very good detective if I didn't.' She was still buzzing about her news, then her smile fell away. 'Hall lived and worked in South Shields at the time, only seven miles from where Joanna's body was found. One night when he was off duty, Control received a report of a disturbance at his home. Uniforms were dispatched. It turns out there was a domestic going on, though his wife denied it when she opened the door, claiming they were messing around, a misunderstanding.'

'Was he spoken to?'

'And given a slap on the wrist. However, I cross-checked his professional record with his personal one, and about three weeks later he applied via headquarters admin to change his address. He was separating from his wife, Jan. Maiden name Welch.'

'Any kids?'

'None, then or since, though he did remarry a few years later. Her name is Sarah, formerly Murray. Unless the records need updating – I'll check that when we get back to base – they're still together. Might be worth speaking to her . . .' Indira had left the best till last. 'She's ten years his junior, guv.'

17

Thirty miles north, nursing a coffee as black as her mood, Frankie sat on her balcony overlooking Amble harbour, listening to the gulls and loose rigging slapping against the masts of the yachts berthed there. One vessel with a French navy hull and pristine white decking glided gracefully into position on the pontoon in front of her, its owner – a man she knew by sight only – giving her a friendly wave.

On land and sea, they were unconventional neighbours.

Even the view of Warkworth medieval castle in the distance couldn't lift Frankie's depressed state that morning. All she could think of was the child she'd left behind. For a moment, she was in his room, drawing a face on the back of her hand, using her forefinger and middle finger to make legs, walking the miniature figure across the child's bed towards the door, then walking them back again, trying to make him understand that she'd return. It didn't help. He cried . . . and so did she when she got outside.

Get a grip.

The kid with no name was turning her to mush.

Convinced that the boy had narrowly avoided being sold on, exploited and abused, she couldn't afford to lose control. If she didn't get her act together, she couldn't help him. Her suspicion that other kids may have been less fortunate would haunt her until she got to the bottom of it.

She'd never admit it to anyone outside of her immediate family, but dogs and children always got to her. Once, she'd very nearly adopted a Jack Russell that had been found wandering the streets and brought to the station by a concerned animal lover.

The dog followed her around, refusing to leave her side, until it saw its proper mum, at which time Frankie became surplus to requirements.

She was hoping to repeat that experience, finding the boy's mother.

If Frankie was reading the situation correctly, the child wasn't lost, he'd been abducted. She wondered if he'd arrived with parents fleeing persecution from abroad, then been snatched. If he'd been smuggled in, as frantic as his parents might be, claiming him as their own would out them as illegal immigrants. Mired in helplessness and despair, faced with an impossible situation, they were unlikely to come forward.

If she was right, the boy was virtually an orphan.

With no known family, doctors pushed for beds would hand him over to social services. Children disappeared while in the care of the local authority, an unbearable thought Frankie had conveyed to Andrea as they left the hospital. While the accident investigation was hers and hers alone – nothing to do with Frankie now – a case of child abduction, if that's what they had stumbled across, was a whole other ball game, a matter for the CID. Frankie should step away and let them get on with it.

There was zero chance of that happening.

When they had finished eating, Indi pushed her plate away, laying a hand on her stomach. 'I'm stuffed. That was so good, guv. Thank you.'

'We have to eat,' David said. 'Don't expect it every day.'

At Middle Earth, he returned to Bright's outer office, while Indira peeled off to the female locker room. As she exited the loo and approached the washbasin, the door crashed open. Pam Bond entered. At six three, she towered above Indi and everyone else in the MIT. She was quite a presence, in and out of her role as receiver. The office anchor, she was the go-to person for information on past and present enquiries. As smart as anyone Indi had met since joining the department as an aide, what Pam didn't know wasn't worth a light.

Through the mirror above the sink, Indi caught her eye.

'I just heard.' Pam turned, offering a high five. 'You must be stoked.'

David's warning arrived in Indi's head: *stick to your legend*.

For a split second, she thought Pam was about to ask what she was up to in Bright's outer office with their boss, or why they had been out together for lunch at Riley's. On both counts, she was wrong. Pam was merely congratulating her on becoming a detective, a note to that effect having reached her desk from admin, confirming her appointment.

Indi should've known better. Pam would never use her seniority to put her in an awkward position. That was not, and never had been, her style.

'Fancy a drink after work to celebrate?' she asked.

Indi relaxed. 'I'd love that.'

'Great, I'll give Frankie a call.'

18

Frankie had only just dropped off – at least that's what it felt like – when a ringing sound pulled her from sleep. Or had it? For a moment, she wasn't sure if she'd dreamt it. Then it started up again, louder this time. Not the doorbell chime on her mobile, alerting her of a text. This was the real thing. Whoever was outside kept their finger on the bell push, confirming his or her intention to get her up.

Throwing off her warm duvet, Frankie hauled herself out of bed, pulling on a silky summer robe as she walked into the hallway to answer the door, the noise increasing as she approached.

'All right, all right!' she yelled. 'I'm coming.'

Christ's sake! This had better not be the postman.

The video entry system showed Andrea looking directly at the camera behind a pair of dark sunglasses, her short blonde hair flattened by wearing a hat all night long. Frankie slipped the security chain from its track rail.

The din ceased.

Yanking open the door, she was about to ask her in-law what the hell she thought she was doing, when she realised that Andrea hadn't been home, or if she had she hadn't stayed long enough to shower and change. Fearing a negative development, Frankie invited her inside.

'Why aren't you in bed?'

Andrea shrugged. 'Couldn't sleep. Don't know how you can.'

'I can't. Some idiot woke me.'

'Don't moan, eh?' Andrea closed the door, following Frankie into her open-plan kitchen-cum-living room. It was bathed in bright sunshine. 'There's something I need to tell you. It can't wait.'

'Don't mind me.' Frankie swung round. 'Who needs sleep?'

'Got owt to eat?' Andy's tone was flat.

Fleetingly, Frankie wondered if she'd argued with Rae and walked out.

'I have bread.'

'That'll do.'

'It'll have to, it's all I've got.' Frankie walked around the island that separated the two parts of the room, noticing that the loaf in her bread bin was well past its sell-by date. Checking it for mould, she cut off the crusts, popped two slices in the toaster, put the kettle on, then grabbed two plates and mugs from the cupboard, butter from the fridge.

'You want milk in your tea?'

'Lemon.'

'Inside or out?'

'Out.'

'Words of one syllable usually means trouble.'

Ignoring the gibe, Andrea opened the patio doors and stepped out onto the balcony, glad of her shades. Nudging the fridge door shut, Frankie studied her closely. Andrea placed her forearms on the balustrade, looking out over the water. Frankie had rarely seen her this downcast. Desperate to know what was on her mind, she hurried with the tea and took it outside, setting it down on a small bistro table.

Despite her low mood, Andrea sat down immediately, scoffing her toast like it was the last thing she'd ever eat, eyeing Frankie's plate afterwards.

Never one to stand on ceremony, she said, 'You going to eat that or just look at it?'

Frankie almost laughed. It was like being in the staff canteen. You snooze, you lose if there was food to be had. She shoved her plate towards Andrea. 'Have it, she said. 'I'm not hungry.'

'Really?'

'Really. And when you're finished, you can tell me what you're doing here.'

'I'm sorry, I should have let you sleep.'

'So, why didn't you?'

Before Andrea could answer, Frankie's phone rang.

She got up to fetch it from the living room where it was on charge and didn't get there quick enough. She'd missed a call from Pam. No voicemail followed. Quick as a flash, a WhatsApp message arrived instead:

Indi made DC. Drinks 8pm. Usual place.

Frankie keyed a reply: On duty tonight. 😔

Bad luck.

Give her my best. x

You'll be missed, Inspector.

Returning to the balcony, Frankie sat down, placing the device on the table.

Andrea stopped chewing. 'David?'

'No, and what's more, I don't care.'

'Could've fooled me . . .' Andy let the sentence trail off.

Frankie ignored the comment. 'I need to crash, so maybe now you've filled your face, you could get to the point of what went on after you left me at the hospital.'

'I went home. Your mum was there.'

Frankie sensed something else coming. 'Is that a problem?'

'No, of course not . . . or should I say, ordinarily it wouldn't be. This morning, Julie took one look at me and knew what kind of a shift we'd put in.'

'Did you forget Rule 6?' Frankie was trying to lift her. 'Low morale is strictly forbidden. Didn't I warn you she can spot it a mile off—'

'You're not wrong . . .' Even now the ice was broken, Andrea seemed uncharacteristically glum. 'Your mum and Rae were talking about the accident when I walked in. Stupidly, I mentioned the boy. It set them off. Rae hasn't even seen him but already she's tearing her hair out over it.'

'She's a softie. What did you expect?'

'Yeah, well, things went from bad to worse.'

'What d'you mean?'

'They're on a mission . . .' Andrea wiped her face with her hands. 'If you're looking to blame anyone for my visit, blame them. They sent me here.'

Frankie screwed up her face. 'To do what?'

Andrea dropped her head, then raised it, her face flushed with guilt. 'Will you hear me out before you start yelling?'

'Depends.' Frankie's teasing failed to land. 'Hey! It can't be that bad, surely.'

Andrea hesitated, wrestling with her conscience. 'We've been keeping something from you.'

'We?'

'Me and Rae.'

'Are you going to tell me what it is?'

Andrea pushed a hand through her hair, biting the inside of her cheek. Her hesitation made Frankie nervous. She wondered if one of them was ill, if they were separating, if they were in financial trouble. Of all the things that flashed through her mind, what came out of Andrea's mouth was not one of them.

'We want to foster the child,' she said.

19

It took a while to calm Indira down. She'd arrived at her desk in a flap, her face flushed, explaining to David that she'd fallen short of her own high expectations by agreeing to meet the team for a drink after work. In hindsight, she regretted her actions, believing that in doing so, she'd opened the door to Frankie's appearance sooner than either of them had hoped or expected.

'Relax,' David reassured her. 'Inviting her isn't the end of the—'

'I didn't invite her, guv. It was Pam. I'm not trying to drop her in it either.'

'It doesn't matter who it was. Frankie was bound to turn up here eventually. Not inviting her on your big day would have raised suspicions . . . hers and everyone else's. Would you be here if it wasn't for her? Would Mitch? Not a hope in hell. Remember, she once had your back . . . and now, by keeping her out of the loop, you have hers. To be honest, I'd rather we saw her before our enquiry is properly underway.'

'Before rumour and speculation are rife, you mean?'

'That too. Like it or not, it won't take the MIT long to realise that something's off. It's human nature to want to be in on a secret op.'

'You don't think they've noticed that we're absent from the MIR already?'

'You perhaps, not me. I'm in and out of there hourly liaising with Dick, complaining that I'm swamped with paperwork, using Bright's office to get some peace. He's been briefed on your boring admin role and asked not to disturb you. So, if anyone asks, that's what he'll tell them. If our enquiry goes on, his pay will increase. He's living the dream. He won't want it to end.'

'Why don't you ask him about Hall? He worked with him then—'

'No, Indie. We don't share this. Not with anyone. You have your instructions. When you turn up tonight, go with the flow, like you did last time, BAFTA style.'

'Will you be there?'

David was desperate to spend time with Frankie – dreading it too. 'Would you like me to be?'

'I would.'

'Then I'll consider myself invited.'

Frankie didn't need Andrea to confirm which child. She meant *the* child, the one they had left at the hospital hours ago. They were staring at one another, in Frankie's case trying to interpret her sister-in-law's expression. If she had to call it, she'd have said it was a mixture of sadness and euphoria, with a touch of trepidation thrown in. Frankie's mum had been playing Mother Teresa, urging Rae and Andy to help a child in distress – a kid with no name and an uncertain future.

The silence got to Andrea. 'Frank, did you hear what I said?'

'I wish I hadn't.' She didn't give Andrea the opportunity to respond. 'In what universe would the powers that be allow you to foster him, no matter how good your intentions? You and Rae have zero experience of kids. And, to get over what he's been through, that little one may need specialist support you're un-qualified to give.'

'Julie said—'

'It doesn't matter what Mum said. You have a full-time job.'

'I know that—'

'Which includes nights like last night.' Frankie spread her hands. 'Are you for real? How many times have you told me that you need your kip to function? As do I. You cannot be serious—'

'Frankie, stop. Rae and I are trained and vetted.'

Frankie's mouth fell open. 'What?'

'That's what I'm trying to tell you, if you'll shut up a moment.'

Frankie wound her neck in. 'Knock yourself out.'

'A couple of years ago, Rae and I decided we'd like to foster kids whose parents, for one reason or another, couldn't look after them. We've since gone through the process and were given the go-ahead recently. Rae wanted to keep it between us until we were matched with a specific child. One that could, potentially, arrive at a moment's notice. So to some extent we are prepared.'

That stung.

Andrea's relationship with Rae had come about through her association with Frankie. They had known each other longer: they had joined the police together, partied together, snuck out of training school against regulations *together*, receiving a bollocking in the process. Until now, they had shared everything, including the love of Frankie's big sister.

'And there was I thinking we were close.'

'Don't sulk. We are, you know we are.'

'Doesn't feel like it.'

'Go on, make this about you, why don't you? You weren't the only one we didn't tell, Frank. Your mum and dad didn't know either, until I stupidly mentioned the kid, then Rae blurted it out to your mum, explaining how well placed we were to help. If you'd witnessed Julie's reaction, you'd think Rae had given birth.'

'Grandma and Grandpa-to-be must be ecstatic.'

Andrea threw her a filthy look that required no explanation. 'You can't help yourself, can you?'

Frankie's eyes found the floor briefly, then she raised her head. 'Trained or not, irrespective of ready-made grandparents, there's no way the local authority or an independent fostering agency will let you practise on that kid. Nor should they. He needs, he deserves, the best care he can get.'

Andy exploded. 'Well, thanks for the vote of confidence.'

The incident room seemed oddly quiet without Frankie in it. David missed her camaraderie, her silly rules and laugh-out-loud humour. Detectives had their heads down in their work, some fielding calls from members of the public, though the usual suspects were milling around the coffee machine.

As David approached, Pam Bond had them cornered. She was collecting cash with which to buy a gift for Indira, calling out Charlie, the office manager, for being a stingy sod. *There was always one.* Reaching into his pocket, David pulled out a twenty and dropped it in the pot as he passed by. Pam was the only woman he knew who could smile at one colleague while glaring at another.

Charlie hurried away, shamefaced.

Pam thanked David for his generosity, without querying when Indira might reunite with the team or what was keeping her away. Relieved, he moved towards his office.

Dick stood as he entered.

'As you were,' David said. 'I'm not stopping. How's it going?'

'With that lot?' Dick flicked his head towards the MIR beyond. 'So far, so quiet, guv.'

'Yeah, I noticed. Enjoy it while it lasts. Will I see you tonight?'

'Yeah, shame Frankie can't make it.'

'She's not coming?'

'No, she's late shift.'

'Bummer.'

David felt an ache in the pit of his stomach. Frankie's absence solved one problem and created another. He'd have to talk to her at some point and had been hoping that a group chat in the pub would avoid any awkwardness between them. He decided to give her a call, an icebreaker. Her number was starred as a favourite.

Tapping on it, he walked down the corridor towards Bright's office.

Frankie's voicemail arrived in his ear.

He rang off without leaving a message. If she was working later, most likely she was in bed and wouldn't thank him for disturbing her. Her soporific voice arrived in his head, a memory of the last time he'd called her out in the small hours when she was half asleep: *Oliver . . . Whoever you are, bugger off. I'm state zero.* Then, as the drowsiness wore off, and in a voice barely audible, she mumbled: *David . . . is that you?*

His smile faded.

Next time he made such a call to his 2i/c, Dick would answer. He was a good detective but no match for Frankie. With that depressing thought lingering, David walked on. By the time he reached his covert incident room, he was in a better mood. Indi had news. Before she shared it, he put her mind at ease. 'Frankie won't be joining us for celebratory drinks. She's on lates.'

'That's good,' she said. 'I mean, sorry – I didn't mean that to sound—'

'Relax, I know what you meant.'

David scanned her desk.

She was carrying out his instructions to the letter. Her notebook was closed. There was no accumulation of paperwork on her desk that anyone entering might read upside down. Her laptop screen was down. There was no doubt in his mind that she'd have bookmarked relevant digital files for future reference.

He'd chosen well.

'So, where are we?' He pulled out his chair and sat down.

'I plotted all the departments Hall worked in over the years, one of which overlapped with Frankie's grandfather, who was then a DS in general CID. Hall was working in South Shields, presumably when he bought a house there, and Frankie's father was the on-call DI within the MIT.'

'Was Hall on duty at the time of Joanna's death?' David knew what was coming.

'I've not been able to establish that yet. I'm still looking. It's going to take time. Her death predated the computerisation of station records. I'll have to trawl through God knows how many boxes of paperwork . . . if they still exist.' Having read his expression, Indira ended by asking and answering a question. 'Unless you know a shortcut?'

20

Frankie got up early enough to visit the boy in the hospital before staff settled him down for the night. He visibly perked up when she entered his room, and seemed generally more rested and relaxed than he had this morning, his new toy pulled tightly to his chest. Frankie had done a lot wrong in her lifetime, developing feelings for her boss topping that list. As gestures go, it seemed she'd got this one right.

Sitting down, she patted the toy.

When the child copied her, she almost wept. She knew nowt about kids, but it didn't take long to work out that the soft toy could serve as a conduit for better communication. Pointing at her chest, she said her name.

'Frankie.'

The boy blinked.

Moving her finger to the toy, and for want of a better name, she said the first to arrive in her head: 'Teddy.' She repeated this game several times, going back and forth between her own body and that of the small bear: 'Frankie . . . Teddy.'

At last, she had the boy's attention.

On the next run-through, she said, 'Frankie . . . Teddy,' then pointed at the boy's chest. He just looked at her. She'd just decided that her idea was naff, when the kid pointed at her. Frankie repeated her name. This breakthrough set her adrenalin surging. She had the kid's interest and tried again: 'Frankie . . . Teddy.'

She pointed at the child.

'Amir,' he said.

*

The pub was heaving, filled to the rafters with cops and robbers. The TV was on in the background, a Sky Sports transmission of a UEFA Champions League Qualifying First Round match: FK Sarajevo versus Celtic. In the summer, during the close season, footie fans would watch anything they could lay their hands on. It had been all square at half-time, a goal apiece when David and Indi arrived. Celtic had scored twice in the second half, Sinclair putting the last one past the goalie in the 85th minute, ensuring the win.

A group of Glaswegians on the next table went nuts.

David asked. 'Who wants another?'

'Won't say no,' Mitch said.

'There's a list behind the bar,' Pam added.

Indi laughed, eyes on David. 'They've done this before, guv.'

As he waited for his order, his phone rang, Frankie's name appearing in the small screen. He tapped to answer, lifting the device to his ear, making every effort to sound upbeat, as if nothing untoward had happened at her party, hoping she wouldn't mention his vanishing act.

'Hey, Frank. Tell me you've wangled the night off. I could do with a hand with this lot.'

'Unfortunately not. I'm heading north.'

He could hear road noise. 'Well, slow down. You don't want a repeat of last night.'

'That's why I'm calling. I could do with some advice—'

'Hold on . . .' The guy behind the bar dispensed David's drinks onto a tray, holding out the card reader for payment. David tapped his debit card against it, holding up a thumb to the server as he passed the receipt across the bar. Frankie's signal was poor, fading in and out. 'Where the hell are you?' David put a hand over his free ear, straining to listen. 'Frank? You still there?'

'Yeah, I hit a dead spot. Sorry to miss Indi's celebration. Sounds like quite a party. Even on a rest day, I don't think I'd have made it after last night's RTA and Andrea beating my door down earlier. Tell you about it sometime.'

Would she though? David hesitated for a moment too long.

'I was wondering if you'd like to meet up,' she said finally.

'I'm flat out, Frank.' Even in his head, that sounded like a brush-off.

'Doing what?' Her tone was brittle.

'Rush job for HQ.'

'Dick said you were quiet. You'd better confirm that I'm more interesting than a pile of paperwork or I'm off to find a tall building.'

Having been caught out, David eyed Dick from across the room, best friends with Frankie since God knows when, thick as thieves, the two of them. He was the obvious one she'd go to for information. Thinking he was being summoned, the DS had risen to his feet and was now making his way towards the bar.

'Listen,' David said. 'It's my shout and the guys are thirsty. I'll call you soon, OK?'

Frankie was already gone.

21

At Berwick nick, Frankie reversed into her parking spot, making sure the automatic sliding gates closed behind her before exiting her vehicle. She entered the building, hoping to get more conversation out of Graham Ross than she had her former DCI. However, the concept of a debrief on the pile-up on the A1 was lost on her sergeant. For him, it was case closed. Nothing more to discuss. The road had been swept and reopened. He'd liaise with Andrea in due course, then it would be job done.

Anything else was none of their business.

For Frankie, the fallout from the RTA was still ongoing, on a personal rather than professional level. Declining to join Graham for another night in the area car – for reasons she made clear were nothing to do with last night and everything to do with getting to know the rest of her team – she wished him luck, telling him to radio in if he needed reinforcements, then waited for him to leave.

Amir and Andrea were in Frankie's head. She asked Control to get Tango 7003 to contact her on her mobile at the earliest opportunity. Andy was more likely to respond to her call sign than a missed text and a conversation she had no wish to repeat.

A few minutes later, her vibrating mobile began to march across her desk.

Andrea was immediately arsey. 'Using Control for a personal matter can get you fired.'

'If anyone asks, I'm after an update. Are you mobile?'

'Stationary.'

Frankie was relieved to hear it.

Driving and arguing didn't go together.

She pictured Andrea parked in a lay-by single-crewed, waiting for a shout that she was required, keeping an eye out for trouble, providing a visible police presence. She hated being in the office and practically lived in her car.

'I've been thinking about our conversation,' Frankie said. 'I didn't mean to upset you. I'm just not sure Rae's right for fostering. You'd need a crowbar to prise Amir off her once she's formed an attachment.'

'Amir? Is that his name?'

'Don't you dare tell Rae. If she asks what he looks like, do not mention that he's cute. Do not personalise him in any way. It will end in tears if you do. Be honest. You know that, right? I seriously think you should consider adoption.'

'Do you? Well, I'll be sure to pass on your instructions.'

'Don't be like that, I'm trying to help . . .'

'Did we ask for help?'

Frankie sighed. 'No, but—'

'Our minds are made up. Stay out of it.'

There was a knock at the door. A female PC stuck her head in. Frankie beckoned her in as she spoke into the phone. 'I have company. Call you later.'

Andrea cut the call.

Olive branches were overrated.

'Inspector, you have a visitor.'

Frankie got to her feet when Bright strode into her office, dismissing the PC who'd shown him where to find her. Of all the people Frankie might have expected to walk through the door, it wasn't him. He hadn't come to congratulate her. He'd done that at her leaving do, while scoffing several of her mum's veggie sausage rolls, sharing a few jars with her old man.

As men go, they were as close as any.

Shutting the door, Bright stood a moment, staring at her. He was a handsome man, impeccably dressed: a charcoal grey suit, white shirt, striped tie. Whatever cologne he was wearing must have cost a packet. His face was relaxed, but he had something on his mind. He didn't travel to see people. They went to him. She smelled trouble and braced herself.

'Sit down, Frankie.'

'You're a bit off the reservation, aren't you, guv?'

'Put simply, I've come to relieve you of your post—'

'Do I need a Fed rep?'

He laughed.

She didn't. 'What have I done?'

He drew up a chair. 'I have a proposition for you.'

'Isn't that against regulations?'

'Behave. I need an experienced detective—'

'Then you're looking in the wrong place, guv.' She circled her hand around the room. 'This is the blue suit department. At least, I think it is. I only just got here. They're a nice bunch.'

'I'm sure they are, but don't get comfy. I'd like you to run the child abduction investigation.' He studied her reaction. 'You seem conflicted. I find that surprising, given that you witnessed the poor bugger's plight *and* have been visiting him in your own time.' He'd been talking to Andrea. 'Distressing, I imagine.'

She nodded. 'It's not something I'll forget in a hurry—'

'Then there's your motivation to do something about it.'

'Guv, I've been here less than two days. I'm not even bored yet. If the request had come up in say three or four months from now, I'd have bitten your hand off. I really feel I should give Berwick my best shot—'

'Don't talk bollocks. The timing could've been better, but I read your report: quote – "Child exploitation is too serious to ignore" – unquote. That's two things we agree on.' He paused. 'I thought you'd relish the opportunity to run with it.'

'I would. I do—'

'Then what's your problem?'

He could answer his own question. He was offering Frankie all she'd dreamt of – an accelerated ticket out of Berwick. A chance to bin her uniform in favour of plain clothes. A DI's post. Not to mention the opportunity to bring down some serious human traffickers. He was in no doubt where her heart lay. But if she accepted his offer it could extend the time that she was out of the MIT, the last thing she wanted.

He'd been there too.

And now she was stating the obvious.

'Guv, as my sergeant pointed out to me earlier, the enquiry you're asking me to undertake has nothing to do with me. The only reason it's landed on my doorstep is because of geography. Whoever takes on the investigation needs to know where that kid's journey began and/or where it was intended to end.'

'And I know you'll hunt down the offenders or die trying.'

'It could tie me up for weeks, if not months.'

'I've already cleared it with your supervision.'

'Without speaking to me first?'

'I'm the boss, remember?' His raised eyebrow put her in her place.

Frankie looked away.

She was luckier than her contemporaries. The most senior detective on the force was almost part of her extended family and had been since she'd sat on his knee as a girl. It had taken her years to stop referring to him as Uncle Phil. An onlooker might accuse her of overfamiliarity, but she didn't mess with him in public. No one respected his rank more than she did, but even here, alone in her new office, she'd overstepped an invisible line. In her shoes he'd have done the same.

'What is it you want, Frank?'

Hope flashed across her face. 'Can I speak freely?'

'Would it help if I said no?'

'I'm a murder detective. I never wanted to come here in the first place.'

'Hallelujah. Those are the first genuine words you've spoken since I arrived.' She didn't crack a smile. He gave her a shove. 'If you're telling me you're not interested, I'll find someone who is.' His strategy worked. 'I want a detective who's jumping at this, not one I'm pushing to show interest. So, consider this your bargaining chip. Do this for me and I guarantee you won't be disadvantaged. Your stint in uniform will be over.'

'Done,' she said.

'Cheeky bugger.' He narrowed his eyes. 'You think I haven't heard of reverse psychology?'

'Old-fashioned terminology, guv. I prefer to call it persuasion.'

'You were always that, even as a four-year-old.'

'Joanna taught me.' Frankie was smiling.

Bright's guts were churning. It wasn't like her to talk about her late sister, even as an aside. He couldn't help wondering if she'd heard something and was giving him the opportunity to come clean. No, he decided. Stone could be trusted to keep his end up. Her comment must be coincidental.

'You can't do this alone, Frankie. It's too big a job. Mitch will be joining you.'

She frowned. 'We'll be working from here?'

'Good idea!' That wasn't what he meant. In truth, he'd given her base little consideration, but was happy to make it sound like her suggestion. Mention of Joanna had demonstrated why it was necessary to keep her away from Northern Area Command. 'If you return to Middle Earth, you'll get dragged into whatever is going on in the incident room and we don't want that. Your focus is the boy, whoever took him. Nothing else. If you stay put, you'll have no distractions.'

'Fair enough.'

'I'm not expecting you to run the show here on top of this new assignment. I'll sort your replacement, so you don't have to.'

'I have someone in mind.'

He agreed to her suggestion. 'Well, that's it then.'

'That's easy for you to say, guv. Apart from the registered keeper of the Mercedes, I have nothing to go on.'

'You do now. On my way here, Andrea filled me in. The dead guys' prints from the van are now with Interpol. There was an Edinburgh postcode in the satnav. Mitch is trying to establish who the mobile was talking to. It was active at the time of the collision.'

'Are Police Scotland on board?' Frankie asked.

'Not at this stage. I'd like you to carry out covert enquiries in the area, intelligence gathering on how many properties there are and what sort, what's the general demographic. Other children could be in the area, waiting to be sold on. If we go in too early, we could spook the traffickers into ending lives. Check your inbox. Your hotel reservation will be there.' He smiled wickedly. 'If you hurry, you'll make it before closing time.'

Frankie laughed, acknowledging the fact that she was never going to win. He hadn't ordered her to jump ship. Neither was he taking no for an answer. A moment later, Bright couldn't fail to notice her expression darken. She'd gone someplace else.

He couldn't guess what was coming.

'There's something else I want, guv.'

'Don't push it.'

'It's important, something that didn't occur to me until you mentioned Andrea. I spent half the morning convincing her to talk Rae out of some ridiculous notion that they might be able to foster the kid I found in the van.'

'What?'

'They're on an approved list of foster carers—'

'Since when?'

Frankie shrugged. 'Recently.'

'You didn't know?'

'Not until this morning. I tried to talk her out of it.'

'How did that land?'

'She told me to fuck off.'

'Maybe you should. Is it such a bad idea?'

'For Amir, no. If the scum who took him want him back, he may still be in danger. He's a traumatised victim. If we can get him to talk, he's also a witness who could identify the guy who escaped from the Mercedes. There's no limit to how low these people will sink. For all we know, he may have been a special order, destined for a paedophile ring. If he was hand-picked to feed a predator's sick perversion and they find out he's still alive, he's vulnerable.'

'They will. It's headline news.'

'Then he needs protection while in hospital, a safe house when he's discharged, a place of safety that doesn't involve social services or a Home Office migrant facility with other asylum seekers, because that's what I think he is.' Where children were involved, Frankie never held back. Never gave in. 'Kids are disappearing every day and what the hell are we doing about it? They have a fundamental right to our protection.'

'I couldn't agree more.'

'Can you pull some strings?'

'You're asking a lot.'

'Is it doable?' Frankie was practically begging.

'Maybe. An application would stand a better chance with people we can vouch for.'

'Well, you know Andy. Once her mind's made up, she usually sticks to it. In which case, there's no one I'd rather endorse than her and Rae. And if anyone can convince a judge to go into bat for Amir, you can.'

22

David dropped Indira at her new maisonette in Sandyford, made sure she was safely inside, then took off to pick up Ben from the city centre, just over a mile away. His nephew wasn't at or near the RV point they had arranged, so David parked on Dean Street, got out of the car and walked downhill towards the House of Tides, where Ben was being treated to Michelin-star dining in a former merchant's townhouse.

Belinda Wells knew how to live.

Lucky them.

David hadn't eaten a thing since his trip to Riley's Fish Shack. His stomach was rumbling, with only a small portion of cold pizza to look forward to at home – if it was still edible – though he had reasons to be grateful. Over drinks, there had been no awkward questions as to what Indi was up to, separated off from the MIT. The team had swallowed her legend, one or two of them commiserating with her for landing such a tedious assignment on the very day that she'd received good news.

The closer David got to the riverside, the more revellers he encountered, toing and froing between the many bars and eateries on offer. One or two lads were struggling to keep up. They'd be in the Royal Victoria Infirmary on stomach pumps by midnight. The rest of the guys were in good spirits, looking to score, in more ways than one: the girls were stunning; the smell of cannabis strong. Stone's twenties had passed him by.

If he was their age now, he'd be in there.

The Toon was rocking tonight.

*

Frankie had no time to plan. After the horror of last night's shift, she'd decided to revert to her old ways, to have a kitbag in the rear of her car with a change of clothes handy in case things went tits up. Before visiting the female locker room, she had stuff to take care of and should remain dressed for the part. First, she tried Andrea's mobile.

The call cut to voicemail.

She didn't leave a message.

Instead, she radioed Graham Ross, asking him to confer with her in her office as soon as he was free to do so. He arrived fifteen minutes later, with a young man who'd got into a minor altercation in the town centre. The lad had come quietly. He was contrite and had no form. Frankie sent him on his way with a caution, the first and last she'd administer in Berwick.

Graham saw him out, then returned to her office.

Handing him a brew, she invited him to sit.

He took the mug of tea but remained standing, no doubt pleased to be out of his area car and on his feet. Though she was buzzing with excitement, she regretted ending their association so soon. 'I don't know quite how to tell you this. I've been given a new assignment by the detective chief super.'

'I heard he'd been in.' Graham caught her surprise. 'News travels faster than you think in the sticks.'

'I'm sorry. It was never my intention to leave so early.'

'No sweat. This outpost is a revolving door, boss. People come and go. We're used to it. When will your replacement arrive?'

'I'm looking at him. As of now, you're officially acting up.'

'Wow.' He flushed slightly. 'I wasn't expecting that.'

'You impressed me last night.'

'I'm impressive most nights. You're the first to notice.'

Frankie laughed. He was as chuffed as she was. 'Can you manage on your own tonight? If not, I'll find someone to help.'

'No need, it's dead out there.' He held up his mug. 'If you're ever in the area.'

'I'm staying put, running my enquiry from upstairs. I'll clear my stuff and you can move in.'

23

Turning right onto the Quayside, David felt the mobile in his pocket vibrate. Assuming it would be Ben ringing to apologise for keeping him waiting, late leaving because Belinda had ordered one last drink, he was surprised to find that the caller was Bright. It was rare for him to call this late.

Intrigued, David tapped to answer. 'Guv? Something I can do for you?'

'You can stop looking over your shoulder. I've put Frankie on something that'll take her further afield and keep her occupied.' He went on to explain what it was and that she'd continue to work from Berwick.

'Thanks, guv.' It was a weight off David's mind. 'How did she seem when you called her?'

'I spoke to her in person. I'm sending Mitchell to give her a hand, assuming that's OK with you?'

'Perfectly. Does he know?'

'Yes, I had a call to make. No time to run it by you. I've told Frankie that when it's over she'll return to the MIT as promised.'

'Thanks for the heads-up. I'm glad you called, guv. If it's convenient, I'd like a moment of your time.'

'Crack on. I'm on my way home.'

With his foot to the floor by the sounds of it. 'Can you hold, guv? I'm not alone . . .'

'So I gather. Where the hell are you?'

'Quayside, picking up Ben.'

Graham seemed pleased that Frankie was sticking around. Northumbria Police was one of the largest forces in the country, covering over two thousand square miles, serving a population of one and a half million. Mathematically, once she took off, they might never see each other again.

After he left, Frankie called the hospital and was relieved to learn that Amir was doing OK. The nurse she spoke to said he was adorable and not a lot else, nothing that might jeopardise her job by saying too much without permission.

Frankie asked for the boy's consultant.

Catherine Acres came on the line.

Frankie identified herself as Detective Inspector Oliver for the very first time, explaining what she needed from the medic. 'I'm not being unkind, nor do I wish to be disrespectful, but I've had the "as well as can be expected" chat. Now I'd like the official line on Amir's prognosis?'

'Physically, the child is responding to an intake of fluids. Emotionally, he's not so good. He's unresponsive when being examined. His breathing is erratic. He's confused for much of the time. These are all indicators of shock. We're keeping close obs on him, Detective Inspector. Can I ask how he was when you were in earlier?'

'He seemed better.'

'Can you hold while l check his notes?'

'Of course.' Frankie heard the tapping of keys.

Acres said, 'After your visit, there was a marked deterioration.'

'In what way?'

'Visible and significant distress. He's been anxiously watching the door since you left. There's a note to that effect here. The staff can't get a word out of him. Is your name Frankie by any chance?'

'Yes, why?'

What Acres said next floored her.

'He cried out for you in his sleep.'

Frankie had no words.

A moving image of the name game she'd played with Amir and his teddy scrolled through her head. After giving Acres further instructions, she disconnected. Bright was expecting a result. She couldn't afford to fold. She called Mitch. He'd already been given the heads-up that he'd be working with her on the abduction.

He was thrilled.

'Me too,' she said.

'What do you want me to do?'

'Meet me in Berwick first thing. Amir's consultant is Catherine Acres. If you need to speak to anyone at the hospital, she's your contact. I've made it clear that we'll need full samples from him: blood and buccal swabs for a DNA match to the two guys who died in the Mercedes and the one who got away, when . . . if he's found. Check with forensics. Just make sure that any intel comes to you in my absence.'

'Will do. Do you want me there when samples are taken?'

'No, I'll do that.'

'I thought you were heading north?'

'I'll be back at dawn. It's not because I don't trust you. I've bonded with the kid. He's uneasy around men. Acres seems to think that he's like that around everyone bar me. I've made it clear that I'm to be informed of his progress, that under no circumstances is he to leave the hospital without my say-so and that if I'm unavailable, she should speak to you. She has your number. I'll text you hers. We'll debrief in the morning.'

'What if someone turns up to claim the lad?'

'Mitch, did you hear what I said?' Frankie lowered her voice. 'No one has reported him as missing yet. Until that happens, the child is in our custody, under our care and control. His security detail and Acres are in the loop. From now on, every doctor or nurse who wants access to that room will need photographic ID to prove they work for the hospital. If Amir is taken away for tests or any kind of examination, the cop goes with him. He's been instructed to call you or me if anyone does turn up. Unless we can prove that they share his DNA profile, they're not getting the boy.'

*

From across the road, David could speak freely with his guv'-nor. From there he'd see his nephew and Wells should they exit the House of Tides. While he trusted them implicitly, what he had to say could never, should never, reach the ears of any journalist.

He returned to his call.

'Guv, Indira and I need to lay our hands on station records for the time of Joanna's death. I happen to know where I can get hold of them.' He paused. 'It's tricky . . . I thought I'd better speak with you first.'

'If you mean from Frankie's father, forget it.'

David hesitated.

In his den at home, Frank Snr had been investigating Joanna's murder since the day she died, both as a serving, then as a retired detective, working incognito. He'd been unable to lay his hands on evidence that had inexplicably disappeared. To this day, his very own major investigation continued. He'd obtained replica case files and station records documenting every officer on or off duty around the time of Joanna's death. Holiday and sickness periods, court attendances or random hours off were marked up. The force didn't use them now. The duty rosters were a station sergeant's bible, amounting to a snapshot of time provided by those loyal to Frank. In his case, that meant all of them. With no authority to do so, Frank Oliver had copied the murder file in its entirety.

The flashback arrived instantaneously, a memory of spending time with Frankie on her candlelit balcony. A glass of wine. A work-related meeting on a weekend evening, a way of escaping the pandemonium of the MIR.

David couldn't recall exactly how their discussion drifted to more personal matters – only that it had and that she'd been gripping a photograph of her dead sister, while he tried and failed to find words of comfort. There was nothing vague about how Frankie looked, the fact that she was traumatised or what she'd said at the time.

Her words were ingrained on the inside of his brain.

My old man wouldn't let me touch it. Didn't want me to see what he saw. There are literally boxes and boxes of evidence in his cupboard behind lock and key. I've seen it all. Every time Mum leaves the house, he's in there. Every time they both do, I am. I know where he hides his key.

David kept his eyes open for Ben while trying to decide if his guv'nor was now hinting that he knew about Frankie's father's unofficial investigation.

Bright put him out of his misery. 'I know all about his silent room. Frankie told me about it. If you breathe a word of it, you'll be in trouble.'

'Understood . . .' David hesitated a moment, unclear on why the detective chief super was keeping Frank Oliver in the dark. 'Isn't it the case that when new evidence comes to light, we're obliged to contact a victim's family and put them in the picture?'

'That's the protocol.'

'But?'

'Common sense dictates which of them can and can't handle it. Give some of them an inch and they want a mile. Frank will fall into that category. He'll demand specifics we can't provide. If we don't come across, he'll call in favours and find out what we're up to. And if you think he won't go off on one, think again.'

'Even with me?'

'Especially with you. If he gets wind of who you're looking at, he'll be unstoppable. Trust me, it's not a place you want to go this early in your investigation. And when he's told, *I'll* be the one to do it. Besides, gut feelings and hard evidence aren't the same thing, Stone. When they are, we'll talk.'

'Indi says those station records are unobtainable from any other source, sir.'

'I'll sleep on it,' Bright said. 'Be in my office at 8 a.m.'

24

Having familiarised herself with Edinburgh, Frankie bypassed the city on the way to the suburb of Leith on the north shore, her first visit to the area. Before she left Berwick, a quick Google search established that it was one of the city's top attractions, a good place for rental property. It would surprise her if the traffickers owned a house. She was ruling nothing in or out. Hiding in plain sight, surrounded by young and old, an organised criminal gang could blend in and get away with murder.

All Frankie had to go on was an EH6 postcode.

She drove on, eventually making the coast road, passing warehouses, retail outlets and lock-ups – some derelict buildings unused for years, all potential hiding places from which to run an illegal operation, but not within her target area.

Entering Leith from the south, she was pleasantly surprised by what she found there, a mix of ancient and modern architecture, Georgian townhouses and new apartments sat side by side, along with cosy pubs and every kind of eatery, none of which she had time to enjoy. Many of them close to water.

Penthouse or warehouse, it was all the same to her.

So long as she got what she came for, she'd return home happy.

Ellen had booked her into the Malmaison near the historic port, off Customs Wharf. After registering at reception, Frankie took the lift to the fourth floor, dumped her bag in her room, then took off again, buying refreshments from a vending machine on her way out to sustain her overnight. Her energy would drop like a stone if she didn't take on food and water.

She was expecting to pull a long shift.

With her voice memos open, Frankie cruised up and down the three streets covered by the postcode, looking for anything incongruous, reading in the number plates of parked cars. It didn't take her long to realise that two of the streets were no through roads, blocked off at one end, an attempt to make them safer and more pleasant places to live in.

Her decision was made.

No right-minded scum would limit their chances of escape, especially when facing a lengthy jail term. The longer the better, she was thinking. Having narrowed her search to what had once been, and to some extent still was, a magnificent stone-built five-storey terrace overlooking a small park, she pulled to the kerb, with a good view either way. Cutting the engine, she reached for the water bottle and drank from it.

A gin wouldn't go amiss.

For the first hour and a half, there was no movement in or out of the houses she was watching. Bored rigid, she checked her watch: 01:30. Satisfied that the coast was clear, she unclipped her seat belt, venturing out of her vehicle for a closer inspection. AirPods in, voice memos open, she gave a running commentary on everything she saw, in as much detail as possible, in case she needed the assistance of Police Scotland. Their main station at Gayfield Square was only a short drive away, the one in Queen Charlotte Street even closer. There was no need for that yet.

For now, she was on her tod . . .

A recon exercise . . .

On the terrace of identical houses, some less well kept than others, one stood out as in dire need of repair. Her old man would call it the worst house in the best street. The one to buy if she was in the market for a new home. The top and ground floors were lit, the middle floors in darkness. On the side of the front door, an original brass bell push was affixed to the exterior wall, dulled with age, engraved with the name J. BYRNE, the property's first occupant perhaps.

Now, the house was split into flats.

The outer entrance was a French door, painted black with windows into the inner hallway, which threw up no warnings. It was tidy, separated from the main house by a solid wooden door. Frankie noticed some large footprints facing both ways on a black-and-white mosaic tiled floor. The rest of the hallway was pristine.

Her eyes travelled to the mailboxes.

What she saw raised the hairs on the nape of her neck. The labels had all been written on the same paper, in the same hand, probably on the same day. One merely said: Flat 6. Frankie looked up. Unless this house had undergone recent renovation – the shabby exterior suggested the opposite – there was little chance that a bunch of tenants had arrived en masse and taken up residency. She stepped away, then looked up, the words 'multiple occupancy' taking on a sinister meaning in her detective brain.

Something was off.

Taking out her mobile, she zoomed in, capturing the names contained there, though she was convinced that they were all dodgy. She repeated the process in neighbouring properties. In those hallways junk mail littered the floor, along with bikes and folded pushchairs, residents claiming this limited extra storage space as their own. More importantly, mailboxes were personalised, each in a different hand, some of the names written in block capitals, some in flamboyant script. Other labels were typed, some scribbled. They were old and new, some faded by the sun, one written in the colours of the rainbow to make it stand out.

Andrea would approve.

She still hadn't returned Frankie's call.

Dismissing the thought, Frankie scanned the labels again to satisfy herself that she wasn't overthinking, exaggerating what she was seeing to fit her point of view. She wasn't. This was life. This was normal. If she had to describe it, she'd say that the house next door was trying too hard.

Crossing the street, she blipped her car doors open.

She was about to start the engine and drive away, when a skinny youth jogged down the street and made his way up the path of the house where she'd been standing moments before. He was dressed in black clothing and white trainers. In his hand, a plastic carrier bag. With his back turned, she couldn't get an image that might ID him.

She captured him on her iPhone, just in case.

He glanced over his shoulder, then rang the bell.

Sliding down in her seat, Frankie watched and waited, wondering if he'd spotted her hanging around and was about to blow the whistle. Light flooded the window of a room on the floor above. An older man appeared behind the glass: tanned, bald, fortyish, built like a tank. He looked down, checking who was at street level. Seconds later, he appeared at the front door, motormouth, yanking the young guy inside.

What she'd witnessed gave Frankie hope.

25

Full of good cuisine and booze, Ben was sending the zeds up, giving David plenty of time to think as he drove home, mostly about the enquiry into Adam Hall. Frankie was there too, weighing him down. She'd been gone a matter of days, already a big miss from his life. There was no doubt that she'd resume her MIT duties. Bright had paved the way for that to happen just as soon as the child abduction case was over. That could be a long way off. And while a lengthy, complex investigation would keep her out of David's hair – exactly what he needed while he investigated her sister's murder – what Frankie had been asked to do was highly dangerous.

The decision to send her single-crewed to Scotland's capital with no backup from local police worried David. Their guv'nor trusted her not to do anything stupid. He got that, but he'd never get over it if anything happened to her – and neither would her family. Frankie had hung up on him during their last call. He could tell from her voice that she was in a bad place. Even though he was similarly impaired, through no fault of his own, he felt guilty for putting her there.

Her happiness mattered to him.

Tapping the WhatsApp icon on his CarPlay system, he instructed the social media platform to send Frankie a message. He made every effort to sound upbeat, even though she'd receive it as text: 'Hey, it's me. I hear you're northbound.' He paused. There was so much more he wanted to say, so much more he could and should say. He stopped short of saying it.

He didn't want to spook her.

'Take it easy, Frank. And watch your back. Call if you need me, day or night.'

When asked if he wanted to send the message, David said, 'No.'

He could do better. He glanced into the passenger seat. Ben was out of it. David composed the message again, repeating it verbatim, advising the CarPlay system to send it this time, then waited . . . and waited some more.

'She's not going to reply.' Ben opened his bloodshot eyes.

David met his gaze. 'Sorry, didn't mean to wake you.'

'Mind if I smoke?'

'No, I'll drop you here.'

'Don't bother.' His nephew sat up straight. ''Fess up, then. What did you do?'

'What do you mean?'

'You know perfectly well. I was there too, remember.' He meant at Frankie's party. 'I bumped into her outside the club. She was looking for you, though she tried to hide it when she saw me. I'd already seen you sneak out. She looked stunning, don't you think?' He was rubbing it in.

David didn't answer.

The ghost of DS Jane Vincent was in his head; a Met colleague he'd worked with at West End Central, an officer he'd grown fond of. There was a moment when he might have shared how deep his feelings ran. He'd bottled it, allowing the thought to float past like an air balloon before plummeting as her killer entered the flat, the sound of gunfire overriding David's inhibition. Four shots fired in quick succession by her lunatic ex.

David held her until she was gone.

That fateful day pervaded his dreams until he left the south, returning to Northumberland, the place of his birth. Not to forget. He'd never do that. Battered and bruised emotionally, he'd come home to heal. He had Frankie to thank for making it possible to live with his grief.

He owed her . . .

And would deliver.

26

Frankie continued to observe the house as the man who'd come to the door watched the street from the floor above. He was smoking and had the window open. A text arrived on her mobile. She sank further down in her seat, snatched it off the charger, dimming the screen so it wouldn't draw the attention of the guy across the road. It was from Andrea, asking if she was available to talk. Frankie called her. Keeping her voice low, she explained that she'd have to make it quick, where she was and what she was doing.

'I know,' Andrea said. 'I spoke to Graham. How's it going?'

'I might be on to something.' Frankie explained what had led her to that conclusion, describing the premises and the smoker leaning on the windowsill. 'I could be a mile wrong. Maybe he's a bodybuilder who likes housework.'

'Bodybuilders don't smoke.'

'Says someone who's never worked the West End.'

Andrea laughed. 'Where are you now?'

'Still watching the house.'

'What do you see?'

Frankie looked out through the windscreen. The street was quiet. Not a soul about. No movement in the houses, beyond flickering TV screens. 'A fabulous Georgian terrace, why?'

'Anything else?'

'Yeah, a shedload of flats. Hundreds of them.'

'High-rise?'

'Google Earth is a wonderful tool.' Frankie checked her rear-view mirror, looking for Andrea's private vehicle. It wouldn't be the first time her sister-in-law had shadowed her movements covertly. Frankie had a feeling that she was about to deliver proper intel. 'Go on then, hit me with it.'

'I've been viewing the video from the eye in the sky to see if the crew captured footage of the guy who legged it out the rear doors of the van. When I zoomed in on the stills they took, I noticed the Mercedes had an identifying number on the roof, like we do.'

'You're kidding?'

'This operation is bigger and more sophisticated than we thought, Frank. These guys are organised. The way I see it, someone with a high vantage point at your location waits for a signal when the delivery van is a few minutes out. When it arrives, the lookout talks to a runner on the ground, exchanges the cargo. Job done.'

'Except the Mercedes didn't make it this time.'

Eyeing the surrounding apartments, Frankie thought of the skinny youth who'd made his way into the house she'd been watching a moment ago and the big bugger who'd come to the door, who may or may not have anything to do with child trafficking. She glanced up at him, wondering if he was waiting for such a signal.

She couldn't make up her mind if he was shifty or anxious.

'You're suggesting the van's driver and co-driver had no idea who they were dealing with or where they were going?'

'Except for a postcode—'

'Clever. What's the number on the van?'

'Eleven.'

'Shit! Are you sure?'

'From a distance, the helicopter crew thought it was two random marks on the roof. Forensics had other ideas. I've been up there and had a look myself. It's an identification sticker, applied after manufacture. There's no doubt about it. Makes you wonder how many more vans there are.'

At least ten, Frankie thought. 'Any prints yet?'

'Coming soon.'

'We need to establish origin of those after-market stickers.'

'On it. Maybe we'll get lucky.'

'I don't feel lucky. I have Mitch. I need more bodies.'

'You have me and as many of my team as I can spare.'

'How you going to manage that?'

'We'll stretch out the accident investigation and work out of Berwick, if that helps.'

'Thanks, Andy, we'll rendezvous there. First thing. I have something to tell you. Don't be late.'

'You're acting like a DI already.'

Frankie laughed. 'Listen, I didn't want to upset you this morning.' The smoker at the window was looking directly at her. 'Shit! I think he made me.'

Andrea was still on the line. 'Get out, *now*!'

27

In Bright's anteroom, David sat back, hands linked behind his head, as he observed Indira. She'd been invested in Joanna's case from the moment he'd taken her into his confidence, hard at it since early doors, making copious notes and much progress, by the look of it. Closing her laptop, she flashed him a winning smile.

'You got something on Hall?' he said.

'Yeah, he didn't move around a lot in the early part of his career, so it wasn't hard to collate a list of personnel.'

'Let me see.'

For security's sake, she'd been instructed not to print anything out on paper that they could view on a screen. She got up and came round to his desk so he could view her laptop. The list of officers Hall had worked with to date was comprehensive. Having spent much of his service in the Met, most meant nothing to David.

'Anyone stand out?'

'One or two . . . both of them female.' She highlighted the names PC Rachel Hart and PC Stephanie Masterson on the second page. 'These two had great qualifications with obvious potential, expected to move up. They were respected. Keen. Nothing about them would suggest that they would put their ticket in early . . . and yet they both did.'

David looked at her, intrigued.

'What I find interesting and more than a tad suspicious is that, in both cases, they resigned for, quote, "Unspecified personal reasons", unquote. Incidentally, both worked with Frankie's dad. They weren't the only women to leave, but they were so high profile they stuck out. After some digging I found out that Rachel went on to take an LLB at Durham.'

'Did she complete her degree?'

'With a distinction. She's now a barrister, specialising in family law.'

'And Stephanie?'

'Went into accountancy. I don't know where though. It could be that they just wanted a total change of career.'

David caught her ambivalence. 'You don't think so?'

'No, I don't.'

'Why?'

'If it was me, I'd never put personal reasons on a resignation form. No ambitious woman would. It's a negative, open to interpretation: childbirth, mental health breakdown or, dare I say, inability to handle the big boys.'

'Good call. Sounds like a place to start making external enquiries.'

Berwick was in bright sunshine when Mitch arrived, keen to hook up with Frankie and crack on. With a view over the car park, Acting Inspector Graham Ross came out to meet him at reception, offering a warm welcome and a firm handshake. Mitch had beaten Frankie in. The office they had been allocated was up a flight of creaking stairs on the first floor, an unused part of the magistrates' court, big enough to accommodate the two of them, plus Andrea's team when they turned up.

She was en route with a colleague.

Mitch glanced around the room.

Left empty for months, if not years, a strong smell of polish indicated that someone had dusted recently. They'd opened the window to air the place, but the smell of mould lingered. He'd experienced worse. The furniture was ancient, the desks empty, with telephones that belonged in the seventies, before he was born; one of them even had a rotary dial. His mood lifted as his eyes came to rest on a modern kettle, coffee, tea, a fresh carton of milk and ginger snaps.

Grateful for the hospitality, he made himself a brew and sat down to wait.

The first thing Frankie would do was ask after the boy. Slipping his mobile from his pocket, Mitch called Acres to check on him. The consultant reported that the child had eaten breakfast at six thirty. He was still showing signs of agitation. This wouldn't please Frankie any more than it did him.

She'd be hoping for better news.

Thanking Acres, Mitch disconnected.

Voices and footsteps reached him through the door.

Andrea entered with one of her crew, Tango 5285, Sergeant Samantha 'Sam' Casey.

Leaving Sam chatting with Mitch, Andrea walked to the window and looked down at the empty space reserved for Frankie's vehicle. With her back to the others, she stared at it, the last words she'd said to Frankie echoing in her head . . .

Get out, now!

It didn't take long for a sense of foreboding to arrive. Even though Frankie had been up half the night, it was unheard of for her to be late for work.

She had no off switch.

Unlike many who lived alone, if she was awake, she was talking within five minutes of getting out of bed and on the phone – usually to Andrea, Rae or her father. As a family, they were inseparable. Andrea checked her watch, then her phone. No missed calls. No message alerts. She clicked the messages icon. Frankie's was the last text she'd received.

Panicking, Andrea called her number.

It rang out, unanswered.

Behind her, unaware of her developing distress, the others were discussing Nigeria's win over South Africa in the Africa Cup of Nations. Football was not her thing. Even if it had been, she had other matters on her mind.

Andrea swung round. 'Mitch, when did you last speak to Frankie?'

He peered over his shoulder. 'Late last night. Why?'

'How late?'

He turned to face her. 'About eleven.'

'What time were you expecting her in?'

'She told me she'd be back at dawn, but even dynamos need recharging. She probably slept through her alarm—'

'When have you ever known her do that? Or not call to explain a delay?'

'Maybe it slipped her mind. She was planning a visit to the hospital. She wanted to be there when samples were taken from Amir, though they didn't mention she'd been in when I called just now.' For a moment, he couldn't speak. 'Andy, you're scaring me. What is it you know that we don't?'

28

David asked Indira to set up a meeting with ex-PC Rachel Hart, then typed an email for Bright, letting him know in writing where he intended to go next and why. In it, he mentioned Indira's progress. A man after David's own heart, Bright recognised excellence and praised those who deserved it, nurturing them, guiding them to make the right choices, giving them a leg-up. Though he could throw his weight around, and often did, he had an undeniable affection for his staff, especially the grafters among them.

Frankie, he adored.

In the last half-hour, Indira had come up with a credible reason why as a force they needed the duty rosters from Frank Snr. She'd put forward an idea on how they might approach him, without tipping him off that they had new evidence in relation to Joanna's murder or raising his suspicions. It was data the Cold Case Unit gathered and reassessed during every review, so much as they were able, information they could do with at their fingertips.

David was convinced this would push Bright over the line.

'Indi, have you seen the guv'nor this morning?'

'No, boss.'

'Hmm . . .' David frowned. 'He was due in at eight.'

'Probably on the golf course.' She grinned. 'I didn't say that.'

David marked the email URGENT and pressed send. He waited a few minutes before glancing at his watch, then left his seat, using the connecting door to access Bright's office. He wasn't there. His newspaper was lying on his empty desk, folded and unread. Where the hell was he?

*

Sam Casey had worked with Andrea for a decade and knew her better than anyone. Though she'd made light of Frankie's failure to turn up on time, she grew more and more agitated as the morning progressed. Taking her to one side, out of Mitch's hearing, Sam lowered her voice. 'You're struggling, boss. When did you last speak to Frankie?'

'Two-ish. She was watching some dodgy guy in a house.'

Sam saw the blood drain from her face. 'And?'

'She thought she'd been made. I told her to get the hell out of there. Seconds later, she sent me a text to stand down.'

'Show me.'

Andrea accessed the message and passed her the phone.

Sam read it – False alarm. x – and looked up.

'It put my mind at ease, but what if it wasn't . . . false, I mean? We'd agreed to rendezvous here first thing. She wanted a word and told me not to be late.'

'Shit! You'd better call David.'

David had just sat down when his mobile rang. Curious as to why Andrea was calling, he tapped to answer, his stomach taking a dive as she asked him if he'd heard from Frankie. He hadn't. Andy didn't let much freak her out, but the pitch of her voice was higher and she was in a hell of a hurry. His imagination was in overdrive, worst-case scenarios presenting themselves.

Noting a change in atmosphere, Indira looked up.

She didn't ask and he didn't tell. Ignoring her concern, he concentrated on the call. 'Has she checked out of her hotel?'

'We don't know where she's staying,' Andrea said.

'Head north. I'll call you back.' David hung up, then tapped on Bright's phone number.

His wife came on the line. 'Morning, David. We're running late . . . about to leave—'

'Ellen, this is urgent. Did you make Frankie's hotel reservation in Edinburgh?'

'Yes, why?'

'I need the details.'

'Is there a problem?'

'Frankie's not turned up for work.'

There was a short pause. When Ellen spoke again, her voice sounded muffled, as if she'd covered the speaker or turned her head. 'It's David . . . Stone,' she was telling his guv'nor.

Bright came on the line. 'What's up?'

'Frankie failed to meet with Mitch and Andrea in Berwick this morning. No one has heard from her. It's probably nothing. I'd like to check if she's still at her hotel. I need—'

'Hold on.'

On the other end of the line, a discussion was taking place, Bright sounding as concerned as he was. David heard heels on a parquet floor moving away at speed, then silence, then Bright's voice introducing himself to someone, the words 'one of my detectives' and 'need to locate her' coming across loud and clear. 'It's urgent. Give her a knock, I'll wait.'

David held his breath as the seconds ticked by.

Instinctively, he knew Frankie was in trouble.

Bright's voice broke as he came on the line. 'Her bed's not been slept in. Her vehicle is not in the car park and her overnight bag is lying unopened on her bed. Now get off the fucking phone and find her.'

29

Andrea was sixty-five miles closer to Edinburgh than David, over halfway there. Before he'd put the phone down, she was on the move, rushing down the stairs and outside to her Traffic car with Mitch. She raced away from Berwick station with David's words ringing in her ears: first stop, the hotel. In the meantime, he'd take care of things his end, doing all he could from Middle Earth with the assistance of Police Scotland. He'd put a trace on Frankie's car and, more importantly, her mobile, in an attempt to locate her.

Andrea joined the A1, her speedometer climbing as she floored the accelerator: sixty, seventy, eighty miles an hour, under blue lights, paving her way through rush hour and with no time to waste. The most difficult journey she'd ever made. Mitch was rigid in the passenger seat, so pale she thought he might throw up, silent for the first twenty miles.

Andrea knew what he was thinking.

If an Organised Crime Group had Frankie, they would never see her again.

Bright had just reached the office, when an urgent call came in from Police Scotland's control room asking to be patched through to him personally. That didn't bode well. Fearing the worst, he took the call, steeling himself for what was to come, already rehearsing how he'd break bad news to Frankie's father if she'd come to harm.

His name and rank was all he could manage when Bright took the call.

'Good morning, sir. This is Inspector Ed Cooper, Police Scotland, Traffic. A vehicle was involved in an accident in Leith during the night, the car written off, its female driver taken to the Royal Infirmary A&E. I found that her vehicle registration number was blocked on the PNC. Further enquiries revealed that it belongs to one of yours. As a result, I've been asked to contact you. The driver had no identification on her, no bag either.'

Bright knew why. If this was Frankie, she had more sense than to carry either while checking out an OCG. 'Did you recover a mobile?'

'Yes, sir. It's with the patient. The device is dead. No use to her.'

'What did she look like?'

'Small, brunette.'

'Bolshie?'

'Sir?'

'Was she talking, man?'

'She wasn't making much sense last night, to be honest. She took quite a knock and was asking for someone called Amir.'

Andrea's mobile lit up: David. Taking a deep breath, she asked Mitch to put it on speaker.

David was rattled as he relayed the information Bright had just given him.

'Where are you?' he said.

'Almost there,' Andrea said.

'Drop Mitch at the hotel. Frankie's in the infirmary: EH16 4SA. Her car was T-boned near your location in the early hours. Go! And let me know when you get there.'

He disconnected.

Andrea screeched to a halt on Customs Wharf. 'Out you get.'

Mitch grabbed his jacket from the rear seat, then reached for the door handle and jumped out, leaning in to speak to her through the open door. 'Collect Frankie's stuff and question the staff, right?'

Andrea nodded.

He was about to shut the door, when she reminded him that Frankie would not have taken her warrant card with her in case she was spotted by the people she was watching.

'Check the safe,' she said.

'How? I don't have the code.'

'You won't need it. Try 2003 – my old collar number. I use hers. She uses mine.'

Mitch pulled a face: *seriously?*

She glared at him. 'What? It works! Share that with anyone and you're in trouble. Also, if her room's not been paid for, tell the hotel admin to take it up with HQ.'

'Shall I make my way to the hospital when I'm done?'

'Depends on what I find when I get there. I'll bell you.'

Mitch took off.

Reprogramming her satnav, Andrea headed south, arriving on Restalrig Road with a new ETA of twenty minutes to cover four miles. Heavy traffic slowed to a crawl. Sod that. She activated her siren. Frankie's condition could deteriorate quickly. She didn't have time to hang around.

30

David's head was in Scotland. He was desperate, gutted not to have been on his way north to Edinburgh. Details on Frankie's condition were sketchy. He'd rather that the information had come from people he knew and trusted, not some polis from another force who might have been tempted to play down her condition to Bright who, it had to be said, was not the easiest man to placate when things went wrong. No sooner had the thought occurred to him than the man himself burst through the adjoining door. 'Any news?'

'We're making headway,' Indira said.

'I meant from Andrea.'

'Not yet,' David said, sparing her blushes. 'Anything further from Police Scotland?'

'That's why I'm here. They have confirmed that Frankie's accident happened on Commercial Street in Leith at around four a.m. adjacent to The Language Institute. Does that tally with where her provider said her mobile went off?'

'Correct. Damaged in the accident, I presume.'

'Which is why we haven't heard from her.'

'Let's hope it's nothing more sinister.'

'It isn't.' Bright's relief was palpable. 'Local police have the incident on CCTV. It was a two-car collision, a Renault hitting the passenger side of Frankie's car, failing to give way at a junction. Otherwise, it may have been fatal. Both occupants in the Renault were also hospitalised. Neither has form, though they soon will. Just two daft kids, as high as kites on a cocktail of drink and drugs. So, rest assured she wasn't followed, nor the target of those she was watching.'

David felt the tension leave him.

Andrea had company. In an area of Edinburgh known locally as Little France, a police vehicle moved into a position behind her, blue lights flashing. It followed her into the hospital grounds, an enormous white building that spelled out EMERGENCY DE-PARTMENT in huge capital letters on its roof at one end. Two up, local officers had spotted her Traffic car, clocking the fact that she belonged on the south side of the Scottish border.

Using her rear-view mirror, Andrea watched a young cop get out, pulling on his hat, adjusting his sunglasses, before swaggering towards her like a Miami cop. *Here we go.* She climbed out of her vehicle, increasing the possibility of him making her life difficult. She outranked him. She was a woman. Taller by at least a foot. More reasons to have a go, should the Scot need them.

'Bonjour!' Her smile was ignored. 'Can I help you, officer?'

'What are you doing here?'

'Same as you, I imagine.'

He glanced at the insignia on her Northumbria patrol car. 'A bit off your beat to be running blues and twos, aren't you?'

An older officer, a sergeant, had joined them, a barrel of a man who'd seen more service than the two of them put together. His presence didn't deter the young cop from reminding her that she had no powers outside of her jurisdiction.

'Technically, that's true,' she said.

'In a hurry, were you?'

'Yup,' Andrea said. 'Over the limit, speed-wise. What are you going to do about it?'

'Knock it off, Sandy . . .' The sergeant gave his co-driver a dollop of wisdom. 'We're on the same side. If you ask nicely, I'm sure the inspector has a reason for being here.'

'Thanks . . .' Andrea thumbed towards the entrance. 'I have urgent business inside, so if PC Protocol has no further objections, I'd like to get on with it.'

'What business?' Sandy couldn't help himself.

'A colleague of mine was admitted in the early hours of this morning after a serious RTA. I need to get in there in case she carks it, assuming that's OK with you?'

She could have said that Frankie was dealing with a major enquiry and might take any intel with her if she didn't survive. That would draw questions. Police Scotland would want chapter and verse. Besides, Northumbria wanted the collar. Bright would go apeshit if she spoke out of turn.

Sandy swallowed the lie, though he continued to push his luck. 'You're in uniform, driving a police vehicle. You didn't think to clear it with our HQ?'

'I did not,' Andrea said. 'I was on duty in Berwick when I heard. Came straight here. Tell me you wouldn't have done the same.'

The sergeant sent the young pretender packing, telling him to wait in the car. He didn't move, just stood there playing blink first for ten seconds or more.

'Go on, piss off,' the sergeant said.

Sandy stared at Andrea, his jaw bunching. He'd lost the swagger as he moved away.

The sergeant turned to face Andrea. 'He's young—'

'And rude,' she said.

'I'm not arguing.' The sergeant continued to make amends. 'I'm sure what he meant to say, what he should have said was, is there anything we can do to help?'

'You did. I appreciate the goodwill.'

Andrea was already walking away.

31

Frankie was completely zonked, a bruised forehead, otherwise uninjured according to medical staff, who were more friendly than the copper Andrea had the gloves off with on the way in. Frankie's head had been scanned as a precaution. No signs of internal bleeding or swelling. She hadn't been sedated but was on strong painkillers. Given that her accident was less than six hours old, the fact that she'd been up all night and kept vigil at Amir's bedside the night before, she'd probably sleep through an earthquake.

Andrea took a sneaky look at the medical chart hanging from a rail at the bottom of her bed. She knew her fair share about vital signs and nothing on it worried her. She called David. Best to keep it in-house until she was sure of her facts. No need to upset the family. Rae would be furious, but what she didn't know wouldn't hurt her. As the call rang out, Andrea checked her watch: 09:37. Was that all? It felt like she'd left Berwick hours ago.

David's concern reached her ear. 'Andy, how is she?'

'OK, I think. Concussed. Kept in for obs. She's asleep now. Probable discharge tomorrow.'

'Discharge now, you mean,' Frankie groaned.

Andrea turned, relieved to see her awake. 'Welcome back.'

'I feel like shit. Get me out of here.'

'Was that Frankie?' David said. 'Can I speak to her?'

'Hold on . . .' Andrea held her mobile to her chest to dull the sound through the speaker. 'David wants to speak to you?'

Frankie shook her head, wincing, no doubt wishing she hadn't.

Andrea turned away, avoiding eye contact with Frankie while she lied for her. 'She's not up to it, David. She said to tell you she's had worse and not to worry. I'll chat with the medic before I leave, see if we can get her home today. There's zero chance she'll agree to stay in, but you can't ignore a head injury, however slight. Will you pass the message on to Bright that I'm with her and that she's OK?'

'Yes, of course.'

David sounded like anyone does when they are surplus to requirements. Left out, offering help to those who'd rather not accept it. Andrea wasn't stupid. Something had happened between him and Frankie since her party. One minute there were furtive looks across the dance floor. The next he was gone. Whatever it was that prompted his quick exit, Frankie wasn't sharing.

Must be serious.

Andrea swung round, this time muting the phone. 'He's worried, Frank. Can't you just say hello?'

Frankie's avoidance tactic was to close her eyes.

'How old are you, five?' Andrea said.

Frankie didn't answer.

She sat up, then instantly laid down.

Apart from Rae, there was no one on Earth that Andrea loved more than Frankie Oliver. They had been through hell together and come out the other side. Like the time Frankie was left unconscious in the rear of the car, an offender setting fire to it before she fled. Andrea could almost feel the intense heat, smell the acrid smoke.

On another occasion, at an RV point on the south side of the Tyne, one minute they were chatting, the next Andrea hit the deck, taking a crossbow bolt to her chest. She couldn't help thinking that one of these days, the wheel would come off permanently for one of them. Which one was open to question. It would come at the most obscure time, when they thought they were safe, when someone off their head would act, putting them in mortal danger.

Today was not that day.

Andrea smiled at Frankie. 'Get some rest.'

32

As he pocketed his mobile, David was aware that Indira had noticed his low mood. He reassured her that Frankie was awake and seemingly unharmed, apart from a nasty bump on the head that would disappear and a stubbornness that wouldn't. He didn't mention that she'd refused to take his call. The rift between them was a personal matter, something he was unable to explain to her or Frankie. He was backed into a corner with no way out.

The script he'd imagined at her party was full of plot holes.

There was no doubt in his mind that they'd been destined to meet, like the poles of a magnet, a force too powerful to ignore; two lost souls searching for a better hand than they had been dealt, the prospect of a happier life. Maybe their relationship would work itself out. Maybe not.

Right now, the odds were against them.

Leaving his seat, he headed next door to update his guv'nor.

Bright was on the phone, arranging to meet with someone, explaining that he didn't have the manpower to protect a child, that he had a plan to secure guardianship and a safe house, somewhere the kid would get round-the-clock surveillance that didn't involve an armed guard, plus the care and attention he was going to need, an emergency protection order if the person on the other end could manage it.

'Yes, sir. The parents are unknown . . . a boy, Amir. Foreign national, I suspect.' The detective chief super paused, listening intently. 'That's all we have. Nothing else is known about him at this stage. I have reason to believe that he's at significant risk, even in hospital. The sooner we can get him out of there, the better. As young as he is, he's a witness.' Another pause. 'I appreciate that, but the circumstances are exceptional. There's a valid reason why this one must stay off the radar of social services.' He checked his watch. 'Would midday suit?'

David had no clue why his guv'nor was handling this, beyond the fact that Frankie was temporarily incapacitated, unable to proceed with the trafficking case until she was fit to do so. It wouldn't be the case for long. Once she was out of bed, she'd crack on. He watched Bright scribble down the name and address of a senior county court judge whose ear he obviously had . . . for the moment.

'Thank you,' he said. 'I appreciate it. Yes, I'll be there.'

He put down the phone and stood up. As he grabbed his coat, David gave him the good news on Frankie. Bright blew out a breath and turned away. What mattered, the *only* thing that mattered – to either detective – was that she'd survived another close call.

'Sir?'

Bright turned to face him.

'I don't suppose you've had time to consider the request I emailed about the duty rosters?'

'Yes, I have. Excellent idea.'

'With your permission, I'd like to approach Frankie's father to discuss it.'

'No, you crack on. I'll do it. I think it best that you keep your distance for now.' Bright paused, a moment of consideration. 'I'll tell him it's a pre-emptive strike, a plan to update our system so it works effectively on historical cases. He won't question that if he thinks it'll help his own case.'

33

It wasn't the drugs. Frankie had suffered nightmares her entire life. They were often about being stranded in unfamiliar places with seemingly no way home and no means of communication, where every stranger was a threat. This time she was holding hands with a lost boy. In the distance there was a distressed woman with arms outstretched, both woman and child begging for help, unable to reach each other across an invisible barrier.

Frankie woke in a pool of sweat.

The first thing she saw was Andrea.

The first thing she said was, 'How's Amir?'

Andy avoided her gaze. 'Don't fret, he's fine.'

'Tell me the truth. Did anyone call the hospital this morning?'

'I said he's fine!' Andrea snapped. 'Mitch rang for an update. If you must know, Acres said Amir's discharge is imminent.'

'What? That's ridiculous—'

'I know. She's out of her bloody mind if she thinks he's anywhere near ready. His physical injuries might be healing, but he's still in a bad place, terribly agitated.'

He wasn't the only one.

Andrea was acting weird. She wasn't stressing over Frankie's RTA either. She'd seen enough survivors to tell the difference between minor and serious injuries. Even after Frankie reassured her that she felt perfectly fine, her mood didn't lift.

This was something else . . .

It was to do with Amir.

The last time they had spoken about him, Frankie had opposed her wish to foster the child, hinting that he needed someone more qualified. Andrea was angry with her lack of enthusiasm.

Now she seemed completely overwhelmed, emotionally drained just hearing his name. It wasn't merely a reaction to Frankie's wisdom. It was something much deeper than that. Normally cool in a crisis, Andrea always found a way out, or a way forward, depending on the circumstances.

Not today.

She was conflicted, panicking almost.

In Frankie's head, they were on her marina balcony, a face-off, anger coming from both sides. In Andrea's case there was another emotion in play. Almost but not quite imperceptible, it had flashed across her face before she could hide it.

Frankie hadn't understood then.

She did now.

Tears pricked the back of her eyes. As much as she hated seeing Andrea this way, she wouldn't, couldn't, shy away from the difficult question on the tip of her tongue as she realised what was troubling her.

'Oh, Andy. Fostering is not something you want, is it?'

Unable to meet her gaze, Andrea looked out of the window, then turned back, almost choking on her words as they spilled from her mouth. 'It's not that I don't want it. Rae and I said we'd take a kid, irrespective of age. I'm ready to commit, I swear, but you were right. Fostering must be tailored to the needs of the child. Amir's are complex. He's so young, so lost, his situation unpredictable. If I were to say no and he goes into care, which we both know he will, Rae will hate me for it.'

'Then you do right to pause.'

'Frank, this is no temporary wobble.'

'Then what is it?'

'It's fucking serious . . .' Andrea stalled. 'I didn't see it at first. I do now. Rae's reaction to Amir's plight was profound. The idea that we could help brought her unadulterated joy. She's expecting us – and by us I mean you and me – to fix this, and I don't know if we can. Even if we could, can you imagine what it would do to her once she's formed a bond with that little one if his parents were to turf up and claim him. Unlike adoptive parents, we'd have no legal rights whatsoever. How would we ever know that his biological parents didn't sell him in the first place?'

'You won't.'

'No, but it happens, even in the UK, right? And if the law is on their side, what's to stop them regaining custody and doing it again? I couldn't live with that uncertainty. Neither could Rae. It would kill her.'

Frankie was reading the subtext. 'You lied to me, didn't you?'

'What? No!'

'Admit it. Rae didn't send you to my place the other day. You couldn't back-pedal fast enough.'

Andrea wiped her face with both hands. 'I don't know how to tell her, Frank.'

'Just tell her what you told me. Neither of you could anticipate this. Rae loves you. She'll understand if you suggest that you wait for a child to come to you as planned.'

'Will she hell!' A tear rolled down Andrea's cheek. 'This will break her, Frank. And where will that leave me . . . us? Is that why you wanted a word? To have another go at me?'

'No . . . Quite the opposite.'

'What? I thought you said—'

'I changed my mind. As we speak, there's a cop stationed outside Amir's room, a precaution in case anyone should try to get to him. I had to consider his immediate future. I don't know how far he's taken it, but I asked Bright to support your case for fostering.'

'Fuck!' Andrea was pacing the room. 'What a mess.'

'Yeah, you'd better tell Rae before she's given the go-ahead. Get the conversation over with. It's for her own good, and yours. Don't worry, I'll sort Bright. No one else knows. If anyone ends up with egg on their face, it won't be you. I'll tell him I got hold of the wrong end of the stick.'

'Frank, if Amir's at risk—'

'Not your problem.'

'Easy for you to say.' She approached Frankie's bed. 'Give me twenty-four hours.'

'To do what?'

'I need to go home and lay it on the line for Rae, then come to a decision . . . together. If she knew we were even having this conversation without her, she'd be mortified. Please, Frank. Don't say anything to Bright yet. You'll have our answer tomorrow.'

Frankie hesitated. 'Andy, I don't want children. Never have. Probably never will, but I know one thing. If I took one on, my life would change immeasurably. They would become my first and last priority—'

'I know.'

'OK, I'll wait, but if this is not something you want with all your heart, now or in the future, you come clean. You cannot mess with a child's life to avoid having to face Rae with the truth – all of it. If you don't tell her, I will.'

34

Andrea left the ward on the pretext that she needed to wash her face. Frankie was right, but their heart-to-heart had taken its toll on both. Andrea felt totally exhausted and wanted two things: to force Frankie to rest and to make a quick exit from the hospital alone. With such a monumental decision to make, she needed space, time to think without Frankie bending her ear.

To that end, she headed for the nurses' station, asking to see the duty consultant.

A few moments later, a middle-aged man swept into the atrium, his white coat flowing in his wake. He was kind-looking, with greying hair and hooded eyes beneath bushy brows.

'Officer? Douglas Munro. You wanted to see me?'

'Yes. Are you looking after Frances Oliver?'

'I am.'

'Are you planning to discharge her today?' She took in his concern. 'I'm Inspector Andrea McGovern, Northumbria Traffic. I'm not here to make an arrest, sir. We're colleagues. Family too, as it happens.'

'I see . . .' Munro appeared relieved. 'She's only been with us a few hours, Inspector. The CT scan was clear, but I'd like to keep her tonight and will reassess her in the morning. A precautionary measure. Subdural haematomas can develop soon after trauma or take days or weeks to appear.'

'That's sensible. In my line of work, I see a lot of bumps on the head and a whole lot worse.'

'I can imagine.' He stared at her for a moment. 'Have you seen Ms Oliver yet?'

Andrea gave a nod. 'I've just come from there.'

'Do you have any concerns? Anything about her strike you as odd this morning?'

'She's odd every morning.' Andrea's humour fell flat. 'You do know she lives alone?'

He bristled. 'That's not what she told me earlier.'

'Figures. She's keen to get home.'

'I'll try and talk her out of it.'

'Good luck with that.'

'Is there anything else I can do for you?'

'I could use a bed, if you have one handy.'

At last, a smile.

Wanting to leave on a positive note, Andrea smiled back, then faked irritation. 'Would you excuse me a second?' Pulling out her mobile, she tapped the home screen, lifting the device to her ear. She took a couple of steps away, remaining in his eyeline.

'McGovern.'

He locked eyes with her.

'OK . . . Text me your location . . . On my way.'

Pocketing the device, she moved towards Munro, apologising. 'Would you mind getting a message to Frances that I've been called away urgently? I don't want to disturb her again.'

He agreed.

She thanked him and walked away. Job done. A quick stop to pick up Mitch in Leith and she'd be heading south at speed.

Frankie rolled onto her side. She'd been watching the door to her room, wondering what was keeping Andrea, concerned that she was even more upset than she'd let on. Frankie hadn't forced her hand exactly, and didn't regret what she'd said, but it had hit her hard. She'd been gone fifteen minutes.

It didn't take Frankie long to realise that she wasn't coming back. When a nurse entered to confirm it, she knew that Andrea's call-out was a ruse. It was a manoeuvre she'd used herself many times when she couldn't face company, including and especially those she was closest to.

Without a mobile, Frankie asked to borrow one.

It surprised her that the call was answered immediately. The number she was calling from was not in anyone's contacts. Cops didn't tend to answer those. She'd thought about calling Dick, who'd bend over backwards to help her out, even if he had to throw a sickie, but another name was in her head.

The ringing tone stopped.

She forced an upbeat tone.

'David, I'm being held hostage. Come and get me.'

35

David arrived two hours later. Frankie almost shed a tear as he walked in, aware that if things had gone the other way during the night, they may never have spoken again. She wasn't being childish or mean, declining to speak to him on the phone earlier. She would have lost her shit for sure.

'Hey!' He was out of breath. 'I got here as quick as I could.'

'Thanks, David. I knew you'd come.'

Even now, as he gave her a gentle hug, she was losing control. His scent was working its magic. She stood there, limp in his arms, dressed in last night's clothes. She didn't know what she looked like. She didn't care. He was used to seeing her dishevelled. Only one thing mattered. He'd come to her rescue.

'I won't ask how you're feeling,' he said. 'I can imagine.'

'I've had worse in the Bigg Market on a Saturday night.'

He laughed.

Over the centuries, the medieval heart of Newcastle city centre had morphed into an area renowned for pub crawls some would describe as a vibrant party scene, others as utter pandemonium. It had seen its fair share of drunken fights. A police presence was essential, part of Frankie's beat when she first joined up.

'You should call home, Frank.'

'How did you—' Frankie got it. He'd been talking to Andrea. 'Anyway, my mobile's totalled.'

'Then borrow mine.'

'I'd rather not, thanks. You know what my olds are like. I'd rather present myself with two arms and legs. There's no point putting them through the wringer when they can't see for themselves that I'm OK—'

'You're not OK.'

'And they'll know that the minute I open my mouth. They'll only fret if I tell them what happened.'

'What did happen?'

'Don't know. One minute I was driving, the next . . . I vaguely remember sirens, flashing lights, the rear of an ambulance.'

'You didn't see the other car?'

'Not that I recall. Were the occupants badly injured?'

'That's you all over,' David said. 'They almost killed you. Your car's a write-off—'

'Well, I'm not, so stop bellyaching.'

He was right. Frankie was not OK, though as they left the ward, he didn't comment on her swift discharge from hospital. He knew the score. No medic had passed her fit to leave. She was going against their advice. Any cop would have done the same in her shoes, though she felt decidedly woozy now she was on her feet.

Despite accepting more painkillers, her head was splitting. She chose not to mention it. If she did, he'd wreck her plans to remain on duty for her own good. If Bright got to know of it, he'd pull her off the abduction case. That couldn't happen. If she'd been made last night, she couldn't afford to hang around giving the offenders breathing space and time to move to plan B. Frankie had no fallback position. An urgent operation had suddenly become critical.

36

David started the car just as a track on Spotify ended and another began, a guitar intro, then the haunting voice of American singer-songwriter Lucy Wainwright Roche. Not all the poignant lyrics of her song 'Call Your Girlfriend' resonated with them, but many did as they filled the airwaves, causing an atmosphere of unimaginable pain and regret, not to mention awkwardness.

In under a minute, Frankie was in bits in the seat beside him.

Killing the sound, he pulled over, stopping the car. He swivelled in his seat to face her. 'Hey! C'mon, Frank.' His smile never made his eyes. 'Don't cry. Hours away from a car crash, you're bound to be emotional.'

'And you're not?' Her bottom lip was trembling.

He didn't answer.

David was hurtling towards a car crash of a different kind. He didn't always show it, but he too had been moved by the music, the opening lines of the track still loud in his head. It was time they had the talk. He wanted to give Frankie reasons, to explain that his pulling back was not her fault. He wanted to take her in his arms and tell her not to get upset, second-guessing everything he'd said and done.

He'd never meant to hurt her.

He couldn't say it.

Frankie dried her eyes, avoiding his by looking out of the window. On the one hand, she was angry that he was holding back. On the other, she'd seen that her sadness was killing him. She couldn't breathe, let alone speak. She decided that the moment they had shared at her party was a pipe dream. The magic had gone. Her heart would mend eventually. He was there for her. They were mates. It would never be enough, but it was the most she could hope for.

She turned to face him, reverting to type.

'Are you going to drive, or did you bring a picnic?'

It wasn't relief she saw on his face as he turned the engine over and pulled out into traffic – it was anguish. Frankie didn't want to add to it, though she did wonder what was going on in his head.

Despite her attempts to quell her anger, it bubbled to the surface. He'd led her to believe that he'd left the past behind. At the time, she didn't question it – she wanted it to be true – but he was kidding himself.

And so was she.

Losing Jane had changed him. When he arrived in the north as Frankie's new boss, he was living alone and was lonely. Two very different things in her book. Fortunately, having Ben in his life had changed him more. When you had a kid, of whatever age, moping around was off the menu. From nothing, with a little help from her, he'd carved out a family life she'd been hoping to be part of. She was proud of that. She was proud of him.

She couldn't bear the silence. 'How's it going at Middle Earth?'

'Fine. Dick said he'd be in touch. He was worried, Frankie. We all were.'

'Not as worried as I am about the kid I found.'

'Want to give the hospital a bell?'

'No . . . I was hoping we could call in on the way.'

'Not like that, you don't.' David was staring at the blood on her clothing. 'Bright told me you'd built up a rapport with him. You really want to tear it down?'

37

Frankie was a brilliant detective, one of the best, but she had no more sense than she was born with. What made her great also made her vulnerable. She'd insisted that David drop her in Berwick so she could change, brief the team and pick up the kit Mitch had collected from her Leith hotel. He could run her to see Amir on his way home, she said. There was zero chance of David persuading her otherwise.

He told her to get her head down.

Once he'd dropped her at the nick, he shot off, something else she might misinterpret as uncaring. If he'd told her that he'd arranged to meet with former PC Rachel Hart at the Old Low Light Café, it would've drawn questions. He'd briefed Indi that he might be late and to start without him.

He just made it, but with little recollection of his drive to North Shields.

Indira was standing against a lamp post scrolling through notes on her mobile phone in readiness for the upcoming inter-view. He parked the car, updated her on Frankie's condition, then set off along the Fish Quay at the mouth of the Tyne.

As they approached the café, Frankie was in his head again, and not because he was near water – though he had happy mem-ories of time spent at her marina apartment less than thirty miles away or at the beach, their unofficial office, where they would often go to talk through complex cases. This was something else entirely. Of all the places Hart could have chosen to see him on a rare day off, this was the worst possible location.

David had been to the exact same spot on a summer's day much like this one, the day Frankie lost her rag in the incident room and began scrapping with a fellow detective. He'd driven her there with the intention of talking some sense into her, to find out why she'd kicked off, an attempt to understand – mitigation should the matter reach a disciplinary.

They fought that day, a heated exchange.

She'd disobeyed an order, said hurtful things, called him names, lied even. Whatever she was covering up was killing her. At the time, he had an inkling that it was to do with her dead sister and couldn't cajole her into a confession. Instead, he'd confided his innermost secrets, telling her how low he'd sunk after Jane's death, how grief almost destroyed him, a defining moment in his developing relationship with Frankie. He'd done it hoping it might prompt her to come clean and explain her loss of control.

His plan failed miserably.

She simply refused to discuss it.

Without Dick's help, David may never have got to the bottom of it. Dunne, the detective she'd fought with, had been slagging off her father's detection rate, triggering a downward spiral, reminding her of her sister's murder and the fact that the perpetrator had never been brought to justice – the very case David and Indira were now investigating.

What goes around . . .

38

Frankie felt better for having taken a nap on the journey to Berwick. As soon as she was out of the car, she was heading for the locker room. Before leaving, she downed a couple of painkillers, then made her way to her office to regroup with Mitch, Andrea and one other; none of them had expected to see her. Frankie had hoped for more personnel. Then again, Sam Casey's work rate was double that of most officers. She had investigative experience too – in the CID and as Andrea's 2i/c.

If Frankie had to pick one of her crew – Sam was it.

She handed Frankie a takeaway coffee and a Cornish pasty in a paper bag. Andrea's lunch, a sandwich, sat on the desk beside her, uneaten. Having abandoned Frankie without money or a mobile in Edinburgh, she was keeping her head down. She knew Frankie well enough to know that she wouldn't gripe about it until they were alone.

The phone rang.

Andrea picked it up, scribbled notes on a pad during what was a short call, thanked the caller and disconnected.

Frankie could tell she had news. 'Who was that?'

'Holly Fenton, technical support. It seems there's an app for everything. The voicemail on the Mercedes driver's phone is Bulgarian. Independently verified by a translator. The message was short, requesting an ETA. It came in two and a half minutes before Control received the first emergency call from a witness alerting them to the A1 crash.'

'Maybe that's what distracted the driver.'

'Very likely. There was no corresponding reply. No call, text, or voicemail. The phone was a burner, a new one. Nothing else on it. No contacts either. Holly is trying to establish where it was purchased. Also, it seems the Mercedes was late for its rendezvous.'

Sam looked at her boss. 'Makes you say that?'

'The person who sent it was screaming for an update,' Andrea explained. 'It sounds like whoever they were talking to had taken possession of Amir, been given a van and the keys to go with it, a clean mobile and a postcode – that's all.'

Mitch brushed puff pastry crumbs from his shirt. 'They were working blind?'

'It seems so. Let's hope Leith was their only destination. One drop-off point—'

'That's one too many in my book.' Mitch turned to face Frankie. 'Want me to find out who the postman is, the names of delivery and taxi drivers assigned to that postcode? We need to know who's going in and out of there, right?'

Frankie was shaking her head. 'Not yet. Andy thinks the postcode relates to a street visible to a lookout. Once the cargo arrives, it's sent elsewhere. That way, the traffickers are protected. I was going to brief everyone when I returned from Leith.'

Mitch didn't yet know the whole story.

For his benefit, she explained that the operation they were undertaking could be much larger than they first thought. 'Andy found an identification marker on the roof of the Mercedes van. We need to work backwards. Starting point Brighton, where the van was nicked.'

'If Amir was lifted from a home nearby,' he said, 'why has no one reported him missing?'

'I don't know. But there's one man who does.'

39

No charges, internal or external, were ever brought against Frankie for decking an officer. Firstly, no witnesses could be found, despite a full house. Second, journalist Belinda Wells had seen to that. She later told David that Dunne had been feeding intel to the press in the brutal murders of four women. The accusation was undeniable. Wells had a recording to prove it and Dunne was removed from the MIT.

He was gone . . .

And forgotten, until today.

Head swimming with memories, David stepped off the pavement, crossed the road and entered the café that was a big part of the location's maritime heritage. No sign of Rachel Hart. He ordered and paid for two lattes and told the woman behind the counter that they would be outside.

She smiled at him. 'I'll bring it out.'

He moved off, Indira following.

'Great place,' she said.

He agreed, though not today.

He led her through the rear door, onto the terrace, into the midday sun. The view was glorious, a Mediterranean blue sky and white fluffy clouds over the North Sea. The smell of salt was strong, the sound of screeching gulls deafening as they flew off towards a fishing boat entering the mouth of the Tyne.

David scanned the tables, all of them taken: a tea stop for four middle-aged cyclists whose bikes were leaning against the café wall, a variety of families and couples, young and old, soaking up the atmosphere, a child sitting astride a three-wheeler, ice cream dripping onto his shorts and T-shirt, hands and cheeks covered in the stuff.

Sensing a presence, a small, slim brunette – the only person sitting alone – looked up. Dressed in casual clothes, cropped jeans, trainers and expensive-looking sunglasses, she raised a hand, confirming who she was. In that moment, Rachel Hart morphed into an image of Frankie sitting in the exact same spot she'd occupied years ago.

Where else?

Hart stood as he made his way towards her, forcing a smile as he neared the table. He hadn't told her the nature of his business on the phone, merely that he needed to speak to her, an urgent matter that couldn't wait, given that she'd already explained that she was due in London for a hearing that might take a week or more to conclude.

'Ms Hart? I'm DCI David Stone and this is DC Indira Sharma.'

'Rachel. Pleased to meet you.'

They all shook hands and sat down.

'Thanks for meeting us at short notice,' David said as their coffee arrived, an elderly waiter setting it down on the table. He noticed Rachel's empty cup. 'Can I get you another?'

'No, I'm good, thanks.'

The waiter moved away.

'How can I help?' Rachel said.

'I believe you were once one of us,' David began.

'In another life,' Hart scoffed. 'I assume you're here about a historical case. I must warn you, my memory isn't as good as it once was, though I still have my old pocketbooks if we get stuck.'

'Before we get into it, I need to make it clear that anything we say is highly confidential, part of a background check on some-one you worked with during your service, which came to a halt quite suddenly. You left for personal reasons, is that correct?'

'Is that what they called it?' Rachel's smile fell away. 'What's he done?'

40

David hadn't expected such an instant reaction from Rachel Hart. What she had to say was illuminating, leading him to believe that he was on the right track. From the look of her, Indira thought so too, though she didn't know what he knew. There were no specific incidences Rachel alluded to, only general comments about her time in the police, how a certain detective picked his moments to hit on her when no one else was around, how he'd made her feel when she rejected his advances.

She sat back, crossing her legs. 'He didn't take it well.'

David had witnessed that himself. 'He was married, right?'

'Oh yes. Misunderstood by his wife, or so he told me. The officers on my shift thought there was no harm in him. In their opinion, it was just his way and that was that.'

'And how would you describe the reaction of your peers?'

'Selective blindness, no doubt about it. They showed little or no support, including the women. I was young and green. The officer in question was abusing his position and my concerns were ignored.' She rolled her eyes, gave a big sigh. 'I simply couldn't take it.'

'Nor should you,' Indira said.

'Don't get me wrong, he was a great cop, lovely with me and charming with the public. Offenders too unless they didn't come quietly. He was personable, fun to be around. After a while, I couldn't handle the unwelcome attention. I could've asked for a transfer, but you know what it's like. The rumours would have followed me, even though nothing happened between us.'

'Mud sticks,' Indira said.

'Something like that.'

Listening to Rachel recall her experience, taking in how uncomfortable it made her to revisit an unhappy period of her life, angered David. As someone who respected women, including and especially those he worked with, he could see how such behaviour would affect her ability to learn on the job, a profession that required her full attention.

'I gather you were not the only one to leave,' he said.

'No, sadly that's true.'

'Same guy?'

She didn't answer.

No one spoke. Indira was the one to break the silence, keen to push on with the interview in more detail. The newly appointed DC was sure that Hart had more to say.

'Did you ever come across Stephanie Masterson?'

Rachel was nodding, a flash of concern crossing her face.

'Are you still in touch?'

'Occasionally. If you're going to talk to her, tread lightly. She had it worse than I did.'

'He got physical?'

'You'd have to ask her that.'

A legal response. Again, she went quiet, reliving a past memory perhaps.

Rachel sighed. 'I'd like to say that being invited to the bar has made a difference. But as you are no doubt aware, behaviour of that type is rife in every court in the land, from colleagues to court officials. Even the judiciary take liberties. Fortunately, I've grown a thicker skin.'

'I gather Steph is now an accountant,' Indira said. 'Do you know which firm she's at?'

'She's a partner at Freeman & Scholtz in Gosforth. I can give you her number.'

'That would be helpful.'

Something troubled Indira, something she couldn't quite put her finger on. The guy Rachel described didn't fit with the in-depth study she'd done on Hall, a man who allegedly assaulted his wife, even though she'd sworn he hadn't. Indira had seen the images of Hall's warrant cards throughout his service. Even as a young man, he wouldn't stand a hope in hell of attracting the woman sitting opposite. She was attractive now, probably stunning when she was younger.

Indira reached for an answer. It flew away, as if caught on a gust of wind. She racked her brains. Nothing made sense. She glanced at David. His expression was hard to read. He was elsewhere, deep in a thought too awful to share. In a moment of clarity, Indira got there. If he wouldn't tell her, then Rachel might . . . if she asked the right question.

Indira gave her a nudge. 'Is there anything else you can tell us, Rachel?' David hadn't shown ID. Indira thought she knew why. 'It's important,' she continued. 'David and I are MIT, looking into a cold murder case.'

'Now hang on, that's a serious allegation.' Rachel looked from the DCI to the DC, thrown by their silence. 'Even I don't think him capable of that.'

Leaning in, Indira looked her right in the eye.

Taking a beat, she asked one final question.

'Exactly who are we talking about here?'

41

By late afternoon, Frankie had completed her strategy, such as it was. With little to go on, she'd come up with a list of priorities for the team, despite a raging headache. She sat back, closing the lid of her laptop. She was flagging, forced to take more medication, unable to hide it from Andrea, who was watching for signs of fatigue, a word that didn't come close to describing her condition.

Sam was similarly concerned.

'How are you feeling?' she asked. 'If you don't mind me saying so, you look pale.'

Frankie lied. 'Nothing a good night's kip won't fix.'

Andrea's expression was scathing. She glanced at the others. 'Guys, Frankie and I need the room a moment.' Sam and Mitch got up, making themselves scarce. Frankie knew what was coming and so did they.

As the door clicked shut, Andrea dragged her chair closer and sat down facing her. 'Look, I'm sorry for leaving you high and dry, but I was trying to protect you . . . from yourself. Obviously, it didn't work, but if you're going to run this investigation you need to up your game.'

'Do I?'

'Just telling it like it is, Frank. I'm not criticising your ability or commitment. When have I ever doubted you? Be honest, you're not a hundred per cent fit. Hopefully, that'll change soon. Go home. See how you feel in the morning.'

'Home is the last place I want to be.'

'Then stay with Frank and Julie for a few days.'

Frankie looked right through her.

'Oh, I get it,' Andrea said. 'This is about David, right? You're worried he'll be waiting for you.'

'How the fuck do you think I got here with no phone, money or warrant card?'

'Oh, I thought you'd arrived on your broomstick,' Andrea joked. 'It's good that he picked you up, isn't it?'

'No!' Frankie lied. 'But you'd pissed off—'

'Then why didn't you ring your old man?'

It was a good question. 'Whether you like it or not, I'm working.'

'Don't freeze me out. I'm trying to help. Falling out with David isn't going to get you back where you belong, is it?' Andrea paused for a moment. 'Look, I don't know what's happened between the two of you. I don't need to. If you don't want to tell me, that's fine, but I'm not stupid. It's obviously upset you. Isn't it time you acted like a grown-up and had it out with him?'

'I will . . . when I'm ready.'

The phone Frankie had purchased on the way south rang. Andrea got to it before she did, turning the device off, continuing the exchange. 'Would it hurt to put him in the picture? He'll not rest until you do. You know that. He's crazy about you, if only you had the sense to realise it.'

'He's crazy all right. I got upset in the car. Long story, but he brushed it off as an emotional reaction to the accident. Hello? I'm a cop and he's full of bullshit. That was his opportunity to talk. He blew it.'

'For Christ's sake. Listen to yourself!' Andrea crossed her arms. 'What is wrong with you? If you learned anything from your near-death experience, isn't it that life is precious, too short to waste? You and David are solid. You've fought before and made up. We all have. Why is this time any different?'

'Back off, Andy. It's none of your business.'

'C'mon, maybe I can help.'

'You can't, so drop it. I have two things on my mind: Amir and cracking this case.'

'Let me tell you something. Your old man was worried about you even before the crash. He knows you're hurting and so do I.

138

If you really want to help Amir, get your shit together and make your peace with David . . . or fuck it up. I don't care.'

Frankie said nothing.

Andrea held her hands up in surrender. 'OK, I tried. Just remember the times he's supported you.'

'You think I owe *him* an explanation?'

'Do you?'

Frankie glared at her. 'Find the others. We have work to do.'

Andrea got up.

Before she reached the door, Frankie spoke again. 'Andy?'

She turned.

'I'm sorry, you have a big decision to make. You don't need this and neither do I—'

'Then do something about it.'

'I will, I promise.'

Andrea left the room, returning with Mitch and Sam a moment later. Frankie planned to brief them on what she wanted them to do in the morning. First, she had a question for Andrea. 'Any news from your witnesses? I thought they were going to send you images taken at the crime scene.'

'No, sorry. I'll chase them.'

'Give Interpol a nudge too, please. How long can it take to process fingerprints? Sam, those ID stickers are equally important. Get on to whoever is trying to find the manufacturer. C'mon, we can do better than this. We need that information.'

'What about me?' Mitch said.

'You're on the guy who escaped from the Mercedes. Liaise with ANPR. See if they can track the vehicle heading north. If they made a stop, we might get lucky. What we need is an image the press office can share, not as a person of interest in an abduction, but as someone involved in a major RTA who may need medical help. I'll not rest till we find him. Now, who's giving me a lift to Cramlington?'

Andrea cut her dead. 'Don't you think you should—'

Frankie spread her hands. 'If you want me to sleep, I need eyes on the boy.'

42

David was impressed, but in no way surprised, with the way Indira had handled herself during the interview with Rachel Hart. On the way to their base, his newest detective sat in silence, shell-shocked by the name the barrister had given her. A name he already knew. Indira didn't move a muscle or give the game away. She didn't sulk either when he insisted that the person in question would be referred to as 'our suspect' from now on, with no need to explain why he'd withheld key information.

'You did well, Indi . . .' He followed the compliment with a warning. 'His name is off the menu, in or outside of our office. If anyone gets wind of who we're investigating and it turns out that he's innocent of anything more than being a chauvinist prick, his career is over, and we'll be to blame.'

'Got it.'

David couldn't help himself. 'How the hell did you know to ask Hart that question?'

'I just did. The man she was on about didn't fit the profile of Hall I'd put together. I've listened to his interviews, trawled through his record. He wasn't the right persona. Our suspect,' she said carefully, 'is the guy Hall was winding up at Frankie's leaving do, right?'

David nodded.

'How did he respond?'

'He didn't . . . and that speaks volumes.'

'Did no one else hear him?'

'One guy I didn't recognise. They arrived together, but without his ID, we're screwed. We can't request a full list of attendees without raising hackles. We've been ordered to leave the Oliver family out of it.'

Indira clasped her hands behind her head, studying him. 'Was Hall pissed?'

'As in angry or drunk?' David didn't wait for an answer. 'A bit of both, I think. Why?'

'Don't know . . . I assumed that he'd blurted out what he said on impulse.' Indira sat forward, more animated than before. 'Do you think it's possible that it was a set-up, that they came to the party with the intention of causing trouble?'

'Well, they achieved that.' David was back in the police club, surrounded by people having fun, his focus on three men among a room full of detectives, uniform personnel and civilian staff who'd come to say goodbye to Frankie. He clasped his hands together, making a steeple with his fingers, propping up his chin. 'This is going to sound weird. There was a moment when Hall and his target stared at one another. Maybe I misinterpreted, but I could swear it meant something very personal.'

'What's more personal than fingering him for Joanna's murder?'

'I know it sounds crazy, but that's what I saw. We've yet to establish whether Hall knew Joanna. We know for a fact that our suspect did. That puts him in the frame and gives Hall an out. Like I said at the beginning, we need to rule him out before we move on, which means interviewing those who knew him then. Our next stop is Steph Masterson. Give Freeman & Scholtz a call. Set up an interview.'

'And after that?'

'We'll move on to Hall's ex.'

'Why, if you know he's not our guy? Sorry, I don't understand.'

David levelled with her. 'Hall said a lot of things at Frankie's party. Like I said when I brought you on board, we don't take that at face value. Before we move on, we need unequivocal proof that he couldn't have killed Joanna, that he's not playing us.'

'Misdirection, you mean?'

'Exactly that.'

They heard someone entering Bright's office, then a weighty silence. The room was carpeted. Still, they could usually hear their guv'nor moving around inside. David gestured for her to stay put, got up and listened at the adjoining door. No sound. Wondering if their guv'nor had come in and gone straight out again, he checked the corridor. Empty. He turned, his voice almost a whisper.

'I'm going in.'

Frankie had planned to visit Amir alone, but Andrea persuaded her otherwise. If Bright was successful in his bid to get the boy made a ward of court and placed in her care, she wanted Frankie to introduce them.

'He trusts you,' Andy said. 'He might trust me if he sees us together.'

'Not a good idea. You need to talk to Rae first.'

'I will when I get home. My eyes are wide open, Frank. Right from the off, I've known the score in terms of his needs as well as the consequences should his parents come looking. When I talk to Rae, I won't sugar-coat it. I've seen Amir before. Seeing him again won't sway me one way or the other.'

That was the plan, but as they walked into the children's unit, they noticed there was no armed guard present in the corridor.

They quickened their step . . .

Then broke into a run, hearts racing.

In seconds, they were at the viewing window. The room was empty. Amir's bed made up. His teddy gone. The space made ready for another sick child. This could not be happening. Frankie swung round, facing the nurses' station. Everyone was going about their business as normal, like a movie in slow motion, while her world tilted on its axis. Consultant Catherine Acres was nowhere to be seen.

The shock, a repeat of last night, caused a flashback, fragmented images of things she hadn't remembered until now. Cutting equipment. A fireman extricating her from her crashed vehicle.

What's your name, sweetheart? We'll have you out of there in a second. And he did. He placed her onto a waiting stretcher, a paramedic asking: *where does it hurt?* Curiously, it didn't. She was numb then.

She was numb now.

Questions came thick and fast. Had Amir deteriorated? Had he been transferred to critical care with injuries that weren't apparent on admission? He too had been in a car crash, his small body thrown around, causing untold injury. Or had he been abducted a second time? Where the hell was the police detail? Why hadn't she been notified?

Slowly, she turned to face Andrea.

'What the fuck?'

'Take a breath . . .' Calm as ever. 'There'll be a perfectly reasonable explanation.'

Frankie couldn't think of one that didn't involve the morgue.

43

Bright's office door opened, then clicked shut. Indira lifted her head, a glance over her shoulder. David was heading in. Retaking his seat, he chucked his mobile on his desk, exhaling frustratedly. For a moment, she assumed he'd caught someone sneaking into the adjoining office, knowing that the detective chief super was not in the building, perhaps trying to find out what she and David were up to, except she'd heard no raised voices, just muffled conversation through the partitioned wall.

'Everything OK?' she asked.

'Yeah, the guv'nor's back. He's taking a breather.' David kept his voice low. 'Looks like he's gone ten rounds with Tyson Fury. Last time I saw him he was off to meet a court official about the kid Frankie found at the scene of the RTA. He said an emergency arose in the middle of their meeting. I've rarely seen him look so drained.' David checked his watch. 'Whatever he was doing, it's taken six long hours.'

'Maybe he went to see Frankie's dad about the duty rosters. Could it be that Frank Snr's not buying the story we fed him?'

'No, it wasn't that. Bright did call on him. There was no one home. He'll try again tomorrow.'

'What else could it be?'

'Check the incident log.'

Indira typed a command, a quick scan of the screen as the page loaded. 'Nothing here.'

'Could be in-house then, or something else he wants off the radar.'

After racing down the corridor towards Catherine Acres' office,

Andrea was about to knock, when Frankie crashed through the door ahead of her, demanding an immediate explanation for Amir's removal. Having seen his empty room, which had undergone a deep clean, she'd already worked out that he wasn't going back there.

Her tone was laced with poison. 'We had an agreement. The boy stayed put until I said otherwise. You knew I needed samples to establish his identity. I left you in no doubt what you should do should his condition deteriorate, or if anyone tried to remove him, including social services.' She was praying that was the case. 'Where is he?'

The consultant stood, taken aback by Frankie's fury, displaying some of her own. She wasn't used to being spoken to as if she were a five-year-old facing a head teacher hell-bent on putting her in her place. 'Keep your voice down or I'll call security. This is a hospital ward, not a cell block. Who the hell do you think you are, charging in, shouting the odds?'

She walked to the door and threw it open, Frankie's cue to leave.

She didn't move, though she'd stopped yelling.

Acres noticed that her hands were shaking, her face ashen, a film of sweat forming on her brow. She'd seen people unravel before. It was happening now. The detective was acting like a distraught parent who feared the worst. She was in denial, mouthing off, looking for a scapegoat. The Traffic officer was equally anxious. She didn't intervene, though she was on the verge of it.

'Please.' Acres gestured for them to sit.

'I'd rather stand,' Frankie said defiantly.

'Do you want an explanation or not?'

Reluctantly, Frankie sat down.

Andrea remained standing, apologising to the consultant, explaining that Frankie was the officer who found the child. 'She's bonded with him, as I'm sure you have. She saw the empty bed and panicked. We both did.'

'And yet you managed to control your temper.'

Andrea sent Frankie an unspoken warning to back off.

'Out of the blue, a woman arrived with a court order,' Acres said. 'What was I to do?'

'What woman?' Frankie exploded. 'And how do you know it was legit?'

Acres passed the document to her. 'I had it verified with the county court. Knowing the circumstances, do you seriously think I'd have let Amir go without looking into it? He was in my care. I'd be struck off.'

'I don't give a stuff what happens to you. He could be in grave danger. D'you think we had an armed guard on his door for fun? Why didn't you call me?'

'I tried.'

'Not hard enough.'

'Back off, Inspector. I called you . . . several times. The number rang out unobtainable. DC Mitchell's number was constantly engaged. The woman produced the court order and refused to discuss it any further. I'm as much in the dark as you are.'

Wondering why the urgency to remove the boy, Frankie asked Andrea to step outside.

'I'm good.' Andrea didn't budge.

'Is Amir . . .' Frankie stalled. 'Is he—'

'He's fine,' Acres said. 'Come with me—'

Frankie's heart leapt. 'They haven't left yet?'

'No, they're in the playroom.'

Andrea and Frankie followed Acres through a six-bedded ward, every bed occupied by a sick child, some of whom looked very poorly. At the far end was a light and airy playroom, the walls decorated with sea creatures on a blue background.

They stood outside, looking in.

Amir was sitting in the middle of the floor, legs stretched out in front of him, arms by his side, a plastic digger truck in one hand, the teddy Frankie had bought for him in the crook of his other arm.

Unable to believe what she was seeing, Andrea locked eyes with Frankie.

They turned to face the room . . .

D-Day had come early . . .

Decision made.

Rae was on her knees, moving cars along a road map rug into a garage made of Lego bricks, neither aware that they were being watched. She said something to Amir. He smiled at her.

Andrea stifled a sob of relief.

'Well, that's a first . . .' Acres said to Frankie. 'Looks like you've been demoted, Inspector.'

Andrea wanted to tell her that, young or old, everyone took to Rae; that she was her partner and Frankie's sister, that they would be looking after Amir. She couldn't reveal it. To do so would breach confidentiality and put the boy and people she loved at risk. It was enough to see him out of bed, relating to someone who'd grow to love him as if he were her own, a process that had already begun.

She'd need a spreader to separate these two.

She turned to face Acres. 'Did you ask her to wait for us?'

'No. In her rush to get here, she came unprepared, without a child seat. Someone is bringing it.'

Behind Acres' back, Andrea and Frankie exchanged a worried look. That someone would be her father, the only person in the world Rae would trust not to give away her identity. Frankie pulled her phone from her pocket and turned it on. There were missed calls from Acres and her old man. She flicked her eyes to the door.

Andrea made her excuses and left.

'I'm sorry,' Frankie said to Acres. 'I was out of order.'

'Apology accepted.' The consultant pointed into the playroom. 'Shall we join them?'

As they entered, Amir looked round, Rae following his gaze. She helped him up. Allowing his teddy to fall to the floor, he ran to Frankie, wrapping his broken arms around her legs. This was too much. She didn't even like kids. She hadn't anticipated that her position might change. With this one it was love at first sight.

44

David collared Dick in the incident room as soon as he arrived for work, checking the murder wall on his way in. There was little on it. Unusual. No new major incidents reported in their area command. He hoped it would stay that way. He wanted no distractions while working on Joanna's murder. Distractions led to fuck-ups. In this instance, one that would buy him a one-way ticket to King's Cross.

'Something I can do for you?' Dick said.

David scanned the room, a lot of empty desks. Mitch, he knew, was otherwise engaged with Frankie on the abduction-trafficking case. As for the rest, he was perplexed.

'Where is everyone?'

'Division have a couple of straights on.' He meant murders where the perpetrator was known but not yet apprehended. 'They have one locked up, the other they're still looking for. They're struggling, guv. You said no interruptions, so I sent Rob to help the statement reader. Pam is running the room on the understanding that if we get anything in, Division are on their own. She said the available detectives are rookies. None have received training on live incidents or HOLMES.' He was referring to the Home Office Large Major Enquiry System. 'And don't get me started on disclosure. What's this bloody world coming to?'

'Sound like a complete shitshow.'

'It's ridiculous.'

'Does Bright know?'

'He does now.'

'Good. Rob and Pam will keep them right.'

'Want a brew while you're here?'

'No, I'll have to shoot.' David was about to turn away, then changed his mind, remembering why he'd come. 'The guv'nor mentioned that there was something going down yesterday. Any ideas?'

Dick shrugged. 'That's news to me.'

'There's nothing on the incident log either. Just curious. Maybe it was Division's request for assistance.'

'Nah, too low level.' Dick knew something.

David said, 'What did you hear?'

45

In the last twenty-four hours, Frankie had experienced the full range of emotions. She stayed with her parents in Woolsington village overnight, too exhausted to go home, and slept in the room she once shared with Joanna. Her bed had gone, but her stuff was there: her artwork, books and CDs; the child-sized guitar Frankie couldn't bear to part with propped up in the corner; a framed original programme of Dire Straits' appearance at Newcastle City Hall on the wall, part of their Brothers in Arms World Tour – a treasured gift from Bright.

During the night, Frankie had a vision of Joanna playing air guitar, strutting around the room as if she were onstage with an audience of thousands. Always the cool one. It sparked a series of memories, one of the last times they spent time together. Joanna had taken Frankie into her confidence about the first and last cigarette she'd smoked. Frankie, barely eleven at the time, had sat up in bed, wide-eyed, begging for more.

'What was it like?'

'Tasted rank.' Joanna acted out a vomit, making Frankie giggle.

She wasn't giggling anymore. She tossed and turned, wondering if Amir had brothers or sisters out there somewhere he might never see again. She had to find out where he'd been abducted. Having lost a sister, reuniting Amir with his family was a big priority. She was conflicted, desperate to return him to his biological parents, aware that it would devastate Rae.

In solving one problem, Frankie had created another.

She hadn't slept a wink.

*

Frankie didn't mention her fatigue over the breakfast her mother had got up early to cook. Poached eggs on brown toast, home-made pancakes with fresh raspberries. Julie poured Frankie a coffee, strong and black – the way she liked it.

'Thanks, Mum.'

'For feeding my daughter? Don't be daft.'

'It all looks brilliant.'

'So why aren't you eating it?' Julie sat down, studying her closely. 'You look tired, love. You sure you're all right?'

'Yeah, I'm fine.' The white lie hung in the air. 'I was dead to the world last night.'

Her father said, 'That's better than dead, I suppose—'

'Frank!' Julie's eyes were like daggers.

'What?'

'You're not helping.'

'She should've told us about the accident—'

'How could I, Dad? I was out of it.'

'Any chance that a bang on the head might have knocked some sense into you?'

'It wasn't my fault . . .' Frankie nibbled at the edge of her toast. 'And before you ask, it had nothing to do with the people I'm trying to find.'

'Says who?'

Julie reached across the table, laying her hand on Frankie's. 'Your dad's right, love. How can you possibly know that?'

'I do . . . He's making it sound worse than it is.' Frankie eye-balled him. 'Drop it, will you? I'm still on the right side of the grass.'

'You may be. I almost wasn't.' Her father always used humour to mask anxiety. 'And I'm not the only one concerned about you, Frankie. I saw David yesterday. He had a face like a smacked arse—'

'Nowt to do with me.' Frankie's warning to back off hit its target. 'I've been busy.'

'More toast, anyone?' Her mother got up to fetch it, steering them in a different direction as she brought it to the table. 'For what it's worth, I think concentrating on Amir was the right thing to do.' She beamed at her daughter. 'He's safe now and that's down to you. I'm proud, even if Mr Grumpy isn't. Mind you, he enjoyed his shopping spree yesterday.'

'Hey, I'll have you know I'm on first-name terms with the woman selling kids' clobber in Fenwick's.' He meant Newcastle's favourite department store. Acting like most new granddads do, he'd leapt into action when Rae called from the hospital to ask a favour. 'I was expecting to buy the lad an ice cream. I was three hundred quid down by the time I left.'

'You were brilliant, Dad . . .' Frankie smiled at her mum. 'He fitted Amir's car seat into Rae's vehicle in a flash. It was the simulation steering wheel that took us all by surprise.'

Julie narrowed her eyes at Frank. 'What?'

He blushed. 'Don't ask.'

'Priceless, he called it,' Frankie scoffed. 'It might even come in useful when Amir's arms mend, which is probably why he didn't tell you. It has flashing lights and talks. Can you imagine the din? It's giving me a headache just thinking about it.'

'Amir was delighted,' her father said. 'So was Andy.'

'Yeah, for the five minutes you were playing with it.' Frankie grinned at him. 'Give her a few days, she'll be taking it back.'

Tuning her parents out, Frankie let her mind drift to the hospital car park the day before. Eyes everywhere, looking for anyone who stood out as suspicious. Satisfied that no one fit the bill, she'd turned to find her dad making funny faces at Amir as he lifted him into the car seat. The boy smiled, even though he was being tethered to a vehicle by a male he'd never seen before, something Frankie anticipated might have made him scream the place down.

Speaking quietly, Frankie said. 'Would you like me to help?'

'Relax, Frankie . . .' Her old man glanced over his shoulder. 'I know what I'm doing. Does he look scared to you? He needs a positive experience of men if he's to conquer his fear.' He refocused on Amir. 'Don't you, little man? Ignoring the issue won't help you, will it?'

Frankie needn't have worried.

Even at such a young age, Amir's instinct kicked in. He seemed to know that the people surrounding him were kind. All set, they took off in convoy, Frankie driving Rae's car so she could keep an eye out for a tail – Amir and Rae in the back, her father bringing up the rear.

The Olivers on tour.

Frankie pushed her empty plate away. Last night's plan worked perfectly. Before they left the ward, she'd made sure of two things: that samples of Amir's DNA were taken and that Rae's private vehicle had been blocked on the PNC. Untraceable to anyone, including a bent copper, should the traffickers have one on the payroll. There was one way in and out of the hospital, a narrow road along which those entering or leaving had to negotiate a mini roundabout. So that no one could follow, Frankie had asked Andrea to use her Traffic car to block it off, giving her a head start, and to contact Control to advise of her position, in case she met a problem.

With Amir on board, Frankie was taking no chances.

She took the minor roads.

Amir was asleep by the time they reached their Morpeth destination, the riverside apartment where Rae and Andrea lived. Frankie stayed with him until he was tucked up in bed, in the nursery made ready for a foster child.

Rae had given her employer prior warning that her resignation, when it came, must be immediate, incurring no notice period.

Frankie had never seen her so happy.

A reality check was required. Andrea had promised to deliver it immediately, reminding Rae that the rocky road ahead could lead nowhere she wanted to go. The family would face that when the time came. As her mother had said, Amir's safety was paramount. They would all pull together for his sake.

'More coffee?' Julie asked.

'No thanks, Mum.' Frankie stood up. 'I need to call a cab.'

'Wait!' Her mother got up and walked into the hallway, returning with a set of car keys to a new VW Polo she'd bought a couple of months back, a runaround for when Frankie's dad was out and about. She pressed the keys into Frankie's hand. 'I hardly use it. You may as well until you have time to replace yours.'

'Are you sure?'

'Take it, pet.'

Frankie threw her arms around her, a warm hug.

'Don't I get one?' her father said. 'If you're not waiting for a taxi, what's the rush?'

As Frankie moved towards him, a worrying thought occurred. No one had yet explained the need to move Amir urgently, not her father or Acres, and there had been plenty of time to do it. There would be a story behind it.

Frankie was desperate to find out what it was.

Acres' voice was in her head. *In her rush to get here, she came unprepared.* She'd been talking about Rae, but that didn't sit well with Frankie. If her sister had been assessed to take a child imminently, there was no way she'd have been caught off guard . . .

Unless . . .

There had been a development.

46

At Northern Area Command, Frankie was about to knock on Bright's office door, when she saw David hurrying along the corridor in her direction. With no cover, she was trapped, too late to disappear inside. She wondered if he'd seen her drive in. Unlikely. He'd have to explain himself. There were two ways this could go. She could make it awkward, or she could just move on. She had no energy to fight. *Who gave a shit, anyway?* His face lit up when he saw her, though his eyes flew to the purple bruise spreading across her right cheek.

He grimaced. 'That must be seriously painful.'

Not as painful as being near him. 'Looks worse than it is.'

David looked genuinely concerned. 'How are you doing now?'

'A damned sight better than yesterday.' She nodded sideways, hoping to make a quick exit into Bright's office. 'Can't stop. Need to see the guv'nor.'

'He's out, which means we have time for coffee in the canteen.'

Frankie said, 'I'm no longer welcome in your office?'

'Dick's prepping a court report in there.'

'It's not like you to share—'

'Ouch.' His eyes could melt a glacier.

To avoid them, Frankie glanced into the stairwell. 'I saw Bob Thompson on my way in. He tells me you're short-staffed. How come?'

'Pam and Rob are helping Division. Harry's off sick.'

'You can't have Mitch. He's all I have, apart from Andy and Sam. And they'll be pulled off soon enough.'

'The way it goes, Inspector.' He was teasing. 'I'm here if you need advice. Beyond that, I have my own show to run.'

'Can you spare Indi?'

''Fraid not. The boss has her on a job involving personnel. She's the only one with knowledge of the system.'

'Your rush job?'

'Yeah, boring admin, though it's something that will help the MIT going forward.'

He didn't elaborate and the floor seemed suddenly to have developed an unexplained fascination. Frankie recognised a snub when she heard one.

Well, if he wouldn't tell her, Dick would.

She didn't have time for that now.

'I get the feeling I'm persona non grata around here,' she said.

'Why? The guv'nor gave you an assignment that got you out of uniform. I'd have thought you'd jump at the chance of a route back here.' Frankie didn't respond and he carried on. 'Anyway, if you need assistance, ask Division. Tell them I said it's a two-way street. We're not helping if they're not willing to return the favour.'

'Thanks. Any idea on Bright's ETA?'

'None. C'mon, may as well take the weight off while you can. My shout.'

The canteen was empty when they got there. David got them both a coffee and then sat down opposite, the table providing a physical barrier between them. Not that they needed one. Only the truth would close the gap between them. Frankie had made it clear that she was feeling sidelined. He alone was responsible for that.

He ached to tell her what was going on.

'Sounds like you have your hands full,' he said.

'And some. There's a rabbit off though. The kid I found at the RTA was moved from the hospital yesterday without my say-so. I'd like to know why.' David didn't hide his reaction quick enough. She put her paper cup down on the table, then crossed her arms. 'You know, don't you?'

He gave a nod.

'Are you going to share?'

'Word is the security detail spotted someone suspicious on the children's ward yesterday. He couldn't leave Amir, so didn't get a good look at him. He called Bright, who I happen to know was organising a wardship at the time. Given that you were in hospital overnight, he handled it. I gather he'd already organised a place of safety. I don't know the details.'

'I do. The less people who know about it the better.'

Touché!

She was hinting that two could play that game. She knew he was hiding something. David was about to change the subject, when her phone rang, a welcome distraction. She checked the screen and looked up at him.

'Sorry, it's Andrea. I need to take this.'

'Say again . . .' Frankie took a small notepad and pen from her pocket as Andrea offloaded new intelligence. 'How are you spelling that?' She wrote two names down: *Stanislav Mitev (driver); Hristo Petkov (co-driver)*. She continued to listen as Andrea added more details. 'OK, good plan . . . You crack on finding their associates.' Andrea had even better news. One of her witnesses had sent her an image. It wasn't great but he'd sworn it was the guy they were hunting. 'Fantastic! Forward it on. I'll be there within the hour.'

As she hung up, David stopped reading her upside-down scribble. 'Persons of interest?'

'Dead persons of interest. No help whatsoever. Plenty of form, including violence and extortion. Interpol confirmed they're Bulgarian nationals. Fugitives on the run, prime suspects in the murder of a young woman. Last known address Burgas, Black Sea coast. They fled via Turkey to Charles de Gaulle in 2018.'

'No sightings since?'

Frankie shook her head as Andrea's text came in.

The image wasn't as bad as she'd implied. If it was taken from the embankment, the witness had zoomed in to capture the mayhem of the accident. The man featured had a beard and long dark hair tied in a topknot. She held up her phone to show David, an automatic response – the way things used to be.

'This one's still breathing,' she said.

'He looks like Andy Carroll.'

'He does.'

It felt like old times discussing a case with David, though more difficult being around him than Frankie had anticipated. He was tense. He'd gone quiet, which meant only one thing. He had more to say. Second-guessing what it might be, she prepared herself for an explanation she'd hoped for yesterday but was now keen to avoid.

He looked away, then at her, a change of heart perhaps.

'Something wrong, Frank?'

'Apart from everything?'

'Are we OK, you and me?'

'Why shouldn't we be?' She threw him a sickly smile. 'Relax, will you? I don't have time to play nice, so don't kid yourself that this is about us. It's not. The only thing I'm interested in is my investigation.'

She'd hurt him.

'What about it?' he asked.

'Child trafficking is a major crime. I don't get why we're not running it from the incident room, given the fact that the MIT are practically on leave. Why the boss is keeping me in Berwick, God only knows—'

'It's halfway to Edinburgh.'

'So?'

'So, if that's where the van was heading, it makes perfect sense to me. You'll have to liaise with Police Scotland when you're ready to make arrests.'

'I suppose.' Frankie was back in the zone. Too late for an apology. Too bloody-minded to deliver one. 'I may need to go south first. ANPR are reverse-tracking the van. I know where Petkov and Mitev were going, not their starting point, or where they took possession of Amir.'

'Yell if you need a hand.'

'I will.' She wouldn't. Scooping her bag off the floor, she slung it over her shoulder, hesitating before she stood up. 'Thanks for the drink.' She forced a smile, an idea presenting itself. 'You must have close contacts in the National Crime Agency—'

'Some . . . why?'

'This is me yelling. I'd like to know if my dead guys were ever on their radar.'

David pulled a calling card from his pocket, wrote something on the flip side and handed it to her. She turned it over: DI Kit Matthews. Under the name he'd written a direct line telephone number of the NCA detective without having to look it up.

She thanked him and stood to go.

'Tell her I still owe her a curry—'

'Is that the best you can do?' Frankie's eyes flashed, though she kept the smile on her face. 'A matter of days ago you said the same to me. It sounded genuine then. Now it sounds like a fucking chat-up line—'

'Frank—'

'Don't kid yourself that it meant that much. It's a game, right? You moved a piece, I moved a piece, then you fucked me over. Well, in case you missed it, this is checkmate.' She saw off her coffee. 'I'm out of here.'

Before she reached the door, he spoke again. 'Frank, listen—'

'No, you listen . . .' She turned to face him. 'Save it for someone who cares. And lose the bleeding heart . . .' She held up the card he'd given her. 'Unless you'd like me to pass it on to Kit . . . I can do without it—'

'I was going to say, take care. Procuring kids for sale is a dangerous game.'

'I can look after myself, David.' She walked away without a backward glance.

So much for keeping her cool.

47

David caught up with Frankie in the corridor. In silence, he walked her to her car, something he'd not done before, and probably never would again if she had her way. Having blown his chance to make amends, he scanned the road as she pulled away from the secure car park, wheels screeching on the dry tarmac.

Satisfied that she wasn't being followed, David went in search of Indira, who he'd ignored for most of the morning, though she'd sent a text, informing him that Stephanie Masterson had returned from the Seychelles and had agreed to meet them.

He intended to go there next.

Indira's excitement was palpable as he walked in. Trying to look enthused, even though he didn't feel it after his encounter with Frankie, he sat down. Her voice was in his head: *save it for someone who cares*. She did care – and so did he.

He stared at Indira. 'Have you seen Frankie this morning?'

'No, why d'you ask?'

'Nothing. Forget I asked—'

'I haven't, I swear! What's wrong?'

'I wish I knew. She just asked me if she was no longer welcome in my office. I think she knows something.'

'She meant your proper office, surely.'

'Maybe . . . but then she asked if she could borrow you. I told her you were busy. Just be on your guard. If you're ready, we'll head off.'

'Guv, before we do that, I found something. Frankie's old man posted images of her leaving do on the retired officers' Facebook group. Don't ask how I got in, just be thankful that I did. Anyway, I grabbed a screenshot you need to see.' Passing her mobile across the desk, she asked: 'Is that the man you saw Hall with at the party?'

David expanded the screen. The guy standing next to Hall was tall, brown hair, dark eyes, a beard. 'That's him.'

'I have a name too.' Indira opened her laptop and began typing, fingers flying across the keys. A page loaded, an alphabetical list of Adam Hall's colleagues with ID images attached. She scrolled down to the very bottom, then looked up at him, triumphant. 'Meet William Welch.'

David had heard the surname recently.

Unable to place it, he looked on as Indira switched screens, this time bringing up Welch's personnel file. He studied it closely, the usual information recorded in an HR file: gender, age, date and place of birth. He was six one. No scars, tats or other identifying marks or features. He'd listed his pastimes as music lover. Piano player. Sunderland FC fan. Reader of crime thrillers.

'Good job! What else do we know?'

'Welch has an unblemished record and quit the force a couple of years ago. He works as an insurance fraud investigator. Married, two sons. Lives down south. Born and raised here. I suspect he's up here visiting family.' Indira had saved the best till last. 'He's also related to Hall by marriage.'

Now David remembered. 'Hall's first wife, right?'

'Yup, he's Jan Hall's brother.'

48

As soon as Frankie reached Berwick, she jumped on a call to the National Crime Agency's DI Kit Matthews, unaware that she'd have saved herself the trip if she'd called her from Middle Earth. The DI answered on the third ring with her name and rank, a soft Irish accent, asking Frankie to identify herself.

'I'm DI Frances Oliver, Northumbria Police.'

'Where are you based?'

'Berwick . . . temporarily.'

'I'll call you back.' It's what any sensible cop would do.

The line went dead.

Still simmering from her spat with David – she'd gone overboard – Frankie looked across the room to where Andrea, Sam and Mitch were working away quietly, two of them on the phone. A couple of minutes ticked by, then her landline rang.

She snatched it from its cradle. 'Oliver.'

'It's Matthews. First question, where did you get this number?'

'An ex-colleague of yours.'

'Name.'

'DCI David Stone. He said to say hello.' Frankie failed to mention the curry.

'Long time, no see. How is he?'

'Pain in the arse.'

'Sounds about right.' Matthews laughed. 'How can I help?'

'I'm investigating a potential abduction. I have two suspects already identified and a third I'm trying to trace. I have an image of him but no name. Could you run the names I do have through your system to see if you get any hits?'

'Always happy to assist.'

Yeah, right. Matthews wore her animosity like a badge.

Still, they had to start somewhere.

Frankie reeled off the names.

There was a moment's pause before Matthews spoke again. 'Why are Petkov and Mitev of interest to you?'

They were known to her.

Policing was a game where knowledge was power. You scratch my back. 'I'd rather discuss that in person, if it's all the same to you,' Frankie said. 'How long will it take you to dig out what you have on them and their associates? I can be in London in less than four hours. Shall we say five o'clock?'

Forest Grange was situated close to Matfen village, probably once a working farm, now transformed into a magnificent south-facing home. Nestled in a four-acre plot, it was accessed via a sweeping driveway, a row of silver birch on either side. Just east of the house was a triple stable block, stone outbuildings, an old barn, and a double garage. Beyond them, David could see horses in a paddock. Further still, glorious countryside as far as the eye could see.

'Wow!' He brought the car to a stop on the gravel driveway, his focus out of the window. 'I can guarantee that Masterson wouldn't have a gaff like this if she'd stayed in policing. You could fit my whole cottage in that barn.'

Indira laughed.

Having followed him out of the car, she rang the bell and stood back waiting for an answer. The woman who pulled the door open was a breath of fresh air, dressed in a loose sleeveless top, cropped linen shorts and espadrilles. Her greyish-blonde bobbed hair was tucked behind her ears.

'Hello . . .' She smiled warmly. 'You must be Indira?'

'Yes, and this is my guv'nor, DCI David Stone.'

'Nice to meet you both.' Masterson flung the door wide. 'Come in, come in.'

She led them further into the house, turning as she reached a huge light and airy room, a modern kitchen at one end, a cosy snug at the other, with a wood burner that reminded David of his place.

'Thank you for seeing us at such short notice,' he said. 'DC Sharma tells me you're just back from holiday. I'm sorry if our timing is off—'

'Don't worry, I slept most of the way. Excuse the left luggage. I can't bear to unpack and put the washer on. I just want to enjoy being home.'

David looked past her through enormous windows. 'It's a great place.'

'I'm lucky . . . and still on wine o'clock . . .' Masterson lifted a bottle of red from the kitchen worktop. 'It's open if you fancy a glass.' They declined and she gestured for them to sit. 'I'm dying to know what it is you think I've done.'

'Ms Masterson—'

'Please, call me Steph.'

'Are you good to talk?' David thumbed through the window. 'I noticed your children in the garden.'

'Grandkids,' she corrected him. 'My husband's, though I appreciate the compliment. I don't get many. They're good girls. Don't worry, Nigel is out there keeping an eye on them. They know not to interrupt while you're here.' She sipped her wine, eyeing him over the top of her glass. 'Why *are* you here?'

49

As Frankie gathered her stuff together, she asked Mitch to book her on the 11:55 LNER Azuma train, an open return to King's Cross, and to send the e-ticket to her mobile. She made the station with minutes to spare. He'd put her in a first-class carriage, Coach L, seat 34, front-facing, on its own where she wouldn't be disturbed by other passengers. After climbing aboard, she opened her laptop, checking that she had everything she needed.

When the drinks trolley arrived, she opted for water, then went to work, hoping that her Met counterpart would have the information she required and the agency to share it. In no way was that a foregone conclusion. Matthews might have intelligence at her disposal but would probably need clearance to divulge it to an outside force. She wouldn't just hand it over to some mug punter she'd never met before . . .

Whether or not they knew David.

Police were often territorial, withholding intel for their own use, sometimes for legitimate reasons like a 'live' operation they might compromise by widening the scope of people in the know. Often because they were too bloody-minded to see the bigger picture. Frankie would be equally guarded about what she said until Matthews showed her hand.

There came a point when David had to take people into his confidence no matter the risk. Hart had left the service because she'd been hit on, probably since the moment she'd entered training school, the state of play for many females choosing policing as a career. She'd hinted that Masterson had left for the same reason. If he was to move his investigation forward, he now had to establish that as fact, not hearsay, and get to the bottom of who or what had tipped the two of them over the edge.

He levelled with the homeowner, repeating almost word for word what he'd told Rachel Hart on the Fish Quay in North Shields, that he and Indira were there to talk about her police service, such as it was. Specifically, the reason for her sudden departure when she'd aced every hurdle during training and was expected to thrive. He was wondering if Hart had warned her to expect a visit, though her demeanour when they arrived would suggest not.

Masterson topped up her glass.

'May I ask why it's important to drag this out of the closet now?'

'I have reason to believe that you were not treated well by one officer in particular.' David deliberately didn't name him. 'Would that be a fair assessment of the situation that gave rise to your resignation?'

'With respect, that doesn't answer my question.'

'At this stage we're background checking.'

'Must be serious to bring a DCI away from his desk.'

'It's highly confidential,' he confirmed. 'I hate to confront you with it so soon after your holiday. It's also urgent.' The temperature in the room seemed to plummet. 'We both know how dangerous it is to the reputation of the service if we don't jump on it.'

'Is he in trouble?'

'The short answer is, we don't know.'

'I knew you'd turn up one day,' Masterson said. 'Look, I'll make this easy for you. There was undoubtedly a power imbalance, but he did nothing against the law. I was a willing participant initially, nineteen and flattered that he was paying me attention. I knew he was married, but the longer it went on, the worse he got.'

'Did he ever hurt you?'

'Not physically. If he had, I'd have made a complaint, no question. The coercive control went on for months. He was manipulative, and jealous as hell if other officers paid me any attention.'

'Protective of his marital status?'

'So much so he bought me perfume and told me to wear it whenever we were together in case his wife found out. It was the one she used.' Masterson sighed. 'As a matter of fact, that was the last straw. He was terrified of her. She was older, a high achiever. He was out of his depth. He preferred submissive women.'

'Doesn't sound like you,' Indira said.

'You win or you learn,' Masterson said.

50

At King's Cross, Frankie got a cab to Citadel Place, the National Crime Agency's HQ. If David trusted Matthews, then so did she, but not before she saw the whites of her eyes. They could both get something out of working collaboratively. Matthews had alerted the main desk of her ETA. The desk clerk checked her ID, then made a call. Matthews arrived soon after: small like Frankie, a slim redhead, hair plaited and worn to one side, tortoiseshell designer specs.

They passed through an open-plan office, with air conditioning, state-of-the-art computers and other equipment Frankie's own force could only dream of. The place was a hive of activity, mostly analysts. There was the odd stare here and there – a stranger in their midst. Within seconds, all eyes were turned in her direction.

'Christ,' Frankie said. 'Is it feeding time?'

'Ignore them,' Matthews said. 'How was your journey?'

'The train was on time. The coffee was gross. That was a hint, in case you didn't catch it.'

They grabbed a drink on their way to a side room, a quiet space where they could talk without interruption, then sat down, sizing one another up. The NCA stood to gain as much as Frankie did. If they were aware of the Bulgarians and what they were up to, that was one thing. If they weren't, that was something else entirely. If the detective she was facing came up with credible evidence that Frankie could use, she was prepared to share.

'So,' Matthews said. 'Must be important to come all this way—'

'And urgent. As I told you on the phone, it's a line of enquiry

I'm pursuing. I need background on the associates of Petkov and Mitev.'

Matthews pointed at Frankie's face. 'One of them give you that bruise?'

'No, but I've made their acquaintance.' She didn't say how or when. 'You obviously have too.'

Matthews didn't admit nor deny it.

'C'mon . . .' Frankie gave her a cynical smile. 'I'm a hick from the sticks. You're a Met detective. How's that going for you?' Matthews said nothing. Frankie was about to take the piss. 'I've got a brain and excellent hearing. I can hardly pronounce their names, yet they rolled off your tongue like water over a weir. Sorry, you walked into that one. Look, I'm on the clock. Shall we start again?'

'You've seen them up north?'

Frankie bent down, scooping her bag off the floor. After removing a file, she located two images inside a flimsy plastic folder. She took them out and slid them across the Formica table, placing them side by side, watching Matthews' face crumple as she picked them up.

She glared at Frankie. 'Is this a joke?'

'They don't think so—'

'Why didn't you tell me they were dead?'

'You didn't ask. Death tends to happen when you drive the wrong way up the A1 in the fast lane. That's your freebie. Now it's your turn.' Frankie waited. 'Stop buggering about. Are we trading intel or not?'

'What's in it for us?'

Frankie leaned in, elbows on the table, piercing eyes. 'I don't think you understand. There's a human at the centre of my investigation. Multiple humans, for all I know. Your remit is to identify and safeguard victims, right? And yet you're not cooperating. Which probably means that I know a lot more about them than you do. Can we proceed? Your poker face is boring the tits off me.'

'He said you were abrupt—'

'Excuse me?'

'David. He cares for you, but you scare the hell out of him apparently. I can see why.' Matthews smirked. 'You don't feel the same?'

'He's my boss, a walking, talking cliché, if you want the truth.'

'So, you do care for him.'

Frankie had no words.

David was closer to Matthews than he'd let on. He might have warned her. It took a while to find her voice. 'Can we leave him out of this? I'm working, even if you're not. You either know something or you know nowt. Which is it?' And still the Met DI didn't come across. 'OK, have it your way. Don't come crying to me when your analysts decide that your operation extends beyond the M25.' Frankie grabbed the post-mortem images off the table. 'Enjoy the rest of your day.'

51

After leaving Masterson's house, David suggested they stop for a beer at the Black Bull, a traditional village pub in Matfen. He went inside where, even in midsummer, the open fire was burning gently in the grate. The bar was small and friendly, a few regulars who obviously knew each other chatting with the barman at the counter, half an eye on a large TV screen showing pre-match commentary of Hearts v Dundee United on Sky Sports.

The world was a better place with football in it.

David ordered a half-pint of Jakehead, a small glass of wine for Indira and salted peanuts. Dinner was out of the question. He took the drinks outside to a picnic bench in the sun with a view of the church over the village green.

His kind of place.

Within minutes they had devoured the nuts and were deep in conversation, trying to decide which way to go next. They still had to rule out Adam Hall's involvement in Joanna's murder. As every second passed, he looked less like a suspect.

They opted to speak to his first wife, Jan.

Indira had dug out an address for her.

Fifty minutes later, a woman opened the door of a terraced townhouse on Broad Landing, South Shields. She was tall, in good shape, short dark hair with an attractive Mallen streak on one side. She had an apron on, a check tea towel slung over one shoulder. Whatever she was cooking made David's stomach rumble.

'Can I help you?' she said.

'Ms Hall?'

She bristled. 'Welch.'

'Jan Welch?'

'Correct.' She kept hold of the door. 'You seem to know more about me than I know about you. You're a cop, right?'

'It's that obvious?'

'I was once married to one. And I haven't shared his name for a very long time.'

'I'm DCI Stone . . .' David flashed ID. 'This is DC Sharma. Might we have a word?'

'What about?'

'It won't take long.'

'It had better not. I'm expecting company.'

Inside, Jan invited them into a pleasant living room with a view over the Tyne, asking them to wait while she checked her oven. When she returned, David explained that what he'd come to discuss was highly confidential.

'Concerning what exactly?'

'A disturbance at your previous address.'

'You wouldn't be here if you didn't already have the details.'

'Some,' David said, 'though I suspect not all.'

'Does it matter after all this time?'

'I'm afraid so.'

She sighed. 'Is Adam in trouble?'

'No. We need to rule him out of the investigation that led us here. I can't give you any details, but it would help if you could tell us what you didn't tell the attending officers at the time. Does that about sum up the incident?'

Jan came clean.

'Look, it was all my fault.' Her face turned red. 'I had an affair . . . with another cop.' She looked away, then at him. 'Adam came home early one night and caught us in bed together. As you can imagine, it didn't go down well. Adam lashed out. I thought they were going to kill each other. A neighbour reported the disturbance to police. We saw blue lights. The cop I'd been sleeping with legged it out the rear window, across

172

the garage roof. Adam was covered in blood. He begged me to answer the door.'

'You told the officers you were just messing around?'

'Yes. They didn't believe me. Adam was spoken to at work. He left me soon after. I put the house on the market. When it was sold, I moved on. We divorced. He didn't name the co-respondent. I didn't contest his claim. How could I? Once the divorce went through, I never saw either of them again.'

So, it was personal.

Indira's voice arrived in David's head: *more personal than fingering him for Joanna's murder?* What Jan had just told them made sense of the weird moment between the two men at the police club, the one David thought he may have misinterpreted.

'Would you mind confirming who the other cop was?'

'You don't want much, do you?'

52

Time-wasters made Frankie angry. She walked at a fast pace, keen to leave the NCA building, another staring contest with detectives on her way out. A narcissistic bunch, male and female. If any of her Northumbria colleagues treated an outsider like that, David would read them the riot act. He must have hated working down here, Frankie thought. There was little give and take with the Met. How he'd survived their bullshit for fifteen years was beyond her.

He'd make ten of them.

Her phone rang as the lift pinged its arrival. Letting it go in case she lost the signal, she took the call. 'Hey, Andy. How's it going?'

'Not good. Interpol have nothing more to offer on the dead guys. Hopefully, you'll do better.'

'Don't hold your breath.'

Footsteps were approaching from the rear.

Frankie swung round.

Matthews came to a stop when she saw the mobile stuck to her ear. Either she'd come to apologise or to see her off the premises.

Frankie wasn't fussed either way.

She turned away, continuing her call. 'Lucked out here too. Parochial mentality. You know how it is. Win some, lose some. Fucking waste of time.' Frankie saw two shadows reflected in the brushed metal lift door. Matthews had stuck around. A one-sided conversation would be enough to whet her appetite. 'Any news from ANPR?'

'They lost the Mercedes at Scotch Corner. Probably changed plates, though there were none in the van.'

'They'll have ditched them. Change plates, take your furry dice away and you're a different vehicle, especially at night. Tell him I want a check on similar vehicles from that location to the scene of the crash. They'll have stopped somewhere. Scumbags eat, drink and piss like the rest of us. Check all southbound service stations.'

'Don't you mean northbound?'

'Possibly.'

Andrea made the jump. 'Is someone with you?'

Frankie didn't answer.

'OK. You lead, I'll follow.'

'Next train out of here. If I text you my ETA and get off at Alnmouth, can you give me a lift? My car's in Berwick. If I don't get home soon, I'll forget where I live.'

'You want eyes on in case you're followed?'

'Yeah, that works,' Frankie said. 'Any update on the package we received yesterday?'

'Amir is fine, Frank. Rae's a natural. No regrets.'

Smiling, Frankie hung up.

Pocketing the phone, she pressed for the lift, Matthews' voice reaching her from behind. Frankie waited a beat, then a beat more. She turned, pointing at her own chest. 'Sorry, you talking to me?'

'I'd like to.'

'Did you get permission?'

Matthews laughed. She'd crossed the line.

Frankie was one up at half-time.

53

Thanks to Jan Welch's willingness to cooperate, David was torn, overwhelmed by mixed emotions. On the one hand, he was in a good place, closer now than he had ever been. On the other, it looked like someone he had a lot of respect for was guilty of ending Joanna Oliver's life, robbing her of a future, her family the pleasure of watching her grow up.

This would kill Frankie.

He left South Shields via the Tyne Tunnel, keen to get to Middle Earth, a fifteen-minute drive at the arse end of rush hour. All he had to do now was prove Hall's innocence, eliminate him from the investigation and crack on. One interview should be enough to find out what he knew, or what he thought he knew, about the open unsolved murder investigation. His motivation for being vindictive at Frankie's party was self-evident, but was David being led up a blind alley?

His phone lit up on the dash as a text came in. 'See who that is, will you?'

Indira hesitated. 'You sure? It might be personal.'

'As sad as it sounds, I don't have a private life. No time.'

Scooping up the device, she read the text. 'The guv'nor's not one to waste words, is he?'

'What does it say?'

'Check the safe.'

'No kiss?'

Indira laughed.

'Tell him we're heading in. No, on second thoughts, don't. If it's the duty rosters in the safe, we could do without the distraction.'

Indi keyed a short reply.

Blinded by strong sunshine as they exited the north end of the Tyne Tunnel, David reached for his shades and put them on. Bright would expect an update ASAP. While he'd made progress, it amounted to very little in real terms.

He needed more.

Replacing the mobile, Indira swivelled in her seat to face him. 'Do you still want me to trace the people Hall acknowledged on his way out of the police club?'

'No, I think we have enough.'

'What about William Welch?'

'If Jan's on the level, and I think she is, I'm guessing Hall used him as a prop to have a go at the man who screwed his wife, maybe acting on impulse after sinking a few. Let's face it, her brother has as much reason to hate him for ruining her marriage and possibly her life. She was regretful, didn't you think?'

'Too late,' Indira's words lacked sympathy. 'She was a willing participant and so was he. And they were married to other people. My brother would've killed us both if that had been me.'

David snapped his head round.

'I didn't know you were married—'

'I'm not.'

'Well, when you are, remember Jan. Illicit affairs are not all they're cracked up to be. What starts in beautiful rooms ends in the parking lot, or words to that effect. So speaks a Taylor Swift fan. Wonderful lyrics. Want to listen?' She nodded. He accessed Spotify on the hands-free, played it to her, then switched it off. 'Now . . .' He chuckled, in a better mood. 'Don't take this the wrong way, but can you stay late?'

54

Dinner was a strange affair. Frankie was used to restaurants where you could hear yourself think, where the accents were mostly northern and – unless you spoke in whispers – people on the next table could listen in. In Central London, conversations were taking place in a variety of languages. Frankie loved the city's international vibe, but would never get used to the bloody noise, inside or out.

They had driven a couple of miles to Covent Garden, DI Kit Matthews dropping her attitude on the way. No longer on an ego trip, she was keen to make amends. Her chat was friendly while they ate at a restaurant of her choosing: Balthazar. The menu was inviting, the food delicious, the company growing on Frankie now battle lines were drawn.

There would be no pretence from now on.

She declined a dessert, ordering a double espresso, eager to press on with the business end of their meeting. Matthews handed over a printout of Petkov and Mitev's associates the National Crime Agency had on their system, then left Frankie to it while she went to find the ladies.

On the cover was a name: Operation Zenith.

Unadulterated shite.

'Who makes this stuff up?'

Frankie was talking to an empty chair. Turning the page, she found what she was after, images of dodgy-looking males no right-minded person would want to meet on a dark night. Next to them was a precis of their criminal records, and details of exact locations where the photographs had been taken, each of them timed and dated.

Gotcha!

The Andy Carroll lookalike stared back at her, caught on camera coming out of a Brighton pub less than three weeks ago. The close-up revealed a deep scar down his right cheek she assumed was the result of a fight, a reminder to stay in line perhaps. The longer she stared at him, the more certain she was that she'd found her man. His name was Ivan Osman. Quickly, she took out her phone, photographing the lot.

She was googling Osman, when Kit reappeared.

'Mobile.' She made a paddle with her hand. 'C'mon, hand it over.'

Rumbled, Frankie laughed. 'Just keeping you on your toes.'

'David was right. You're a piece of work.'

'Nevertheless, he'd approve.'

Frankie's iPhone remained firmly in her hand. She turned the printout to face her Met colleague, then tapped the Messages icon on her mobile, accessing the image Andrea had sent through. She laid it on the table side by side with the image of Osman she'd been looking at a moment ago.

'Bottom right,' she said. 'Tell me that's not the same bloke.'

'Yeah, I agree. There'll be more images to prove it.'

'Were they operating out of Brighton?'

Kit sidestepped the question. 'I get the impression you're not surprised.'

'It's where they knocked off the Merc – their first mistake. There will be others.'

Kit reached for the wine to top them up.

Frankie covered her glass. 'Not for me. Tell me about them.'

'They came on to the scene relatively recently. Europol alerted Sussex Police that they might be heading to the UK via France, asking us to assist with intel. Irregular migration is growing every week. It's horrendous down here. Out of control. These guys aren't fleeing persecution. They're thugs who couldn't give a shit about anything but money.'

'If you knew Mitev was wanted for murder, why didn't you pick him up and deport him?'

'Sussex asked us not to. They were keeping an eye on him.'

'Were they, really?' Frankie said. 'Look, I get it, I do. But they took a kid, tied him up, intending to sell him on. Osman left him in that van. I want him to pay for that.' She withheld Amir's name and didn't mention that he was a toddler. She would if she had to. 'If the Merc hadn't ploughed into oncoming traffic, God only knows where he'd have ended up. You're OK with that?'

'No, of course not.'

'I'm sorry, this is not on you.' Frankie rolled her eyes. 'Whatever happened to crime prevention?'

'What can I say? It's a mess.' Matthews studied her. 'What are you *not* telling me?'

'How long have you got?'

'As long as it takes.'

'This is bigger than you think, Kit. You need to take it seriously. I found one kid. My guts are telling me that there are many more. If I'm right, this is large-scale human trafficking.' Frankie gave in, picked up the wine, pouring herself another drink. 'Kit, the boy is about four or five years old. Doesn't speak English. I've already checked the PNC for missing persons. There's no one there fitting his description.'

'He belongs to someone.'

'Yeah, and I have zero idea of where he was taken from or how far their operation extends.'

'There's no geographical limit, is the honest answer. We have reason to believe that they are part of a network that extends across Europe. In the UK, nineteen different force areas are on board, feeding intel into Operation Zenith. We know the group are involved with sex trafficking. This is the first I've heard of anyone as young as the kid you're on about. Migrants are easy pickings. Some are unaccompanied minors, separated from parents fleeing persecution. If they had papers at the beginning of their journey, they've inexplicably gone missing by the time they reach the UK. Organised crime syndicates are exploiting them for their own ends. If you have hard evidence, it could be critical in bringing them down. We can help, but it won't be easy—'

'Will you at least try?'

'Can you stick around?'

'No, there's more. I need to head north. We recovered a burner from the Merc. It had a voicemail on it in Bulgarian. The sender was yelling at Mitev that he was behind schedule. That's how we knew his nationality. Interpol gave us the rest. There was an Edinburgh postcode in the satnav. I've been up there to investigate. There are warehouses, tenement flats, hundreds of brand-new high-rise apartments. It's an impossible task for a couple of detectives.'

'That's your team?'

'Welcome to Northumbria Police. We're four up, one DC, the accident investigator and another Traffic cop lending a hand temporarily. That won't last. On the plus side, I have pertinent intel I doubt your team are aware of.'

'Such as?'

'While inspecting the Merc, we found a number eleven stuck on the roof, a crude aftermarket addition, recently applied. Forensics are working on it. I have someone trying to find the provenance of the tape they used. It's not taken us anywhere. It's sold nationwide. I checked with the Merc's owner. The stickers weren't on the van when it was stolen. I don't think Mitev's crew had an actual address they were heading to, just a postcode that leads to a no through road, overlooked by the high-rise apartments I mentioned. They probably have a runner on the street to do the business.'

'Blimey! This is gold.'

'If we jump on it now, we're in with a chance of taking them out,' Frankie said. 'They're unaware that they're under surveillance, otherwise they wouldn't have risked moving the boy. That gives me hope that we can close them down sooner rather than later.'

'You're dreaming,' Kit said. 'They'll have moved on when the Merc didn't arrive.'

'Not necessarily. The RTA made the national news. They'll have heard about it. I made sure the press release was creatively worded. Vehicles up in flames. Two dead men we couldn't identify. It didn't mention the guy in the rear or the child. The OCG may be under the impression that Osman still has him.'

'Good move.'

'Any chance we can split the team?' Frankie had a plan. 'You come north with me and get your guys to do what needs to be done down here. They can explore the south coast and other areas housing migrants. You've got nowt. I have an end point. I'm working out of Berwick, a stone's throw from Edinburgh. Why not begin there and work backwards? I don't care who brings the enquiry to an end, so long as it's cracked. You have authority I don't have. Your NCA warrant card will open doors. Are you up for it?'

Kit raised her glass. 'I'm in.'

55

At Middle Earth, David peeled off to check in with the MIT, telling Indira he'd be along in a few minutes and to get started. Both apprehensive and excited, she felt a rush of adrenalin as she sped along the corridor, a sense of pride that he trusted her to carry on without him. After unlocking their office door, locking it behind her, she dumped her belongings, then opened the safe, keen to locate the relevant duty roster, knowing that it would determine Adam Hall's innocence or guilt in relation to Joanna's murder.

There were forty-three rosters in total, rolled not folded, detailing every station force-wide for the night in question. Indira unfurled them in turn until she reached the one for South Shields, Command Unit: Lima 1.

Spreading it out on her desk, she sat down, slipping on her reading specs.

The A2 document was a work of art, detailing the day in the life of Hall's station. Officers were split by rota – A to D – down the left-hand side of the page, almost a hundred in total. Shifts were written across the top, split by earlies, lates, nights, rest days, with an additional miscellaneous column covering a multitude of reasons why each officer was doing something other than their normal duty: court attendance, sickness, AL indicating annual leave, TO for time off (other than a normal rest day), TC for training courses.

Hall was here somewhere.

Finding his name in the side column, Indi established that C rota were on nightshift . . . except there was no tick against his name in that column. She ran her finger across the sheet to the miscellaneous column.

Bingo!

What she found there gave her an idea.

Drawing her laptop closer, she tapped a few keys, entering the personnel system. As she happened upon what she was after, David entered from the corridor, his eyes seizing on the roster spread across her desk, held down with empty coffee mugs acting as paperweights.

'Any joy?'

Indira couldn't contain herself. 'Adam Hall's shift was on nights. He wasn't. He was seventy-five miles away, instructing on a crime management course, a cross-border initiative led by Cumbria Constabulary. It began on Friday, June twelfth 1992 and ran throughout the weekend.'

'Assuming he turned up—'

'He did.'

'You sure about that?'

She gestured towards her laptop. 'Take a look.'

David walked towards her.

On screen was an image of an internal memo from the course leader to Hall's supervision complimenting him on a job well done.

'The perfect alibi,' David said. 'Except his input was timed at three p.m. Saturday. He could've arrived that morning, or registered on the Friday, then slipped out unnoticed. It doesn't rule him out—'

Smiling, Indi brought up a new page.

'Read on, guv.'

After last night's revelations, David and Indira decided to knock off and work the weekend. Next morning, they drove to Hall's home, an unremarkable semi in Shields, arriving at 10 a.m. The door was opened by his current wife. Sarah was in her dressing gown – a lie-in, they supposed. Introductions complete, apologies extended, she saw them into a living-cum-dining room and went to fetch her husband. He arrived a moment later, hair sticking out at odd angles, a pair of tracksuit bottoms, a creased T-shirt hastily pulled on to greet his visitors, nothing on his feet.

He shook hands with them, showing no sign of stress, more a healthy dollop of intrigue.

'Sorry to arrive unannounced,' Indira said.

'No problem. What's this about?'

'An old case . . .' David pointed to the dining table. 'Mind if we sit?'

'Sure.' As they took their seats, Hall glanced at his wife. 'You couldn't make us a cuppa, could you, love?'

Without argument, she disappeared into the kitchen, closing the door behind her.

David didn't hang around. 'You're not in trouble, Adam. I have reason to believe that you have information regarding an open unsolved case.'

'Which one?'

He knew.

David sidestepped the question. 'Everything we discuss is off the record and cannot be shared. Understood?'

'I'm the epitome of discretion, guv.'

David stared him down. 'We both know that's not true.'

Hall's face flushed, a hint of recognition reaching his eyes. 'You were both at Frankie Oliver's leaving do last week, right?'

David said, 'You'd had a few.'

'Apologies if I embarrassed anyone.'

'We're not here to lay one on you for having a go at someone we all know.'

'So why are you here?'

David made him sweat. Hall leaned his elbow on the table, rubbing at his forehead. He'd already worked out why the detectives had come knocking. Time to put him out of his misery. 'We now know why you were making your mouth go. We spoke to your ex—'

Hall was instantly riled. 'What the fuck for?'

'We needed to know about the call-out to your home before the two of you split up—'

He wasn't expecting that. 'What is there to say? It was years ago. What's it got to do with you anyhow? Or a cold case, for that matter?' His body tensed as he jumped to the wrong conclusion. 'Is Jan all right?'

'She's fine,' Indira reassured him. 'Just answer the question.'

'Look, there was an altercation, which which led to the breakdown of our marriage. That's all you need to know . . .' Again, Hall made the wrong jump. 'Christ, what did she say? I didn't touch her—'

'Relax, Adam . . .' David said. 'No such allegation has been made. We know about her affair. She named her lover, the guy you were hassling the other night. For what it's worth, she has regrets.'

A dark shadow crossed Hall's face. He also had regrets. He opened his mouth to speak but was interrupted by the loud whistle of a kettle from the kitchen, presumably the old-fashioned type you boil on a stove.

'Look, as far as I was concerned, Jan and I were happily married. She broke my heart. I couldn't live with it.' Hall cleared his throat. 'Did she tell you I decked him?'

David confirmed it with a nod.

'The fucker deserved it.'

They paused the conversation as Sarah entered with a tray of refreshments no one had the time or inclination to drink. Hall was avoiding the awkward look she threw his way. Telling him she was going for a bath, she left the room. They heard her climbing the stairs, a door slamming shut on the floor above.

'We're not here to cause you grief,' David said. 'We can do this elsewhere if it's easier.'

'No. Sarah knows.'

'Everything?'

'Yeah.'

'Look, I understand why you hate the guy,' David said. 'That's not my business. What is my business is whether there was any truth in what you were mouthing off about the other night. This is your chance to put the record straight – assuming you recall saying it.'

'I do . . .' Hall looked suitably ashamed. 'It wasn't planned, guv. I didn't go there looking for trouble, if that's what you think. Last time I saw him, my fist was in his mouth. And there he was, talking to some foreigner, Anna someone or other, with his tongue halfway down her throat. I couldn't resist telling him what a useless piece of shit he was . . . useless detective too, in my opinion. He might be different now, but much of what he knows, I taught him.'

'So why the comment on a missing jacket, the white van?'

Hall stroked the stubble on his chin. 'He was on Bright's team. Thought he was God's gift. Only I knew he was too busy shagging other people's missus to concentrate on finding either. The guy's a sleaze.'

'Not the person we know,' Indira said in his defence.

'Well, maybe he got his fingers burnt and grew the fuck up.'

As Hall looked away, the detectives exchanged a fleeting look. Was he hinting at Joanna's murder? Bright had confirmed that Hall wasn't selected to investigate. David's gut was telling him there was more to the story. To find out what it was, he asked a question he already knew the answer to.

'Adam, were you involved in the enquiry in any way?'

'Should've been. Would have, had I not been spoken to about a so-called domestic a few weeks earlier. Having heard a scream, a neighbour called our lot thinking Jan was in danger. When the attending officer arrived, I begged her to fob him off and she did. When he asked to see me, she refused. He wasn't buying it and filed an unofficial report. I received a verbal warning, was told not to let it happen again.'

'Why didn't you tell anyone?'

'Would you?' Hall's eyes were angry. 'And guess who got the job, his big break—'

'Ouch.' David winced.

'Yeah, double whammy: loss of wife and dream job, a case that every detective wanted in on, so excuse me if I came across as a resentful prick the other night. Your man has a lot to answer for.'

Indira jumped in. 'What exactly are you saying?'

'I'm saying he used Jan and shafted me on the same night.'

David wanted more. 'What do you know about the investigation into Joanna Oliver's murder?'

'Not much. I was in Carlisle when it happened.'

David flashed Indi a brief smile. 'I'll let DC Sharma explain. She deserves the credit.'

Indira's face flushed. 'We know you stood in for the after-dinner speaker that Friday night. There's a thank you in your personnel file. Did you know Joanna?'

'I knew of her and saw what her death did to her old man. Outside of that, I can't help you.' Hall focused on David. 'Are you reopening the case?'

'Not until we have fresh evidence.'

'Good luck with that. Are we done?'

'For now . . .' Thanking him, David got up. 'I have one final question. What was the feeling about this missing jacket?'

'It was one of the first pieces of evidence to be sent to the lab for testing. Negative result. Years on, when it was to be re-examined forensically using new techniques, it was not in the exhibits room when detectives went to look for it. By then, HQ had relocated. Things got lost. Frank Oliver was incensed. He kicked up a fuss. Who wouldn't? If it looks and smells like a cover-up . . .'

56

Kit Matthews had submitted a hand-written report to her guv'nor and was given permission to assist Frankie up north. They had been promised sufficient human resources to locate Osman and put him away. They had taken an early train from King's Cross; Kit's first visit to Berwick, a four-hour journey. When they passed through the Northumberland coastline, heavenly on a summer's day, she realised she'd been missing out. Much of the time, she seemed lost in the scenery as it flashed by.

Frankie studied her.

On the way up, Kit had told her that the NCA and Police Scotland worked collaboratively out of Glasgow. Troops were assembling. Already, it felt like they had known each other for years, even though they had only met yesterday. Frankie wondered why David had chosen to confide his innermost thoughts to Kit when it had taken him so long to be honest with her.

He cares for you.

Frankie would never understand men.

She'd had her bitch face on the last time she'd seen David. The word *'checkmate'* echoed in her head. *Outmanoeuvred. No fucking escape. Game over.* She couldn't have made it clearer that there was no way back for them.

The train slowed.

She had no idea how long she'd been sitting in silence. It wasn't until Kit spoke that she realised she'd been ignoring her counterpart.

'What?' Kit said. 'You were staring at me.'

Frankie's brow creased. 'Was I?'

'I still have the daggers if you want them back.' The smile slid off Kit's face. 'So, what's the plan, assuming you have one?'

'Not now. This is our stop.'

The heavens opened as they got off the train, a crack of thunder in the distance, neither of them dressed for torrential rain. They'd be drenched if they made the ten-minute walk to the nick.

Taking shelter, Frankie made a call.

Within minutes, Graham Ross arrived to pick them up.

When he pulled into the police yard a few minutes later, it was full of unmarked cars: a personnel carrier, motorcycles and pushbikes that hadn't been there when she left. Inside, Frankie's office was cramped. She could work with that. Detectives, new and old, had been busy. Desks had been set up with additional computers. Surveillance equipment was being made ready. There was a real buzz about the place. A mini command centre. Everyone waiting for instructions, including Mitch, Andrea and Sam.

Kit introduced DS José Rodríguez, and DCs Ari Hassan, Sheena McKenna and James Robertson. Frankie welcomed them, telling them all to grab a brew before she briefed them, then took Andrea to one side. Facing away from the others, she kept her voice low.

'How's Amir?'

'Settling in. Bright offered to find us an interpreter, multilingual, to help us communicate with him and hopefully ID where he's from.'

'Good idea. Everything OK here?'

'Yeah, no complaints.'

'You've briefed them?'

'Mitch did . . . I didn't want to step on his toes. They're keen to get moving.' Andrea leaned against the wall, crossing her arms, a concerned expression. 'You OK?'

Frankie shrugged: *I guess*.

'What about Matthews?'

'What about her?'

'You seem pally. I thought you said she was a cocky shit.'

'Rude.' Kit was laughing as Frankie swung round to face her. 'Also true on occasions.'

Andrea laughed, always the practical joker.

Frankie did too, glad of police humour. It would carry them through what she knew would be a difficult operation. They were now as one, in complete harmony, a small team with the same priority.

She called for phones to be switched off.

The team complied.

Those who were standing sat down and paid attention.

Frankie thanked the Glasgow detectives for deploying so speedily. 'We'd be screwed without you.' She perched on the edge of a desk, thanking Mitch for briefing them. 'If the offenders in Edinburgh think Osman still has his cargo, they might assume he'll make his way to them as soon as he's able, so that Leith postcode is our best bet. Given that he doesn't have the child, my guess is he'll be lying low, perhaps not far from here.'

Graham's hand was up. 'Want me to circulate Osman's photo?'

'Yeah, brief your crew to keep a lookout. If anyone asks, he's suspected of child trafficking. I'm as sure as I can be that he was employed to do the grunt work. There were no firearms in the van, so no suggestion he'll be armed. Tell your guys to approach with caution though, just in case.'

'Won't he be making his way south?' Sheena asked.

'I don't think so. As young as he is, the child we found is a witness. Leaving him alive in the van wasn't smart, nor was leaving the dead guys' phones for us to find. Osman has reasons to be fearful – and not just of us.'

'Where's the kid now?' José asked.

'In a safe house being well looked after . . .' They had too much experience to ask where. 'Let me be clear. The boy has not been reported missing. There's been no ransom demand. My guess is he was smuggled into the UK as a commodity, like counterfeit cigarettes or drugs. No idea what they intended to do with him. I don't want you to dwell on it. Speculation won't help us find who took him.'

The room fell silent.

The detectives facing her were under no illusions. Hopefully, what she'd said would spur them into action. Frankie carried on. 'I won't lie to you. Yesterday, I'd hit a brick wall. With DI Matthews' help, I've turned the corner and I'm not letting go. We're on the clock. NCA have given us a week.'

'What?' Andrea's face was easy to read: *what use is that?* 'I know these ops cost, but it's unrealistic to expect we'll get it in under the wire in seven days.'

'All the more reason to crack on,' Kit said. 'Pooling resources equals a fortnight. Right, boss?'

'And not a minute to waste,' Frankie said, grateful for her enthusiasm. 'Before our time is up, we need something I can kick upstairs, enough evidence to justify a request for an extension—'

Kit grimaced. 'It'll probably be denied.'

'Not by my guv'nor . . . but thanks for the reality check. If yours objects, ours will deal with it when the time comes.'

Aware that they were facing an uphill struggle, a task bordering on the impossible given the time frame, faces were grim.

'Hey, we're still in the game,' Frankie said. 'Besides, when have you *ever* known those on the top floor to make an important decision without a working party?'

A ripple of laughter made its way around the room.

'While they argue over budgets, we're still rolling. The rest is down to you . . .' Frankie hadn't quite managed to lift morale yet. 'We all know that right across Europe, right across the world, task forces are working to stop the trade in humans. We can't solve all the problems. We can try to solve this one.'

57

'I believe him,' Indira said as she climbed into the car, looking out at Hall, who was watching from the window with a dispirited expression. 'He didn't enjoy being forced to relive an unpleasant memory, that's for sure. I feel sorry for him, don't you?'

'Why?'

'He's the victim in all this and he still cares for Jan. Did you see how emotional he was when you told him we'd seen her? I honestly thought he was about to lose it.'

David didn't argue.

He fired up the car, moving off at speed, head-checking the road as he joined the main carriageway. 'Now he's ruled out, we move on. Where we go next is another matter. When we return to base, you carry on with what you were doing. I'm going to give Anna a call. She was closer to the conversation than I was.'

'That missing jacket bothers me,' Indira said.

'Me too. Frank Snr will have explored every avenue to find it. If it was taken deliberately and not lost in transit, I cannot believe it still exists. Only an idiot would hold on to it. As we both know, our suspect is no fool.'

Indira stared at him intensely.

Sensing the weight of her gaze, and simultaneously spotting a lay-by, David pulled over. Killing the ignition, he turned to face her. 'What is it? Do we need to go back?'

'No, that's just it, guv. Hall had every reason to throw mud. That doesn't make his target guilty of murdering Joanna though, does it?'

'Correct, so we exercise caution, but Joanna was fifteen years old. If he took her life' – David stressed the word *if* – 'he's destroyed many more. I don't give a fuck if he's tried to make up for it since—'

'Didn't Hall explain that? Why are you so sure that their spat had anything to do with murder? His wife confirmed it independently. She struck me as genuine, someone deeply troubled by her own behaviour.'

'Then why mention it?'

'To get at him. To rubbish his detective skills. Hall thought he'd done enough to make Bright's hand-picked team, then the opportunity was given to his adversary. That's a big deal. No wonder he's jealous. That aside, shouldn't we explore other suspects, not just the convenient ones?' Indira paused as a Traffic car sped by with sirens blaring. 'I'm playing devil's advocate, guv. I don't like what's going through my head any more than you will.'

He waited for her to elaborate.

'Promise not to lose your rag until you hear me out?' When he didn't answer, she opened the window for some air. With the air con off, the vehicle stationary, it was stifling in the car. She swivelled in her seat to face him. 'You said yourself that Frankie's dad was a suspect in the initial investigation—'

'That's always the case.'

'Yeah, but if he was called out to the scene, he could already have been in the area.'

'He wasn't,' David reassured her. 'He was dealing with another job when he received the call-out.'

'Was he though? Didn't you say he rowed with Joanna on the night she died?'

'Indi, I want you to question everything. I'd expect nothing less, but on this occasion you're wrong. There were witnesses who verified that call.'

'Then give me access to the murder file.'

'Done. And if you continue to have doubts when you've studied it, we'll talk again. Frank Oliver has spent almost three decades trying to chase down Joanna's murderer. He's obsessed by it.'

'A good ploy if anyone raised him as a suspect further down

the line. A grieving, loving father who couldn't let go would garner sympathy and throw investigators off the scent, right?' Already Indira was thinking like a detective. 'And this is going to sound even more crazy, but what about Bright?'

'As a suspect?' David scoffed. 'You're off your trolley—'

'He's Joanna's godfather—'

'How the hell do you know that? I didn't until this week.'

'Frankie mentioned it.'

'When?'

Indira shrugged. 'Can't remember. Weeks, months. I don't recall how it came up. She said it wasn't common knowledge, though why anyone would keep it a secret is beyond me.'

'Bright will have advised her to keep it quiet when she joined up, in case he was accused of favouritism, or she got it in the neck for being too close to him. You'll be accusing me next. I'm also close to the family, though I'd never heard of the Olivers until a few years ago. You want to throw in Joanna's granddad for good measure? Besides, you just answered your own question. How Bright and Frankie handle their relationship is their business, no one else's—'

'What if it turned out to be true, guv?'

'Then I'd deal with it.'

'You wouldn't make it go away?'

'You're questioning my integrity now?' David studied her.

Indira was conflicted, stressed out for having raised her concerns, not to mention red in the face. 'I'm sorry, I shouldn't have said that. I overstepped the line.'

'Don't *ever* apologise for doing your job. It takes guts to suggest corruption. I won't lie. It felt like a slap in the face.' He was smiling. 'Rest assured, I'd never look the other way, whoever we finger as the culprit. That includes Frank, Bright or the bloody chief constable. Now, back up a moment and explain where all this came from? It didn't just randomly arrive in your head. You know something I don't?'

'I do. Joanna's jacket isn't the only thing that's missing.'

'What do you mean?'

'Some of the rosters I was expecting to see weren't in the safe. There were none from headquarters CID.' Indira stopped talking, allowing that to sink in. Assuming they were like that when Frankie's father received them, only one other person had access to them before they were passed on.

She meant Bright.

58

Frankie had witnessed many an internal scrap during her service when there was more than one officer of the same rank working together – often from neighbouring forces. There was no power struggle in play here. Kit and Andrea were happy that she should lead the abduction-trafficking investigation. From the outset, it was clear that her newly formed team, such as it was, would work collaboratively. She'd asked them to chip in with ideas. They were as keen to shut down the gang who'd taken Amir as she was. She still hadn't shared his name, nor would she.

He was safer that way.

She noticed that Matthews was deep in thought.

'Kit, you want to say something?'

She looked up. 'Am I right in thinking that Petkov and Mitev were never identified publicly?'

'Correct,' Frankie said. 'We didn't have ID at the time. It served our purpose to keep the information to ourselves when we did.'

'What about the women who died at the scene?'

'Their families asked for their names to be withheld. We respected that.'

'Good, which means that whoever's waiting at the Edinburgh postcode won't know who did and didn't make it. What's stopping us from sourcing a similar Merc? Replicating the plates and the identifying number on top, passing it off as the original. Driving it to Leith.'

'Risky,' Frankie said. 'There were loads of people out of their vehicles that night, standing on the embankment, taking photos. If just one of them posted images of that van, we're screwed.'

'The fact that it was stationary means nowt—'

'I'm not disputing it's a great idea. Worth a shot if we'd done it the day after the accident. It's too late now.' Frankie picked up her mobile, scrolling the images Andrea had sent her of the crash scene, landing on one of the Merc. She handed the device to Kit. 'As you can see, it was a hefty front-end shunt, almost head-on.'

'Yeah, I see what you mean. Anyone can tell it's a write-off.'

Frankie moved on. 'Our best chance is to stake out that Leith postcode. If the offenders are using the apartments overlooking that location to spot a numbered vehicle, then so can we. They could be waiting for another assignment. I want us there when it arrives. Operation Zenith is very much a live enquiry.'

Kit showed no aggro at being shot down. 'I'll get my guys in the south to put an eye in the sky to see if they can spot any other vans with ID numbers on top, paying close attention to where the Merc was stolen and any locations housing asylum seekers.' She turned to face her NCA colleagues. 'Frankie thinks the kid she found is a migrant. If our luck holds, the next van that leaves, we'll be right behind them.'

Everyone agreed it was a good call.

'Andy, did you get a result on the kid's blood sample?' Frankie asked.

'Yeah, it's disappointing. There's no match on the database.'

'Well, that's that then. Let's hope the interpreter can get the boy talking.'

Grabbing a detailed map of the location, Frankie described the set-up as the team gathered around to view it, keen to get her take on the place. On the train, she'd downloaded the images she'd taken in Leith to a memory stick so they could view them if she was not around. Inserting it into her laptop, she zoomed in on the house she'd been concerned about, the scruffy exterior, the mosaic-tiled floor, the tidy front porch.

For a moment she was back there, viewing mailboxes, while telling the others about the man mountain who'd come to an upstairs window to check the street before opening the door. Moving the cursor, she clicked on his image.

'This is him.'

'I'll check him on our system,' DC Ari Hassan said.

'Thanks. The guy spoke in a foreign language, hauling his visitor inside like he was in a hurry.' Frankie clicked on another photograph. 'This is the skinny kid who knocked on the door. It's not a good image, but the best I could do. I've seen more meat on a cocktail stick. Ari, keep an eye out for him.' She eyeballed Mitch. 'Did you visit the service station where ANPR lost the van?'

'Yesterday. The company that owns the car park is checking their CCTV.'

'It takes seconds when they want to slap you with a fine. Follow it up, now please.'

Mitch was already pulling out his mobile. Andrea was checking hers too, a frown developing as she slid the device into her pocket. Frankie jumped to the wrong conclusion: a potential problem at home with Amir?

She had to ask . . . in code.

'Andy? Got anything else for me?'

'No, that was my guv'nor. Traffic are flat out and need a hand.'

'Sam too?'

''Fraid so. We've gotta go, I'm sorry.'

'It is what it is. Hand off any outstanding actions to Mitch before you split. Go careful out there.'

Andrea had read the shorthand of her words, a warning that didn't involve roads and fast cars, just a wee man who needed her. She'd be liaising with Rae as soon as she was out of there. The Traffic officers brought Mitch up to speed, then grabbed their gear, pivoting to face the NCA detectives before they left.

'Guys, it's been a pleasure,' Andrea said. 'Flat out doesn't mean incommunicado. My phone's on 24/7. Anything you want, just yell.'

Having rubbished Indira's take on Bright as a suspect for Joanna's murder, David drove to the coast, unable to get the notion out of his head. He'd taken a short walk, time to think more on the subject. The idea was inconceivable, but now he was asking himself how Joanna Oliver had ended up in Southwick on the north bank of the River Wear, so far from home. The conclusion he'd drawn was that she'd known the person who'd driven her there, accepting a lift without realising that she was exposing herself to danger.

What kid chooses the bus over a ride home with someone they trust?

Before Joanna left the house that night, there had been an argument. She'd been rude to her mum. Her dad had lost his rag, grounding her. When she apologised, he'd changed his mind in favour of a curfew.

Frankie had told David that Joanna was bound for Newcastle city centre to meet friends for a pizza, calling their old man from a coin box an hour before her estimated time of death. On duty that night, he'd ignored the call, a decision he'd lived to regret.

Next time he saw her, she was dead.

Later, when David offered his assistance to Frankie, she was in tears: *don't help me, help him*. The thing that haunted her the most was that her father would die before the truth came to light, before the person who killed her sister was in a cell serving a full life sentence. She'd begged David to give her dad closure.

The weight of that responsibility was killing him.

Hearing young voices, his attention shifted from the inside of his head to a seashore safari taking place in front of him; a group of toddlers gathered around an adult, rock-pooling, intrigued and curious, mini explorers with enquiring minds, also searching for answers.

As he continued to watch their smiley faces, his mind flew back in time. Frankie had shown him a newspaper cutting, flimsy and browned with age, referencing Joanna's final night out. Before leaving her friends to return home, she'd moaned that her dad was hard on her because of what he did for a living. One of the group, Jack Gale, could relate. His old man, known as 'Windy' within the CID, was also a detective, one her father

200

accused of losing evidence to protect his son, an allegation he later retracted.

In any case, in David's mind the person who took Joanna would've been older than her by a few years. Old enough to drive and have access to a vehicle. Jack Gale was her age. That didn't rule him out. A lot of rebellious kids drove illegally, were guilty of vehicle theft – two wheels or four. Having met his father, David didn't think it likely that Jack was one of them. Nevertheless, he would re-interview him.

Now an adult, Jack could no longer hide behind his old man.

Hoping that he might get more out of him, David called Indira. 'I'd like you to trace a witness in the original enquiry. He used to hang out with Joanna and was with her on the night she died. His name is Jack Gale.'

'Boyfriend?'

'In his dreams.'

'She wasn't keen?'

'Put it this way, he was more interested in her than she was in him. Set up a meeting . . . discreetly. You'll see why when you look him up.'

'On it.'

David cut the call.

59

At the end of a long day, Frankie left Berwick, Morpeth-bound. When she reached her destination – Rae and Andrea's riverside apartment – she rang the bell, smiling as she looked up at the recently installed CCTV. It was not the only addition to home security. She heard a bolt slide back on the door, the safety chain come off, her father allowing her inside. It didn't surprise her that he was there. He'd insisted that Rae and Amir would never be left alone until he was satisfied that they were out of danger.

If Andrea was out, he was in.

Had it been legal to carry a firearm, he'd have done that too.

Putting his forefinger to his lips, he led Frankie to the living room, pausing at the door. Rae and Amir were sharing a picture book on the sofa in a room that could easily pass for a small toyshop.

Rolling her eyes at her old man, Frankie whispered: 'Toys R Us?'

'Closed down. Went to Toytown instead. Could've spent all day there.'

'Looks like you did.'

'Guilty as charged.' He winked at her. 'Don't tell your mum.'

Frankie refocused on the readers cuddled up together, inseparable already. 'Jesus, she's a natural. Gaining his trust when there's no shared language is nothing short of incredible. If that's the only barrier between them, they'll soon overcome it.'

Her father's hand found hers. 'Be proud, Frank. You paved the way for that to happen.'

Standing in the doorway, observing, she listened as her sister pointed to an image contained within the pages of the book, explaining to Amir that it was a 'FROG,' keeping it nice and simple, as Frankie had in the hospital.

Feeling a tug on her sleeve, she turned.

With a flick of his head, her father gestured towards the kitchen. She followed him. He put on the kettle, then sat down to wait for it to boil, speaking in low tones so as not to interrupt story time going on next door.

'The interpreter came—'

'Wow, super quick.'

'And super young.'

'Is that relevant?'

Frankie glanced at the business card he pushed across the table: *Penelope Wardman, PhD, CIOL, DPI*. She recognised the acronyms: Chartered Institute of Linguistics and Diploma in Police Interpreting. She looked up at her father. 'What's your problem? She has more qualifications than we have put together. It says here she specialises in kids who've suffered trauma.'

Her old man scoffed. 'She looks about ten.'

'So did I when I joined up.'

'True.'

'And I made DI before you did. A personal best.' Her smug humour turned to modesty. 'No need to sulk, Dad. I'll never be the legend you are.'

'You underestimate yourself.'

'Much as I'd like to sit here and trade compliments, I don't have time. I'm on the clock with a very short window before the NCA bods are recalled. I need to check in with Kit and spend time with Amir before I leave. Did Wardman give any indication of his nationality, or even hazard a guess?'

'No, but Bright claims she's the best there is. She did say it would take time, that we should allow Amir to go at his own pace. Kids his age soak up new languages quickly, love. I'll have him talking Geordie in no time.'

'I'm sure you will. That's not the point, nor is it helping me identify where he's from or how he ended up here.'

'Have you traced the witness who ran away?'

'Not yet. I'm hopeful now I know his name.'

'You'll get there. You aways do.'

Her mobile vibrated on the table. Lifting it, she checked the screen, then looked up at her father. 'Sorry, I'll have to take this.'

'Crack on. Tea?'

'Please.'

As her father got up to make it, Frankie took the call. Kit Matthews sounded upbeat. 'I've deployed our lot, north and south, and secured an empty flat overlooking the postcode we're interested in. If anyone so much as breathes the wrong way, we'll know about it.'

Finally, things were moving.

60

As David wandered along the beach, other questions came thick and fast. In a rebellious mood, had Joanna gone willingly to Southwick, extending one finger to the curfew her father had imposed? Why and how she'd travelled there had never been clearly established. Frankie had once told him that Joanna was sophisticated for her age, could easily pass for eighteen. Had she been mistaken for an adult, abducted by a stranger or groomed by someone she knew and trusted, innocently accepting a lift, then taken advantage of? A relative or close associate, perhaps. Someone she liked and looked up to. Had that individual listened to her tale of woe, siding with her point of view, treating her as an adult, not a kid, extending a sympathetic ear?

Someone like Bright.

Or was the man David and Indira already had eyes on responsible for her death? Either way, they had no time to waste if they were to apprehend her killer. David sat down, taking in the wide stretch of golden sand in front of him. Like Frankie, he did his best thinking among crashing waves and soaring gulls. A conversation with Icelandic DCI Anna Jónsdóttir was one he was keen to conduct away from Middle Earth.

Anna was a cop David rated and respected. He imagined her in her smart office, with an unrivalled sea view from the window, feet on her desk, with far fewer 'live' cases than a UK major crimes SIO had to deal with.

He found her number and tapped on it.

She picked up on the first ring. 'David, what a nice surprise!'

'Maybe not when I tell you why I'm calling.'

'Sounds grim. Has something happened?'

'My life is about to implode, does that count?'

She laughed.

Though she'd take it as a given, he stressed the need for confidentiality. 'No exceptions,' he added. 'It could have devastating consequences for people we both care for. I would have called sooner, but I wanted to be sure of my facts before involving you.'

'How can I help?'

'At Frankie's party, I witnessed an altercation between two of the guests standing close to you. Did you hear it?'

'It was hard not to.'

'Then we're on the same page. From where I was standing, I only overheard the tail end of the exchange. I was hoping you could fill me in. Anna, I wouldn't drag you into this shitshow if it wasn't important.'

'It was unpleasant,' she said. 'Name-calling, mostly. I'm no psychologist, but it seemed deeply personal for both men. There was bad blood for sure. Moments earlier, I'd been chatting with the guy on the receiving end. He seemed nice enough.'

'Can you recall specifics?'

'It was an accusation of professional misconduct, screwing around when he should've been at work.'

'I heard, married or single,' David said. 'The younger the better.'

'"Anything with a pulse" were his exact words, an expression I'd never heard before but one that required no interpretation. The target of the abuse was avoiding eye contact with me. Other than telling the instigator to keep his voice down, he didn't retaliate, which I thought was odd. Given the same circumstances, I'd have reacted, or taken it outside to speak in private.'

She would too.

Like everyone David had met in Iceland during their joint operation – detective, uniform personnel or witness, male and female – Anna was kind and thoughtful, but direct, unafraid to speak her mind. It was a cultural difference he applauded. British politeness and tendency to apologise for fear of upsetting others was an irritating trait that led to ambiguity. The police service knocked that out of you.

Blunt was not a dirty word in his world.

'It was about an old case,' Anna was saying. 'An undetected investigation only one of them was involved in. I recognise professional jealousy when I see it and there was definitely some of that. To be honest, I didn't understand much of it. The accusations were one-sided. I made a quick exit, as you would have seen if you were observing.' She paused for a moment. 'Is that why you left early?'

'It was.'

'I guessed as much. Your vanishing act didn't go unnoticed. I'm sure you had your reasons.' She paused for a long moment. 'Does the case involve a close relative of Frankie's? When she confided in me about her late sister, she mentioned missing evidence and so did the instigator of the argument. We're talking about Joanna, right?'

'Yes.' There was no point denying it.

Anna was too smart not to have worked it out.

'David, I'm so sorry. What an appalling situation for you to deal with. It can't be easy keeping it to yourself, knowing what it means to Frankie.' There was a weighty silence on either end. 'How is she?'

Wishing he knew, David sidestepped the question. 'You didn't mention it?'

'To Frankie? Hell, no. I wasn't wearing body armour. You know what she's like. I didn't tell her or anyone what had happened. If she'd caught so much as a whisper, she'd have gone berserk.'

Anna was right . . .

There would have been a riot.

David was about to thank her, when she spoke again.

'She was looking everywhere for you. You didn't want to be found, did you?'

'No, not really.' He pictured Frankie across the dance floor. She looked radiant but perturbed by the fact that he was keeping his distance, her mouth turned down in a frown. He wasn't fooled by her attempt to make light of it.

Anna's voice drew him into the present. 'David, are you still there?'

'Yeah, sorry. For what it's worth, I felt like a shit leaving,' he said. 'It was the only way out of a conversation the two of us couldn't get into.'

'Don't beat yourself up over it. It was better you left.'

'I wish I'd not turned up at all.'

'Well, you did, so deal with it.'

'The more I dig, the bigger the hole—'

'She'll thank you one day.'

'Perhaps . . .' David heard someone enter Anna's room, probably her sidekick, Emil. A good bloke he'd met during a case that had taken him and Frankie to Iceland on the hunt for a killer. Anna didn't ask him to wait, so he carried on. 'What worries me is the pretence. She'll think—'

'Listen, I'm due in a briefing.' Anna was on the move. 'And does it matter what she thinks?'

'It does to me.'

'Then give her the result she needs.'

The line went dead.

61

Frankie had spent longer than she'd anticipated with Amir. Seeing how well he'd taken to her family, she felt satisfied that he was doing OK. As young as he was, he seemed to sense that the Olivers were good people he could trust. That would speed his recovery from the accident and whatever had gone on before the Mercedes ploughed into oncoming traffic.

Frankie didn't want to think about that.

The fact that he was out of hospital, under observation, protected by people who knew what to do in an emergency, was a big plus. Frankie's old man would lay down his life for the boy should anyone attempt to do him harm. Andrea arrived home, looking exhausted, ending his shift as minder.

'What's wrong?' she asked Frankie when her father had gone.

'I feel awful leaving Amir. I won't see him or you for a good few days, maybe more.'

'We'll take care of him, Frank. I'll be in touch every day.'

'Promise?'

'Promise.'

When Frankie finally left, there were no tears from Amir. Before she took off, she called Kit from the car. The Met detective was as good as her word. She'd put Frankie in touch with a named officer at the National Crime Agency and organised round-the-clock surveillance in Leith. 'We have spotters on foot, on pushbikes, in unmarked cars,' she said.

'Any visits to the property?'

'A couple, including the skinny guy you observed. We have a better image of him now. Sheena is chasing that up. They're being cautious, Frank. The door is never opened before someone on the second floor checks out who's there. The general area is busy. No numbered vans leaving or arriving, nor any sign of Ivan Osman.'

'Any other problems?'

'José almost had his cover blown. A uniform arrived on foot with his taser ready, asking him to step out of his vehicle, wanting to know why he was hanging around. Obviously, no idea what a blocked vehicle was, or didn't have the sense to check before making his play. Could have compromised the operation.'

'Shit.'

'Don't panic. They weren't seen. José showed his warrant card and told him to sling his hook. So now we wait. I'll give you a shout if there are any developments this end. Rest assured Operation Zenith is shit hot in the south with drones in the air.'

'Does Mitch have any news from the service station?'

'No. The van drove in, then out again.'

'Displaying the correct number plate?'

'Yeah, looks like they changed it elsewhere.'

'Bugger.' Extending her gratitude, Frankie told Kit to stand down for the night, then tried to contact David, twice. He didn't take the call, which didn't surprise her. Keen to make amends, she tried a third time with the same result. Bored with that game, she called Dick instead.

He picked up immediately. 'Hey, stranger! How's it going?'

'I was about to ask you the same thing.'

'It's dead this end. You're not missing much.'

She was. 'Are you still in the office?

'Only just.'

'Fancy a drink? My shout.'

'When have you ever known me to refuse? I thought you were up north?'

'Not tonight. Is Linn expecting you home?'

'No, she's out. A late one. I'm all yours.'

They arranged an RV point, the Cumberland Arms, a popular pub overlooking Newcastle's historic Ouseburn valley. Frankie keyed her ignition and moved off.

62

David had been gone for hours. He wondered if Indira would still be hard at it when he reached Middle Earth. A few minutes later, as he drove under the security barrier, he could see that she was. The north-facing window where she sat was open, the light on.

He needed to speak to her . . .

Urgently.

She closed her laptop as he walked through the door. He could see that she was deeply troubled, probably stressing over the missing documentation and the idea she'd put forward as to who might have taken it. Once she'd planted a seed of doubt in his mind, it grew. He didn't take a seat at his desk.

He just stood there, internal dialogue in full flow.

Their guv'nor was the most senior detective on the force, the best of his generation. If he'd removed paperwork that might implicate him in Joanna Oliver's murder, they were in deep shit. David couldn't ask Frankie's father without raising his suspicions, yet he hadn't been able to discount the idea, let alone write it off as over enthusiasm from an inexperienced DC – accusing the very man who, at his request, had sanctioned her step up to detective grade. Already she was proving to be worthy.

'We're done for the day,' he said. 'Grab your stuff.'

Her face crumpled. 'Where are we going?'

'Out. I need a drink, even if you don't. We need to talk. I'd rather it wasn't here.'

Indira locked everything away, then grabbed her jacket and bag off the back of her chair. In silence, she followed him out and down the stairs, practically running to keep up with him.

He was in a hurry, unlocking the doors to his vehicle as they walked towards it. He started the car and moved off, exiting Middle Earth as if they were running blues and twos.

'Guv, if I spoke out of turn earlier—'

'Relax, you didn't.'

'What I said has been preying on my mind. I've thought it through and still have reservations.'

'Join the club, I have several.'

'Can I ask a question?'

'Crack on.'

'Was it Bright or you who suggested that only the three of us should handle a deep dive into Hall's affairs?'

'It was me.'

What she said next was everything he'd been chewing over since he went out. 'Didn't he forbid you to go anywhere near Frankie's father? Guv, he knows the family. He adores Frankie. He's helped her. Mentored her throughout her career. Couldn't that be interpreted as a guilty conscience?'

'That would make a lot of sense, were it not for the fact that he's done the same for other detectives, other SIOs, including Kate Daniels.' She was an exceptional murder detective.

'I get that, but the stakes are too high to ignore it, surely. Couldn't he be keeping his enemies close? He's a powerful man. Only a fool would dare challenge him. Don't we owe it to Joanna, to Frankie and her family, to explore anyone who comes up on our radar?' Indira's next line was a killer. 'Guv, no one is in a greater position to manipulate.'

'Agreed, and he's too smart to have involved anyone else. You realise we're playing with fire keeping this from him?' When she didn't speak, he glanced into the passenger side. She was rigid in her seat. 'Indi? Are you in or out? I need to be sure, because it's not just my neck on the line.'

'I'm in,' she said. 'You?'

David looked at her, remembering Bright's reaction when he told him it wouldn't take a genius to work out why he wasn't utilising the MIT to investigate Joanna's murder. His jaw was set like a blade, his eyes flashing angrily, and yet he didn't bite back or put him in his place – unheard of for a man who liked the sound of his own voice.

'We discount no one,' David said. 'This line of enquiry is explosive, with far-reaching consequences for the MIT, the CID, the whole force if there's any truth in it. We're finished if we get it wrong. The guv'nor's already threatened to can us if we cause the family a nanosecond of angst.' Feeling the weight of her gaze, he paused before delivering an admission. 'Maybe I missed the subtext. Maybe what he really meant was if we cause *him* any.'

63

Dick was pulling up outside the Cumberland Arms when Frankie arrived. They entered the Victorian pub together, making their way to the bar. She indicated a vacant table, telling him to take the weight off and that she'd bring the drinks over. No live music or comedy tonight, so not too busy.

'What do you want to drink?' she asked.

He scanned the pumps. 'Grolsch.'

'Food?'

He shook his head. 'I'm good, thanks.'

Frankie watched him walk away, then ordered, wondering how she'd quiz him without making herself sound desperate for information – or just desperate. Checking in with other old colleagues hadn't answered her questions, the fact that they had nothing to offer adding to her frustration. The party line was that everything was hunky-dory in the MIT . . . It wasn't, not with David anyway.

She had to know.

Dick smiled as she sat down, pushing his pint across the table towards him. He downed half of it in one gulp, raised his glass, toasting her, asking how she was doing in Berwick.

'Well, as you probably know, my uniform stint was short-lived—'

'Yeah, I heard. Sounds grim. You look wrecked. Is there anything you want from me?'

'Not for the moment. I'll give you a shout if that changes – and before you ask, I didn't go looking for trouble. It came looking for me. The NCA are involved now. I'm not hopeful. Their guv'nor has given us a week.'

He almost choked on his beer. 'In their dreams.'

'Exactly.'

Frankie sipped her wine, people-watching, thinking time. Ordinarily, Dick was up to speed on circulating rumours, her ally in times of crisis. If he didn't know something, he'd make it his business to find out. She was counting on him, dying to discover what David was up to and why she'd been dumped – because that's what it felt like.

She kept it casual. 'How's it going with the boss?'

'What boss?' Dick laughed. 'I've hardly seen him. Have you?'

'Once or twice. I dropped in to see Bright and bumped into him while I was there. I'd have called in for a chat. David told me you were busy.'

'You should have given me a nudge if you needed a shoulder to cry on.'

She feigned confusion. 'Is that what you think this is?'

'Isn't it?' He sat back, crossing his arms, eyeing her across the table. 'How long have we known each other?'

'Sorry, you've lost me.'

'Well, if this is going to take a while, I need another pint.' He thumbed towards the bar. 'You want a refill?'

'No, if I have another, I'll fall over.' Frankie held up a finger to the bartender, pointing into Dick's empty glass. He nodded his understanding. She assumed he'd bring it over. When she turned around, Dick was studying her intensely.

'What?' she asked.

'What's the boss done to upset you this time?'

'Dunno. He's freezing me out. We had words. Harsh ones. He's stopped taking my calls. I'm beginning to feel like a stranger. Andrea's clueless, Rae too, though he's been in touch with both.' Frankie dropped the pretence. 'He told me what he's working on. I'm not buying it. What's he really doing?'

'Why are you so interested?'

'You know me. I like my finger on the pulse.'

Dick opened his mouth, then closed it again as his second beer arrived.

215

He pulled out his wallet.

'Put it away, I've got this.' Frankie paid the barman.

Dick waited until he'd gone before continuing. 'Stone's hunkered down in Bright's outer office with Indira. Why don't you ask her?'

'That wouldn't be fair. It'll put her in a difficult position if she's working with him. He's decidedly cagey, don't you think? Maybe it's me he has an issue with, though I'd love to know why I'm being sidelined from his work and his life.'

'Are you two—'

'What? Fuck no! Not my type.'

'You have a type?'

She sidestepped the question. 'Maybe he's decided not to have me back and hasn't got the balls to tell me—'

'Nah . . .' Dick rubbished the idea. 'Probably can't wait to get shot of me.' He stared at her. 'Now you mention it, he is acting weird.'

'In what way?'

'I offered to assist, but he declined. Odd, given that he's allegedly on a rush job and I'm doing nowt. If *you* had asked, I guarantee he'd have bitten your hand off.' A long pause followed. 'And another thing . . . none of the MIT are allowed in.'

64

David pulled the door open, stepping aside, allowing Indira to enter first, scanning the bar as they got inside to see if there were any familiar faces, good or bad. His stomach took a dive when he noticed Frankie and Dick deep in conversation in the corner furthest from the door, where they too could spot trouble should it arise.

'Shit!' Indira whispered.

David didn't look at her.

Her anxiety was infectious, bubbling in his gut like a witch's cauldron. Of all the pubs he might have chosen, this was the wrong one. He'd rather know about their get-together than not. It was Dick who'd told him about Frankie's dark past, the fact that her father was the detective who responded to a call-out to a fatal stabbing, only to identify his eldest daughter as the victim. David owed him, but this meeting could spell trouble if she was on a fishing expedition.

Indira had read his mind. 'Shall we make a run for it, guv? I don't think they've seen us.'

'Oh, they've seen us.'

Dick glanced over Frankie's left shoulder, spotting them at the door. A cautious look she responded to. Her eyes met David's. A stand-off. Neither one enjoying the experience of seeing the other.

If awkwardness was a colour, it was red.

Whatever the nature of the conversation she was having with Dick, it had made them both wary. David knew right away that they had been discussing him. Acknowledging Frankie with an upward tilt of his chin and a smile he didn't feel, he tilted an imaginary glass in the air. Frankie shook her head, pointing at her watch: *no time.*

Dick lifted a full pint, a heavy hint that he was sorted, though he looked like he could do with another – and probably one after that.

Aware that he'd walked in on a heavy conversation, David turned sideways, so they couldn't lip-read. 'Too late to back out now. Stay cool and stick to the script. A quick drink and we're out of here.'

'Do we *have* to join them?'

'It'll raise a red flag if we don't. You can do this, Indi. See you over there. Make me proud.'

Nodding, she moved off, a big smile on her face.

David approached the bar – a moment to compose himself. Ordering two halves of lager, he wandered over to join the others in shoes that felt like they were made of lead, every step slowing him down. Accepting her drink, Indira remained standing and so did he.

Dick pulled out a chair for her, an invitation she ignored.

'Thanks, but I've been sat on my arse all day,' she said. 'Much as I'd like to, I can't stay.'

'Me neither.' Frankie's tone was clipped. 'I need to crash.'

'Crash' was an interesting word. Coupled with 'burn', it was where David's journey into his covert investigation began. He wanted it to end. He wanted to explain. Mostly, he wanted to take Frankie's pain and resentment away. For the next few minutes, they engaged in meaningless small talk, something he knew she hated and would avoid at all costs. Like the rest of them, she was keeping up appearances – a bloody sitcom.

Not one of them was being straight.

Seeing off his drink, David put his empty glass down on the table and cut the conversation short, using the excuse that Ben was waiting for a lift home. Leaving Dick and Frankie to it, taking Indi with him, he made for the door, grateful that he'd not been forced to answer any unwieldy questions.

He had many of his own.

Indy asked, 'What do you think that was about?'

David said nothing, though he was as concerned as she was.

If Frankie was trying to establish what they were up to, Dick would make it his business to find out. They had almost reached David's car, when Frankie called out to him. They stopped walking, turning to face her. Beneath a calm facade lay an unexploded bomb. She focused on Indira.

'Can you give us a moment, Indi? I need a word with the boss.'

'Sure.'

David handed Indi his car keys.

She couldn't get away fast enough.

Turning her back on the retreating DC, Frankie's eyes flashed. 'David, I'm going to be tied up for a while, so I'd like to get this over and done with and concentrate on work, something I'm not able to do while we're at war. I apologise for being mean, but I have a question. What the hell was that "moment" at my promotion do? Did I imagine it?'

'No, it was real . . . you know it was.'

'Then why are you ignoring me?'

'That's three questions.'

She wasn't smiling.

'I've been busy.'

'Nice try. What did I do to deserve the cold shoulder?'

'Nothing.'

'Then look me in the eye and tell me we're still mates, because it doesn't feel like it.'

He didn't answer quick enough. Already, she was on the move, racing towards her mum's VW. Pulling her iPhone from her pocket, she tapped on his number and turned to face him. His mobile rang simultaneously. They were no more than twenty yards apart, staring at each other across the car park.

It felt like twenty miles.

'Fuck's sake, David. Tell me!' Her voice broke. 'Is it Jane? Because I cannot compete with a dead woman. I thought we were past that. I thought you were.' His silence made things ten times worse. 'What then? If it's not her, it must be me.'

He looked away, then at her. 'It's not about us—'

'I told you, there is no *us*. Not now. Not ever. It was a rubbish idea. Relationships hurt. I'm bailing. I'd . . .' Her voice broke. 'I'd like to think our friendship can survive this blip, that we can still work and hang out together.'

David had lost the power of speech.

Even from this distance he could see how upset she was. Before he could think of something meaningful to say, the line went dead. He looked on as she pocketed her mobile. She kicked out at the wheel of the VW and got in, slamming the door shut. He wanted to approach her. Thought better of it. He couldn't explain himself. She knew he was covering something up. The best he could hope for was that she'd calm down, remember what they'd once shared and get over her tantrum.

Anna's voice arrived in his head.

She'll thank you one day.

David wasn't so sure.

65

Indira didn't know what to say to David when he climbed into the car beside her, strapping on his seat belt. He didn't start the engine. Staring through the window, he watched the VW merge with the traffic, heading towards the river. Its tail lights disappeared and Frankie was gone. He was both tense and pissed off. Whatever had been said was his business. Indira kept her mouth shut until she noticed his fists close around the steering wheel, his knuckles turning white.

He might not be aware of it, or even want it, but he needed to talk.

With the window down, Indira hadn't heard much of the conversation, but she'd seen enough to know that it was a full-blown row. Frankie was livid – not in tears exactly, but not far off.

'Guv, do you want me to drive or are we going to sit here all night? You look like you're ready to lamp someone.'

'Count yourself lucky it's not you . . . or Frankie. She blows hot and cold sometimes.'

'I've never seen her lose it like that.'

'Nor me.'

'Why was she so angry?'

'She's under a lot of pressure.'

He may as well have said: *conversation over*.

David started the car, pulling out of a tight parking spot, making no attempt to answer her question. Reverting to type, he changed the subject, burying himself in work-related chat.

'I'll drop you at Middle Earth. From now on, it's you and me. Be wary of the guv'nor. If he complains that we're dragging our feet, I'll deal with him.' He overtook the car in front. 'Did you manage to trace Jack Gale?'

'I did. He's a locations manager within the film and television industry, currently in Frankfurt, research for an upcoming production.'

'Damn it. Any idea when he's getting in?'

'Tomorrow afternoon.'

'Married, single?'

'He lives alone, according to his neighbour,' Indira said. 'So do I, so did you until you took Ben in. Is that relevant?'

'*Everything* is relevant. It's the little things people miss. Did you find anything in the case file that stood out?'

'Yes, and it bothers me. *A lot*. There was less CCTV in and around Sunderland when Joanna died, but no sighting of the white van the MIT spent time and a great deal of money looking into. The witness described it as transit size with a distinctive corporate logo on the side, like the front end of a blue Concorde and three tapered lines indicating speed at the rear.'

'No name?'

Indira shook her head. 'The SIO's best guess was that it might have belonged to a logistics company, but none could be found bearing that logo. The original investigation team questioned several hundred drivers, examining their vehicles, and didn't come close. They spoke to garages and service station personnel and drew a blank there too. As time went on, they stopped looking. The action was put in for referral.'

David was intrigued. 'Who's the witness?'

'Anonymous female. That's what bothers me.'

David snapped his head around. 'And the call taker?'

'Don't know yet.'

'Find out.'

66

Frankie was seething as she drove home to Amble, desperate for her bed. She'd asked David outright and he'd declined to answer. It suited her that she wouldn't see him for another week or longer. The chemistry was gone. She wouldn't dwell on it. She had a job to do. A plan. Pack a bag. Head north. Immerse herself in Operation Zenith. There was more at stake than a relationship she'd have to keep to herself anyhow. Lately, it had felt toxic, undermining her confidence, making her unhappy.

Bored now, she vowed not to give it another thought, but as she sped along a dual carriageway locals called 'the Spine Road', David's words echoed in her head. She glanced in her rear-view mirror, his ghostly image superimposed in the glass. It wasn't only the physical distance between them that was stressing her out. Emotionally, they were poles apart.

Her eyes flew to the mirror.

David had vanished. He was never there, but the memory remained. A forlorn face staring intensely at her from across a dark, empty car park, a strange expression: a cross between relief and regret. It had her wondering if Bright had warned him off. A relationship with a subordinate officer was, and always had been, frowned upon.

This from a man who'd slept with his PA . . .

One rule for those on the top floor . . .

Another for everyone else.

Except that didn't fit the man she'd known since she was a young child. Bright wouldn't go behind her back. If he'd thought her actions unwise, he'd have fronted up and told her to her face, without a word to David, expecting her to let him down gently.

Who else could persuade him that he should cool it?

Not her old man to the son he'd never had.

He had a lot of time for David.

Before she wrote him off altogether, closing the page, putting any chance of fixing their non-existent love lives out of reach, Frankie had an idea. Accessing Ben's number, she called him on the hands-free, feeling slightly guilty that she might drag him into a situation that was none of his business, something that would put him in a difficult position should David find out.

'Hey, Frank! Thought you'd gone off me.'

'As if. Sorry, Ben. I've been busy.'

'You're beginning to sound like Dave.'

Frankie took the roundabout at speed. 'Where are you?'

'At home, waiting for a carry-out. There's bugger all in the fridge.'

No lift required then.

David should've known better than to tell a provable lie. She'd destroyed his pathetic excuse with three simple words, but where was he now? And why the secrecy? Had he taken Indira to another pub to get away from her? Why were they so tight-lipped about the job they had on? Ordinarily, nothing was off limits. David took her into his confidence, sharing everything, apart from his bed.

He trusted her integrity.

Well, he used to.

'You should complain to management,' Frankie said.

'Yeah, fat chance. He's like *The Invisible Man*.'

Frankie kept her tone light so that Ben wouldn't become suspicious. 'In my book that's bordering on neglect.' She paused. 'I saw him earlier. Now you mention it, he looked washed out and seemed oddly distracted. Any idea why?'

'No clue, unless he's found himself a woman . . .' He let the sentence trail off.

Was he fishing?

'Well, if he has, he didn't seem too chuffed about it,' she said.

'You can say that again, not that he tells me anything. Our roles are reversed since you were last here. I'm the one who should be communicating in words of one syllable. If I ask him owt, he grunts. I'm feeling proper grown up.' Ben laughed, then fell silent, leaving her wondering if he'd picked up on her disappointment. Before she could steer him in a different direction, he spoke again. 'Tell me to do one, but I thought you and he—'

'No! And since when was romance your specialist subject?'

'I wish. A surname isn't all Dave and I share. When it comes to women, we fuck up every time. With you, I thought it might've been different. I told him if he has feelings for you, to get in quick—'

'You're my pimp now?' Frankie scoffed at the suggestion, even though it was breaking her heart. 'I'm too young for all that nonsense. No time. No inclination. I can't be doing with the hassle.' That was partly true.

She heard a doorbell chime, the phone go down, feet crossing the hardwood floor. Ben's delivery had arrived. That suited her. She'd got what she wanted, confirmation that David had given her the heave-ho. She heard a door open. Muffled voices before it closed. It surprised her that takeaway food was a thing in the sticks.

Ben's voice hit her ear. 'Frankie, I'd love to chat, but my body needs fuel.'

'Mine too, if I could be arsed.'

'Any message when Dave gets in?'

Frankie said the first thing that came to mind. 'Ben?' She paused for effect. 'Ben, are you there . . . ?'

She cut the call – when in doubt, lose the signal.

67

The altercation had been going on for a while. A hate-filled atmosphere. Bright and David were on their feet, head-to-head, neither willing to back down. Painfully aware that his career was in jeopardy, if not over, David intended to go out with a bang. He'd dared to question Bright's authority for reasons that became too big to ignore, amounting to an accusation that he'd killed Joanna Oliver, then engineered the investigation to go his way, knowing it would come to nothing.

Bright was in his face. 'Are you out of your fucking mind?'

'You said yourself you headhunted the team, keeping Hall out of the loop—'

'I was the SIO. He'd had his card marked.'

'That we can agree on. Isn't it also the case that he was the better detective, one that might have exposed you?' David looked him straight in the eye, a river of sweat soaking his shirt. 'You knew, didn't you?'

'What did I know?'

'That Hall suspected a cover-up.'

'He was resentful of his exclusion, if that's what you mean.'

'You could see why that might upset him, why he was banging on about it at Frankie's party, years after the event. And yet you failed to mention it when I drew it to your attention. If he wanted to keep his job, maybe he was leaned on—'

'Was he shite! Where the hell is all this coming from?'

'There's more. You could easily have removed Joanna's jacket from the evidence room—'

'So could any other fucker.'

'They couldn't do the same with incriminating paperwork you took from Frank Oliver, could they? What did you do? Burn it?'

'No, but I'm about to burn you, Stone. You're finished. You can forget the pension you worked so hard for.'

'Don't threaten me, sir.'

Bright was yelling now, playing right into David's hands, the best form of defence being attack. Unlike his boss, David rarely lost his temper. When he did, he didn't rant or rage. He went deathly quiet. And when that happened, when the curtain dropped, woe betide anyone who got in his way.

'There was no credible evidence on the white van because the anonymous female informant was bogus, wasn't she?' David said. 'Was that you or did you get someone else to do your dirty work?'

'Where's your proof, Stone? I live in the real world, where the only thing that counts is hard evidence. You are way out of line, so if that's all you've got, get the fuck out of my sight—'

'I'll have more when I've spoken to Frank.'

'You'll go nowhere near him. You're off the case.'

'Firing me won't help you, sir. I'm following orders, keeping you abreast of developments, like you told me to. I didn't question it then. I am now. I offered to pick up the rosters from Frank's house. You instructed me to go nowhere near him. And you've just repeated that. No wonder you wanted the collar.'

'Of course, I owe it to Frank.'

'From where I'm standing, you owe him a damn sight more than that. Is that why you were taking a breather when I was in here the day before yesterday? I know anxiety when I see it. Were you wondering how to handle being discovered when I found out that some of the documents were missing? You're a disgrace to your office.'

'Right, I've heard enough. I want your warrant card.'

'No, I think I'll keep it, thanks.'

Bright marched to the door and held it open. 'Get out! And if I see you again, you'll wish I hadn't.'

David stood his ground.

Bright flipped, launching a ferocious attack.

David hit the deck before he saw the right hook coming. Blows rained down on him, kicks too, then he lost consciousness. When he came to, he had no idea how long he'd been out. Straining to open his eyes, he could see dark squares, indistinct shapes, a shadow hovering above him.

He couldn't move his body. He was shivering. Really cold. Lying in a pool of liquid. As the shadow moved closer, he made a vain attempt at self-preservation, a flailing fist finding nothing but fresh air. A thought lingering as the figure moved away. Those who've killed have nothing to lose the second time around.

68

Frankie's mobile rang loudly on her bedside table. Following her usual fingertip search to locate it, she drew the device towards her. Half-asleep, lying face down with her eyes closed, she expected David's voice to hit her ear, telling her that they'd been called out to an incident, a sudden and violent death, giving her the heads-up on location. Then she remembered that she'd fallen out of favour, that her return to the MIT was no longer a foregone conclusion.

C'est la vie.

She yawned, pushing the thought away. 'Oliver.'

'It's me,' Mitch said. 'Were you asleep?'

'Still am. What's up?'

'I'm downstairs.'

'Shit!' Opening her eyes, Frankie glanced at her iPhone. She'd asked him to be there at six thirty sharp. Already it was twenty to seven. She apologised, telling him she'd slept through her alarm. 'Come up if you like. I just need five.'

'It's fine, I'll wait here. This is some view.'

Though they had worked together for a while, Mitch had never been to her apartment. Everyone who had been there commented on how lucky she was. Luck had nothing to do with it. She'd saved for years and bought it off-plan. A smart move. Her apartment had almost doubled in value. The marina may not have the knockout backdrop of Monaco, Capri or Montenegro, but it was stunning in its own way.

She couldn't imagine ever moving.

'Can you hold a second,' Mitch said.

'Going for a dip?'

He laughed. 'Bit chilly for me, boss. I just got a text from Kit . . .' He paused the call to access it. 'She's been trying to get through to us. I'll give her a bell and find out what she wants.'

He rang off.

Intrigued as to why the Met DI was so keen to speak to her this early in the morning, Frankie decided that there had been a positive development in the south. While waiting to find out, she took the opportunity to wash her face and clean her teeth. Before she'd finished brushing, the phone rang again. After spitting toothpaste in the sink, grabbing a towel to wipe her mouth, she padded barefoot to her bedroom, tapping on her phone.

'You're on speaker, Mitch. I need to get dressed. What's the story?'

'Ivan Osman was spotted on foot in Brighton at three a.m.'

'Yes!' Frankie punched the air. 'Where is he now?'

'Kit didn't say.'

Frankie opened a cupboard, finding something appropriate to wear, clothing that would blend in when she joined her new crew at the Leith postcode. She preferred a hands-on approach, rather than riding a desk issuing instructions, something she'd learned from her father, who also led from the front.

'What about our end?' she asked. 'Anything happening?'

'Dead as a stone. Any idea on our ETA, if Kit asks?'

'Nine, if I get a wriggle on.' She pulled on a pair of skinny jeans and a dark T-shirt, slipping on a pair of comfy trainers before grabbing the holdall she'd packed the night before. 'Tell her we're on our way.'

69

When David wandered into the kitchen, the place was a mess. Ben was making breakfast, or trying to, something he'd never done before. The concept of looking after himself hadn't landed yet. He'd usually get ready, then sit around like a baby bird waiting for David to drop food in his mouth. He'd starve otherwise. Or wait until he got to work and eat whatever crap he could lay his hands on, usually at Belinda Wells' expense. She spoiled him, making David's life more difficult.

Ben was hopeless in practical ways, but he'd turned his life around since his father died. David was grateful for that. Frankie had been right: taking him in was a good call, a way to honour his brother's memory. The day Luke died had changed their lives for ever. To give Ben credit, this morning he was making a fist of it – until he swung round, realising he had company.

'Jesus. You look awful.'

David's right eyebrow shot up. 'Take a look in the mirror, mate. You don't look so good yourself.'

'That's because some prick woke me up yelling his head off in the middle of the night. You took a swing at me. Even a dodgy parent should know better. I've reported you to Childline. They say I might need counselling.'

David gave him hard eyes. 'Not remotely funny. That's a reality for some kids—'

'Lighten up, man. It was a joke!'

'So are those burnt eggs.' David pointed at the frying pan. 'Thought you didn't like them crispy.'

Turning away, Ben swore.

A strong back, like his father's.

The same dark sense of humour.

Ben glanced over his shoulder. 'Want to take over?'

'No, you crack on. No pun.' Ben didn't laugh. David said, 'Dude, if you can't take it, don't give it.'

Ben scooped up the greasy mess, flipping the eggs onto a slice of over-buttered bread, and sat down, slapping another slice on top. The concept of plates had also passed him by. Slicing the sandwich in two, he looked up.

'Want halfers?'

'Of that?' David grimaced. 'I'll pass, thanks.'

Devouring his breakfast, egg yolk dribbling down his chin, Ben spoke with his mouth full, a mumble that was hard to decipher. 'You scared the shit out of me last night. I thought you were having a coronary. What the hell were you dreaming about?'

'Can't remember much of it. That's the nature of bad dreams. They don't make sense.'

The truth was, David could recall every bit of it.

He had a vague recollection of Ben's worried face coming into focus.

Deeply troubled, his nephew had stayed put when told to go back to bed. In the dead of night, his likeness to his father was so pronounced, it could have been Luke watching David recover from his nightmare.

Just how long had Ben been standing there?

And had David mentioned Bright's name?

He was about to ask, when a text pinged into his phone from Indira.

The short message made his heart race:

I was wrong.

70

Texting his ETA, David asked Indira to meet him out of the office at Links Art Gallery, just off the promenade at Whitley Bay. He'd rubbished the idea of Bright's involvement in Joanna's murder at first. The more he thought about it, the more he realised he must give it due consideration. Her theory had shot to the top of the pile. Only a forensic examination of their guv'nor's movements would shut her up. If he was in any way implicated, David wouldn't put it past him to have bugged their office.

To avoid heavy traffic, he took a detour as he headed across country through the villages of Seghill and Seaton Delaval, Bright's culpability weighing him down. Wouldn't a man who stood to lose everything he'd spent his life working for simply refuse his request to reopen an undetected case? He'd already said that his team had pulled out all the stops to find Joanna's killer. It was in his power to write off a case review as a waste of time and resources.

So why hadn't he?

David had to concede that when he'd approached him initially, he had little more than a hunch to go on. His new intel was paper thin and yet his guv'nor had told him to push on. Was he that arrogant? Unless, with a team of two, he'd decided that David stood zero chance of bringing the open unsolved investigation to a close. Only a man who'd covered his tracks would dare give such an experienced detective permission to review a murder investigation that could, potentially, lead to his downfall.

David slowed in the village of Old Hartley. After negotiating a mini roundabout, he floored the accelerator, his speed climbing along a straight stretch of road, St Mary's Lighthouse visible in the distance.

If evidence existed, with Indira's help, he'd damned well find it.

On the last few minutes of his drive, having weighed up his options – conscious of lines of enquiry already in the mix – a plan began to form in his head to put his guv'nor in the frame or eliminate him from the enquiry, as he'd done with Adam Hall. That would satisfy his own curiosity and Indira's.

Minutes later, he spotted her vehicle as he drove into the car park. She was sitting outside the gallery's café, a table sheltered from a stiff breeze coming off the North Sea, making the most of a dry spell of weather. Dressed casually, she was wearing super sized sunglasses and red lipstick, her hair tied in a messy bun. She waved as he got out of the car and walked towards her.

'Morning,' he said.

'Morning.' Having clocked him driving in, she'd ordered them both a double espresso. 'I can change it if you'd rather have something else.'

'No, I need the extra shot.'

'No sleep?'

'Something like that.' He failed to mention his nightmare.

The drinks arrived as he sat down in the sunshine. Table 13, he noticed. He wasn't superstitious, but from the moment he'd picked up on Hall's behaviour at Frankie's leaving do, his luck had deserted him.

He scanned the café, hoping that might change.

A crowd of middle-aged walkers were enjoying breakfast that looked and smelled more edible than Ben's. Not hard to achieve. Music was playing gently in the background, a compilation album that was Mediterranean in style. Whoever had put the soundtrack together, David approved.

If he closed his eyes, he could be anywhere in Europe.

It was a great place to chill, a favourite of Frankie's, though today she was unlikely to make an appearance. She was heading north to deal with an equally important investigation of her own, one he hoped she'd solve without putting herself in danger. She didn't think the OCG were responsible for her accident. True or false, it wouldn't stop them from trying to take her out if she got too close. Pushing the unsettling thought aside, he focused on Indi.

'So, your text said you were wrong. About what?'

'Boss, I misled you . . . about the detective chief super. I'm sorry.'

'So am I, because now you've raised him as a suspect with such a compelling argument, we can't cross his name off the list and pretend it didn't happen. We need to rule him out.' He studied her. 'Why the sudden change of heart?'

'Three reasons. One: at the time Joanna was murdered, the rosters didn't include headquarters CID, which means they're not missing. Senior supervision kept their own diaries. It might take a while to locate them. I'm looking into it. Two: because of his close association with the Oliver family, he insisted that diaries were checked for the time of the offence.'

'Good move for someone with a lot to hide.'

Indira's face flushed. 'I get where you're coming from, but he has an alibi—'

'Cast iron?'

'No, but I've seen the documentation. It's genuine. The guv'nor was fastidious, David. In addition to his own movements, he demanded that every member of the murder squad gave an account of their whereabouts on the night in question to rule themselves out. Neither was he the detective who took the anonymous call about the white van investigators couldn't find and were suspicious of from the off—'

'Whose signature was on the call slip?'

'You're not going to like it.'

71

Mitch dropped Frankie off in Berwick before heading north to join the others. When she entered her office, Kit was sitting alone at her desk, scrolling through a file of images taken overnight, forwarded on by the National Crime Agency. Frankie pulled up a chair, buoyed by the news that Ivan Osman had been found, the first significant breakthrough in the child-trafficking investigation.

The detectives high-fived.

'The NCA have eyes on?' Frankie asked.

Kit threw her a nod. 'My lot followed him to an address already on our system, one we've had on our radar for some time, though this is the first time we've had it under round-the-clock surveillance. We don't have the manpower.'

'No movement since?'

'No, he's still inside.'

Frankie studied the images on-screen. Osman had lost the beard, but his long dark hair was still tied in a topknot, his scar clearly visible. It was him all right.

'Do we have any video footage?'

Kit closed the stills file, tapped a few keys to open another and pressed play. Frankie watched Osman closely. He was walking normally, seemingly uninjured, no visible signs of having been involved in a fatal RTA.

That bothered her.

'Can I see the house?'

'It might surprise you.'

'In what way?'

'You'll see.'

Kit opened another file containing several hundred images of the front and rear of a high-end detached Georgian property. Ostensibly, a family home on a quiet street, like any other.

'Jesus! That's impressive,' Frankie said. 'I was expecting a shitpit.'

'It's a fictitious company rental that changed hands a year ago,' Kit told her. 'The owner lives in Mauritius. Verified as kosher. His letting agent is in for it when this is over. The rental on that house won't be cheap.'

'Where is it?'

'Not far from the Hove promenade, with parking for several cars at the rear—'

'Or numbered vans.' Frankie's tone was flat.

'We've been watching the location for months, on and off, photographing visitors, going in and out, by day and night, mostly via a rear door.'

One of the images made Frankie's blood boil: a young female caller holding the hand of a small child, not that much older than Amir. Wondering if she was the one who'd handed him over to his captors, Frankie picked up her mobile to check the home screen.

No notification from Rae or Andrea.

'The team are on strict instructions not to enter without your say-so,' Kit said.

'Good. Osman could be getting ready for another run to Edinburgh. A journey that will take, what, eight, nine hours?'

'About that,' Kit confirmed. 'Wonder how he'll explain his missing cargo.'

'I thought about that on the drive up. As I told you, there were four fatalities announced in the press. Osman's mates and the two women in the car they collided with. He'll probably think one of them is the child, that he's free to continue as before. That gives us scope to keep watching, or do a hard stop on the motorway, but only as a last resort. We need to be extra vigilant up north to see if things change now he's surfaced.'

*

Indira was pacing the office, unable to get her head around the fact that the man whose signature was on the call slip was still in post while under suspicion for murder. To set her straight, David sat her down, to explain his rationale.

Aware that Bright was in his office next door, he spoke quietly. 'Indira, I don't wish to stamp on your enthusiasm, but you need to slow down and listen. Yesterday, you pointed the finger at someone you later found out was entirely innocent and had the guts to apologise for that this morning.'

She was about to speak.

He held up a hand. 'Let me finish, please. It's an indisputable fact that the original investigation team were looking for what we now suspect was a non-existent white van. That doesn't prove it was done deliberately. The vehicle may or may not exist. We don't know for sure. It may have been carrying a dodgy logo an offender removed afterwards. Our suspect's signature on an anonymous call slip means very little. We get scores of those during a lengthy murder enquiry.'

'Yes, but no one else reported seeing the van and we have no hard evidence to back up the caller's claim, assuming she was real.'

'We can't assume she wasn't. And if she was, memories are complex. It was a week after Joanna's body was found when the witness allegedly called the MIR. She might have seen a white van. The question is, how well did she see the logo?'

'She was very specific, guv.'

'Because that's what she thought she'd seen. Even genuine callers who don't wish to be identified make mistakes.'

'You're saying the message was passed on in good faith?'

'I'm saying I have reservations on the credibility of our suspect. We have no proof that he sent the MIT in the wrong direction on purpose. If we were to make an arrest, he'd walk in twenty-four hours – and he'd know we were on to him. We don't move until we have a watertight case.'

'Imagine the fallout if he's guilty and the press find out that you didn't take steps to have him removed.'

'Are you going to tell them? I'm not, because we don't have the evidence to suspend him. And even if we did, that would be my problem, not yours.'

'Understood, guv. I won't jump the gun in future.'

'It pays to be cautious, Indi. That's all I'm saying.'

She nodded; no offence taken. 'So, where do we go from here?'

'We stick with the plan: review the murder file in its entirety, including the physical evidence.'

Indira narrowed her eyes, frown lines appearing on her brow. 'Won't that raise unwanted speculation? We have a list of forensic exhibits in the safe. There aren't that many, but removing them from the exhibits store will leave a paper trail—'

'I'm going to ask Bright if there's any way he or I can bypass the normal route. We need to examine them ourselves, not rely on someone else's list. Only then will we know if anything was missed.' As he reached the adjoining door, he turned and spoke again. 'What time does Jack Gale's flight get in?'

'Five.'

'I'd like us both to be there.'

72

Frankie and Kit had been waiting patiently for further positive news from the south. There had been no movement from the house Osman had been seen going into. DS Steve Braithwaite, the OIC at the southern end of Operation Zenith, had decided that the target was lying low.

As time ticked by, Frankie's frustration increased. She began to wonder if Osman had made the NCA detectives, escaping out of the rear of the property before they could organise a round-the-clock surveillance detail.

'It's rare to see anyone enter or leave that property on a Sunday,' Kit said. 'Osman's appearance was highly unusual, perhaps more significant than we first thought. Relax, Frankie. Steve has it covered.'

Frankie couldn't sit on her hands and wait.

Scooping her mobile off the desk, she checked in with Andrea. Amir continued to settle well. He wasn't talking, in any language, though he'd found other ways of communicating, a tug at their sleeves to grab their attention, a pointed finger if he saw something that pleased him.

'We got smiles,' Andrea said. 'Lots of them.'

Frankie felt a stab of pride, though she was conflicted.

On the one hand, she was desperate to find the boy's blood relatives; on the other, she'd like nothing better than to see Amir become part of her extended family. Those cable ties were in her head, his battered body tethered to the van. The absolute horror of finding a small child left to die alone would never leave her. Had Amir not managed to cry out before losing consciousness, had she not been standing in the right place at the right time, he may not have made it.

Whatever Osman's role was, he'd pay.

That was Frankie's driver.

'Is Penelope with you?' she said into the phone, wanting a word with the interpreter.

'Been and gone,' Andy said. 'She joined us for breakfast. Don't you want to speak to Rae?'

Frankie was about to make an excuse, when Kit's ringing mobile did it for her.

Kit checked the screen, then met her gaze across the desk. 'It's Braithwaite.'

'Not now, the NCA are on the line.'

'Go!' Andrea disconnected.

Kit put the phone on speaker to enable Frankie to listen in, Steve's deep voice filling the silence. 'Guv, an unidentified male just left the target property in a taxi. He must already have been inside when Osman arrived. Whoever this guy is, he's never seen grunt work. Check your inbox. He's now on the A23, heading north. We're on his tail with ample cover.'

'Thanks, Steve. Keep us posted.'

As the line went dead, Kit pulled her laptop towards her, checking his email, clicking on the attached video. The white male in question was well-dressed in a good suit and tie, the type you'd expect to see coming out of a house like that. No luggage. He walked confidently, like any businessman going off to work. Steve was right. The guy stood out from other individuals the NCA had seen entering and leaving the property in the past.

Thirty-five minutes later, Steve was on the line again, informing them that the taxi had turned off, heading for Gatwick Airport. A few minutes more and he confirmed that the target had been dropped off at the terminal. The surveillance detail were on foot, watching his every move.

Steve patched them through to the running commentary between detectives on the ground. Their target had smoked a cigarette before entering the airport. One of Braithwaite's guys, Unit 1, had taken possession of the butt end he'd discarded on the ground.

In her earpiece, Frankie heard him joke: 'Smoking kills.'

'Let's hope so,' she replied.

'Unit 2 has the eyeball.'

Frankie was getting excited.

In her mind's eye, she imagined Unit 2 peeling off, following the target into the terminal. There was a long pause in transmission, then a crackle as a female voice said, 'Unit 2: target has checked in on a British passport in the name of Simon Thorne. Checks underway. EasyJet flight, departing 15.50, Edinburgh bound. Unit 3 on his tail.'

After what seemed like an age, Frankie pressed to transmit. 'Any update, Unit 3?'

'He used the gents, ma'am. No purchases made airside. Currently en route to the boarding gate. He's cutting it fine. Gate closes in five.'

Another twenty minutes passed with no further update, then: 'Unit 3, Thorne is aboard. Taxiing for take-off. Standing down.'

Lightning fast, Frankie was on the phone to Mitch with clear instructions to take NCA detectives James Robertson and José Rodrígues to meet the plane when it touched down, leaving Sheena McKenna and Ari Hassan in their high-rise position overlooking the Leith drop point. Kit was on her way to join them.

Frankie felt her adrenalin kick in.

These were the moments she lived for.

73

At Newcastle International Airport, an inbound Lufthansa flight landed bang on time. David and Indira waited at passport control to waylay Jack Gale. The locations manager was first through the door: good physique, deeply tanned, casually dressed in jeans and a dark T-shirt. He was wheeling a brightly coloured Samsonite backpack, cabin luggage that had seen some wear by the looks of it, the best friend of a frequent traveller.

Once through security, David stepped forward, introducing himself and Indi by name and rank, asking if they might have a word, adding that they wouldn't keep him long. As an afterthought, he added, 'Assuming you're not in a rush to retrieve a pre-booked vehicle from the car park—'

'No, I came by cab.'

'You don't have one waiting?'

'Not yet.' Jack frowned. 'What's this about?'

'We're not airport police, sir. We're Northumbria detectives. Murder Investigation Team. We need a few minutes of your time.'

Jack's prominent Adam's apple moved beneath the skin as he swallowed. His deep blue eyes lost their sparkle instantly. 'Is this about Jo?'

'If you mean Joanna Oliver, yes.'

'You've reopened the case?'

'We're reviewing it,' David said. 'Something we do regularly.'

'And yet here you are, delaying the final leg of my journey. That would suggest urgency to me.' Jack paused, having made it perfectly clear that he wasn't buying David's bullshit. 'You and Frankie Oliver work with my old man, right?'

'Not anymore.'

'Lucky you.'

David acknowledged the comment with a half-smile.

He didn't rate the man either. There was no sense hiding it.

Frankie's feelings ran even deeper. She hated Windy, not because of her father's unfounded accusation that he'd covered for Jack at the time – there was zero evidence to suggest that he'd followed Joanna when she left the others. He'd already taken off. Other teenage witnesses confirmed independently that he'd boarded a bus a few minutes before Joanna left the group, the rest remained together for the whole evening.

Frankie's beef with their ex-boss was professional, not personal. He was ineffectual, lacking in leadership. In a meritocracy, he should never have achieved such a high rank. He wasn't a man to forgive or forget either. Under his command, he'd made her suffer for the sins of her father – and some.

They couldn't stand one another.

Other passengers were making their way towards passport control.

David met Jack's gaze. 'Fancy a Starbucks?'

'I could murder one.'

David couldn't make up his mind if that was a cliché or a dig, a reminder not to treat Jack like a dimwit. They moved through customs, turning left into the concourse. Unusually, the café had few customers and no one waiting at the counter to be served.

'I'll get this.' Indira asked for their preferences, then went straight to the till to order while the two men found a table.

David sat back, one leg resting on his other knee, eyes on Gale. 'Good trip?'

'Productive. Frankfurt is a great city.'

'Yeah, I was there for a conference a few years ago. Wish I'd had time to explore. Your job must be interesting.'

'It gets me about,' Gale said. 'I've been doing it for years. Story conferences are what float my boat. I get to meet inspirational producers and writers who share my passion for good story-telling. Got my first break after leaving university, much to my father's disappointment. Your job doesn't interest me.'

'How is he?'

'No idea.'

'You don't talk?'

'He's a difficult man to like.'

'His own worst enemy.'

David didn't say that his father had never mentioned a son. No point rubbing salt into an already gaping wound.

Indira approached, juggling their drinks. She handed them out, then took a seat, finding a pen and small notepad in her bag, ready to write down anything not contained in the file.

'Shall we get on with it?' Jack said. 'I'm meeting a mate for dinner.'

David detected a slight nervousness in Jack, though no reluctance to answer his questions. 'I know you used to hang out with Joanna, that you were with her on the night she died. That's well documented. I'd like to know more about her frame of mind that evening. Assuming you remember.'

'How could I forget?' Jack said. 'She was angry. Her dad had imposed a curfew. She was bitching about having to go home early. Unlike mine, her father cared enough to impose boundaries.'

'And she resented that?'

'Didn't we all at that age?'

David didn't say that he'd lost his parents way before he reached his teens. 'I'd have thought your father would be as strict, if not a downright autocrat.'

Jack shrugged. 'When he was at work, I had free rein. My mum pissed off for a better life. Wish she'd taken me with her.'

David wondered why she hadn't. He kept the thought to himself. 'So, you and your pals were surprised to learn that Joanna didn't make it home?'

'We couldn't believe where she ended up. I mean, where her body was found. It took us all a long time to get over it. I'd offered to take her home that night. She told me to do one, so I did. No point hanging around if she was leaving.' Jack wiped a thin film of perspiration from his brow. 'Can't tell you how many times I wish I'd hung around.'

'Don't torture yourself. You weren't to know what would happen.'

'Still. I felt partly responsible. We all did.'

'You didn't get the impression that she was meeting anyone else that night?'

'No. Last I saw her was from the rear seat of the bus I was on. She must have realised she'd hurt me. She waved.'

Indi spoke for the first time. 'How would you describe your relationship with her?'

'What relationship?' Jack saw off his espresso. 'I wasn't her type. Too young.'

'And how did that make you feel?'

'Pissed off. She was cool. I wasn't.'

'Just now you said you were too young. What did you mean by that?' For the first time, Jack faltered. His jaw bunched and he looked across the empty café. Indi had hit a nerve. David gave her a nod to continue. She wasn't letting go. 'Jack? Are you saying Joanna was into older kids at school?'

'No . . .' He turned his head, took his time to answer. 'He was an adult, mid-twenties, at least. When you're fifteen, that seems ancient. I saw her getting into his car once.'

David had read the file in its entirety. The original MIT had raised multiple actions to trace vehicles, but no enquiries relating to an older friend, let alone a man. He took over the questioning, with Indira taking notes.

'What kind of car?'

Jack grimaced. 'To be honest, I didn't notice. Don't drive. Never have. I'm sorry, I can't tell you the exact make or model. A Ford . . . maybe.'

'Colour, size?'

A shrug. 'Dark, I think. Not big.'

'Registration number? Even a partial would help.'

Jack answered with a slow shake of his head. 'I'm sorry. My focus was on her and him.'

'Describe him to me.'

'He was on the other side of the car.'

'You said he was mid-twenties. You must have seen his face.'

'I dunno. Brown hair. Slicked back. The dude wore a suit.'

'Have you ever seen that car before or since?'

'No.'

'Did you tell investigators any of this when questioned?'

'I didn't tell anyone . . . except my old man.'

David couldn't hide his frustration. 'Why not?'

'For the same reason you're acting weird now.'

'Weird?' David frowned. 'It's a perfectly reasonable question.'

'If it means anything at all, I've been waiting for years for you guys to show up, so I could own up.' Jack was distraught now, eyes misting up, bottom lip quivering, unable to control his emotions. 'Look, I was into Jo. She wasn't interested in me. My old man said that gave me motive, that if I mentioned an older guy, Jo getting into his vehicle, it would look like I was trying to shift the blame, inventing someone who didn't exist. He told me to keep my gob shut, stay out of it or risk being thrown in a cell.'

'What?'

'Yeah. Imagine that.' Jack sighed.

'He suspected you?'

'Until police found a witness who saw me exit the bus at the end of my journey. By then my father's odd behaviour had raised a red flag for Jo's old man. Frank Oliver knew my dad was hiding something – and he was. I don't blame the guy. He was heart-broken, looking for someone to blame.'

'He still is, Jack. After all these years, he still is.'

74

Having missed its slot, the EasyJet flight from Gatwick was delayed on departure, frustrating passengers who were made to sit and wait on the runway and those waiting for it to land half an hour later than scheduled in Edinburgh. Mitch was leaning against a column in the arrivals hall, looking suitably bored, sipping from a bottle of water. He spotted Thorne the minute he emerged through customs with a mobile stuck to his ear. He was walking at a fast pace, his expression serious, like a man with a problem he was keen to fix.

Mitch relayed that information to Frankie, who was directing both ends of Operation Zenith from their Berwick office, her very own Gold Command.

'Any sign of Kit?'

'Yeah, she got here just before touchdown.'

'Great,' Frankie said. 'Whatever you do, don't lose him.'

While she waited for an update, Frankie called Steve. 'Anything doing in Hove?'

'Not a thing. Officers are on standby waiting for your signal, as and when required.'

'Cheers. We have eyes on Thorne. I'll get back to you with anything relevant.'

As she hung up, she received a text message from Sheena:

I got facial ID on your skinny runner. Craig Lewis. DOB: 05.04.2000. He has form.

You don't say. All quiet your end?

As a grave.

Get ready, you may be getting a visitor.

Frankie wanted to be out there, getting her hands dirty, like old times. However, she'd been tasked to run the show and that's what she'd do. Using her warrant card, she logged on the PNC to check out Lewis, a low-level offender who'd been kicked out of school at fourteen, entering the care system for a couple of years before taking up residency in HMYOI Polmont, an institution that began life as Scotland's first borstal.

Different name, same clientele.

If Lewis had graduated to trafficking humans, in whatever capacity, he'd be back inside before long. Frankie wasn't about to have him lifted. She'd sit tight and pick him up when the time was right.

Jack Gale understood that the Oliver family were desperate for answers, that they would never rest until Joanna's killer was found and brought to book. Jack, the adult, wanted that too, perhaps as much as they did. Even though his feelings weren't reciprocated at the time of her death, it was obvious he'd cared deeply for her. His reaction to David's words was hard to handle. He wept openly, apologising for having taken so long to come clean.

His father had a lot to answer for. He'd frightened Jack – the boy – into withholding vital evidence in a murder enquiry for his own ends, perverting the course of justice, failing to support his son to do the right thing.

Unforgivable.

On the way to his office, David pictured Frank Oliver at the crime scene, his world falling apart. He'd been slowly destroying himself ever since, unable to forgive himself for not answering Joanna's call on the night she died. Frankie's crumbling voice arrived in David's head: *what scares me the most, what I really can't bear is the thought of him dying without knowing the truth.* Though David was only one step closer to avoiding that, with new lines of enquiry to pursue, it felt like a giant leap forward.

Frank Oliver hadn't failed to notice a vital clue.

It was never there to miss.

75

Walking along Berwick's medieval defences had become part of Frankie's routine while she kept in constant contact with her teams in Hove and Edinburgh, praying for something, *anything*, to happen at either end of the UK. She'd known from the start that she'd be playing a waiting game. She was tearing her hair out, thoroughly depressed by her work situation. She'd heard nothing she could act on for three long days.

From a positive start on Sunday, her excitement had fizzled out. Kit had followed Thorne to a townhouse in Stockbridge, where he remained for the rest of the day, forcing Frankie to split the team to cover both addresses. On Monday morning, at around eight o'clock, Thorne had taken a taxi to an office in Edinburgh city centre, repeating that journey the next day and the next, seemingly an executive going about his business.

Graham said, 'I take it you're no further forward?'

She'd glanced sideways, a wry smile. 'How did you guess?'

'The clock's ticking and we have time to waste.'

Frankie stopped walking, eyes out to sea, hair whipping away from her face in a stiff wind. She turned to face him, leaning against the old town wall. A frustrated shrug. 'Thorne's not set foot on Leith soil. And I just got the nod that there was no DNA match on our database from the tab end Met Police lifted from Gatwick. He's Mr Clean. In two days, Kit and her Glasgow crew are back to normal duties. It's not looking good.'

'Anything I can do to help?' Graham said. 'I'm beginning to miss my area car.'

'The steering wheel on your desk not doing it for you?' Frankie smiled. 'Join the club. I'm itching to get stuck in.'

'Maybe Thorne's nothing to do with your case?'

'He came out of the house Osman went into. Call it gut feeling. Beneath that cool facade I reckon he's up to his neck in it. He may be hiding in the shadows, but he has links with both ends of Zenith. You need money to transport people across borders and, by the look of the guy, he's got plenty. It wouldn't surprise me to learn that he's the architect behind the whole thing, using his power to exploit the vulnerable and voiceless. The lad we found is exactly that. So traumatised, he's hardly spoken a word since.'

In the aftermath of a violent death, families coped in a variety of ways. Some fell apart. Others set up charities, keeping their loved one's name alive. Many victims' bedrooms had morphed into shrines, with favourite belongings never touched or were put in a special box to look at occasionally. It was different when a murder remained undetected for years. In such cases, personal possessions were untouchable, locked away by police in case they were of evidential value, linking victim and killer.

In Joanna's case those possessions merited closer inspection.

David looked at Indira. 'Ever been in the evidence room?'

She shook her head. 'No, not yet.'

'The office is manned 24/7. There's a small offshoot where we can look at everything in situ, without flagging up Joanna's case if we're smart. Malcolm, the night-shift admin clerk, seems to think he owns the place. He's not the brightest in the bunch. Call him. Ask if he's busy and tell him we're on our way down.'

'He's bound to ask why.'

'I'm counting on it.'

'I don't understand.'

'Stick to your legend and be sure to mention who's giving the orders. Tell Malcolm there have been complaints that it's a nightmare to find anything down there. Bright's had the gloves off with him once or twice.' David chuckled. 'I'm betting he'll be keen to avoid round three.'

'Like your style, guv.' Indi picked up the internal phone, punching in a number, repeating David's suggestion word for word, then hung up, a broad grin on her face. 'It worked. He's on the back foot.' Locking everything away, she grabbed an A4 pad and made herself ready to leave.

76

Steve was upbeat. 'We're on, Frankie. A detective viewing drone footage spotted a van in Hove, moving at speed through the town, a number seven clearly visible on the roof. The vehicle is now stationary and under surveillance, less than half a mile from my location. Driver and passenger still in the cab.'

'Clean faces?' She meant unknown to the National Crime Agency.

'Yeah, no ID on either. They appear to be waiting for someone.'

'Let's hope that someone is Osman.'

'I'll let you know. I've got a good feeling about this.'

Thanking him, Frankie disconnected and made another call. Any operation involving an OCG could go seriously wrong. The fact that hers involved minors made her want to consult with David. He'd know what to do. His phone rang out unanswered. Where the hell was he when she needed him?

Ignoring the mobile vibrating in his pocket, David told Malcolm to bugger off for twenty minutes. If the phone rang, Indi would answer. The exhibit's clerk didn't argue. As soon as he was gone, David stuck a notice on the door: Back in half an hour. In the canteen if it's urgent. After locking the door from the inside, he slipped the key into his pocket.

He and Indi gloved up and got to work.

Their luck was in.

Joanna's personal effects were on a shelf at the far end of a musty aisle not covered by CCTV. Good news for them and for whoever removed Joanna's Levi jacket. There were two boxes, a large one containing forensic exhibits; a small one full to the brim with items considered less significant by the SIO, retained in case new evidence came to light. Before lifting the boxes down, David took off his jacket, laying it across the top should anyone check the video recording to see what he was carrying into the side room.

Malcolm might be a donkey, but he was also a nosy sod, prone to gossip.

David happened to know that the CCTV had no audio feed and didn't extend to the side room he intended using. The offshoot was for officers to examine evidence, often for hours on end. No need to spy on them once a file had been signed out and entered in the logbook Malcolm called his bible.

They'd be safe there.

After placing the boxes down on a Formica table in the centre of the room, David removed his jacket from the top of the box, hung it on the upright of a chair, then turned to face Indi, offering a word of well-meaning advice to his recruit.

'This is not going to be a walk in the park,' he said. 'Switching intellectual gears is never easy.'

'Guv?'

'Nowadays, we sweep a victim's room looking for computers and mobile phones. We contact providers and comb social media platforms to understand their lives. A lot of that is at our fingertips. In the early nineties, none of that was available. CSIs would've lifted what they thought might be relevant. Bearing in mind Joanna wasn't killed at home, the SIO probably didn't bother with much of it. So, if anything strikes you as odd, flag it.'

'Gotcha.'

'Ready?'

Indira gave a confident nod.

As they removed each item from box 1, Indira checked the reference number, comparing it to the exhibits list. David noticed her hand shaking, a slight flinch as she handled Joanna's bloodied clothing in its cellophane bag. She closed her eyes for a split second, her mouth turned down at the edges, trying to keep her emotions in check.

David had never known her to look so tense.

'You OK to continue?' he asked.

A nod, though she didn't speak.

'It's never easy, Indi. You'll get used to it in time. If it's any consolation, the fact that these items of clothing were worn the last time Frankie saw Joanna getting ready for a night out is making my stomach churn. Stop me if it gets too much. It's not a two-person job. I can manage on my own.'

'No, I'm good, guv.' She quickly regained her composure. 'No weapon?'

'No, it was never recovered.'

77

As darkness fell, the phone rang. Frankie's father was not at home in his den. He was on security duty at Rae's place in the market town of Morpeth when the call came in, Andrea having been kept late, a regular occurrence given the nature of her job. Frankie made it clear that she wanted to talk in private – without interruption. What she meant was, without Rae earwigging.

The call was work-related.

He slid open the balcony door, telling Rae he wouldn't be long, and that she needed more outside space for the little 'un.

'Yeah,' she said. 'I'm on it.'

He smiled. 'Mum and I will help.'

Frankie's voice in his ear. 'Dad, I haven't got all day.'

'Hold on.'

Before Frank managed to slide the door closed, Amir squeezed through the narrow gap to join him on the balcony. Rae made a funny face through the glass as Frank sat down, lifting the little man onto his knee.

They were practically inseparable.

Amir held up his new toy truck.

'Good boy,' Frank said.

In her Berwick office, Frankie almost wept, still stressing over her nearest and dearest playing happy families with Amir, wondering how on earth they would cope if she found his blood relatives. More importantly, who'd get the blame if that became a reality. The answer was all too obvious.

'Is that Amir with you?'

'No, it's your uncle Arthur.'

Frankie laughed. He'd passed away ten years since. She checked her watch. 'It's almost seven thirty. Shouldn't Amir be in bed?'

'Try telling him that.'

Frankie laughed. 'Are you good to talk? I need your advice.'

'Clearly. When else do you ring your old man?'

'That's not fair, Dad.' She explained what was going down in Hove, that the NCA were observing another numbered van, which may or may not have a second cargo aboard. 'It's two-up, like the first one. The OIC reckons it's a goer.'

'Isn't that what you've been hoping for?'

'Now it's here, I'm . . .' She didn't finish the sentence.

'Losing your bottle?'

'A little.'

'Frankie, I'm pulling your leg.'

'I know, but it's a huge responsibility, Dad. I'm working blind, with personnel I hardly know. Kit seems confident that they can pull it off, but it won't be her neck on the line if they don't. I can't afford to fuck it up or allow another kid to face the same fate as Amir.'

Amir's ears pricked up when he heard his name spoken. He made a grab for the phone, which slipped through Frank's hands, crashing to the floor, cutting off the call in the process. The child's eyes grew big, a pet lip appearing.

'It's OK, mate. No sweat. I'll call her.' Frank redialled.

Frankie answered immediately. 'What was that?'

Her father ignored her in favour of Amir, speaking like the kid could understand every word. 'There you go, it's Frankie. She's calling to see how you are.' Then, to Frankie, 'He heard your voice and got excited. I dropped the phone. I know you're busy, love, but would you say hello? Then I'll ask Rae to take him inside, I promise.'

Frankie spoke quietly. 'Hello? Amir? It's Frankie.'

'Well would you look at that,' her father said.

*

Frankie didn't hear the rest. An image pinged into her mobile. A selfie of her dad and Amir on Rae's dimly lit balcony, the river behind them. The kid was dressed for bed, a pair of green PJs with a mechanical digger on the front.

He was smiling.

Frankie shut her eyes, dark memories of the last few days scrolling through her head like a movie, flashbacks that had consumed her every day and every night since. His tiny foot poking out from beneath a filthy blanket, exposed by flashing blue lights. His tethered wrists. His limp body as GNAAS medics worked on him in the chopper. Emergency nurses sedating him.

Frankie could've thrown up.

Checking the image again, she reminded herself that Amir was safe in her father's arms, her mind trip dissolving. She was about to speak, when she heard the patio door slide open, a few mumbled words between Rae and her father, before it clicked shut and he came back on the line.

'OK, it's bedtime. Rae coaxed Amir inside with a glass of milk and a treat. He's getting lots of those. Don't tell your mum.'

'She won't care. Can we please get to my problem?'

'What problem? If you didn't have doubts, I'd be worried. The op you're running is a big deal.'

'Don't I know it. I tried calling David. He's not picking up.'

'I'm second choice now?'

'Be serious.'

'You don't need either of us, sweetheart.'

'I do when kids' lives are at stake, Dad. I can't get my head around the idea that another kid will suffer like Amir did. It terrifies me.'

'It should. Frankie, don't let what happened to him cloud your judgement.'

'I'm not!'

'Aren't you?'

'Dad, it's too risky. I can't do it. As a cop, I get it. As a woman, I have grave concerns about leaving minors in the rear of that van with people who might abuse them.'

'Leadership means not copping out, Frankie. It's never easy.'

'I'm finding that out.'

'Was Amir abused?'

'Not sexually.' Amir had undergone a thorough examination by Acres.

'Exactly. He was a commodity. They are traffickers. Delivery drivers. Out to make money. The criminal justice system forces us to stick or twist, love. The window for interviewing is short. You need evidence before you jump. Pile in there with none and they'll have a lawyer quicker than you can spell it. If time runs out you'll have to release them. Once they're in the wind, you're done for.'

'I have one shot at this.'

'Don't waste it. You won't get another.'

Frankie said nothing as she wrestled with her conscience.

Her father's voice filled the silence, sharing the cold, hard truth. 'If you want to make an omelette, you need eggs, sweetheart. Your choices are limited. Stick to your plan. Your endgame is to catch them in the act, so hit pause and rewind. Let Zenith run its course and close them down.' He nudged her over the edge. 'If you don't, there'll be many Amirs for years to come.'

78

Apart from Joanna's denim jacket, everything in the first evidence box tallied with the list Indi had recovered from the safe. Finding nothing untoward, David closed it and moved on to the second. As before, everything in there was also bagged, sealed and labelled. Indira looked up as David passed her Joanna's diary.

'How are we going to read that without breaking the seal?'

'We don't need to. At Bright's insistence, every page of the diary and Joanna's notebooks were copied in their entirety, as were her photographs. Hard copies. Remember them?' He smiled. 'There's a file in here somewhere, one we can remove without drawing unnecessary attention.'

'Does Frank Oliver have access to the file?'

'I doubt it.'

'You don't know?'

'I'll check with Bright, but I can't see it. If Joanna mentioned her killer in there, even if she only used his initials, Frank's had twenty-seven years to hunt him down. Believe me, that's not something he'd miss.'

Once all the items were out and on the table, David placed the diary, notebooks and hard copy photographs to one side, then began flipping through the pages of the file he'd just mentioned. It was split into sections, with named tabs and side notes on every page indicating where each item had been found, all captured by the CSI photographer before they were removed.

David examined the diary pages first.

Like most people, Joanna had begun the year well. On the first of January, she'd made a note of Frankie's birthday in neat handwriting. She'd kept up the diary, religiously at first, but as 1992 progressed she became less interested, the entries tailing off to nothing. Had she found an older boyfriend, one she'd kept secret, knowing her parents wouldn't approve? In June, the month she died, there was only one entry, her father's birthday. After that, the only things he found were significant birthdays and her grandparents' upcoming wedding anniversary on the tenth of October.

Another family celebration she'd missed.

Indira continued to tick off the items on her list as David waded through the file, switching his focus to a tab named: artwork. It contained drawings of landscapes, seascapes and portraits – her preferred art form. They were of schoolmates and family, all realistic and compelling, including one of Frankie, copied from a photograph that had been pinned to the inside cover of her sketch pad. Joanna had captured her perfectly, especially the warmth in her eyes.

The likeness made his chest tighten.

'Look at this,' he said. 'What a talent.'

Indi looked across at the sketch. 'Wow!'

David turned the page, avoiding her gaze.

Indira turned away, none the wiser.

She continued to examine Joanna's jewellery and other objects collected from her room, her eyes shifting to bottles of cheap fragrances and oils, some she'd never heard of: Dewberry, Tramp and Tribe. The last bottle she looked at stood out as a household name: N°5 by Chanel. She held it up, noting that it was almost full. It stood out from the rest of her belongings, like a beacon of hope in an otherwise bleak landscape.

Indira felt a rush of blood to her head.

Something wasn't right.

David's mobile rang.

He stopped browsing and moved away to answer it. With his back turned, Indira pulled the file towards her, turning to the relevant pages to find an image of Joanna's dressing table, eventually finding one. Wishing it was digital so she could zoom in, Indira peered at it for some time, then turned a few more pages.

'Jesus!'

David hung up, eyeing her curiously. 'What's up?'

'This . . .' She held up the Chanel, so he could see it clearly through the cellophane.

'What about it?'

'Isn't it a bit old for a kid of Joanna's age?'

'It's a well-known brand.'

'Yeah, if you can afford it. Call me suspicious, but I don't believe any kid of fifteen would buy that, let alone wear it.'

'Maybe it was a present from her mum.'

'So, where's the box . . . and why was it hidden?'

79

Frankie's old man talked a lot of sense. He always managed to see the bigger picture, however unpalatable it might be. Risky though it was, Frankie had to face facts. To take down a gang who'd caused so much suffering in exchange for untold wealth, she had to let the action play out. Only then might she discover the extent of Simon Thorne's involvement. She suspected that he was bankrolling the trade in humans, hiding behind a dodgy Edinburgh address and an office her team couldn't get access to without showing their hand. This was her opportunity to end his high life and put him away.

'I'm ready,' she said. 'Thanks, Dad. Your support means everything.'

A notification arrived on her mobile, two discreet tones. Someone was trying to reach her. Asking her father to wait, she glanced at her screen. Thinking it might be David returning her call, her finger hovered over the decline button.

She couldn't take that chance.

'Dad, I have a call waiting. Gotta go.'

'Be careful, Frank.'

It was almost an echo of David's warning.

Disrupting an OCG was serious shit. She was dealing with people with nothing to lose if they were caught. They had muscle. They were ruthless. They would kill anyone who got in their way – and enjoy doing it.

'I'm riding a desk,' she reminded her father. 'Nowhere near the business end of the operation.'

'Yet,' he said. 'You're an aunty to Amir now, so no heroics.'

*

Had that status been permanent, Frankie would have embraced it. She didn't remind her father that it might not be. 'Love you, Dad.'

'Love you, sweetheart. Keep those plates spinning. This is your chance to get the bad guys. I'm with you every step of the way. If you need anything, call me, day or night.'

'I will.' Frankie ended the call, accepting the other. 'Oliver.'

Steve Braithwaite didn't stand on ceremony. 'Osman is on the move, boss. Looks like he's in a hurry, heading for the van. ETA three minutes. Drone in the air. Vehicles standing by to follow.'

'I'll hold,' she said.

As the seconds ticked by, Frankie pulled her laptop towards her, logging on to the video feed, watching Osman in real time. He was wearing black jogging pants, a black T-shirt, maroon trainers. When he reached the vehicle, he slapped his hand against the driver's window, then proceeded to the rear, looking over his shoulder before opening the back door, climbing in.

The van pulled away from the kerb.

Steve said, 'It's a go!'

David placed the Chanel bottle on the table. 'Where was it found?'

'In the very back of a drawer where Joanna kept her jumpers, not on display with the cheaper brands taken from her dressing table. A gift from the unidentified adult Gale alluded to, perhaps? A man the original investigation team didn't know about. And we've already had a hint about perfume from Masterson. It's him, boss.'

Indi didn't mention a name.

David knew who she was talking about.

Snippets of their conversation with Masterson entered his head – *He preferred submissive women* – an opinion loaded with subtext. What she meant was young and impressionable. Girls of Joanna's age would fit the bill perfectly.

How could he stoop so low?

Indira asked, 'Will we get DNA or prints from it this far down the road?'

'We won't know unless we try. I have no doubt you're on to something, but we need another word with Masterson, in person. She's the key to all this. I have a few calls to make. Give her a bell and set it up.'

Indira checked her watch. 'Now?'

'Right now.'

'Target vehicle taking the third exit onto Devil's Dyke Road,' Steve said. 'Will keep you posted, boss.' The line went dead.

As Frankie walked to her vehicle, she called Kit to update her. 'There's no intel on destination, so I don't have an ETA. Steve will let us know the route they take.' She opened the car door and climbed in, placing her laptop in the passenger footwell, starting the car. She didn't move off. 'Let me know if Thorne makes a move in Stockbridge, or if anything goes down in Leith.'

'Will do,' Kit said. 'If the van is heading to us, Steve will tip us off.'

'Assuming he's heading your way, I have seven or eight hours to kill. I'm heading home, but don't hesitate to get in touch. Sorry you got the thick end of the wedge.'

'What?' Kit snorted. 'You've gotta be kidding. We love this shit. Eating takeout every day. I'm in fish-and-chip heaven.'

'I'd do anything to change places.'

'Hey! We take them down. You take the credit. The way it goes. This is your case, remember?'

'I'd rather be there slapping the cuffs on Osman.'

'I'll make sure they're good and tight. If he resists, I'll break his arms. How's that?'

Amir's tethered, bleeding wrists entered Frankie's head. 'You reap what you sow.'

80

With the offices of Freeman & Scholtz closed, Indira had no choice but to arrange a second interview with Stephanie Masterson at her Forest Grange home. It was pitch-dark when they got there, an eerie drive on unlit roads, under the dark skies of Northumberland. A starry night. Clear of any cloud.

Indira rang the bell.

Steph's husband answered the door – a tall man with short-cut greying hair that matched his kind eyes.

'Sorry to trouble you so late,' David said. 'I'm DCI Stone and this is my colleague, DC Sharma.'

'Yes, we spoke earlier.'

'Then you'll know it can't wait till morning.'

He invited them in. 'Good to meet you both.' He glanced into the kitchen. 'I was cheffing tonight.' Nigel Masterson rolled his eyes. 'It looks like a bomb has dropped in there. Please, come through to the living room.'

David glanced around the room as they entered. It was vast, nicely lit, a great entertaining space, with large sofas facing one another on either side of a huge stone fireplace Indira could walk into without banging her head. The grate was empty, with logs stacked neatly on either side of a wood-burning stove. On the hearth, dried flowers in a gigantic vase added a splash of colour.

The level of detail was exquisite.

A latte glass sat empty on a low coffee table along with a pair of designer specs. Copies of the day's newspapers were strewn across the floor, the *FT* reporting on looming interest cuts. US banks were feeling the pinch.

Steph's homework, David presumed.

He caught a whiff of Indian food. 'We're not interrupting your dinner, I hope.'

'No, we've eaten. I'm on clear-up duty. I'll fetch Steph . . .' Nigel hesitated; his eyes fixed on Stone's. 'Go easy on her, eh? She was upset after you left on Friday. She told me everything. Believe me, she's not proud of her behaviour.'

David nodded.

Masterson disappeared.

Moments later, his wife arrived looking tired. 'Back so soon?'

'We're here to take a statement this time,' David said. 'We have more questions.'

Her face paled slightly at the formality. He waited for her to sit. She took the armchair, lifting a pair of what he presumed were middle-distance specs onto the bridge of her nose.

'I told you pretty much everything there was to say.'

David knew the who – a truth that would break Frankie's heart when it was made known who'd killed her sister – now he wanted to uncover the how, which he suspected would embarrass the woman looking daggers at him.

'Steph, I appreciate this isn't easy for you. What I'm after is information that'll hold up in a court of law when I'm able to make an arrest.'

'Are you sure he's your man? I feel so guilty, naming him.'

'You wouldn't if you knew what I know.'

'I understand.'

'Good, because he doesn't deserve your sympathy. If it's any consolation, you're not the only one to point the finger.' David wasn't looking forward to what he was about to ask and what her reaction might be. He shook his head, an apologetic expression. 'There's no other way to say this. Did your relationship with him take place during working hours or in your own time?'

She dropped her head into her hands, then looked up, a mixture of guilt and shame visible. This interview was killing her. 'Mostly at work. I knew it was wrong and was stupid enough to go along with it. After the initial excitement wore off I became terrified that we'd be seen and reported. He laughed it off. I was in uniform. He wasn't. That's the real reason I resigned.'

'I'm sorry, I need specifics.'

She cleared her throat. 'It began as these things do, with a bit of office banter, and turned into a sordid affair. He'd drive somewhere quiet. We'd have sex in the car, then go back to work as if nothing had happened.'

'We're not judging you,' Indira said.

'That's kind. I think you probably are.'

'We're not the morality police, nor Professional Standards,' David reassured her. 'Unlike the instigator of the affair, you weren't taking advantage from a position of power. You made a mistake and owned up to it. The job can't touch you now. We're murder detectives, Steph, which means that anything we discuss is embargoed—'

She blushed. 'I told Nigel.'

'I know. He's not likely to mention it, is he?'

'No. If this comes out, it'll destroy me.'

'I'll try to keep your name out of it, but I need to know anything and everything you can tell me.'

'Like what?'

'Did this affair take place in his private vehicle?'

'Hell, no. A CID car.'

David knew from experience that detectives favoured high-performance cars that were new and fast-moving. They were pool cars, not allocated to individuals, so what you got was often dependent on whether you were working earlies or lates, first or last in the queue.

'It would help us a lot if you can remember any of those vehicles.'

'I don't, specifically. They were generic and compact . . .' She blushed. 'Astras, Escorts, one or two Metros. He often used a dark blue Escort. I don't remember plates, if that's what you're after. One of them was a J reg, I think. We never left the station together. He'd pick me up just off Northumberland Road near the entrance to John Dobson Street multistorey.'

As he'd done with Joanna, David was thinking.

This was where Jack Gale had last seen her.

She could take a bus home from Eldon Square or Haymarket, just a few minutes' walk away. The thought of his suspect cruising up and down, looking for fresh meat, made David feel physically sick. He'd pulled a few strokes in his time, but the guy Masterson was describing was not the one he knew.

'That's really helpful,' he said. 'What about when you met up outside of work?'

'It didn't happen often. We'd meet in a place of his choosing. Often he'd arrive in a cab. He never took me home. Now I know why.'

'You said on Friday that he bought you a specific perfume and asked you to wear it. Can you remember the brand?'

'Chanel . . . N°5.'

81

At her Coble Quay apartment, Frankie took a hot shower. Wrapping her wet hair in a towel, she wandered barefoot into her bedroom to collect her mobile from where she'd left it to charge. It was now at full power. There was no news on Zenith, north or south. She threw it down on the bed. On edge, she got dressed, dried her hair, then went outside onto her balcony to wait, counting herself lucky that things were moving.

They almost weren't.

A brief telephone conversation with Bright earlier entered her head. He'd called to tell her that Kit and her crew had been denied extra time by the Met's top floor. They argued over it. When pushed, Frankie stood her ground, demanding an explanation.

'Really, guv? What's more important than *this* job?'

'Calm down! You knew from the outset that you were on the clock. Matthews was told to close it down when the seven days expired. No argument. She didn't tell you?'

'Of course she did, but she'll be begging her bosses for more time, and I told her you'd be doing the same.'

'Did you clear that with Ellen?'

'No! Guv, Kit's crew have worked tirelessly at both ends of the investigation. They're all knackered, but they know what they're doing and they're up for it. Have they, have I, got anything better to do than save lives?'

'I assume that's a rhetorical question—'

'You must intervene. You—'

'I have. They're. Not. Listening. And neither are you by the sound of it. Suck it up and move on.'

'Did you hear a word I said?'

The row ended when Bright told her to stay in her lane, a stark reminder of who she was talking to, a warning not to overstep the invisible line between enthusiasm and disrespect. She had apologised. He'd have fought her corner and some, though it riled her that a critical operation came down to funding, money that should be ring-fenced for these kinds of cases. As her father had so eloquently pointed out, nothing else mattered.

When lives were at stake, you pushed on.

The echo of negativity died away, along with the conversation.

Now, things were looking up. Though their deadline was fast approaching, Kit's superiors could hardly refuse her request for an extension with a van in transit, potentially with human cargo aboard.

Frankie checked her laptop, watching the target vehicle proceed on its journey north, a live feed from the surveillance team's onboard cameras. She needed a plan should the van veer off course to a different city, a different town. She may have to ask another force to deploy resources at a moment's notice. That was no easy task. She needed Bright's authority and support to make it happen.

She couldn't afford to piss him off.

Sick of waiting, she left the balcony and went inside, locking the door behind her. She considered a catnap and discounted it. She was too wired to sleep. Scooping up her car keys, she grabbed a coat and left the house.

Reversing at speed from her undercroft parking space, she turned the car around and drove away, a plan to surprise David before he left for the evening, to make her peace with him. The situation between them had caused her untold anxiety when she could least afford it.

If Bright found out what she was up to in the middle of a critical operation, she'd be told to focus or ship out and let the National Crime Agency take over. That's what they were already doing. She was geographically remote, unable to assist, waiting for news.

Sod it.

On autopilot, she turned off the A1 to call on Rae and Andrea, a flying visit. She found Rae asleep on the sofa, Andrea watching TV, snacking on crisps, toys strewn across the floor waiting to be picked up.

Parenthood was exhausting.

Declining a drink – no time and even less inclination – Frankie snuck into Amir's room. He was sleeping on his back, his angelic face peaceful, a far cry from the jumpy child she'd watched over in hospital whose eyelids continually moved beneath the skin as if he were in the middle of a nightmare she could only guess at.

Kissing his warm cheek, she covered him up, leaving his nightlight switched on, his door slightly ajar. She left the house, satisfied that all was good, that he was making progress and that his short-term foster family had everything under control.

A worthwhile detour.

If David wasn't at Middle Earth, Dick might be. Since being asked to hold the fort, he often stayed late. Reaching her destination, she was delighted to see David's car in its designated spot. She was about to get out of her vehicle, when Steve called.

The NCA detective reported that the surveillance operation had gone without a hitch. 'Targets stationary,' he said. 'They pulled into a service station.'

'What are they doing?'

'Driver is out of the van, changing plates.'

'No sign of Osman?'

'Still in the rear.'

'And the co-driver?'

'He's gone inside. Officer on foot. Hold on . . . The co-driver is jogging to the car. They're off!'

As Steve hung up abruptly, Frankie spotted David exiting Middle Earth, making his way across the car park with Indira. They stopped walking, had a few words, an intense conversation by the looks of it. This late, Frankie expected them to go their separate ways, and was surprised when they both climbed into David's vehicle and took off. Whatever they were doing for Bright, it wasn't admin.

82

Over a late dinner at a local restaurant, David and Indira's conversation inevitably drifted into shop talk. They may have found their gun. It wasn't yet smoking. Before leaving their base, Indi had sent the Chanel exhibit to forensics for examination, a rush job. Without doubt they were closing in, their suspect more credible than ever before, though there were no high-fives or congratulations. Only copious amounts of misery and rage . . .

And, in David's case, a feeling of betrayal.

He was struggling to row back on that.

'In our hearts and heads, we know who we're after,' he said quietly. 'As keen as we are to gather all available evidence to throw at him, we must do it responsibly. As an organisation, we're often castigated for trying to fit evidence around a suspect. We want none of that. We're beginning to build a case. In doing so, we must show that we're being fair and transparent, not just hanging this on a suspect for convenience.'

'You're saying we need more before we make a move?'

'A lot more. What I'm also saying is we need to demonstrate our honesty and openness on paper. Our investigation will be scrutinised to the nth degree, by Bright, the press, the CPS and the offender's defence team. They'll spot circumstantial from a mile away and have it discounted.'

'We have evidence from the women he dated' — Hall's first wife, Jan Welch, and former cops Rachel Hart and Stephanie Masterson — 'all consenting adults who'll make good witnesses,' Indira reminded him

'That makes him a creep. But unless his DNA or prints are on that perfume bottle, we have no proof of an association with Joanna.'

Indira didn't argue.

If their suspect had ended Joanna's life, he couldn't be allowed to sidestep the sentence he deserved. 'Identifying the CID car Masterson referred to would be a good start, guv.'

'Locating it so long after the event isn't a realistic prospect. It'll have been sold on several times since . . .' David forked a piece of chicken jalfrezi, then put his cutlery down, pushing his plate away. He'd lost his appetite. 'The car may not even exist now. Probably ended its life in a scrapyard years ago.'

Indira wiped her mouth on a serviette. 'I'll consult with the DVLA on the history of the vehicle in the morning. There'll also be records of cars bought and sold in the archive somewhere, including which stations they were allocated to.'

'Good shout. Gale and Masterson gave us a start, possibly a dark blue Ford, J reg. If we can pinpoint our suspect's favoured vehicle, talking to other detectives who used it might work to our advantage.'

He fell silent, a pensive mood.

Indi caught his eye. 'Something on your mind, guv?'

'Masterson was in uniform, with no business being in a CID vehicle. It happens, I get that. At her own admission, she was anxious about being caught, so much so that she put her ticket in, while he carried on with his career intact. If he was indiscreet after she left, that might also work in our favour. The problem is, we need him in cuffs before we go poking around.'

'You think it likely that he'd brag about his conquests?'

'His police ones, maybe. A lot of cops do. It's like a badge of honour to some. Imagine the leg-pulling, the name-calling. Imagine what that would be like for a nineteen-year-old rookie trying to make a good impression. We could be in with a shout here. If our suspect's relationships were made known, his former colleagues will be queueing up to tell us about them when they find out why he's under arrest.'

David glanced at the clock above the bar.

'It's late . . . See your drink off. I'll give you a lift to your car.' As she raised her glass, he raised his to toast her. 'Be proud, Indi. You did good today.'

83

Frankie had no idea how long she'd been standing in the shadows outside the restaurant, looking in at the cosy candlelit table for two. She felt guilty stalking David, poking her nose into his private life, watching his body language, the way he looked at Indira, the smile on his lips reaching his eyes.

A toast?

Really?

They had had their heads together for the whole time, hardly a pause in the conversation. Indira had got more out of him than she ever had. The thought that they might be romantically involved, that Frankie was no longer his new golden girl, stung. Why else would they meet, away from their workplace, outside of office hours?

It had taken him forever to even suggest that to her.

His voice hit Frankie's ear: *Tell her I still owe her a curry.*

It surprised her that he wasn't more creative. Again, she wondered if he and Kit had ever been an item. She decided not. The woman had more sense than to get involved with a fellow officer, especially one she worked so closely with. Professionally, it was dangerous. Personally, as Frankie had come to realise, it sucked.

Kit's voice replaced David's: *He cares for you.*

'Bollocks,' Frankie said.

'What's wrong, bonny lass?'

Frankie swung round.

The guy standing over her was hammered, the smell of second-hand alcohol almost knocking her over. He looked through the restaurant window, then at her. 'You been dumped . . . by that streak of misery? You can dee better than him, pet. I'm clammin,' if you fancy a bite to eat. If he sees us together, he'll soon realise what he's lost.'

Ordinarily, she'd have laughed at his banter. With David and Indira on the other side of the glass, she held up her warrant card.

'Push off.'

'Suit yersel . . .' Holding up his hands, he backed away. 'Nee need for that, like.'

Frankie watched him weave his way down the street, plaiting his legs as he went, taking his beer belly with him. She took one last look through the restaurant window. Ever the gentleman, David was helping Indira on with her jacket. And to think, *she'd* gone there to apologise.

Fuck that.

Why did she even care?

With no time to indulge such thoughts, she raced to her car and tried to forget what might have been. As she drove, a voice message arrived from Steve advising that the target vehicle was flying. Eighty miles out, it had left the M25 at junction 21, taking the M1 exit to Luton airport.

No!

Trying to control her panic, she called him on the hands-free. The phone rang out for a while before he picked up. 'Steve, whatever you have to do, do not allow them to board a plane.'

'I misled you, boss. They're now on the M1, heading north.'

Frankie relaxed.

So far, so good.

84

As soon as he got in, David went straight to the kitchen and grabbed two beers from the fridge, taking them through to the living room. Handing one to Ben – the squashed cans on the wooden floor proof that he'd already had several – David sat down to join him. Ben was lolling in an armchair, his fist propping his head up as he watched TV, a sports channel reporting on the £20 million transfer of England right-back Kieran Trippier from Spurs to Atletico Madrid.

When the piece ended, David looked across at his nephew. Seeing him in profile made his heart flutter, like looking at his late brother in this very room when he was Ben's age . . . only less bored. Like his father, Ben had mastered the art of good conversation, unless he couldn't be arsed, which seemed to be the state of play this evening.

'Have you eaten?' David asked.

Ben's eyes remained fixed on the set. 'Cheese sandwich.'

David felt guilty for declining his leftovers at the restaurant, though he kept that thought to himself. 'Heavy day?'

'Not especially.'

'Something wrong?'

'No, I'm good.' Still no eye contact.

'You don't sound it.'

Ben picked up the remote to mute the sound and turned to face him. 'Dave, I don't expect you to like what I'm going to say, but I'm moving to town.'

It came as a shock. 'You're right, I don't like it. Can I ask why?'

'Why would I live here when I can get a place of my own? You're hardly ever in and there's nothing for me to do when I'm on my tod. My mates are out on the hoy several times a week. I'm missing out.'

'What? It's not five minutes since you were begging me to let you stay.'

After Luke's funeral, surrounded by mourners, David's nephew acting like a dick, smoking dope openly, discarding his roach end on the ground. A row had ensued, Ben continuing to whinge that he had nowhere to sleep and needed a bed, David making it clear that it was not his problem.

'I can't bunk in with mates,' Ben said.

'Why not?' He didn't have any, David was thinking.

'I dropped out.'

'Well, you'd better drop back in sharpish!' David asked him if he was born clueless. 'When your compensation claim goes to court, you'll be expected to prove your commitment to your university course, or you'll get bugger all in terms of a settlement from the arsehole who was driving the lorry that killed your dad.'

Ben glared at him. 'I'm finished with uni—'

'Pat yourself on the back, son. Your old man would be real proud. You finally got what you wanted.'

'What's that supposed to mean?'

'It means you're on your own.' David leaned in, lowering his voice. They had company, including Frankie. 'Listen to me, you piece of shit! Of the many bad moves you've made in your relatively short and aimless life, this one takes the biscuit. Have you any idea how much your mother wanted you to get a proper education? How much your father sacrificed to put you through university?'

Ben didn't answer.

'No, I didn't think so. What exactly is it you want from me?'

'You said you'd sort out probate.'

'Give me one good reason why I should.'

'You're family—'

'Not anymore.'

*

David blew out a breath. He looked across at Ben, unsure of what to say. Try as he might, he couldn't shake the memory of that terrible day. So much had changed since then. He might still have a lot to learn, but Ben had grown into a young man David admired for turning his life around, a young man his parents would have been immensely proud of.

'We're company for each other,' he said. 'I thought you liked being here—'

Ben made a face. 'Did you, when you were my age?'

He had a point. At nineteen years of age, David had left his grandmother's countryside cottage at the first opportunity for the bright lights of London. He'd travelled the world before joining the Met. Since coming back, he'd learned to live without long holidays in exotic places. He'd got used to having his nephew around. For the first time since he'd become a surrogate father, he realised how much he'd miss Ben's company if he took off.

'I'm sorry. I've been flat out lately.'

'Me too, considering my future.'

'C'mon, dude. Don't give me a hard time. My job isn't nine to five. You knew that when you moved in.'

'Well, now I'm moving out.'

In his mind's eye, David could picture the graveyard. Friends and family beginning to move away, stopping to shake his hand on the way out, heading back to work, heading home, some walking off through the archway of the central clock tower and into the garden of remembrance, taking a moment to remember Luke, his wife, Ruth, and others who'd gone before.

Out of the corner of his eye, Ben had stood glaring at him.

David turned to face him. 'Probate, eh? Your dad's place is worth a few quid. It should make you a tidy profit and you'll be sorted. Is that the plan?' He narrowed his eyes. 'You're a property tycoon now, right? Wrong.'

Ben's cocky stance fell away. 'What's that supposed to mean?'

'It means you should check in with your solicitor before you book that cruise.' David was readying himself to leave. 'I think you'll find that I'm holding the purse strings.'

'I'm his next of kin,' Ben said. 'He can't do that!'

'He can and he did. It's his last gift to you, Ben. All legal and above board, signed in the presence of his brief. Any provision he made for you comes via me from now on, when or if you play ball. So, I suggest you get your arse in gear and buckle down. If you do that, you'll get the exact same allowance your father was paying you. Except, unlike your dad, I'll be checking on your attendance every week . . . No show, no dough.'

And that had been the case until Ben turned twenty-one. Until then, he was as much an orphan as the kid Frankie had found in the back of a stolen Mercedes van. They were both lucky enough to have someone on the bench to take over as temporary guardians. David couldn't deny that he hadn't wanted Ben initially – and would never have taken him in had it not been for Frankie's intervention – but now he understood.

It was for both their sakes.

It would be a wrench if he left now.

'Why don't you think on it?'

'Too late. I'm grateful for everything you and Frankie did for me, seriously I am, but living here isn't working for me. It hasn't for a while. It's too remote. I paid a deposit and signed a contract this morning on an apartment on the south side of the Tyne—'

'Without telling me first?'

'I don't need your permission.'

'No, but you could've given me the heads-up.'

'I tried.' Ben glanced at the mobile lying on the arm of David's chair. 'Check your recent calls list.'

David found four missed calls, all arriving before 10 a.m. He apologised again. 'I had an early meeting. Listen, if the idea was to lay a guilt trip on me, congratulations. You win. You're not seriously telling me you'd rather piss off than live here practically rent-free.'

'Think of it as an investment—'

'It's not just a mortgage you're facing, son. Did you factor in council tax, utility bills, grub? Your inheritance might seem like a huge amount now, but it won't last forever.'

'Back off. It's my money, to spend how I see fit. I'm not a complete idiot.'

'At least stay until you join up.'

Ben took a swig of beer before firing off another missile. 'I've changed my mind about that too.'

David knew that his words were not designed to injure. That was not Ben's style. They were merely a statement of fact. He was considerate and thoughtful, a lad who thought before opening his mouth or making big decisions. If he hadn't made up his mind unequivocally, he'd never have mentioned it.

'I thought you were keen.'

'I was, but I've come to realise that policing requires its officers to make too many sacrifices. Admit it, you have no social life, no love life, no room for family.'

That hurt David.

Seeing his wounded reaction, Ben said, 'That's not a criticism. I get how important it is, to you and Frankie, but all work and no play isn't for me. I'm staying at the paper, at least for the time being.'

'Look, I have leave to take. Why don't I book a flight out of here when my case is over—'

'What case?' Ben's glare was like an accusation. 'You said the incident room was dead, that you were doing something boring for Bright.'

If Ben were to find out what he was doing – and who was under suspicion for Joanna's murder – he'd go apeshit. Unable to tell him, berating himself for slipping up, David lied. 'Bad choice of words, I meant assignment.'

'For a cop, you're a rubbish liar.'

'It's confidential—'

'As per . . . unless you want my help, or Belinda's – then you're willing to share.' Ben paused. 'D'you think we're stupid? Do you think Frankie is? She knows you're hiding something. Looks like she was right.'

85

Frankie paced her apartment, her mind focused only on Operation Zenith. She sat down to check the video feed. The image switched as surveillance vehicles changed places. She watched the footage for a while, relieved to see the target vehicle take, then leave, the M18, merging onto the A1M, almost halfway to Leith – if that's where they were heading.

Mentally, she crossed her fingers.

Having been involved in lengthy pursuits, she knew the score. Every team member would be on high alert, ready to react to a situation that could change swiftly and dramatically, forced to speed up or slow down as directed. If they were ordered to stop, they might take the opportunity to change the appearance of their vehicles with kit they were all equipped with. The game was to stay clean or bow out if spotted.

It was fun . . .

It was exciting . . .

Nothing matched the thrill of the chase.

On the flip side, the men they were following were highly dangerous. Operations like this could go seriously wrong if they perceived a risk and made a run for it, endangering others in the process: civilians, officers and anyone inside or outside the target vehicle. The surveillance team would avoid any movement that might force a change of strategy for Osman and his drivers, compromising the safety of their human cargo. If spooked, the offenders could jump out, set fire to the van and leg it.

Unimaginable horror.

Amir's face flashed before Frankie's eyes. She'd never forget the state he was in when found, and had reasons to be grateful.

It could have been a whole lot worse.

Anticipating a long night, she attached her laptop to a wall socket. The surveillance team would maintain radio silence unless there was something to report. Leaving the video feed on, she laid down for a kip. She'd be awake in seconds should anyone speak.

Frankie was drifting in and out, when she heard the next shout. 'Target vehicle indicating left into Moto Washington Northbound.' The voice was female. 'I have enough cover to follow. All units, hang back.'

Frankie sat up, rubbing her eyes. She'd been out for hours. The video footage jumped as the trailing vehicle took the slip road to follow. One headlight, Frankie noticed, a motorcyclist, her headcam active.

'All units, stand by,' she said. 'Target vehicle reversing on the western periphery of the car park. It's busy, guys. Could someone take up a position at the north-east exit to the A1?'

'Unit 3: I'll take that and put Terry out on foot to observe.'

'Units 4 and 5: we're off at Chester-le-Street, south of your position. Give us a shout when you're ready to roll.'

'Copy that.'

Frankie's heart was pounding.

Pursuit vehicles could shift. If necessary, at speeds in excess of a hundred and thirty miles an hour. However far behind they were, when given the go-ahead, they'd tank up the motorway, catching up with the others in a flash.

These guys were pros.

Unit 1 had a good view.

The van was parked away from other vehicles, the driver and co-driver taking a leak in the bushes behind it. When they were done, they returned to the tarmac, one of them pulling out a pack of cigarettes, banging his fist on the side of the van.

Osman climbed out to join them, a big stretch, as if he'd pulled a heavy shift. Accepting a cigarette, he was laughing and joking with the others, his back to the camera, a maroon sweatshirt to keep him warm, the same shade as his trainers. Frankie's hatred for this man knew no bounds.

He'd go down for trafficking Amir.

Unit 1 was on the move, her voice dead calm. 'Stay alert, guys. I have eyes on. Looks like the targets are having a quick tab and will soon be on their way.'

One by one, all police units restated their individual positions. They were ready and so was Frankie.

From an operational point of view, she'd made her decision and would stick with it, though it made her feel physically sick to think of a child or children like Amir secured to the interior of the van, cold and alone, in the dead of night. She couldn't believe that they had slept a wink since leaving Hove.

She took her laptop into the kitchen, grabbing snacks and water from the fridge, shoving them into a small backpack. The van was just over forty miles away. She had time to make it to Alnwick, where she'd lay in wait and join the rear of the convoy. Kit had told her, 'We take them down. You take the credit.'

No way.

86

Frankie's phone rang unexpectedly at 2 a.m. Thinking it was one of the surveillance team, she answered without checking the screen. 'What's happening?'

'Nothing good . . .'

The voice in her ear was not one she expected. 'David? You do know what time it is?'

'Yeah, I know. Ben and I were up late, a bit of a disagreement.'

'Is he OK?'

'Yeah. I'm not so good. Thanks for asking. Tell you about it sometime. Couldn't sleep. Just checked my messages. Mitch tells me things are kicking off your end. And before you ask, I asked him to keep me in the loop.'

'Well, he had no business doing it.'

'Hey! Don't go all Shiv on me—'

'I'm not!' Frankie smiled at the *Succession* reference. The TV series had been the talk of the MIT since it was first broadcast in 2018, the character of Siobhan (Shiv) Roy portrayed by Sarah Snook topping a list of favourites among her old colleagues. 'Anyway, as bitch faces go, hers is good. Mine is out of this world.'

David's mood lifted. 'You don't have to tell me. I've seen it often enough. And leave Mitch out of this,' he added. 'He still works for me, remember? I hear the OCG is on the move, heading north.'

'Yeah.'

She'd been so pleased to hear from him, all thoughts of his cosy dinner with Indira had evaporated, though now she couldn't help wondering if it was really Ben who had kept him up. Whatever the story, the man she'd worked with and grown fond of was his old self. The distant, uncommunicative version could do one. Their friendship meant everything. She'd hate to lose it.

'Where are they now?' David was asking.

'Stationary at Moto Washington, northbound. Looks like we're on.'

Her good mood was replaced by a much darker emotion as Unit 1's voice came over the radio, a slight tremor this time.

'Unidentified Ford transit has reversed alongside our target. Registration: November, Papa, Six, Nina, Mike, Lima, X-ray. Stand by.'

Everyone held their collective breath, including David. He'd offer to lend a hand if they needed an extra body. Frankie wouldn't need to ask. He'd heard every word. If he *was* doing something boring for Bright — and that was by no means a certainty — he'd be dying to get involved.

For now, he remained silent so she could listen in to her team. Frankie changed down, accelerated round a sharp bend, grateful that the B roads leading to the A1 were empty. The radio sprang to life again.

'I repeat, unidentified vehicle alongside. Headlights on. Engine running. Driver exiting the vehicle. White. Male. Middle-aged. He's approaching Osman. Potential transfer of cargo.'

Frankie swore under her breath.

'Take five, Frank.'

David never lost control.

She allowed herself a smile: maybe he should, now and then.

Another radio transmission. 'On way to you, Unit 1.'

The officer she assumed was one of those who'd pulled off at Chester-le-Street had used his initiative, a decision not to leave his oppo exposed. Like her, he'd have his foot to the floor, racing to Unit 1's location.

It's what she'd have done.

What David would've done.

'Unit 1: Osman is shaking his head. Whoa, his driver is going for his pocket. Handing something over.' She paused her running commentary. 'False alarm. The new guy is lighting up. Returning to his vehicle. Stand down. No, wait. Osman's not happy. Targets on the move. Osman making his way to the rear. Two up in the front, as before. It's an off, off, off. I repeat, it's an off, off.'

'Unit 3: I'm with you. Terry, do a forensic sweep. The tail-end car will pick you up.'

'That's received, boss.'

'Jesus!' Frankie said into the phone. 'If they get cold feet, we're in trouble.'

'Not necessarily,' David said.

'You reckon? They'll be on the look if they think that idiot was police. He could have compromised the whole operation.'

'The question you should be asking yourself is, did he?' David told her to get inside their heads, to think of the situation from their point of view, reassuring her that all may not be lost. 'Hold off and let it play out, Frank. They're bound to exercise caution, but they'd be doing that already. And, given what happened on the previous run, the last thing they'll want is to abort a second shipment—'

'I'm not even sure there are kids inside. Since their vehicle was spotted, it's been manned. No chance for the NCA to check it out. We must assume they're carrying. Why else would they be travelling?'

Frankie parked up just off the A1 on the outskirts of Alnwick, the surveillance team keeping her abreast of developments. There had been no detours, no sign of Osman's crew changing plans. As the last surveillance vehicle passed her location, she fell in behind.

In Leith, Mitch was ecstatic, also watching the live video feed. 'We're ready, boss.'

'Good.' Frankie failed to mention her location, though he'd probably guessed that she was mobile. 'Where is everyone?'

'Sheena, Ari, James and I are at the high-rise. José and Kit are watching Thorne's place.' He failed to mention the skinny kid who'd been in and out of the terraced house several times in the past couple of days, photographed on each occasion.

'Any sign of Lewis?' she asked.

'He delivered four pizzas earlier. So at least that many inside the house. Lewis is in his flat now, hopefully keeping his eyes peeled for activity. Otherwise, all quiet this end.'

'Fifteen on their way to you,' Frankie said.

Sixteen if she included herself.

'Cannot wait, boss.'

By the time she reached the outskirts of Edinburgh, Thorne had taken a taxi, Kit and José recording its journey. It had stopped in a side street and so had they. Thorne didn't get out. Frankie suspected that he was waiting for a signal.

En route, the surveillance team had negotiated six roundabouts, some doing a reciprocal to change places, then re-joining at the rear. Four miles further on, the target vehicle entered Constitution Street and pulled to the kerb, also waiting, just a minute or two away from the five-storey terrace Frankie had staked out before involving the National Crime Agency.

This was her time, her moment.

She was hell-bent on making it count.

'Unit 1: I'm stationary. Driver is on the phone. Get ready.'

Frankie lifted her radio: 'Silent but deadly, guys. Right behind you.'

87

Frankie had shed tears of rage just moments before keying in David's number. It took him a while to pick up, answering with his surname only, as he'd done so many times when she'd called him in the middle of the night to report another violent death requiring their attendance – an all too frequent occurrence. Struggling to contain her emotions, she failed to find her voice when he picked up.

'Frank? . . . Frank, is that you?'

'Yes.' She kept her voice low. 'I had to talk to someone.'

'What's wrong?'

'I've been had—'

'What d'you mean?'

'Exactly what I say.' It all came spilling out then, the tension of the past two hours, the euphoria of thinking she was closing in on Osman, then the crushing disappointment and anger that followed. 'Our targets both stopped short of what we thought was their destination.'

'Did you react?'

'No, it would have meant ripping out all our gear. Changing tack. We waited and waited. Nothing happened. Thorne returned home in the same taxi he arrived in. If we speak to him now, he'll just say he was meeting someone who stood him up. This whole operation was a decoy, the OCG testing us, leading us to the location they somehow knew we were watching.'

David swore under his breath. 'And the van?'

'Still there, parked up. They've been one step ahead of us all the way and our time runs out in less than twenty-four hours. We thought Osman was in the rear, until one of the surveillance team we left behind spotted him at Moto Washington South-bound. He's crossed the motorway footbridge twice. With access to the A1 north and south, that's a major headache with the personnel I currently have at my disposal.'

David asked: 'What's he doing now?'

'He's on the south side, under close obs.'

'Then your operation is still live, Frank. Osman wouldn't sit in the rear of that van for three hundred miles just to piss you off. He's here for a reason—'

Her stomach took a dive. 'Could that reason be Amir?'

'I don't think that's likely.'

'Then why are you so anxious?' When he denied it, she exploded. 'Stop lying to me! I can hear it on your voice.'

'Frank, calm down. I'm sorry, you're right. We can't afford to make assumptions. Andy and Rae will be warned to prepare themselves. I'll take care of it myself.'

'Would you? I'm stretched here. If anything happens to Amir, it'll break their hearts.'

'What about yours?'

'Mine's already broken.'

It was out of her mouth before Frankie realised what she'd said. She missed his company, at work and at play, the laughs and camaraderie, a dynamic that was no longer there. Nothing was the same and probably never would be, even if she returned to the MIT. Perhaps she should reconsider and take a posting elsewhere. Kit had already suggested a secondment to the National Crime Agency that could last two to five years. Could she take it up? Should she?

The idea had been percolating . . .

She bit down on her emotions.

Focus!

'I've left the NCA up north watching their end,' she said. 'We can't move on the van until Osman is in custody and we daren't arrest him until we know what he's up to. It's an absolute shit-show, David. Hold on . . .' Osman had reappeared in the café. Behind him, Mitch hung back, pretending to take a call, at the same time observing him. Frankie spoke quietly. 'That's interesting . . .'

'What is?'

Frankie eyed Osman over the top of her laptop, which was open on the table in front of her, cover should she need to drop her head if he glanced her way. The maroon sweatshirt had gone. Shoes too. He was now wearing a plain grey T-shirt, black jeans, black trainers. 'He took nothing with him to the gents, yet he's changed clothes.'

'You're at Washy?' It was his nickname for Moto Washington service station. They often stopped there to fill their faces with Greggs pasties or grab a coffee to go when they were on their way back to base from a sudden death in the early hours.

'Where else?' she said.

'Christ, you must have been shifting.'

'I may have broken one or two laws getting here.'

'I bet. What's Osman doing now?'

'Checking his watch, making a call, giving someone earache, by the looks of it. Nothing seems to be going to plan for either of us. That's about to change. He can count on it. I'd like to rip his head off.'

David warned her to be careful.

'I'll be fine . . . Mitch is with me. I'm too old for him, but we make a lovely couple.' She smiled at her protégé as he retook his seat, returning her greeting. 'He's in character, three pasties up and one waiting.'

David's laughter evaporated. 'Who else is there?'

'We have two bodies stationed outside. Reinforcements on their way. I hope they get here before Osman takes off. We have one NCA car, one motorcycle and my vehicle.'

'Listen, if there's anything else I can do—'

'No, you've done plenty. Thanks for listening. We've got this. We're not there yet, but I know what's required. Until I say so, this isn't over.'

88

David put the phone down, alarmed that Frankie was so thin on the ground, having pulled the mother of all shifts, directing operations remotely to more than one location. She could do anything she set her mind to, except be in two places at once. It was mentally exhausting. Tiredness equalled mistakes. Mistakes that could, in this instance, prove fatal.

She had to stop doing this to him.

As a precaution, he advised Andrea that Osman was in the area before calling her father-in-law, telling him what was going down. Reassured that Frank Oliver would take it from there, David contacted the control room, identifying himself and the reason for his call. He didn't often raise his voice. Sometimes it was necessary to trigger the right response.

This was one of them.

'Where the hell are DI Oliver's reinforcements? This is serious shit, not some Mickey Mouse operation. She needs backup. Now.'

He heard the controller tapping keys, checked his system for the incident. He reported with good news. 'On way, guv.'

'ETA?'

'Three minutes.'

'Make it two.'

On edge, David slammed his mobile down on the bedside table. Sensing a presence, he swung round. Ben was standing in the doorway, wearing only boxer shorts. For a split second, neither spoke, the gravity and urgency of the situation like a dark cloud hanging over them, a serious issue they were both aware of that neither wanted to discuss.

Ben took the lead. 'What's going on?'

'Go back to bed,' David said. 'This doesn't concern you.'

'Like hell it doesn't! I was wide awake. I heard every word you said.' He stood his ground. 'You think you're the only one who adores her, Dave? She gave us both a second chance. We've got our shit together because of her.'

'You think I don't know that?'

'And, just so you know, I'm not leaving because of you, so don't take it personally. I'm ready to move on. That's all there is to it. You know that too, right? I don't care what you're up to either, but Frankie's like a big sister to me. If she's in danger, I have a right to know. I swear on her life, it won't go any further.'

Frankie felt foolish for having been duped. In policing, it had happened more times than she cared to remember, though never on such a large scale and with so much at stake. The O in OCG was there for a reason. She wondered if she'd underestimated Osman. He appeared to have moved swiftly up in the pecking order. He was highly organised. She couldn't deny that he had the upper hand. It wouldn't happen again. From now on, she'd shadow every move he made.

On her instruction, one of the National Crime Agency officers, posing as a toilet cleaner, had retrieved the clothing Osman had dumped in the bin in the gents toilets. It was a calculated risk; one she'd considered carefully before making her call. Anyone with any sense would go back and check if it was still there. She didn't want to think about that. If there was evidence to find, DNA to collect, she couldn't afford to miss it.

Osman hadn't spoken to a soul in the service station since he'd been spotted by the NCA, which raised the question over his new wardrobe. She looked across the room, wondering if while she watched him, one of his crew was watching her.

No one stood out.

Didn't mean they weren't there.

She had no way of knowing if Osman or any of his cohorts might be armed, though there were no weapons found on the driver and co-driver of the van involved in the head-on collision from which he made a miraculous escape. Then again, he may have removed them before he fled the scene.

A Northumbria detective Frankie knew walked past the window, throwing her an inconspicuous nod that doubled as a thumbs up. Her reinforcements had arrived. She relaxed, eyes on Osman. Whatever this low life's plans were, she would see to it that they failed – and that wasn't all. If Simon Thorne was Osman's guv'nor, she'd bring him down too.

To do that, she needed assistance.

It was on its way.

89

Andrea's call sign, Tango 7003, hit the airwaves reporting a white transit van with a Hastings registration plate heading into Moto Washington Southbound, a vehicle that had been reported stolen two days prior, only thirty-five miles east of Brighton. She had no details of any identifying number on the roof of the van but, having checked the VRN, she put two and two together and hit the jackpot.

Andrea was stationed in an unmarked police vehicle at the entrance to the car park; fellow Traffic cop, Tango 5285, Sam Casey, taking up the same position northbound. To have these two reliable officers on her team would give Frankie the edge in a car chase, though that was the last thing she wanted if kids were inside.

Still, it was her job to consider all possibilities, not only the obvious ones.

If the worst came to the worst, the van would be stopped safely using a rolling road. There were no officers more skilled at slowing and stopping a vehicle travelling at high speed. The precious cargo, if there was one, would be uppermost in their minds, whereas Osman would prioritise his freedom above all else.

Therein lay the rub.

Frankie had witnessed many a stop go horribly wrong, injuring officers in the process, and on more than one sad occasion, even ending lives. Her plan was to follow the target vehicle to its destination, not panic its driver into doing something that could cause a major RTA like the one she'd experienced on her first outing in Berwick.

She'd never forget it.

A few minutes earlier, Osman had taken a call, immediately leaving his seat, again crossing the footbridge with Frankie tracking his journey this time, leaving Mitch on the southside. Her target appeared to be in a hurry, checking over his shoulder every now and then. With no hiding place on the well-lit footbridge, and few people about, Frankie had to time her entry with precision.

Having negotiated that obstacle, the worst scenario she could imagine became a reality. Osman turned. He was now heading towards her, a dangerous moment, for her and Operation Zenith. She was alone and exposed with nowhere to go . . .

Except down.

Should Osman manage to break a window and throw her over the side, with vehicles thundering past in both directions on the motorway below, she wouldn't stand a chance. The road noise she hadn't noticed, until now, was deafening.

She stopped walking, looking down at the traffic.

It brought on a second flashback of where her investigation began: torrential rain, car headlights, onlookers, a mass of mangled metal and casualties with no hope of survival. Frankie was more fortunate.

But for how long?

Pulling her phone, she tapped the hash key several times, a pretence. Keeping her voice steady, she alerted Mitch. 'Hey, Mum. What are you doing up at this hour?' He wasn't on the other end of the line. He'd receive her coded message through his earpiece from the covert microphone attached to her clothing.

She received his response the same way. 'You in trouble?'

'Maybe . . .' She forced a laugh, her heart kicking a hole in her chest, beating a rapid rhythm in her ear. In her peripheral vision, Frankie estimated that Osman was just twenty metres away. 'Should be with you soon.'

'Osman?'

'Yeah, really good journey.'

Fifteen . . .

'You want backup?'

'No breakfast, Mum. I'm stuffed.'

Ten . . .

'That's received, boss.'

Five . . .

Breathe, breathe.

Frankie slid the mobile into her pocket in case she needed two hands, her body convulsing involuntarily as Osman passed her. He didn't see her reaction and kept walking. She'd make sure he didn't see her again until she was slapping the cuffs on.

Mitch's voice arrived in her earpiece. 'All clear, boss . . . Move it. Osman's making his way to the stolen van. I'll follow. Tango 7003 will swing by and pick you up.'

Frankie took off at speed, slowing as she reached the door to the car park. Right on time, Andrea pulled up in a covert surveillance vehicle, rather than her usual liveried patrol car, a grey hoodie concealing her uniform.

Frankie jumped in. 'Fuck me, that was a close call!'

90

Frankie looked on as Osman reached the van. Even from a distance, she could see clearly. He climbed into the front, slamming the door, pulling his seat belt across his chest, barking orders at his driver, his hands going twenty to the dozen. She lifted a pair of 8x40 binoculars, adjusting the focus, the better to see her target.

He gave the driver a backhander.

Frankie thought she knew why.

He'd been made to wait and soon it would be dawn. Osman's plan to carry out his odious business in the dark had failed. In daylight, the risk would increase exponentially, especially where children were involved. The public tended to notice kids. If they were crying, were being roughly handled, or were of an age when a right-minded person would consider it appropriate that they should be tucked up in bed, they might call the law. At this unearthly hour, Osman was done for unless he got a shift on, a thought Frankie shared with Andrea.

'Depends how far they're going,' she replied. 'Sadly, they have options.'

Waiting for the off, Frankie turned to face her. 'Where are Rae and Amir now?'

'The less you know about that the better.'

'Don't you start. I've had all the cloak-and-dagger I can handle.'

'Where do you think they are, dozy?'

Frankie relaxed.

They were with her parents, no better place to be.

Her father would be wide awake, his firearms cabinet unlocked, a shotgun that rarely saw the light of day, prepared.

Should someone burst through the door to retrieve their lost cargo, he'd use it, no matter the consequences. What he wouldn't do was rest until Frankie brought her investigation to a close. She was hoping to do that in the next few hours, avoiding a bloodbath, and incarceration for her father should he take such action. As a former cop who should know better, any term of imprisonment would be lengthy.

He'd do whatever was necessary.

In his eyes, it would be worth it.

Sensing her unease, Andrea leaned across, squeezing Frankie's hand.

She expelled her anxiety with a big sigh. 'Amir looked so settled when I called at your place. I was hoping he could stay put. After what he's been through, I can't begin to imagine what it was like being dragged from his bed in the dead of night and moved to yet another location. Poor bugger.'

'I agree it wasn't ideal. Couldn't be helped, Frank. He's fine. He's safe. So is Rae. Your dad will take good care of them.' Andrea made a funny face. 'I reckon they have their fingers crossed that you'll find more kids who need help. I get the impression they'd like a houseful.'

'That's not even remotely humorous.'

'Not even a little bit?'

Now, Frankie smiled.

'That's better,' Andrea said. 'We need our minds on the job, not on worst-case scenarios.'

In dire circumstance, they had the power to lift each other. They had formed an unbreakable bond in training school, unaware that they would eventually become in-laws. Frankie was about to say something, when her mobile rang, cutting off the conversation.

It was David.

Her index finger hovered over the home screen.

'Don't mind me . . .' Andrea had spotted David's image as the phone lit up. She never missed an opportunity to play Cupid. 'Take it — I won't listen in, I promise. And if I accidentally on purpose hear something I shouldn't, I'll keep it to myself. How's that?'

'Stay out. How's that?' Frankie swiped the screen to answer. 'Hey! How come you're still up?' It was a daft question she knew the answer to.

'You're awake, I'm awake,' he said. 'And so is half the force, by the sounds of it, including the guv'nor. He asked me to let you know that he's obtained a warrant for your Leith address. He has a sheriff on hand to issue more should you require them urgently. I have a judge on standby locally. I'm kicking my heels for a couple of hours if you need me.'

'Nah, go back to bed. Lack of sleep is a killer.'

Andrea whispered. 'Lack of sleep?'

Frankie whispered back. 'Nowt to do with me.'

'I heard that,' David said.

'Big ears!' Andrea laughed as she started the car. 'Here we go!'

Through the front windscreen, Frankie saw the tail end of the van disappear onto a slip road shrouded in mist. 'Gotta go, David. We're moving. And don't worry. You can't get shifted for our lot. Once she knew where I was, and what I was doing, Andy couldn't help herself. You can stand down. We're winning.'

'Never figured you for a loser, Frank.'

She hung up, a smile developing.

Andrea was staring at her.

Frankie shrugged. 'What?'

'Never said a word.'

91

Beyond the service station, on the open road, they were faced with dense fog. The carriageways looked eerie, traffic slowing due to restricted visibility and the added complication of congestion from roadworks that seemed to have gone on for years, a nightmare for locals and visitors alike.

'We could do without this.' Frankie meant the weather.

'Every cloud, Frank. That's not a euphemism, it's additional cover I didn't expect. It was clear when I arrived.'

'You must have X-ray eyes. I can't see a bloody thing.'

In complete control, Andrea was doing what she did best, directing operations over the radio, advising all units that the target vehicle had pulled off the A1(M) southbound at junction 63. Two cars behind, she followed to a T-junction its driver unexpectedly ignored. Failing to give way, he shot across a roundabout, completing a 360-degree turn, re-joining the same motorway, travelling in the opposite direction. He was changing lanes, driving above the reduced speed limit in the fast lane.

'That's a traffic violation you can add to his charge sheet,' Andy said.

'The least of his worries.' Frankie feared another major RTA if he didn't slow down. 'What the hell is the idiot doing? If that's his best anti-surveillance technique, he'd be rubbish as a getaway driver.'

'Harsh. He's giving it a go, exactly what I'd have done in his position.' Andrea was poised, her eyes glued to the road ahead, her voice flat calm. 'That's what I meant by options. No worries, we have the advantage. My team know this area like the back of their hands. We have unmarked cars stationed at every possible exit. Our targets are leading us where we want to go. Believe me, this'll be a breeze.'

Frankie wasn't so sure.

As the thought entered her head, the van suddenly veered across three lanes of traffic, off at junction 65, onto an A-road, entering a populated area, adding complications for pursuit vehicles, not to mention putting other road users and anyone inside the van at risk.

Andrea updated her team.

A few miles on, she suggested that Osman was heading for Sunderland.

'How d'you know?'

'That's what the sign says.'

Frankie laughed. 'He could double back—'

'Call it sixth sense. Isn't it time to check where the shite lives?'

Frankie grabbed her laptop from the rear seat. Opening it up, she logged on, searching the force-wide intelligence system to find which areas of the city were home to known paedophiles or anyone convicted of crimes against children. The numbers were hard to take.

'Cancel that,' Andy said. 'He's heading for Pennywell.'

After a bit of persuasion that included pulling rank, Control had patched David into the designated radio channel of Frankie's incident. He listened intently to the chat before deciding what to do. He had his own investigation to conduct, but Frankie's was critical. And Indira was probably still asleep. He sent a text she'd see the minute she woke:

Might be late in. Our suspect was involved in some high-profile cases. He may have been interviewed by the press. Check it out.

He was surprised to receive a reply:

Will do, guv. Anything else?

Don't forget the vehicle logbooks from the archives. I'll be in later to give you a hand.

Got it.

David grabbed his jacket and car keys. Slipping his ID into his pocket, he cancelled the alarm on his mobile. Switching off his bedside light, he left the room and came face to face with Ben. He looked like shit, sweaty hair stuck to his forehead, dark circles under his eyes, his face pale.

'Not now, son. I must go—'

'Where to?'

'To help Frankie. We both want that, right?'

Ben was nodding. 'Can I come?'

'Not without a warrant card.'

92

By the time Osman arrived on the outskirts of Pennywell, a large post-war housing estate in the central-west area of Sunderland, Frankie had all the intel she required on offenders who might involve themselves in the kind of operation her target was conducting.

Andrea was taking care of everything else.

Legitimate employment was hard to come by here, the chance to make easy money too great a temptation for those who couldn't afford to eat. Social and financial deprivation was rife, though Frankie had dealt with honest, incorruptible folk trying to eke out an existence in the face of such a harsh environment.

'Any hits?' Andrea asked.

'A few.' Frankie had honed her search the closer they got, first by area, then street by street.

She didn't know why, but one of the names flagged was familiar. Perhaps someone she'd locked up when she was in the CID. She'd check it out later. Instead of heading further into the estate, Osman's van veered off.

Andrea was on it immediately. 'Tango 7003, they're taking a left-left into the industrial estate . . . Anyone fancy a KFC?'

'I do, I'm bloody starving.' Sam Casey didn't bother with her call sign. 'Boss, I know the estate well. There's a lot of wasteland and dense woods to the north and playing fields beyond. If they get in there we'll have a problem finding them.'

Andrea pulled over, eyes on the satnav. 'If we get runners, we might need an eye in the sky, Frank. Your call.'

Frankie requested the police helicopter. 'I have a major incident with numerous suspects. If they run, we may need help. What's their status, Control?'

'They're on the ground, Newcastle airport.'

'ETA?'

'Thirteen minutes.'

'Get them in the air . . .' She gave coordinates, explaining briefly what was going on. 'Dog section also required. Silent approach. Park on Hylton Road and await my shout.'

'That's received, Inspector.'

Andrea took over. 'You heard that, guys. We need bodies on foot and the place surrounded at once. There's one way in, one out, in a vehicle. Plenty of options on foot. I want cars at either end. And officers in position to the north. Unit 2, park up in Hastings Hill. Unit 3, take Hylton Road. Unit 4, drive through and observe. On two wheels you'll look like someone arriving for work.'

In a flash, the motorcycle overtook.

There was a short pause before she reported: 'Unit 4: there's an unidentified van parked on the northern perimeter road, two up.' She gave the registration. 'I just passed them. Target vehicle is parked at the northern extremity of Prestbury Road. No movement yet. Large derelict building to the north-west of them. Pulling away now.'

'Unit 3: in position, I have the eyeball.'

Andrea was on it. '7003: all patrol cars make your way to this area. Do not, I repeat, do not approach from the east or the north. Park out of sight. Units 5 and 6, drop your passengers on Penistone Road. All officers on foot to cover the wasteland.'

Again, Frankie waited.

'Unit 3: nothing happening, boss.'

As the seconds ticked by, Frankie wiped her face with her hands, then rotated her head to ease the tension in her neck and shoulders.

Things that felt right often weren't.

'Unit 3: target and his driver are out of the vehicle having a tab. The unidentified vehicle maintaining its position. No, wait, his lights are on. He's driving away. One male, one female. Early morning shag, I reckon. Nowt to do with us.'

Once out of the industrial estate, they'd be stopped.

'I'm on the southern edge of the woods,' an officer reported. 'Roller doors being lifted. All units, stand by for an update.'

'Unit 3: target and driver making their way to the rear.'

Frankie slapped the dash, lifting her radio: 'We have at least three, possibly four in play, potentially more inside. No one move until I say so. Osman and his driver are the prime movers. We take them first.'

93

David smiled. Parked in a lay-by near the industrial estate, he waited. When the chips were down, Frankie excelled. Her voice, like those of her crew, carried a mixture of excitement and tension. That was good. It would keep everyone alert. They'd all be pumped up, adrenalin surging, focused only on their targets. Taking them down would be a big milestone for a recently promoted detective inspector. Frankie wasn't anyone's DI. She was *his*. David wouldn't interfere. He was there as insurance.

She could pull this off . . .

She would.

The words — *we take them first* — echoed in his head. That was her all over: professional, committed, fine-tuned to danger. She'd found Amir in a sorry state. In time, David hoped she'd forget the trauma of that terrible night. For now, as the OIC, there wasn't a hope in hell of her letting Osman escape justice.

Reading the situation, she wouldn't need a warrant. She'd wait to see what came next. If any minors were taken from the target vehicle and led towards the derelict building Unit 4 had mentioned, as soon as they crossed the threshold, that's when she'd rush in and make arrests. Except that wasn't happening.

With no sight of the scene, David was feeling the strain more than most, imagination in overdrive. Though he was willing it to happen, nothing was going down.

The radio was ominously quiet.

94

'Unit 2: we are three up behind the derelict building. We've got scaffy bars and heavy-duty pallets in case they try and slam the roller doors shut before we get in there. No rear exit. Small, high windows. Can't see in. They're covered with newspaper. Boss, the date on one of them is recent, only a month old.'

'7003 to Control: I require an ambulance on standby. Please have this channel monitored. Coordinated strike required. Alert DI Kit Matthews on my GO signal. She'll hit the Leith end of Zenith.'

'Understood.'

Andrea glanced across the car.

Frankie was like a lion, ready to pounce.

Andrea was about to wish her luck, when Unit 2's raised voice hit the airwaves. 'Two distressed minors visible. One boy. Fair hair. Around six years old. One girl. Long blonde hair. Similar age. They're resisting. Targets dragging them inside—'

'Control and all units, go-go-go!' Frankie was out of the car before it came to a stop. She ran towards the building as two unidentified males ran out. She yelled, 'We have runners!'

The shutter door was closing. She wasn't going to make it. The first on scene jammed it open. It stopped only two feet from the ground. Frankie rolled underneath, probably the only one who could.

'Police! Police!'

She scrambled to her feet, listening.

It was dark inside, a cavernous space much bigger than it looked from the outside. Someone was using a scaffolding pole to lever the shutter door open, swearing when it held fast. She could hear one of her team crawling in behind her and kids weeping, a sound that instantly transported her to the crash site she'd attended on her first shift in Berwick.

Amir was in her head.

Using her flashlight, she aimed it at the roof void to check that no one was up there ready to pounce, then down again, a sweep of a brick wall at the rear that looked ready to collapse. Two boys were cowering in one corner, wide-eyed, their faces filthy, one wearing wire-rimmed specs with a lens smashed . . . both had dark hair.

Shit.

These kids were Asian, nothing like those described by Unit 2. Looked like they'd been held captive for days. A slight vibration passed through the broken concrete beneath Frankie's feet as India 99, the police helicopter, flew overhead, a deafening roar.

Movement.

Frankie pointed the flashlight.

Osman's driver ran to the rear of the building, leapt onto an old wooden crate, ripping down the newspapers taped to the rear window, using his elbow to smash the glass, an attempt to flee. The uniform who'd followed Frankie in dragged him kicking and screaming to floor level. With a slither of glass, held like a dagger, the driver fought hard, slashing the cop across the cheek.

There was mayhem as they wrestled with each other. Frankie made no move to intervene in the fight or assist her wounded colleague. As bad as his situation appeared to be, she was facing a more imminent complication. Osman had pushed the fair-haired boy away, grabbing the girl, a knife to her neck.

Witnessing the girl's terror first-hand, Frankie felt responsible. She could've stopped the van earlier. She'd chosen not to. The thought vanished as quickly as it came. What her father had stated when they last spoke was now so obvious. If she didn't take this evil sociopath down, he'd continue to trade in humans.

Making no attempt to run, Osman smiled at her, a flash of recognition from the moment he'd passed her on the Washington footbridge, a sinister smile that required no interpretation. He had nothing to lose and would go down fighting.

She'd seen that look a thousand times . . .

Was he willing to die, though?

Was he willing to kill?

A stand-off.

A second officer crept under the roller door.

Frankie spoke without turning round. 'Don't. Move.'

Seeing what she could see, whoever was there froze. She could feel the officer breathing down her neck. A shard of glass slid across the floor, kicked away by her injured colleague. Whether he'd sent it her way, deliberately or accidentally, she didn't know. He'd got the better of Osman's driver, who was pinned to the floor, his face pushed hard against broken rubble.

The squawk of her radio filled the air.

Outside, runners had made it as far as the wasteland. Air support and dogs were in pursuit. With Osman's back turned, the boy took his chance to run towards Frankie, the other two following his lead. One by one, she gently passed them to whoever was standing behind her.

'Get them out of here. Tell everyone else to stay back.'

He urged the boys to leave. 'Go, you're safe now! That's it, join hands, now go!'

As they scrambled through the gap, the officer relayed her instructions to the outside team. Frankie heard no reply, or if she did, it didn't register. Her eyes remained fixed on the little girl in front of her.

'I want Mummy,' she sobbed.

'It's OK, sweetheart. We'll have you out of here soon, I promise.' Frankie looked at Osman, her anger matched only by her courage. 'Is that the best you can do, hide behind a defenceless child?'

He understood perfectly.

She was aware of her colleagues breaking in behind her and wished they would hurry. Right on cue, the roller door was forced open, intermittent flashing blue lights illuminating Osman's cold, dark eyes.

'I reckon that's checkmate, don't you?' Frankie looked on as he tightened his grip on the girl. A trickle of blood ran down her neck. 'Easy, Osman. Don't make this worse than it already is. This will not end well, you know that. Lose the knife. Get down on the ground.'

He threw his head back, laughing.

He flung the girl to the ground.

'Run!' Frankie yelled.

The bairn was frozen to the spot, shaking uncontrollably.

Osman flew at Frankie.

Her self-defence training immediately kicked in. She turned her body in time to avoid a knife in the chest, the blade striking her arm instead. Unimaginable pain as it passed through, even worse as Osman pulled it out – and enjoyed doing it. Feeling dizzy, she fell to the concrete floor, clutching her arm, trying to stem the bleeding. He lifted the knife and was about to strike again, when he was overpowered, bellowing as he was manhandled outside. Frankie rolled on to her back, looking into the roof void, a glimpse of the sun through a dirty skylight that might easily have been her last.

95

Shrugging off the paramedic's attempt to get her in a wheelchair, Frankie walked to the ambulance. David was the first person she saw as she made it outside. He was standing with his back to her, talking to Andrea. She said something, nodding over his shoulder. He turned to face Frankie. As their eyes met, she smiled. He waited for the ambulance crew to apply a tourniquet and dress her wound before taking his leave of Andrea.

She hung back, allowing them a moment's privacy.

'You OK?' David asked.

'You're a bit late if you've come to save me. It would've been quicker calling the coastguard—'

'You didn't need saving, Frank. You smashed it. Proud of you.'

'Is this the part when you tell everyone you taught me all I know?'

'No, you did the hard yards. You deserve the credit.'

His eyes travelled down her body, coming to rest on her bloodied clothing. She could tell he was upset, probably back in that room with Jane bleeding from a gunshot wound, reliving a trauma he'd been trying so hard to forget, another relationship cut short.

Now, he met her gaze. 'Christ, he could've killed you.'

'Hey, lighten up. I'm still here.' She dropped her head to one side. 'If only I'd known that a near-death experience would be enough for you to make time in your busy schedule for me, I'd have got a shift on.'

'Frank—' His mobile rang, killing the moment. He checked the screen before looking up at her. 'It's Indi. I'm sorry, I need to take this.'

'Go on, piss off. I'm fine.'

A half-smile. 'I'll see you around.'

'Not if I see you first.'

'Get going . . .' He nodded towards the ambulance. 'I'll call you later.'

She watched him walk to his car, a glance her way as he climbed in, his mobile stuck to his ear. As he drove off, others wandered up to check on her, exhaustion replaced by elation and relief that she'd got off lightly. Five arrests had been made: the two runners who'd legged it, a guy who'd been hiding in the rear of the van, Osman and his driver. The building had been searched; the scene preserved.

Receiving confirmation that the place was secure, Frankie gave the go-ahead for a team of CSIs to enter the building to do their stuff. The offenders were en route to the cells, in separate vehicles so they had no chance of getting their story straight before the interview process could begin.

She suspected they wouldn't all speak English.

She'd been told that Osman pretended not to.

He'd soon be persuaded otherwise.

If not, he could go to hell.

Last to arrive at Frankie's side, unable to give her a proper cuddle, Andrea gave her a gentle pat on the back, using humour to comfort her. 'I always knew you were a headcase. Before I met Rae, I pulled a few strokes in my time to attract women.' She grinned. 'Getting stabbed is a bit OTT, isn't it? Mind you, it worked. I saw how David looked at you—'

'It's called concern—'

'Is it shite!'

The fog had lifted by the time David reached the main road. He'd been close to losing his shit at the crime scene. Now he was out of sight, he dropped his window, sucking in a lungful of fresh air. Indira was upbeat on the phone. Having received his text, she'd gone in early. He could tell from her tone that there had been a significant development.

She'd found something.

Too wired to ask what it was, his head filled with images of Frankie's blood-soaked clothing, the truth was he wasn't ready to hear what Indi had to say, let alone process it. Frankie had survived. She was on her feet, still breathing, still talking, keeping it together. If it had gone the wrong way, he'd be on his way to give her father the death message.

'Guv, you still there?'

'Yeah, signal's crap. Heading in now.'

Indi bought his body swerve. 'ETA?'

'Ten, fifteen, no longer.'

'Use your blues, guv. It's dynamite.'

Three of the four minors had been taken to hospital – the boy who'd just arrived in one unmarked car, the two who'd been there longer in another, uniformed officers on hand to comfort them. Frankie couldn't take her eyes off the little girl in the ambulance. She was pale and traumatised, her neck receiving attention from a female paramedic. Her blonde hair was tangled and bloodied, her enormous eyes fixed on Frankie, whose anger rose to the surface.

She looked away to hide it.

The child would be seeing Osman in her dreams for months, if not years to come. She'd feel his vice-like arm across her throat. She'd smell his skin. She'd hear his maniacal laughter – as would Frankie. It had sent a chill right through her.

She turned to Andrea. 'Can I borrow your jacket?'

'You cold?'

'No, I want to speak to the girl before they take her to hospital. I can't do it looking like this.'

Andrea slipped off her jacket and handed it over. Frankie put it on, buttoning it up. Like the high-viz jacket Graham Ross had given her to put on the night this shitshow began, it was too big.

That didn't concern her.

A female paramedic was kneeling beside the little girl, holding her hands, talking gently to her. Like Amir, the kid wasn't responding, though Frankie hoped she would. She'd already spoken.

I want Mummy.

Andrea said, 'What's wrong?'

'Nothing . . . everything.' Frankie sighed, wiping her eye. 'Sorry, I'm a bit emosh, that's all.'

'I'm not surprised.' Andrea gestured towards her vehicle. 'Get in. I'll drive you to hospital. You're in no fit state to see the girl now.'

'No, look at her. She's staring at me. Waiting for me. She saw him stab me, Andy. I can't just disappear. As soon as they're done with her, I'll have a quick chat, then I'll go, I promise.' Frankie didn't dwell on it while they waited, though she did sit down in the wheelchair she'd refused earlier. Her arm was sore. Her hand was tingling. She felt shaky. 'Any idea what's happening in Leith and Hove?'

'I do . . .' Andrea explained that hitting all locations simultaneously had been successful. 'Kit moved in as soon as you did. She has five in custody, including the bloke you saw at the window of the Leith property and a woman, mid-twenties, neither of whom have yet been identified.'

'Did they get Lewis, the skinny kid?'

'Yeah, though he resisted arrest . . .' Andrea grinned. 'Sheena flattened him, a fine rugby tackle Kit said was worthy of Sam Underhill, whoever he is.' Frankie was smiling. Unlike Kit, she and Andy were footy fans who thought that anyone who played with an odd-shaped ball was off their trolley. 'Let's just say our pizza delivery boy learned a lesson in physics,' Andrea added. 'As Kit put it, his nose is out of joint in more ways than one. He'll never look the same again.'

'An improvement then.'

Andrea laughed.

Frankie asked, 'What about the Hove property?'

'The NCA captured four. Both scenes are being processed.'

'And Thorne?'

'In custody. As soon as he was made aware of what was going

315

down, the sheriff issued search warrants. Kit found nowt at Thorne's home.'

'What about his office?'

'It was a front. She discovered enough there to arrest him on suspicion of child trafficking, over a million in cash, several mobiles—'

'None of which is against the law,' Frankie said.

'Hold on! I haven't told you the good bits yet. Thorne is no more Scottish than you are Welsh. His passport was good enough to allow him to come and go, but it's fake. Remember the tab end he discarded at Gatwick?'

'What about it?'

'Kit sent the sample to Interpol. His real name is Victor Ivanov. No previous. Born and brought up in Burgas on the Black Sea coast, which links him geographically with Petkov and Mitev's last-known address. No judge alive will believe that's a coincidence. All you need to do is prove it.'

'You can count on it.'

96

Ben called David's mobile as he reached Middle Earth, asking what was going on. Getting out of his car, he downplayed Frankie's injuries so his nephew wouldn't worry unnecessarily. He'd rather tell him face to face than have him sweat over it. This parenting lark was difficult. Shielding a lad of Ben's age from the darker side of life was as crucial as it was exhausting. Making an excuse that he was due in a meeting, deflecting any awkward questions coming his way, David disconnected.

Inside the building, he took the stairs two at a time, keen to liaise with Indira. As he neared Bright's office, the double doors along the corridor crashed open. Dick rushed towards him, a grim expression, the weight of the world on his shoulders. Only to be expected. Like wildfire, word would have spread that Frankie had been attacked by Osman. Details would be sketchy, her injuries non-specific. She was popular among the MIT. Every one of her former colleagues would be desperate for news.

'Guv, I've been trying to get hold of you,' he said. 'Frankie's been stabbed—'

'Yeah, I know. I was there.'

Dick didn't ask why. 'How bad is it?'

'She sustained a nasty arm injury. No arterial damage.' Had there been, she'd have quickly lost consciousness and died within minutes. David kept that to himself. 'Relax, Dick. She's in no danger. Probably on her way to hospital now, assuming the paramedics managed to drag her from the crime scene—'

'You didn't think to go along?'

'Andy's with her. Reassure the team that she's OK—'

Dick frowned. 'Wouldn't you rather do it?'

David resented the dig. 'You're my 2i/c, so do your fucking job and deputise, unless you'd like to update the guv'nor and call her father before someone else does?' It was a lie. Both Bright and Frank Snr had been notified. 'What's it to be?'

'I'll summon the team, guv. Apologies.'

David ran his fingers through his hair, leaving his hand on the top of his head. 'I'm sorry for being a twat. Between Ben and Frankie, I've had zero hours' kip in the last few days. I'll let her know that you're all asking after her.' He reached for the door, dying to get away, with no calls to make. His real priority was Indira's explosive revelation.

As soon as Frankie reached hospital, she had an MRI, then was whipped into theatre to undergo a surgical procedure to reattach the torn edges of a damaged nerve. Coming round, she'd received a visit from the consultant surgeon, who told her that her operation had gone well. Osman had missed the brachial artery. She'd probably make a full recovery.

Frankie looked at him. 'Probably?'

'There's a small chance of peripheral neuropathy.'

'Which means?'

'You may experience residual numbness, muscle weakness from time to time. You're fit. It'll not affect your ability to do your job. Mind you, it'll take three or four weeks to heal properly. You've been lucky, Detective Inspector. We'll give you something to ease the pain and an outpatient appointment to remove the stitches, another for physio.'

'When can I get out of here?'

'Tomorrow, if you feel up to it.'

Frankie didn't argue.

As he left her bedside, she shut her eyes, still groggy from the anaesthetic. Floating in the space between sleep and consciousness, she found herself back at the crime scene, staring into the eyes of the terrified little girl Osman had taken hostage. She'd told the paramedic that her name was Lexie.

No surname.

It occurred to Frankie that Lexie could be a given name or a shortening of Alexandra, Alexa or Alexis. She reached for her mobile and sent Mitch a message to run it through the system and make it a priority to trace her family. The girl was a little older than Amir, equally distressed, as concerned about Frankie as she was about her.

'Does it hurt?' Lexie had asked.

'Not much.' Frankie smiled. 'How are you feeling?'

Again, the girl asked for her mummy.

'I'll find her, sweetheart. We'll get you home real soon.' Lexie started to cry, her eyes scanning the scene, expecting company of the worst kind. It was pitiful to watch. Frankie had crouched down. 'Lexie, listen to me. The bad man has gone now . . . He's never ever coming back.'

Lexie hooked her little finger, holding it out. 'Pinky promise?'

The words nearly broke Frankie. Her old man used them when she was a kid. She locked little fingers with Lexie, a promise never to be broken. Now, in her hospital bed, Frankie felt a warm tear roll down the side of her cheek. She brushed it away as someone knocked on the door. Her parents entered, approaching her bedside, her father pulling up a chair for her mother to sit down.

Her eyelids were red and puffy.

'Oh, Mum . . .' Hiding her own emotions, as much as she was able, Frankie reached out her good arm to hold her mother's hand. 'I'm bulletproof, you know that.'

'That's just it,' Julie said. 'You're not. None of us are.'

'I took one for the team, that's all.'

97

Indira lifted her head as David entered the room. He looked more tense and dishevelled than she'd ever seen him, his shirt collar open, his tie askew, his face gaunt. His short ETA had stretched to almost two hours. She didn't know where he'd been, or why the delay, only that he'd been ignoring all calls.

A moment ago, in the locker room, Indira had overheard a row developing in the corridor beyond. David had put Dick Abbott in his place. It was unlike him to lose his temper . . . with anyone. While she was on tenterhooks, keen to deliver news that would impress and shock him equally, she got up and made coffee, strong and black.

Handing it to him, she enquired after Frankie.

'She's out of surgery,' he said. 'I just got off the phone with her old man.'

'She's going to be OK though, right?'

Answering with a nod, David took a sip of coffee, then put his mug down on the table. 'What have you got for me?'

'You asked me to look at historical press releases. It wasn't an easy trawl. None during our timeline were computerised, which was unhelpful. I spent three hours searching through microfiche and found nothing before Joanna's death—'

'And afterwards?'

'An entirely different story. I have something you should see.'

Turning her laptop to face him, she watched his reaction as he zoomed in on the screen. It took him a moment to process what he was looking at, an old press release for a good collar, their prime suspect standing in the police pound, posing for the camera, a dark-coloured Ford in the background, a J plate visible.

The image included a date stamp . . .

It was as clear as day.

'What do you think?' Indira asked.

'Not quite enough, but halfway home.' It was a bittersweet moment for them both. He slid her laptop towards her. 'Did you share it with the guv'nor?'

She shook her head. 'I thought I should talk to you first.'

'Keep it to yourself.'

'I was wondering if Jack Gale might ID our suspect from that photo. Until now, his evidence was peripheral, not even circumstantial: white male, mid-twenties, brown hair. That doesn't fit with what he looks like now, but it does with what he looked like at that time.'

'Agreed. We're homing in on what's important. And what's important is all pointing in the same direction. Did you get hold of the vehicle logbooks?'

'No, but I did locate them. They're at headquarters.'

'You carry on, I'll go.'

'You sure, guv?'

'Absolutely.' Shuffling his chair away from his desk, David stood up, straightening his tie, tucking the tail of his shirt into his trousers, trying to make himself presentable. 'I need to get out of here.'

98

Frankie's parents left her to rest. Uneasy, unable to settle, her eyes travelled around the soulless room. She'd spent too long as a patient in clinical places like this, so had Andrea and other officers injured in the line of duty. There had been times when the rubber heelers had come knocking. The first question most Professional Standards detectives asked was had the officers concerned done their jobs properly? Could their injuries have been prevented?

They made her sick.

On each occasion, she been quick to point to the fact that their injuries were criminal, not accidental, and that some had not survived to tell the tale. It was beginning to hit home how fortunate she'd been. There was no doubt in her mind that Osman had meant to kill her and would be facing a charge of attempted murder, on top of everything else. Contemplating her mortality was draining, until a text arrived from David, lifting her spirits, giving her something less morbid to think about.

Hey, I hear you've been stitched up.

Well and truly. Feel like I've downed six G&Ts.

Lucky you. Feel like I've been hit by a bus.

You got any gear you could spare? Clothes, not weed.

No, and I know where this is leading. Not a good idea, Frank.

C'mon! Dad took mine. I'll look like a wally if I walk out of here in what I'm wearing.

Then do yourself a favour. Stay put.

You used to be fun.

Still am. 😉

Frankie smiled at the winking emoji. She waited for more. None came. Before she could send another text, Kit stuck her head around the door, bearing gifts: magazines, chocolate and soft drinks, enough to last a week.

'You can take them home,' Frankie said. 'I'm out of here as soon as I can find some clothes.'

'Don't look at me,' Kit said. 'I'm under strict instructions not to aid and abet your flight from here . . .' Placing her unwanted gifts on the bedside table, she flung herself down in a chair, staring at Frankie. 'No point asking how you feel. I've seen better-looking stiffs.'

'Have you looked in the mirror lately?'

Kit looked tired, as would the rest of her crew, including and especially the surveillance teams who'd been driving all night. Frankie was grateful for their intervention. There was no way she'd have coped without them.

'What's going on?' she asked.

Kit blew out a breath. 'Scientific aides are working hard at all three locations. They're turning Thorne's place over, recovering any items we can use to convict him further down the line, including financial records.'

Frankie nodded.

She didn't need telling that the National Crime Agency's focus would be on instances when money changed hands, identifying where it came from, and whether those transactions coincided with human-trafficking operations. It went without saying that Thorne's assets, physical and financial, could and would be seized.

'Did you manage to ID any of the offenders up north?' Frankie asked.

'Some. It'll take time to identify them all.'

'There will be a media blackout in the meantime?'

'Yes, it's all in hand. The Scottish lot will be interviewed by the NCA in Glasgow. I'd like to transport Osman and his cohorts south and put them before a court down there. I'm guessing Andrea filled you in on numbers?'

'Yeah. Great job.'

Kit hesitated.

Frankie knew what was coming.

It didn't take long to arrive.

'You're going to be out of action for a while, Frank. I need to take the wheel. If we don't crack on, anyone we haven't yet picked up will be in the wind. In any case, you can't interview Osman, much as I'm sure you'd like to.'

Resigned to her fate, Frankie told Kit she understood the need to capitalise while the opportunity was there. 'Operation Zenith was always yours,' she said. 'I'd have liked the collar, but I'm not precious about it.'

'Hey, it's still your collar. My crew know it. So do yours. You'll be our star witness when the case gets to court. You rescued five kids single-handed. Not many can say that. If you don't end up with a handful of commendations, I'd be surprised.'

'I couldn't give a shit about that.' Using her good arm as a prop, Frankie hauled herself up the bed. 'I'm concerned about Lexie, the little girl Osman grabbed—'

'Don't be. Mitch already traced her family. They're on their way up.'

'That's great news. How long was she missing?'

'Three days . . . It would've felt longer.'

Frankie was nodding. 'No wonder she was terrified. Where was she taken from?'

'A playground in Hastings, close to where the second van was stolen. Osman's lot were getting cocky, taking unnecessary risks, exploiting domestic and foreign victims. We've linked him to Lexie—'

'Don't suppose that was hard.' Frankie's tone was sour. 'He had his paws all over her.'

'It's better than that, Frank. We can prove that he was directly involved in her abduction, *before* either of them arrived up north.'

'How come, when you had him under surveillance in Hove?'

'We thought we did, until we picked up his doppelganger. The identifying scar we saw on Sunday was fake.' Kit shrugged.

'It was no happy accident that he looked like Osman either. He was chosen specifically to throw us off track and said as much in interview.'

'Yeah, but Osman's not stupid. If it fooled us, he'll use it to deflect the blame onto his evil twin. At the very least it'll put doubt in the minds of a jury when he comes to court.'

'It won't work.' Kit smiled, oozing confidence. 'Lexie's DNA is on the gear he discarded in the men's room at Washington services – and you followed him directly to the scene. He was never out of your sight.'

Frankie's excitement rose. 'A body double explains why he didn't act like the casualty of a horrific RTA.'

'According to the MO, the real Osman is covered in bruises. We've got him. There's no way he can escape justice now.'

Frankie's elation was fleeting. What they were dealing with was the tip of a bigger iceberg. She imagined the parents of those lost children, and countless others, pinning posters to lamp posts; asking complete strangers if they'd seen their offspring, pleading, begging, waiting for a knock at the door or the telephone to ring with the worst possible news – the only type anyone got to hear about on TV or in the press.

Success didn't sell newspapers.

'What about the other kids?'

'We're still trying to reunite them.' Kit paused. 'That goes for all of them, Amir included . . .' She spotted Frankie's dread before she could hide it. 'Relax, Frank. Given that I'm taking over, Andy felt obliged to share his whereabouts. I gave her my word that it will not appear in any records. She understands that his rights trump all. I'll not stop looking for his family. If they're breathing, I intend to find them.'

Frankie said nothing in return.

What had she done?

99

David drove to Northumbria HQ, satisfied that Frankie was on the mend. As a girl, her life had taken a devastating turn, an incident that had defined her as she grew into the amazing woman he knew. He'd seen her grief materialise on many occasions during murder investigations. Often when she looked at him, all he could see was a tortured soul, driven by a need for justice, despite what it took from her, piercing the armour she hid behind. And yet, she was a survivor with a big heart and compassion for victims few detectives could match.

All David wanted, all he'd ever wanted since discovering the source of her pain, was to give her closure. Her wounds would heal, but the psychological scars of losing Joanna would remain. Pushing away that disturbing thought, he parked his car, entering headquarters under a sky as anaemic as Frankie's complexion when they had spoken at the crime scene.

With help, he located the vehicle logbooks in a small, dusty archive, somewhere deep in the cellar of the building, a windowless room as claustrophobic as the office he shared with Indira at Middle Earth – a space that was beginning to drive him mad.

He scanned grey metal shelving, a bin full of discarded notes and fingerprints in the grime, evidence that someone else had been there recently, a thought that perturbed him. He checked the notes in the bin. None related to his case.

He'd been overthinking.

There were as many reasons to revisit the logbooks as there were for keeping them. They were pink, the size of school exercise books, well-thumbed and grubby from being handled by mechanics who maintained the vehicles. The front covers listed the vehicle registration number as well as the dates they pertained to.

David began with those completed in 1990, two years prior to Joanna's death. He worked chronologically. The hands on the wall clock wound round several revolutions before he was done.

He relaxed into his seat, scanning his handwritten notes.

They included the details of several vehicles favoured by his suspect: times, dates, along with officer IDs and signatures, one of which flew off the page. It gave a first name of his suspect and five words, scribbled in the margin:

Fill your fucking mileage in!

David stared at the entry for a long time. It bore the initials WW and a collar number he'd seen before. This was someone he hadn't anticipated finding, someone he'd not yet interviewed and may have overlooked: Adam Hall's one-time brother-in-law, insurance fraud investigator. William Welch.

100

For four long days, Frankie had been stuck in her apartment, staring out of the window at a world going by without her, with little to keep her occupied. Moping was the perfect way to describe her current mood. She'd been warned not to drive, to keep her injured arm clean and elevated to avoid infection and the possibility of a blood clot, advice she'd been forced to take seriously. Her mother and grandmother had developed deep-vein thrombosis post-surgery which had led, in her nan's case, to a pulmonary embolism requiring immediate medical intervention. Keen to get to work, in whatever capacity, Frankie wanted no such complications.

A potentially serious side effect was a frustration she could do without.

She'd passed the time, keeping in touch with Kit, though hearing and reading updates on the trafficking case in no way made up for the feeling of being out of the loop, unable to contribute. Frankie felt rudderless, lacking a clear sense of direction. The offer of a move to the Met was still on the table, though she'd given no definitive answer. Her future depended upon what she was offered locally.

That was up to David.

He was conspicuous by his absence, though a stream of visitors had come and gone in the past few days, family mostly, keeping her fed and entertained. She was sick of all the care and attention, but what could she say that wouldn't sound ungrateful? Then Rae arrived with Amir, like a breath of fresh air in an otherwise dull existence, lifting Frankie's mood.

Amir stopped dead when she opened the door, his big eyes staring at her bandages. He called out to her, then ran forward and gave her legs a hug, a smile so wide it almost brought her to tears.

They moved through to the living room, Amir breaking off to look through the window at the boats bobbing up and down in the marina. 'I've been showing him old photographs. Didn't want him stressing about not seeing you until you were up to it,' Rae whispered. 'It's one thing seeing the olds, another thing entirely coping with an enthusiastic toddler—'

'Dad's not so bad!'

Rae laughed out loud.

It was good to see her so blissfully happy.

Turning away from the window, Amir tripped on the edge of the carpet, tumbling to the floor. There were no tears, though to distract him, Rae took a picture book from her bag. The sisters sat on the floor either side of him. In a very short time, he'd learned a lot, pointing out his favourite farmyard animals, speaking their names.

Frankie was gobsmacked.

'I know,' Rae said. 'Honestly, he's like a sponge. Andy and I treated him to a visit to Whitehouse Farm on Saturday. He fed the animals, rode on a tractor, met other kids in the soft-play area. We had fun seeing Snowy Owl, didn't we, Amir?' She turned the page. 'Can you find Mr Owl, for Frankie?'

Without hesitation, he used his finger to demonstrate that he understood.

'Good boy!' Frankie turned to look at her sister. 'You're working wonders, Rae. A stranger would be forgiven for thinking that you'd been a family unit for a very long time. I can't believe how far he's come.'

'Penny's great with him. She thinks he's almost certainly Albanian.'

Frankie had been so busy she'd almost forgotten the interpreter supporting them, helping with identification. 'He talks back to her?'

'No, but he responds to the language in other ways. Not all positive, I have to say. Sometimes, he turns away, making sure she gets the message. Makes you wonder what's going through his mind. Which reminds me . . .' She checked her watch. 'I'd love to stay, but she's visiting in an hour or so. We need to get going.'

Rae and Amir had only just left, when someone rang the intercom. Thinking they had forgotten something, Frankie looked around. Nothing stood out. Making her way into the hallway, she checked the spyhole. Ben was on the landing, waiting for her to buzz him in.

She opened the door.

'Ben! Come in. It's great to see you.'

'You sure it's convenient?'

'Since when d'you need an appointment?'

'I don't, but you look worn out.'

'You really know how to compliment a girl—'

'I didn't mean—'

'I know what you meant. If I look like shit, blame my old man.' She smiled. 'I can't get rid of him. Can I get you anything – tea, coffee?'

'No, I can't stop. Belinda's expecting me. I'm heading into town and thought, as I was passing—'

'You're not passing, though, are you?'

'What?' His face flushed.

'You moved out. David told me.'

'OK, so I'm busted. Look, I know you hate a fuss, so I decided not to make one. Just thought I'd give you a knock to see if there's anything you need.'

'What I need is a lift. You're right on time. It'll save me the price of a taxi.'

'Where do you want to be?'

'Middle Earth.'

101

After examining the logbooks at Northumbria HQ, David had updated Bright, then called Jan Welch, a brief conversation. He needed to speak to her brother urgently and was prepared to travel to do it. She immediately scuppered his plan. She and William were attending a family wedding in Berkshire at the weekend, a flash do, by all accounts, one she'd begged him not to ruin.

'His daughter's getting married,' she'd said. 'They've been planning it for months.'

The delay was a source of frustration. 'I can wait . . . on one condition—'

'Which is?'

'He must make himself available on Monday.'

'That won't be a problem. He works from home mostly. I'll tell him. He knows you've been to see me.'

There had been no doubt in David's mind that she'd wait until her family celebrations were over. She'd be curious, maybe even anxious, that a cop of his rank was prepared to make the journey south, not send a DS or DC to do it for him. On the other hand, he hadn't asked her not to warn her brother, which may have allayed her fears.

'Can you give me his address and mobile number? I'll text him my ETA.' As she reeled them off, he'd written them down on a yellow Post-it note that he'd folded in half and shoved in his inside jacket pocket.

Now, two days later, exiting a delayed train from Alnmouth to King's Cross, he pulled it out and jumped in a cab, asking the driver to take him to Fitzjohn's Avenue, Hampstead. The address seemed to ring a bell with him, probably a throwback from his Met days.

Something niggled deep inside his brain.

Over the weekend, Bright had called him at home, insisting that as all the evidence was pointing one way, it was time to level with Frankie's father, something the head of CID planned to do himself today, knowing full well that David would be in London.

That bothered him.

As the SIO, it should fall to him to update the family. Bright had overruled him. Indira's theory that he was well placed to manipulate any or all evidence was in David's head, including his alibi, if it came down to it. He wondered if they were being played. Was their suspect about to take the fall for something he hadn't done?

Welch would nail it one way or the other.

Texting him to say that he was on his way, David looked out of the window at the city he'd lived in for the best part of his career. He'd grown fond of the vibe, the pace and energy, a stark contrast to his current home and life in the slow lane. Feeling nostalgic, he called Matthews. Kit answered on the second ring. He didn't bother with an introduction. She wouldn't have picked up without number ID.

'I have a bone to pick with you,' he said.

'Again?' She was smiling as she said it. 'What did I do?'

'You were on my patch and didn't say hello. I'm now on yours. Want to meet up?'

'I'd love that. Where are you staying?'

'I'm not, but I have a late train. We could have an early dinner. I'm buying.' The cab turned into a leafy avenue and slowed, pulling to the kerb outside a red-brick period conversion with impressive architecture, a domed entrance and steep marble steps leading to the front door. 'Kit, I've gotta go. Message me where and when. I'll be there.'

Disconnecting, he paid the driver and got out.

There were only two cars on the block-paved driveway. Welch's apartment was on the second floor. David rang the bell

332

and waited. William opened the door, extending a hand, inviting him in. Welch was the double of his sister, tall and dark, the same Mallen streak in his hair, though the rest would soon catch up.

The apartment was immaculate inside, tastefully decorated, open-plan with a private balcony overlooking the tree canopy of a sizeable garden, a combination of vintage and modern furniture, a design that made it feel special.

'Good wedding?' David asked.

'My head says so . . .' Welch smiled, pouring coffee. 'I'll be paying for it later.'

David scanned the room. 'Nice place. I'm in the wrong job—'

'Jobs,' William corrected him, handing David a brew. 'Freelance pays well.'

They sat, David getting stuck in immediately, an interview that would last the best part of an hour. He made it clear that everything they talked about was confidential, that it involved the officer who'd fled from his sister's home following an altercation with Adam Hall.

William didn't hold back. He had no time for the man, and there was no denial that he too had used the dark-coloured J-reg Ford mentioned by two eyewitnesses.

'A mechanic bought it eventually,' he volunteered. 'Our lot were asked if we were interested. There were no takers. Put it this way, you didn't need to look in the logbook to check who'd last been in it. It smelt like a brothel. We found all sorts in the rear of that vehicle—'

'Anything specific?'

'Use your imagination.'

'Help me out, man.'

William's expression was unreadable.

David gave him a shove. 'Look, one of my witnesses walked away from the force and from what she told me, she had good reason. When I interviewed her, it occurred to me that she might have dropped something someone else found, ammo for the grapevine.'

'You're talking about Masterson, right?' When David didn't

respond, Welch took it as confirmation that his guess had been correct. 'She was intelligent, well-liked, not to mention stunning. Could've done better. If I'm honest, most of us had a thing for her. She chose the wrong one.'

'You knew about their affair?'

'You're kidding! Everyone did. When she left, we all knew why. Some of the guys felt guilty. When they slept around, they were just guys. When women did it, they were slags, fair game. Steph soon became known for all the wrong reasons, especially on her shift.'

'You didn't put a stop to it?'

'And risk him spreading rumours about my sister? How could I? They were willing volunteers. Jan should've known better. Steph was young and vulnerable. I felt sorry for her. Has she made a retrospective complaint?'

Welch was playing games.

'You know I can't comment on that,' David said.

'Fair enough. Are we done? I have work to do.'

'Not quite. I haven't got what I came for . . .' David showed him the logbook containing his scribble in the margin: Fill your fucking mileage in! 'Did you write that?'

'Yeah, I wrote it. I picked up the car on several occasions when that prick failed to fill it in, probably covering his date nights – and there were plenty. I didn't mind the odd mile. When it extended to twenty or thirty, I boned him about it. Ask around, I wasn't the only one.'

David stood. 'Thanks, you've been a great help.'

William gave him hard eyes as they shook hands. 'Guv, if we meet again, don't patronise me. I don't know why you're here. I don't want to know. Whatever it is, you'd better make it stick. He'll own up to screwing Jan, Steph Masterson and a stream of other women while on duty.' He tapped the logbook. 'You do re-alise his barrister will use this against you, alleging sour grapes on my part, trying to sway a jury into thinking it's payback.'

David took the logbook. 'I'll make sure that doesn't happen.'

102

Before Ben shot off to meet Belinda Wells, he dropped Frankie at the main gate of North Area Command HQ. She watched him drive away, then looked up at the building, excited to get inside. It felt like a homecoming. This was where she belonged. Where she was meant to be.

When she opened the door to the incident room a few minutes later, it was a cauldron of activity, phones ringing off the hook, detectives' heads down in their work.

She noticed that those who'd been loaned out to Division were at their desks, including statement reader Rob Mather, the receiver Pam Bond and several civilian indexers keeping HOLMES fed. Mitch was also there, his NCA secondment ending his involvement in the abduction-trafficking case. Frankie could see from the murder wall that a new investigation was underway.

She was missing out.

Charlie, the office manager, downed tools, breaking into a spontaneous round of applause. The rest looked up and joined in, putting their hands together, getting up to greet her. The racket brought Dick out of his temporary office to see what all the fuss was about. A huddle of bodies had formed around her, everyone keen to extend their congratulations for a job well done.

Dick held off, a big smile on his face as he waited in line to do the same.

As her former colleagues moved away, he stepped forward. 'You're flying, Frank. Great collar. It's bound to lift your profile.' They had had their differences, but he didn't begrudge her a moment in the spotlight.

He'd had plenty of his own.

'Thanks.' On the way there, she'd been wondering how to tell him that she was hoping to be reinstated as soon as she was fit for duty. Because he'd been so nice to her, she decided it could wait.

'Shame you can't finish the job you started,' Dick said. 'Christ knows why. You're here. You may as well be there.'

'I've been ordered to rest.'

'Yeah, like that's going to happen.'

Frankie smiled.

He knew her too well.

She glanced over his shoulder.

The team were back at their desks, getting on with important work with no time to waste. The first twenty-four hours of any major enquiry was crucial. The offender could still be kicking about, might even be wearing the same clothes. Information from the public would be critical before memories faded.

Dick's eyes fell on her injured arm. 'How is it?'

'Not too bad . . .' She looked away as the door to the incident room swung open. The person she most wanted to see wasn't the one who walked through it. She was gutted and it probably showed.

'You seem distracted.' Dick missed nothing.

'I am a bit. Can we talk in private?'

'Make it quick.'

She nodded towards David's office.

They moved into it, closing the door behind them, taking a seat on either side of the desk. Frankie hesitated before taking him into her confidence. 'Working with Matthews has opened doors. Between us, the National Crime Agency have offered me a secondment.'

'Are you going to take it?'

She could see that he was conflicted. If she moved, he stood to benefit, almost certain to continue in his role as David's bagman. On the other hand, they would miss working and hanging out together.

'Not sure,' she said. 'Depends on the boss.'

'Does he know?'

336

'I've not told him. Where is he?'

'At home, I presume. He called in sick—'

'Wow, that's a first, though it explains why I've not seen him over the weekend.' Her tone was laced with antagonism. 'What's wrong with him?'

'Dunno. Indira didn't say.'

'Is she around?'

'No, I saw her leave an hour ago.' Dick paused, another glance at Frankie's injured arm. 'Look, I didn't say this, and will deny it if you repeat it, but the boss didn't look good when I last saw him. Could be delayed shock. A bit of déjà vu. Give the guy a break, Frank. He's worried about you.'

103

Took Took in the heart of West Hampstead was Kit's restaurant of choice. Despite the early hour, when David walked in it was packed to the rafters, the clientele consisting of locals, corporate diners, mixed-nationality tourists.

Pan-Asian street food was David's favourite. They had eaten there before, sometimes alone, more often as part of the West End Central crowd, celebrating this or that.

It was good to be in her company.

When he took a demotion to head north, she was the one he missed the most. She was wild and funny, occasionally insubordinate, but also tough and uncompromising, a detective unafraid to speak her mind. She'd been fishing for details the whole time they had been eating, skirting the subject of Frankie Oliver, trying to lure him into a disclosure he had no intention of delivering.

He engineered a change of direction. 'How's Zenith going?'

Cleverly, she managed to turn the tide while still responding to his enquiry. 'Slowly. We'll get there. We have Frankie to thank for that. Without her intel, we'd be nowhere.' Kit refilled their wine glasses, declining the dessert menu he passed across the table. 'You do know she cares about you?'

'Yeah, I know.'

'So, cheer up. Last time we spoke, I got the impression that her feelings were reciprocated. Is that no longer the case?'

He ducked the question. 'I care about all of my team.'

'Nice sidestep . . .' She met his gaze over the rim of her glass. 'You're right though, it's not my business. You can do whatever you want. Getting too close to colleagues is a pain in the arse, right?' Realising what she'd said, she quickly apologised. 'I didn't mean—'

'Kit, relax . . . I know what you meant.'

Her eyes remained fixed on his. 'Do you still think about her?'

'Jane? All the time . . .' For a moment, he stared blankly at the mosaic-tiled floor, not seeing the random design, just taking a moment before looking up. 'The nightmares are less frequent. Mostly, I wonder what might have been.'

'She was very special.'

'A one-off.' He rubbed at the stubble on his chin. 'I went to see her parents this afternoon.'

'What?' Her expression needed no explanation.

'I know. Insane idea.'

'I wasn't aware you'd kept in touch.'

'Who else is going to do it this far down the line? They're struggling . . . and what are the Met doing about it?' He gave her a disparaging look, then apologised. Kit didn't deserve to take the flack on behalf of her force for failing to support the family.

'How are they?'

He blew out a breath. 'Jane's mum is a drunk. Her father is on antidepressants, trying to keep it together. The fact that the lunatic who shot her will be out one day is destroying them, and me too, if I'm honest. Getting even seems like a good idea.'

'David, you need to move on. I thought you had—'

He spread his hands in protest. 'I have—'

'Until Frankie got stabbed.' It was a loaded statement.

He didn't deny it.

'I'm not stupid, David. The first thing I thought of when I heard the news was how it would affect *you*.' When he didn't speak, she nudged him harder. 'Is that what prompted you to visit Jane's parents and to ask me out to dinner, because you thought that only we would understand?'

'No, that's ridiculous.' He'd protested so loudly the couple on the next table turned to stare at them. When he spoke again, he dropped his voice low. 'Them, maybe . . . not you. I had a few hours to kill and thought we'd hang out—'

'Hey, I know where I stand in the pecking order. There's no need to underline it. And don't lie to me . . .' She glared at the couple earwigging. 'Is there something I can help you with?'

Mortified, they looked away.

Kit refocused on David. 'You realise you'll lose Frankie if you fuck it up, like you did with Jane—'

'How many more times do I have to say it? There's nothing going on between me and Frankie, so stop suggesting there is. She's a mate, a close colleague, no more, no less.'

'Yeah, keep telling yourself that—' She broke off, though she had more to say.

'What?' he said. 'Go on, spit it out.'

'You're not being honest, with me, yourself or Frankie. She means a damned sight more to you than that, and you know it—'

'Believe what you like. I don't care.'

'That's it, right there. You do. You know you do. David, I know how much you loved Jane. I was there to pick up the pieces, don't forget. You cried like a baby because you didn't tell her how you felt before she died. And here we go again. History repeating itself.'

He said nothing.

'Why are you so afraid to admit what Frankie means to you?' She sat quiet for a tense moment before pulling the pin. 'Did she tell you my boss has offered her a stint on the NCA down here?'

He didn't answer.

'She didn't, did she?'

Struggling to control his emotions, it took him a moment to respond. 'It doesn't surprise me. She's a good operator, an asset to any team.'

'Oh, save me the management wank words, David. You are your own worst enemy sometimes. What is wrong with you? It's as clear as day that you don't want her to leave, so why not give her a reason to stay? This isn't the first time she's had a near-death experience, is it? You said as much last time we met. Love hurts. Take it from one who knows, but I know one thing. Life without it hurts a damned sight more—'

'Drop it, will you?'

'OK.' Kit's hands were up. 'If you don't want my advice, let's have some fun—'

'That's why I'm here,' David said, 'not to get heavy. You're not making it easy.'

'I can change that . . .' Kit parted her lips, looking deep into his eyes. What she said next floored him. 'I'm not buying your self-confessed free agent bollocks. Why don't you drop your baggage here and come back to my place for round two? No Frankie. No strings. I'll drop you for an early train in the morning.'

'I don't need a sympathy fuck.'

She laughed. 'You did last time.'

104

With David unavailable, Frankie left Middle Earth disappointed not to have spoken to him. In the car park, she called Ben. He didn't pick up, so she called Wells. When she answered, Frankie could hear the buzz of the editorial office going on behind her. It sounded like the incident room she'd just come from, full of energy, a million conversations going on simultaneously.

'Hi, Belinda. I need to speak to Ben. He's not answering. Is he tied up?'

'Not guilty. I've decided he's too young for me. He just nipped out. Is it urgent? Anything I can help you with?'

'Not really. I was just wondering why he didn't mention that David was unwell when he came to my place earlier.'

'He said nothing to me.' A male voice called out to her. Belinda told him to give her five before resuming her conversation. 'Sorry, it's bedlam this end. I'll ask him to call you when he returns.'

'Owe you one. Listen, I'll be kicking my heels for a few days. Fancy a drink soon?'

'That's like asking if I fancy men.'

'Tried that, wasn't keen. I've gone off them. The way I'm going, I might be heading to the dark side.'

'Tried that, wasn't keen.'

Frankie laughed. 'Give you a bell later?'

'Sure . . .' Another shout for her attention. 'I assume you heard that. Gotta go.'

The line went dead.

With no vehicle, a big decision to make on her future and no one around who might give her a lift, Frankie called a taxi. In times of crisis, there was only one place to go to share her troubles. Her dad wouldn't be happy when she told him she'd been offered a position down south with the NCA, even less when he heard that she was seriously considering it. He'd support her, though it would kill him if she moved away. They saw each other every couple of days.

The mere thought of not doing so was unthinkable.

Frankie considered this as the cab sped up the A19, merging with the A1 south, then west on the A696 towards Woolsington, her childhood home. The Oval was a quiet tree-lined avenue. As the cab turned in and pulled to the kerb, the front door opened.

She smiled, thinking that her father had seen her arrive.

Her jaw dropped as Indira exited alone, gently pulling the door closed, a tormented expression as she trundled down the garden path. Handing a twenty to the driver, Frankie told him to keep the change. She leapt out of the car, racing towards the front gate, cutting Indira off before she reached it.

'Indi, what are you doing here?'

The DC was visibly shaken, unable or unwilling to meet her gaze.

Frankie glanced through the window of her father's den. His pained eyes stared at her, reflecting an emotion she didn't understand.

She refocused on his visitor.

'What's going on?'

An ominous silence.

Indira shifted her weight from one foot to the other. She was uneasy, bordering on anxious, unsure of what to do or say. Frankie wondered why her father hadn't shown her to the door.

Unless the news was so bad he couldn't.

Frankie's heart was in her mouth. A cold sweat crept across her body, chilling her to her core, lifting the fine hairs on her good arm. She glared at her former colleague. 'Indi, I asked you a question. Answer me.'

'Boss, please don't—'

'What's happened?' Frankie thought she might vomit. 'Is it Rae? Please tell me it's not Rae or Amir—' Indira's mouth was moving, but Frankie didn't hear a word she said. She pictured Rae and Amir in her apartment a matter of hours ago, so happy and contented. This couldn't be happening . . .

Not again.

'Frankie, did you hear me? I said they're fine.'

'Is it Mum?' Her mother was out. They had spoken earlier. She was at work, unable to get home till late.

'No, Julie's fine.'

For a second, it occurred to Frankie that it might be David, that his absence was serious, that Indira had come looking for *her*, thinking that her parents would be looking after her while she recuperated. She discounted the idea as quickly as it arrived. If that had been true, Indira would be a basket case. Her eyes were sad but dry, no sign of having been upset.

Frankie had no time for guessing games.

Her patience had run out.

'Tell me!'

105

Caught like a rabbit in headlights – under strict orders from David and Bright to stick to her legend – Indira made the fatal error of repeating that garbage, then elaborating on it, telling Frankie that her father was helping with a cross-border investigation into a cold case of a dead teenager Durham Constabulary had resurrected.

'He's given me some advice,' she said.

'Has he? Well, good for him.' Frankie's tone was poisonous. 'You couldn't find a detective that didn't have a murdered child?'

Indira was kicking herself. It was a rookie mistake. The detective she was facing could spot a lie at a hundred yards. Given that she was there, was it even necessary to trot out the party line? Keeping up the pretence was killing them both. Frankie would find out what she and David had been keeping from her soon enough.

Indi was tempted to put her out of her misery, and would have, had her father not agreed to keep it from her until their suspect was under arrest. He'd begged Bright to identify the perpetrator. He'd refused, which meant that Indi was caught in a web of deceit that she couldn't untangle.

'I'm sorry,' she said. 'It was a shortcut. I didn't think.'

'No,' Frankie said. 'But you're thinking now, aren't you?'

Indira failed to regain her composure. David's voice was in her head, telling her to hold the line: *if they're unhappy, decline to answer further questions . . . shut up shop and refer the matter to me.*

'You need to talk to David.'

'I'm talking to you.'

'Call the MIR. He'll explain.'

'I don't want to call the fucking MIR. You know fine well he's not there. You told Dick he was sick. I'm not swallowing that, so don't you dare lie to me. Where is he?'

Indira tried to step around her.

Frankie countered, blocking her in beside the gatepost. Her anger at being messed around was all-consuming. Other than to defend herself or make an arrest, she'd never laid hands on anyone in her life.

Now, she was out of control, hanging on to Indira's clothing.

She didn't struggle. 'Boss, you don't want to do this. Let go of my arm. You'll hurt yourself.'

'Frankie!' Bright's furious bark reached them from the front door. He took off at a fast pace, moving up the garden path towards them. 'What the fuck do you think you're doing? Get your hands off her!'

'Well, if I didn't know before, I do now. Was this fucking masquerade your idea?'

'Careful, Inspector. You're way out of line. You heard me. Let her go!'

Frankie came to her senses, releasing her grip.

Indira adjusted her crumpled jacket, smoothing down the material. Frankie looked small, worn out and defeated. Had Bright not been there, Indira would have pulled her into a hug and confessed everything. She hated that the detective chief super had observed the altercation and come outside to intervene.

Disgusted by Frankie's behaviour, he focused on Indi.

'You OK?'

'Yes, sir. It was nothing. A difference of opinion, that's all. No harm done. Frankie's been through a lot lately—'

'Don't you dare make excuses for her. I just witnessed an assault.'

'It wasn't an assault—'

'Watch your mouth. It's whatever I say it is.'

Defiantly, Indira stuck her chin out. 'I won't make a complaint, guv.'

'Then I'll do it for you . . .' His temper flared. 'My detectives don't shout the odds on a quiet residential street and get away with it. Clear off. I'll deal with you later . . .' He rounded on Frankie. 'You! Inside!'

Neither budged, empowered by female solidarity.

Frankie was exhausted, the challenges of the past fortnight finally catching up with her, though that did not excuse her appalling behaviour. She'd allowed her emotions to get the better of her, upsetting a colleague she loved and respected.

She'd lost the plot.

It was time to make amends.

She found her voice, directing it at their guv'nor. 'If you're getting the whip out, it's my back you want, not hers. I don't know what came over me. I apologise' – she looked from one to the other – 'to both of you.'

Welling up, Indira sent a silent message: *I'm sorry too.*

As she walked away, Frankie looked through the window of her father's den. He was still there, motionless. If she had to describe him, she'd have said he was anguished, crushed, a broken man. She'd seen him like this before. Unable to look at her, he turned away. Frankie began to unravel, joining dots.

In that moment, she felt the world tilt.

She knew.

106

Was it even possible to feel vulnerable and empowered at the same time? There were no tears. Frankie had dreamt of this moment throughout her teens and adult life, for herself, but more so for her family — her father especially. She found him in his den, staring at a photograph of Joanna taken not long before her death, swallowed up in the grief of that fateful night. Neither of them said anything. They just held one another in the very room where he broke the news that her sister was never coming home.

He was as upset as she was, possibly more so.

Raking up the past was going to be a rough ride for the whole family. As much as she trusted David to make a case, Frankie didn't want to count on a result. Trials were complicated. Verdicts could go either way, depending on the make-up of a jury.

Patting her father's back, she pulled away, eyeing her guv'nor.

She had no fight left in her but somehow found the strength to look him straight in the eye and ask him outright to confirm her suspicions and explain the need for stealth that had left her so isolated. He'd obviously told her father.

She wanted it first-hand.

Bright sat forward, elbows on his knees, hands clasped together. He was dead calm and didn't hesitate to come clean. 'When David came to me with what was a very weak suspicion, I told him to reopen Joanna's case and investigate under the radar. I took the decision to protect you until the time was right. Believe me when I say that what just happened outside was the one thing I wanted to avoid. For what it's worth, David argued against keeping it from you.'

'I knew he was lying to me,' Frankie said.

'And now you know why.'

She stared at Bright.

Her guv'nor had two sides. He was tough and uncompromising, a detective who could go the distance with anyone, in the most hellish of circumstances. His heart was also in the right place, showing compassion and consideration to people in desperate need, in and outside the job. They had gone ten rounds often enough, but he was a good man, an honest man, a friend as well as her guv'nor.

Under the circumstances, Frankie was confident that there would be no fallout from her outburst. Not for her or Indira, who'd fronted up to him. He admired spirited detectives. Above all else, he valued loyalty. Indi had stood up for Frankie who, moments before, had her pinned to the garden gate, demanding answers.

Now, her guv'nor was gauging her reaction.

'I can see you want to punch someone,' he said.

'Damn right I do.'

'We have one shot at this, so don't fuck it up. You go nowhere near it, understood?' Without waiting for an answer, he turned his attention to her father. 'That goes for you too, Frank. No calling in any favours. If this gets out, all that David has achieved in the past two weeks will be for nothing.' Bright was watching her old man like a hawk, taking in his distress. 'What would you have him do? Raise your hopes only to have them dashed? You know how sensitive these things get—'

'These things? These *things*?' Her father sprang from his seat. It was the first time he'd opened his mouth. It was unlike him to remain silent for so long. His brow was furrowed, fists clenched, fear reflected in his eyes, the past and present vying for his attention. 'Fuck's sake, Phil! That's my daughter you're on about. Mine!'

'And my goddaughter,' Bright said. 'I mourned her death, same as you. Same as every parent of a murdered child.'

Frankie tried to take the temperature down.

'Sit down, Dad. You'll give yourself a coronary.'

He remained standing, full of pent-up emotion.

'The boss is right, Dad. If the roles were reversed, we'd have done the same thing.' She turned to look at Bright, wanting, needing answers to so many questions. 'Was Dick lying when he told me that there was nothing going on in the incident room?'

'No, until yesterday, that was the case—'

Her father cut him off. 'Then why is David not utilising the whole team to investigate Joanna's murder? That makes no sense. What's wrong with you? You got a bad case of amnesia? You gave your word to prioritise Joanna's case – an obligation, you said.'

'Tone it down, Frank. We're on the same side.'

'Stone and a rookie, that's all she's worth? You've got to be kidding me.'

Bright didn't need to justify his decision but did it anyway. 'Pam, Dick and Charlie were on the original enquiry team. I didn't want them queering David's pitch or influencing him in any way. He was a clean pair of eyes. We were trying to protect you and at the same time keep the investigation locked down to avoid speculation. You know what the grapevine is like. If one cop knows, they all do.'

Frank raised his voice.

'You could have told us. Should have. We're friends—'

'You're also parents, siblings.'

'We're pros. We'd have handled it—'

Bright cut him off. 'Like you're handling it now?'

Frankie exploded, eyes on Bright. 'You weren't going to tell me, were you, guv?'

'No. I knew Julie was out. I came here to warn Frank that David was close. I didn't figure on you turning up.'

'Well, thanks for having my back. Appreciate it.'

'Drop the sarcasm. You just proved my point. You're too close to this, Frankie. You're angry, I get it, but know this: I acted in your best interests. You'll have questions—'

'Damn straight we do. If David has a suspect, we also have rights.'

'Not yet you don't.'

'She has a point,' her father said.

'I can't tell you who's in the frame. I'm sorry, you'll have to be patient for a little longer.'

'We've been patient long enough.' Frankie spat the words out. 'Let me get this straight, you're telling us that David and Indira are the only ones in the know, apart from you?'

'And that's how it must remain until an arrest is made.'

'David's no sicknote,' Frankie said. 'So why isn't he here doing his job?'

'He's in London, following up a lead. He'll be back tonight.'

Headlights drew Frankie's eyes to the window, panic setting in. 'Shit! Mum's home.'

Bright wasted no time. Grabbing three beers from Frank's fridge, he flipped the tops off, handed them out and sat down. 'I know it's a big ask, but it would be wise to keep this conversation between us. No point upsetting Julie – or Rae or Andrea, for that matter – until we have something concrete to tell them. So get your smiley faces on.'

Frankie's eyes were on her father.

He nodded. 'Not a word.'

107

Frankie didn't know how her father managed to mask his feelings for the next couple of hours, keeping up appearances for her mother's sake. He'd played a blinder and so had she, but when she climbed the stairs to her room, she was wiped out, with one thing on her mind. Waiting until her parents' bathroom routine was over, their bedroom door clicking shut, she sat on the edge of her bed, punching in a number she knew by heart.

The phone seemed to ring out for an age before David picked up. He was mobile, out of breath, walking at a fast pace, by the sounds of it. She heard the familiar sound of a British Rail employee announcing the recent arrival of an Edinburgh-bound train on platform three. He was at Newcastle Central Station, just in from King's Cross.

'Frank, you there? Sorry, couldn't hear myself think. Is everything OK?'

'Nothing is OK . . .' She kept her voice low, her tone assertive. 'I need to speak to you. Tonight. I know what you've been up to. I also know that you were once locked out of an investigation of a murdered loved one, so you're well aware of where my head is right now. Don't you dare try to talk me out of it.'

'I understand, I do, but—'

'No buts, David. I'm in bits here.' There was a beat of time while neither spoke. 'I'm begging you. I know you're under a lot of pressure and that I'm not being fair or logical, but I can't help myself. Please tell me what you've got.'

'Frank, don't do this. I can't give you what you want.'

'For once in your life, bend the fucking rules!'

He was talking, though she ignored the content. After so many years of holding her feelings in, she was incapable of listening to reason. She lost it then, weeping uncontrollably, trying not to let it all out and wake her mum. There wasn't a hope in hell that her old man would be asleep. He'd be wide awake, staring at the ceiling, going over and over Joanna's case in minute detail, trying to figure out what he'd missed that David had found in a relatively short space of time.

Frankie couldn't speak, let alone breathe.

There was silence on the other end, though she could tell David was still on the line. Hanging up, she lay down on her bed and sobbed into her pillow.

The flashback arrived unbidden, Joanna in the leading role. Seconds later, Frankie's phone began to vibrate, marching across her bedside table, David's profile picture appearing on the screen. She sat bolt upright. Heart still racing, she grabbed the phone.

'Meet me. End of The Oval. Twenty minutes.'

David disconnected.

She waited ten minutes before pulling on her coat. Opening her bedroom door, she peered around it, along the hallway to her parents' room. No lights beneath their door. No sound.

The coast was clear.

She crept downstairs.

In the hallway, she waited.

No movement from above.

Moving swiftly through to the kitchen, she reached for the back door key, then swung round, retracing her steps, heading for her father's den, turning on a lamp. A few minutes later, having found what she was looking for, she turned it off, heading back to the kitchen. She let herself out of the house via the rear door, relocking it once she got outside.

There was a warm breeze. The night sky was streaked with cloud, the moon peeping through as she made her way along the street. She'd asked too much of David, putting him in an impossible situation, one that could and would have consequences if discovered. In that moment, she didn't care.

What she was about to do was for Joanna.

108

Frankie reached their rendezvous point. No sign of David's car parked at the junction. She glanced along the road. Seeing headlights in the distance, she stepped out of the shadows of an overhanging tree, hopes soaring. The vehicle didn't slow. It flashed by, heading towards the airport.

A few moments ticked by.

Frankie began to wonder if David had bottled it. She'd be gutted, though she wouldn't blame him. He was taking a huge risk . . . for her. Then, out of the darkness, another car appeared.

This was his.

He swung the wheel, pulling over, leaving the engine running. She checked the B road – nothing coming either way – and jumped in. As she struggled with her seat belt, he leaned across to help, so close they were almost touching.

He didn't say a word.

Nor did she.

All set, he drove on for a short distance, turning left onto Callerton Lane, then sharp left on a country lane, stopping on the side of the road a short way along. He got out, walked round to her side of the vehicle, opened the door then stood aside like any good chauffeur would, slamming it shut afterwards.

There was an awkwardness as they stared at one another.

Slipping a hand in his trouser pocket, he pulled out a pack of cigarettes. Removing the cellophane, he put one in his mouth, offering her the open carton. She shook her head, watching him light up. Now he was pacing, blowing a cloud of smoke high into the air, proof if it was needed that he was in a state.

He walked back towards her. 'How's Frank holding up?'

'How do you think?'

Frankie wasn't being unkind, just taking a verbal shortcut, though she may as well have said: *get on with it*. David got the message. He didn't tell her where he was when he first became suspicious – she'd put the thumbscrews on every party guest – so, without mentioning the names of witnesses, he laid out the evidence he'd gathered with Indira's help.

He'd never seen Frankie look so vulnerable.

She was no fool. He'd left out details that might identify his suspect. She knew where and when Joanna had met her death. He'd given her the how, but not the who. He expected that would be her next question, though she didn't push him.

She would . . .

Crossing her arms, she leaned against the car, head tilted slightly, hair blowing free in the wind. She pushed it back, tucking it behind her ears. 'How solid is your evidence?'

'Very,' he said.

'Enough to make it stick?'

'I need more, but I think so.'

'You think?' Her eyes flashed. 'Either it is, or it isn't.'

'Give me some credit, Frank. Trust me. Would we have told your old man if we weren't certain of our facts? I just need to clarify one or two things before I start the clock running.'

He waited for the red mist.

It took no time to arrive.

The last time they'd faced one another across a pub car park, with Indira looking on, their conversation was upsetting. This one was about to escalate into a full-blown row. Frankie pleaded with him, begging him, accusing him of holding out on her.

He told her to back off. 'I've given you all I can.'

'You've given me nowt. David, I must know.'

109

Under the moonlight, David couldn't fail to notice her welling up. He flicked his cigarette butt away, sending sparks flying as it hit the road. If he had no feelings for her, it would have been easy. He'd have pulled rank, telling her to wind her neck in or ship out. As it was, they were mates. More than mates. He should've stuck to his guns, not called her back.

As dilemmas go, this was a killer.

'Frank, don't cry.'

'I'm not.' She sniffed.

He wanted to tell her that he understood, how he'd pleaded with his Met colleagues to share sensitive intel on Jane's case; how it made him feel when they refused; how it felt when they eventually stepped up, keeping him abreast of developments; how he'd wished they hadn't.

Jane's killer had been pleading provocation, shoving the blame *his* way, making himself out to be the victim, a man driven by jealousy and rage when the balance of his mind was disturbed. Knowing that made David feel worse, not better. He wanted to save Frankie that trauma. His protection wouldn't last, but he'd be ready to pick up the pieces when she finally learned the truth.

'David, please . . . I won't breathe a word of what you told me. Not that it amounts to much.' Raising her head defiantly, she added, 'A few crumbs wasn't what I was after.'

'That's not how Bright will see it.'

'Fuck's sake! It's gone midnight. We're in the back of beyond. How's he ever going to know?'

'I can't identify my suspect, Frank. If you went anywhere near him he'd walk, and so would I.'

'I'd never put your job in jeopardy.'

'That's what it amounts to.'

'Then use me . . . Off the record.'

'I can't do that.'

She hit him with a comment that would appeal to the detective in him. 'Would it make a difference if I had something for you?'

'What can you possibly add that I don't know already?'

'Insight. Background information you may not be aware of. When Bright told me you were closing in, I was so emotional it jogged memories I can't get out of my head. There's not a person alive who knew Joanna like I did, and yet because of my age at the time she died, I was hardly questioned.'

'Go on.'

'She was cool, David. A kid in a hurry to grow up. A risk-taker. Clever or sneaky enough, depending on your point of view, to wear clothes she knew Dad wouldn't approve of, then chuck an old tracksuit on top before she went out. She'd go to a mate's house, put on make-up and wash it off before she came home.'

'Typical teen, then.'

'Yeah, a rebel I looked up to.'

'All kids push boundaries. Are you suggesting she put on different clothing that night? Because that's not the case. Your mum ID'd the clothes she was found in as those she wore when she went out, including the denim jacket that mysteriously went missing.'

'I know.'

'How d'you know?'

'I snuck into Dad's den on my way out and checked his murder file. The point I'm making is that I was Joanna's sounding board. We shared a room. She took me into her confidence, told me stuff she'd never share with anyone.'

110

David could have said that he and Luke were much the same growing up. Forming an alliance, they had kept all sorts from their grandmother. He didn't go there. Though Luke had died before his time, he'd enjoyed years of his company, years that Frankie and Joanna had been denied. His parents were dead. Hers were very much alive, though in the past she'd alluded to a time when they were so caught up in the drama of her sister's death, it felt like she was invisible, like she didn't exist.

Now she was in the moment, with more to say, knowing that she'd piqued his interest. They were talking like they used to.

Two detectives. One goal. A single entity.

'My old man wasn't wrong, David. That jacket didn't get lost in the HQ move. The killer panicked when he knew scientific advances were afoot. So, either he's a cop, a former cop or someone with access to exhibits.'

He said nothing.

'That's what I thought,' she said. 'He'd be bricking it to get in there and cover himself. The way I see it, he had two choices. Remove the jacket or hide it among other exhibits. That's what I'd have done, facing life imprisonment.'

'No, he'll have snuck out with it while the exhibits officer's back was turned.'

She shook her head. 'No, he wouldn't. My old man told me that the exhibits officer back then was shit-hot. You couldn't walk in there and remove a pinhead without her say-so. She checked every box in and out, the contents too.'

'Except Bright put detectives on the jacket the minute he

358

discovered it was missing. If it was there, the MIT would have found it.'

'Not if your suspect was given the action,' she said.

Recognising a pivotal moment when he saw one, David fell silent for a long moment, staring off into the distance before turning to face her. 'I'll check it out.' He sensed her stress. 'Something else on your mind?'

'The timing. He'll have buried Joanna's jacket among the items in a detected case. After five years, any clothing would have been handed back to the family of the victim it belonged to, or sent to be destroyed, which means your suspect will think he's free and clear.'

'Not if I can link him to the action.'

'Can you?'

'I don't know.' David didn't want to give her false hope.

He watched her thinking it through.

Saw her eyes light up.

'What?' he said.

'Unless he witnessed the handing over or incineration of that jacket, he won't know for certain that you have no physical evidence to hang on him. Doubt is a killer, so if you can't find it and you want to scare the living shit out of him, I have a plan.'

'Frank, I don't want to hear it—'

'Hear me out. Remember I told you I wanted to be Joanna. I wasn't kidding. I idolised her, begged Mum to buy me the very same jacket. They didn't do them in my size, so it was a bit big, but I didn't care. After . . .' She stalled. 'After Joanna's death, I couldn't bear to part with it. I hid it in the loft in case Mum and Dad saw it. The jackets were identical in every way, bar one. Mum marked our initials inside, so they didn't get mixed up.'

He lit another cigarette.

This time she joined him.

Her information had been useful. Irrespective of the earlier search, and what she'd said about exhibits being destroyed when they were finished with, he'd tear the exhibits room apart to find

359

that jacket. She was staring at him, waiting for him to speak, no doubt wanting something in return.

He got in first. 'Did Joanna wear perfume?'

'Yeah.' The question surprised her. 'Why?'

'CSIs recovered a bottle of Chanel N°5 hidden in a chest of drawers in your bedroom. It wasn't sent to forensics at the time. It's with them now. I'm waiting on a result. Did you ever see her hide or use it?'

'No! David, she was fifteen, a trendsetter. Chanel was not her style.'

'That's what Indi said. I thought it might have been a gift from Julie—'

'You can't ask her. We haven't told her.'

'Good to know. I'm just off the train. I've not spoken to Bright yet.'

Frankie hit him with it. 'I want a name.'

'Frank, let it go.'

'I can't, you know I can't.'

David wiped his face with his hands. She'd brought him back from the brink. His conscience wouldn't allow him to abandon her now. And finally, he caved, giving her what she'd asked for. He was about to say more, but his words had knocked her sideways, literally and metaphorically.

Her legs buckled.

She cried out in excruciating pain as she hit the tarmac footpath, nudging her injured arm on the side panel of his vehicle on the way down, everything happening in slow motion. He knelt beside her, cradling her in his arms. She sobbed into his chest. Of all the names he might have come up with, this one cut right through her.

'It's OK,' he said. 'I've got you.'

She continued to bawl, unable to speak, the betrayal too hard to bear. He stroked her hair, making no attempt to lift her off the ground. He'd been here before. She didn't need to look at him to know that he was unravelling. He offered a profound apology.

'I'm so sorry,' he said gently. 'It was a mistake telling you.'

She was trembling, paralysed by a lifetime of deceit, his warning hardly registering. It came out as a broken whisper – a plea not to do anything that might compromise a conviction. She looked up, tears replaced by pure rage as their eyes met. 'And risk him legging it? No, David. What happened here will die here. You have my word. I hope you crucify him. I'll drive the fucking nails in myself.'

111

With much to do, David was finding it hard to concentrate. Every time he got stuck in, an image of Frankie arrived in his head. She was walking down The Oval, alone in the darkness, head down, utterly broken. He'd called her mobile on his way in. No answer. He didn't call again. She needed time to process what he'd told her. She was planning to be home by now – up at dawn and in a cab – unable to look her old man in the eye.

There was zero chance he'd miss her upset.

He'd know.

David had completed his interview strategy, fed back on his chat with Welch, then set Indira to work on vital mileage calculations he intended to cross-check himself. At this stage in the game, they couldn't afford mistakes. Now Frankie and her father were aware that things were moving, they needed to move fast.

'The guv'nor's not in yet,' Indira said. 'I'll grab us a coffee before we get started. You look like you need one. Rough night?'

A nod was all he could manage.

Indira went next door to fetch it.

Checking his notes, David logged on to HOLMES, looking up every incident where denim jackets had been mentioned. The page loaded a list of live and cold cases, less than he was expecting, given the time-lapse. It was lengthy, not insurmountable. Like the perfume bottle, finding Joanna's jacket was a long shot, one he intended to explore. He was about to reduce his list further, when his phone rang.

He snapped it up. 'Stone.'

'Sorry to interrupt, guv. Your nephew left something for you at the front desk. Said he couldn't hang around to see you. Want me to send it up?'

'No, I'll be down in a mo.'

Curious, David put the phone down. As he stood to leave, the connecting door opened.

Indira entered, empty-handed. 'Sorry, guv. The machine's on the blink. I'll try the canteen.'

'Not for me, thanks.' Leaving the page open, he logged off.

'You sure?' She screwed up her face. 'It's not that bad.'

'Your memory must be playing up.' He grinned. 'Take your key. I'm nipping downstairs. I'll lock up when I leave.'

'Anything I can do?'

'No, grab your coffee then crack on. I need those calculations asap.'

On his way past the incident room, David poked his head round the door. That was more like it. He was enjoying Indira's company but preferred the cut and thrust of his usual domain, the camaraderie, the chat, everyone working together with one aim in mind.

He closed the door, leaving them to it.

At the front desk, he took the package, thinking it might be an olive branch from Ben, a gesture of appreciation before he moved out. It had been wrapped hastily in brown paper; gaffer taped. Ripping it off, David slid a finger beneath the flap, then teased it open. He saw the denim material and went no further.

Frankie had been in the loft.

That didn't worry him. She'd taken steps to ensure that his nephew couldn't look inside, no doubt made an appropriate excuse to avoid awkward questions. She'd promised not to queer David's pitch. She'd keep her word. He took out the jacket, checking the label: F. It could come in useful if he couldn't find its twin. Frankie was right. The mere sight of it would strike fear into a guilty man, unless he'd burnt the original.

Worth a punt.

Setting it aside, he logged back on, interrogating HOLMES, cutting the list down by two thirds by entering the word 'female' in the search field. He sat back, considering how he might reduce it further. Joanna's jacket had been examined forensically soon after her death in 1992. It wasn't there five years on when Bright ordered a search of the exhibits room, so David entered those parameters, discounting everything after that date, sending the result to his printer, getting up to collect the list as it spewed out.

He was in business.

112

In Amble, Frankie had been sitting outside the RNLI lifeboat station with a view along the waterfront, not really taking it in. She often sat there, enjoying the sea air, eating doughnuts for breakfast purchased from a van in the town's square. Today, she had no appetite, though she'd bought a coffee from one of the quirky pods in the harbour to sustain her while she waited for news from David.

Getting up, she binned the paper cup, then walked on, passing The Old Boat House restaurant, skirting the picturesque harbour and along the quayside, pausing a while as the day's catch was offloaded from fishing boats and taken ashore. She carried on, past the pastel-painted beach huts and onto the wooden pier, a circular route she took every morning before she set off for work. Only today, she was so lost in her thoughts, instead of turning back, she kept on walking south . . .

At Druridge Bay, a stunning stretch of sweeping sand four miles from home, Frankie realised that she'd overdone it. She'd left her sling at home. Her arm was aching from being down by her side. She rang a taxi, then cut through the dunes to the country park pick-up point, the cab arriving as she did.

In her apartment, she lay down on the sofa, exhausted. She hadn't heard from David, nor did she expect to. He'd be careful not to call her now, for fear that anyone might suspect they were in cahoots. She could handle that. She trusted him to press on, though being left out of the loop was more and more difficult as every hour passed. Before he'd left her last night, David had hinted that if things went his way, an arrest was imminent. It didn't lift her mood or quell her rage.

The word 'if' terrified her . . .

It was ambiguous . . .

'When' was better.

A text arrived from Ben, lifting her spirits:

Birthday pressie delivered.

Smiling, she keyed a reply:

Thanks. Hope he likes it.

Drink when you're mobile?

Yes! Need time to recover.

It was a heavy hint not to call. Mitch had already mentioned how drained she looked, suggesting she take the weight off for a few days. He didn't know the half of it. She didn't feel guilty for deceiving him. David needed that jacket, and she'd send his real present before Ben thought to ask . . .

Before David brought Joanna's case to a close.

Frankie prayed that it would be soon.

113

The feeling of euphoria was strong. The evidence was mounting. David was closer now than he'd ever been. The internal phone rang again. Annoyed by another distraction, he hesitated before answering.

The call was brief.

Disconnecting, he blew out a breath.

Assuming he'd hit a glitch, Indira looked up. 'Problem, guv?'

'The exact opposite. No DNA on the perfume bottle, but forensics managed to lift a partial print, which is a definitive link between our suspect and Joanna. The CPS might argue that it's weak. We may need a fingerprint expert to change their minds. Together with a body of circumstantial evidence, I'm going to run with it.' Even as he said it, he had doubts. 'I want you to do something for me.'

'Name it.'

'Bright raised an action to search the exhibits room when it came to light that Joanna's jacket was missing. I need to know who received it.'

Indira was on it, typing furiously, eyes fixed on the screen. He walked round to her side of the table, looking over her shoulder, breathing down her neck. She'd accessed the enquiry. A raised actions page loaded. She scrolled down. Two names only: DCs Roger Barclay and Audrey Grant.

'Damn it,' he said. 'Never heard of them, have you?'

'Grant rings a bell.'

'Find out where they are now. I need contact numbers.'

He returned to his side of the table and sat down.

Indira was again typing. Lifting her fingers from her keyboard, she found what she was looking for and sat back with a grimace. 'I'm in the personnel records. Barclay died two years ago, a boating accident. Grant is now an inspector. Her married name is Howe. She's based at Central Area Command.' She typed some more. 'Well, we were due some luck. She's on duty now, guv.' Indira gave him a four-digit extension number.

David picked up his landline, punching it in.

It rang out, but not for long.

He ID'd himself to Howe, explaining why he was calling. 'Do you recall the action to find that item of clothing?' She did, unsurprisingly, given that the victim was the child of a fellow officer. David gave Indira a nod. 'It was an important job, a massive undertaking, I imagine.'

'It took weeks, with only two of us on it initially.'

The word 'initially' took his breath away. Howe was still talking. 'Bright was none too pleased that the search was taking so long. He was down there once or twice, shouting his mouth off.'

'Is that right? I didn't realise that Bright was so hands-on.'

David and Indira locked eyes across their desks. His newest recruit was like a coiled spring, earwigging his side of the conversation, trying to gauge his reaction. He was wound up too. Howe placing their guv'nor in the exhibits room raised his hackles.

'So, you had help?'

'Unofficially,' was Howe's answer.

'Unofficially?' He held his breath. When she named his suspect, he forced himself to stay cool, so as not to raise any awkward questions. 'Nice of him to volunteer . . .' David gave Indi the thumbs up. 'No reason . . . I'm just fact-checking . . . Yeah, it does. Thanks for your time.'

He hung up, a huge smile for Indira.

She slammed her fist on the table. 'Yes!'

He'd never seen her so animated.

114

With another brick in the wall, David glanced at the parcel containing Frankie's jacket, then sat back considering whether it was worth looking for Joanna's. It could take weeks he didn't have. Though things were often missed, the chances that it had been destroyed were too great to ignore. He wasn't prepared to waste precious time on a doubtful outcome. They were good to go the minute Indira completed her calculations.

'How long will it take?' he asked.

'Almost done.'

'Get to it. I'll organise the rest.'

He spent the next couple of hours studying the murder file he'd created at the beginning of the investigation. It contained witness statements, newspaper cuttings, photographic evidence, including an image of the partial print forensics had sent through, and handwritten notes to refer to in his interview.

Indira arrived at his side, handing him her calculations.

He double-checked them, adding them to his file. Lastly, he arranged his exhibits box to follow the order of his interview agenda. Closing the flaps, he went downstairs, locked everything in an interview room, pocketing the key.

When he returned to the office, he couldn't fail to notice that Indira was stressed out, using a tissue to dab away a thin film of sweat that had formed on her brow. He put it down to first-time nerves. Few had witnessed the arrest, interview and detention of a murder suspect so soon after making detective grade.

'Something on your mind, Indi?'

'Have we got enough? I appreciate the need to investigate under the radar till now, but shouldn't we consult with the original investigation team in case they have any insight to offer?'

'We can do that later. Like I said, they'll be queueing up to talk to us when it all kicks off.' He checked his watch. 'I have a call to make, then we're ready to roll.' He called Mitch's mobile, asking if he was busy.

'Flat out,' he said.

'Sounds like it . . .' David heard Charlie crack a joke in the background. He wouldn't be laughing soon. 'Where are you?'

'Briefing room. Guv, hold on . . .' Mitch said. 'Can't hear myself think in here.' He turned his head away, raising his voice. 'Oi! I'm on the phone. Give it a rest.' The noise died down behind him. He apologised to David for the interruption. 'You want me to swing by when the briefing is over?'

'No, it's not important.' David made up the first excuse that came to mind. 'I rang Frankie earlier. She's not picking up.'

'Probably zonked. I spoke to her this afternoon. She's at home recuperating, where she should be. Rae's going round with Amir later. That'll put the smile on her face.'

David doubted it. 'If you speak to her again, tell her Indi and I are asking after her.'

'Roger that.'

He disconnected.

Indira spread her hands, a frown on her face. 'What was that about?'

'You'll see.' David straightened his tie. 'Jacket on. Come with me and bring your detective constable face with you.'

She followed him out of the room.

He locked the door behind them.

Instead of turning left towards the stairwell that would lead them down to the custody suite, he turned in the opposite direction. Without questioning why, Indira fell in step. Bright was hovering at a pre-arranged meeting point. The nod he threw their way was a signal that Frankie had been collected and taken to her parents' home, where he intended to head next to inform the family of what was about to happen before anyone else could.

'Let's go,' Bright said. 'The squad need to hear this.'

David nodded.

They entered the room together, seconds before the evening briefing got underway. The room was heaving, all eyes turned in their direction. Detectives waited, with odd looks passing between them: *What's this? Who died?*

Bright peeled off to stand at the back.

David moved to the front, about to address them, then turned to the man who arrived by his side. He wouldn't save him the humiliation of removing him before administering the caution. He wanted him to suffer the indignity in public and for the MIT to see him for what he was, a cold-blooded killer.

David stood over him.

'Richard Abbott, you know who I am.' He swept a hand towards Indira. 'You know who my colleague is. You do not have to say anything. But it may harm your defence if you do not mention when questioned something which you later rely on in court. Anything you do say may be given in evidence. I'm arresting you on suspicion of the murder of Joanna Oliver.'

There was an audible intake of breath in the room, some detectives visibly distressed. Mouths fell open. Heads turned. Faces were pale. Incredulity from the young among them, less from those who had more years in, those who'd known Dick the longest. Their collective reaction spoke volumes.

Dick had seen it too.

'Nice one!' He was smiling. 'This is a wind-up, right?'

As instructed, Indira scribbled a note of his reply.

David's hand closed like a vice around his arm.

'Come with me.'

115

In the custody suite, Abbott had been processed. He declined a solicitor and Federation rep. David and Indira walked him to the interview room and sat him down. Switching on the tape, David stated the time, date and location. He and Indira identified themselves, inviting Dick to do the same. He did not, so the DCI did it for him, repeating the caution, asking him again if he wanted representation.

He seemed supremely confident for a man under arrest.

'Why would I need a brief, guv? I've done nothing wrong. You, on the other hand, are making a grave mistake. I don't know where this is coming from, but you've got the wrong man and will end up with egg on your face, as well as a bill for compensation for destroying my reputation.' He eyeballed David. 'How long have we known each other? You really think I'm capable?'

He did, or they wouldn't be sitting there.

Dick's bravado would get him nowhere.

David wasted no time. 'Where were you on the evening of Friday, the twelfth of June 1992?'

'That is a matter of record, guv.' He reminded David that the original team of investigators had been alibied.

'I'm aware,' David said. 'Humour me. I'd like to hear it first-hand.'

'Can't remember. It was a long time ago.'

David jumped on Dick's first mistake. 'I find it completely unbelievable that you can't recall where you were when your guv'nor's daughter was stabbed to death. Especially since he was the on-call detective, the first on scene to view the body, unaware that Joanna was the victim. So why don't you trot out what you told Bright, one last time.'

'As I said, the mind's a bit foggy.'

'Then let me help you with that.' David consulted his file, then looked up. 'You were working out of Etal Lane, correct?'

'I was.'

'You stated that you were seeing an informant in Jesmond. Tell me about that.'

'Normal day at the office, guv. I was general CID. Went out to see my snout, came back and spent a couple of hours at my desk, catching up on paperwork.'

'Did anyone verify that?'

'I don't recall.'

'But you did work late?'

'Yes, that's how I heard about Joanna, same as everyone else.'

'Must've been very upsetting.'

Dick looked right through him. 'It was . . . very sad.'

'You must've been proud when called upon to investigate the murder—'

'What can I say? Every detective on the force wanted to be part of it. Bright hand-picked the team—'

'And in doing so, handed *you* the opportunity to manipulate evidence.'

'Is there a question in there, guv?'

'No, it's a statement I intend to prove in due course.' David let him sweat. 'Let's backtrack to your informant. How did you travel to Jesmond on the night Joanna died?'

'CID car.'

'Make any detours?'

'None.'

'That's interesting, because I recovered the logbooks from the archives at HQ.' David watched him closely. 'You seem surprised that we still have them. We do . . .' Lifting them from his exhibits box, he placed them on the table, opening the one on top where he'd marked a page for easy viewing. 'According to this one, exhibit DS15, you took the car at 19:04, returned it at 21:20.' You logged nine miles that night, recording a start mileage of 14,317, end mileage of 14,326.'

'Sounds about right.'

'Look for yourself.' David turned the logbook around to face him. 'I'd like you to look at the entry after yours, halfway down the page. As you can see, it shows the collar number of the detective who used the vehicle after you.' Their eyes met. 'Does anything about those two entries strike you as odd?'

Dick shrugged, pushing the logbook away.

David pushed it back. 'Take another look.' He used his finger to indicate the correct lines. 'Your end mileage was 14,326. Her start mileage was 14,348. That's twenty-two miles unaccounted for. Added to the nine *you* said you travelled makes thirty-one. I'd like the discrepancy ironed out before we go any further.'

Dick almost smirked. 'She'll have written it down wrong, guv. Or someone took the vehicle before her and failed to record the trip. On a busy shift, it happens.'

'That's not how it was. I traced that police witness. She told me you favoured that vehicle, a J-reg Ford. And that you used to keep the keys in your pocket, as you did on that night. She had to find you to retrieve them.'

Dick didn't attempt to hide his cynicism. 'She has a better memory than I do.'

David said, 'She made a note of it when she discovered that the mileage was incorrect. In fact, so concerned was she that she'd get done for a parking violation or receive a speeding ticket, she kept her own logbook, which I have possession of. It makes interesting reading.' David paused. 'She claims that you frequently wrote down the wrong mileage or didn't fill the logbook in at all. I gather she wasn't the only one who noticed. On one occasion, following a complaint, you were spoken to by your supervision, were you not?'

'Sloppy, what can I say?'

David had been biding his time. Leading him down the road. The problem was, Dick didn't know the destination. He wasn't stupid. David hadn't produced a tangible link to Joanna Oliver, but he'd be wondering why he'd been arrested. David hadn't yet hit the right button. Now seemed like the perfect opportunity.

'Do you know how far the return journey is from Etal Lane to Southwick?'

'Not off the top of my head, guv. Maths was never my strong point. Still isn't. You of all people should know that.'

'It's thirty-one miles, the exact mileage from your base to the crime scene and back.'

Dick sprang to his feet.

David yelled, 'Sit the fuck down!'

Dick did as he was told, cool as you like.

David carried on. 'Do you remember the J-reg Ford you were driving that night?'

'Not particularly.'

'Then I'll jog your memory.' David took two images from flimsy document folders at the back of his file, placing them side by side in front of Dick. 'Exhibit IS17 is a photocopy of a press release. Exhibit IS19 is a newspaper article where that image was also used. As you can see, they show you standing next to that very vehicle.'

'What can I say? It was shiny and new, not a piece of shit. The press office probably waxed it specially.' He was trying to deflect David's attention.

It didn't work. 'We have evidence written contemporaneously, reminding you to record your mileage. I'd like to show you exhibit DS8, another logbook. As you can see, former detective William Welch has written in the margin, quote, "Dick, fill your fucking mileage in" unquote.'

'He's a cunt.'

'I'm sure the feeling is mutual. You screwed his sister and scarpered when her husband turned up.'

'Since when were extra maritals against the law?'

116

Aware that an arrest had been made, Frankie opened the door when Bright turned up. He gave her a sombre nod as he walked in. She said nothing. In the living room, they sat down, her parents on the sofa, Frankie in one armchair, Bright in the other. Frankie's father met her gaze. When she'd arrived in a police car, he knew instantly what was going down. A pre-warning that Bright was on his way in no way prepared him. Though he'd dreamt of this day for a very long time, he wasn't ready for what was to come.

He never would be.

Not even close.

His hand found Julie's.

He gave it a gentle squeeze.

In time, he'd learn the truth of what had eluded him for years, but it was too early for details. He was facing a gut-wrenching, apocalyptic disclosure it would take months, possibly even years, to come to terms with, a truth more painful than murder that Frankie was trying so desperately to hide to protect David's job.

She braced herself.

Bright's eyes were on her parents. Frankie had never seen her guv'nor so tense. He chose his words carefully. 'You all know why I'm here.' He breathed out heavily. 'In the last hour, David has made an arrest. There's no easy way of saying this—'

'Just say it,' Frank said. 'No preamble. We need a name.'

Bright caught Frankie's eye, sending an unspoken apology for what he was about to say, then turned his head, concentrating on her parents.

'It's Abbott,' he said.

'Oh, God!' Her mother's hand flew to her mouth. She looked at her husband, at Frankie, then at Bright. 'Phil, there must be some mistake.'

He shook his head. 'There's no mistake, Jules.'

She broke down then, as Frankie had, utterly horrified. Frankie knew what was going through her head. Joanna's killer had been under her roof, treated as an extended family member for years. Between marriages, Dick had come for Christmas dinner. He'd been invited to every party they'd ever thrown. They had laughed, danced and celebrated together, even set off fireworks on Joanna's birthday, a day they still revered.

Her mother's tears were good. They were healthy. Her father's fury manifested itself in a different way. He said nothing. Under his shirt, Frankie could see his chest rising and falling rapidly. He too was bereft, but his overriding reaction was anger and bitterness.

Bright said, 'David is tied up interviewing or he'd have been here in support.'

'Fucking hell,' Frank broke in. 'Why didn't I see it?'

Julie looked confused. 'What are you saying?'

'You know what he was like as a young detective. It was an open secret. If it was wearing a skirt, he was in there – but I never once suspected him.'

'No,' Julie said. 'I don't believe it.' In denial, she glared at her husband. 'Have you forgotten that at great risk to his career, he helped you get hold of the murder file, anything you wanted. You begged him, Frank.'

'Yeah,' he said. 'Which in hindsight gave him free rein. A bloody good reason to stick his nose in, collecting evidence on my behalf . . . or hiding it to save his skin.'

'You should've come to me,' Bright said.

'Yeah, that would have worked. You wouldn't let me near it, remember? The twat played me. He took Joanna's life, then made mine easier by helping me.' Unable to hold his emotions back, Frankie's dad let out a piercing scream. 'I trusted him. We all did. He must've thought I was a mug.'

Understanding where he was coming from, Frankie dropped her head in her hands, unable to hold back her emotions, even though she was hearing the revelation for the second time. She'd thought about nothing else since David had given her Dick's name.

Bright's voice bled into her thoughts. 'I'll leave you now.'

He got up, placing a hand on her shoulder as he passed her chair.

She stood, following him to the door.

On the threshold, he turned, dark eyes reflecting his inner state of mind. He'd disclosed such information to grieving families a hundred times, but this one was different. This time it was personal. He loved Joanna so much. He dropped his voice low, telling Frankie that he was there when David made the arrest, inflicting maximum shame with the MIT looking on.

She was welling up.

Bright pulled her into a hug, quietly reassuring her that Abbott was going down and would face the ultimate punishment.

She pulled back. 'I hope he rots in hell and never gets out.'

'I'll let you know when he's charged. In the meantime, if there's anything you need, anything at all, Frankie, call me.'

'I will, guv.' Before he turned away, she spoke again. 'There is something you can do for me.'

'Name it.'

'Make sure he's placed on suicide watch. We've been suffering for years. He doesn't get to rock himself off and take the easy way out.'

'Done,' he said.

She watched him drive off before closing the door, taking the stairs to her room, allowing her mum and dad some time alone. None of them expected that the killer would be someone who'd hidden in plain sight.

Least of all her.

Dick had robbed her of so much more than a big sister whose beautiful, cheeky face stared down at her from a framed photograph on their bedroom wall, an ever-present reminder, not that Frankie needed one.

Joanna's effervescent personality lived on . . .

In her.

Frankie wept as her anger towards Abbott flooded out. He was no longer Dick. He was a child-murdering scumbag whose defence barrister would attempt to mitigate his sentence, telling a jury that since that night, his client had lived a blameless life in the service of his community, that he was truly repentant.

Only part of that was true.

The Dick she'd known was good and kind. He'd helped hundreds of victims, but he'd also taken a child's life. Had he moved away, she might have believed the rest, but he'd not done that. Instead, he'd offered his friendship to her and her family, a friendship that was fraudulent, derived from guilt and shame. Even if Joanna's death had brought him to his senses, Frankie didn't care.

She hated him.

She hoped he lived till he was very old. He deserved to exist in a state of fear for what he'd done, locked away, looking over his shoulder for the rest of his days, waiting for the handmade weapon to rip him open, a cop-hating fellow inmate walking away without a backward glance while he bled out on a cold, hard prison floor.

117

Every interview with a murder suspect was like a game of chess, the police making a move, the suspect countering, each with their own agenda. David had given Abbott the benefit of the doubt from the outset, and Indira the lesson of her police career. She was tense, Dick less so, but there was something odd about his behaviour.

Anna's voice arrived in David's head: *the target was avoiding eye contact with me.* David had noticed that Dick was doing the same thing with Indira. He hadn't looked at her once during the interview. He was clearly uncomfortable in her presence and the SIO intended to exploit that.

He held Dick's gaze, making him sweat. 'While we're on the subject of extra maritals, let's talk about women. That should be right up your street—'

'Did you have someone specific in mind?' Abbott was winding him up now.

David wouldn't give him the satisfaction. 'Let's start with PCs Rachel Hart and Stephanie Masterson. I gather they left the force because of you.'

A shrug. 'That's news to me—'

'Hart spurned your advances. Masterson you had a relationship with, having sex with her in that CID vehicle. She made a statement to that effect. Sounds like evidence of system to me. You fiddled the logbooks to conceal affairs you were conducting while on duty. Is that why you doctored the mileage? There are many instances when you did that.'

'No idea what you're on about.'

David hit him again. 'Your first wife was a lot older than you, wasn't she?'

'What's *she* got to do with it?'

'We have reason to believe that you were terrified of her, so terrified you asked Masterson to wear a particular perfume, so if you went home smelling of it, your wife would think it was hers.'

'Guilty as charged. I was playing away.'

'Did you ask all your dates to wear Chanel N°5?'

'Only when the wife was home. She worked away a lot.'

'Let's leave women aside for a moment and concentrate on girls.' Dick almost recoiled at the word girls. 'Did you ever buy them that perfume?'

'I did not date girls.'

David eyed the logbooks, then looked at Indira. 'I'm finished with these for now, DC Sharma.'

He pushed them towards her.

She took her cue, reopening his exhibits box, leaving the logbooks on the table. Frankie's denim jacket had been folded and placed inside an evidence bag with a cellophane front, clearly labelled. It was on the top, the perfume bottle underneath.

David held his breath.

His suspect would jump one way or the other. If he wasn't sweating at this point, he'd destroyed the jacket. If he was, they would know he hadn't got rid. Curious as to what they would bring out next, Dick sneaked a look.

David saw the tell immediately.

Indira had seen it too.

He gave her the nod, watching her key a text to Bright.

A long shot was still a shot. The guv'nor had an army of personnel on standby to find Joanna's jacket – if it could be found.

Dick had recovered his poker face.

David continued. 'As you know, one of the crucial exhibits in Joanna Oliver's case was her denim jacket. You'll also be aware that it was required for further examination at the lab some years after her death and wasn't where it should have been. An action was instigated to find it. Did you have anything to do with that action?'

'No. Barclay and Grant took it.'

'Fog's clearing, is it?'

Dick had begun to wobble as soon as he set eyes on the jacket.

David piled on the pressure. 'Grant is now Howe. Inspector Howe. She said it was a mammoth task and that you volunteered to help. Is that correct?'

'Not true.'

'I firmly believe that you were desperate to help with that action. You moved Joanna's jacket into a detected file you thought would be destroyed. As we've already alluded to, it's surprising what gets left that should have gone to the incinerator.' David couldn't lie, but as Frankie said, doubt was a killer.

Dick was wavering.

'We've got you going in and out of the evidence room on several occasions,' David continued. 'We don't know what you did there, but I don't think that'll bother a judge too much. Let me guess, you checked the forensics box and left the unexamined items where they were. Big mistake.'

David's expression said: *not so arrogant now, are you?* 'As I said earlier, you were put in a position of trust, in the centre of a murder investigation that afforded you every opportunity to remove, plant, or should I say, invent evidence. There was no white van with a distinctive logo, was there?'

'Where's your proof?'

At the beginning of his interview, Dick's answers had been free-flowing. Now, they were short. He was thinking hard. He'd told provable lies when given the opportunity to tell the truth. He should have known better. David's strategy was simple, to hear his version of events, then dismantle it. At this point, he expected one of two outcomes. Dick would either lose his shit or stay silent.

He chose the latter.

David upped the ante. 'For the tape, Richard Abbott is on edge.' He leaned in, taking the perfume bottle from the exhibits box, holding it up. When Dick clocked it, his face paled. Indira's hands were fists beneath the table.

They didn't expect Abbott to roll over.

Only a decent man would do that.

'I'm now showing the suspect exhibit IS20, a bottle of Chanel N°5 that was recovered from the bedroom of Joanna Oliver. It was among her effects, concealed in a chest of drawers, an item that was never forensically examined . . . until a few days ago.' He looked at Dick, deadpan. 'It has your prints on it.'

No reply.

'Furthermore, I have a witness who saw Joanna with a man fitting your description. You groomed her, didn't you?'

'No, I did not.'

'Do you want to tell us what happened?' David had no sympathy. He was merely playing the game, breaking him down to get a confession. 'I can't imagine what it's been like, living with the guilt.' He stared at Dick for a long moment, then gave him a nudge with something he knew would hurt. 'Frankie knows we're questioning you. Bright's with her.'

Dick made no reply.

'We know you didn't rape Joanna. Did she reject you, threaten to tell her old man? Not a good place to be – enough to push a young man over the edge. You were a cop who should've known right from wrong.'

Clocking the revulsion on David's face, Dick hung his head. Not in shame – David didn't believe that – he was feeling sorry for himself, as anyone would facing a whole-life term.

Dick looked up. 'It wasn't like that.'

'So, tell me,' David said.

'I didn't plan it, guv. I dropped my snout in town and saw Joanna at a bus stop. I stopped, offering her a lift. She was whingeing about being on a curfew, having to leave her mates early. She'd called Frank asking if she could stay out. He didn't answer. That riled her even more. She said if she arrived home late, she'd persuade Julie not to tell him. I told her to cool it and took her for a drive.'

'You disgust me. She was fifteen—'

'Yeah, fifteen going on eighteen. Look, I didn't force her. She came willingly. When we got out of the car, she came on to me. When I responded, she took out a knife. We wrestled. She was screaming. I tried to shut her up. Honestly, she was going berserk, calling me a perv.'

'So, you're trying to tell me that she attacked you. She was Frankie's size – eight stone wet through. Do you seriously expect me to believe that with all your training and expertise you couldn't disarm her? Other than a stab wound, she had no injuries on her body.'

'She fell on the knife during the fight.'

'Did you check her vitals?'

'What do you take me for? She was beyond help.'

'What did you do with the knife?'

'I got back in the car, drove to the Riverside Industrial Estate and chucked it in the drink.'

'Why, if it was an accident? Your story could have been proven if it was true.'

'It is true, I swear.'

'You are lying. Your escalating behaviour is well documented. Hart and Masterson ended their careers because of you. You ruined the marriage of Jan Hall and ran away following a fight with her husband, Adam. That's why you carried a knife, to protect yourself if things went wrong. All these witnesses are willing to testify.' David paused. 'And lastly, having killed Joanna, knowing that her father was the on-call DI who would attend the scene, you kept quiet, returning to your desk as if nothing had happened, allowing him to sleepwalk into every parent's worst nightmare.'

Pausing the interview, David turned off the tape.

'You fucking piece of shit.'

118

Frankie now understood David's sudden disappearance from her party and the need to keep her at arm's length while he investigated an open unsolved case off-book. It was too close to home. Too close to bear. He'd kept his promise to find her sister's killer. He hadn't done it for her. He'd done it for her family. Mostly, he'd done it for Joanna.

Deep down, Frankie believed that.

David looked drawn the next time she saw him, almost a week after Abbott had been remanded in custody on a murder charge. They met on mutual ground. Safer that way. Frankie's gratitude was absolute. His and Indira's tenacity in hunting down the man who'd escaped justice for the best part of three decades was commendable.

While they told her everything, David had spared her old man the sordid details of his interview with Abbott, leaving out the parts that would stay with him for ever, like Joanna carping about her curfew, the fact that he'd ignored her call on the night she died, both of which left her vulnerable to a predatory male Frankie no longer recognised.

She clung to the hope that Abbott, a man she'd worked alongside and loved throughout her police career, would fess up at court, sparing her father the indignity of hearing it played out in public, reaping yet more damage on people she loved.

Frankie wouldn't hold her breath.

A guilty plea would seal his fate. Without one, it would take a jury to convict him. The uncertainty was a worry, something she had no control over, beyond spending every day in court studying him throughout the trial, watching him squirm. The best she could hope for was that a partial print on a perfume bottle and the substantial body of evidence gathered slowly and meticulously from so many witnesses would be enough. Abbott admitted taking Joanna to Southwick but denied her murder. As a detective, Frankie knew that his incarceration was by no means a done deal.

During her convalescence in the weeks that followed, Frankie had thought long and hard about her own case. She'd had flashbacks of her near-death experience with Ivan Osman standing over her, ready to finish her off. Mostly, she'd thought of the bloody mayhem at the epicentre of the RTA where she found Amir. It was the wrist restraints that broke her, though in all probability they had also saved his life.

The National Crime Agency, north and south, were still dealing with Operation Zenith, Kit Matthews reporting that, with the help of Interpol, over and above the organised crime syndicate they knew of – Thorne (real name Victor Ivanov), Osman and their cohorts – thirty-seven arrests had been made in four countries: Bulgaria, Albania, Pakistan and the UK.

There would be more.

Working with international police forces in those territories, NCA detectives had managed to identify all the children Frankie had found in the lock-up in Pennywell. Like Lexie, they had been reunited with their parents.

Only Amir was unaccounted for.

Questions remained over where his journey began and indeed where it would end. The NCA's work would go on. Tracing his relatives could go on for his lifetime. For now, he was making progress. His English improved daily. He was happy, no longer fearful of men, surrounded by people who loved him.

Frankie thought of Amir as a gift, however temporary, giving Rae, Andy and Frankie's parents something positive in their lives at a time they needed it most.

In bright sunshine, a small crowd gathered. Frankie laid fresh flowers on Joanna's grave, tracing the inscription on the headstone. For the first time since her burial, her late sister could now rest in peace. As her parents moved away, leaving Frankie and David alone, she thanked him for giving them their lives back and for all he'd done for her.

'Are you going to take the NCA job?' he asked.

Frankie felt her face flush. 'How long have you known?'

'Why didn't you tell me?'

'I haven't decided yet. The offer is still on the table.'

'I don't want to lose you, Frank. I can't go there twice. You pulled me out of a hole. If it hadn't been for you, I'd be nothing. Besides, we're a team, right? The MIT want you back. I want you back. I'd get down on my knees and beg if we didn't have company.'

Frankie scanned the graveyard.

Her old man was loitering close by.

She turned to face David, unable to speak. His words were open to interpretation. She didn't know how to respond. He was frustrated by an impossible situation, his disappointment a mirror image of her own.

'Frank, talk to me.'

'I can't, not now. I'd rather work with you for ever than sleep with you occasionally.' She managed a weak smile. 'Does that sound as pathetic in your head as it does in mine?'

He sidestepped the question. 'We can make it work.'

'For a time perhaps . . . and then there'll be nothing. You and I . . .' She stalled, unable to utter what felt like a jumble of words on the tip of her tongue.

He waited, lost and alone.

She wanted to let him down gently. 'David, I think the world of you, but you and me was a daft idea. I know that now. In investigating Joanna's murder, you investigated me.'

'You're saying I know more than I should?'

'A shedload. That knowledge will crush us eventually.' She was choking now, on the edge of tears. 'Our pasts have cast long shadows. I couldn't bear to live in the dark, not with you—'

'It doesn't have to be that way.'

'Please, David.' A tear fell to her cheek.

He stepped forward, wiping it away gently with the back of his index finger. 'Hey . . . it's OK, Frankie. I understand. I do . . . Friends?'

'Always.'

'That'll do me.' His smile didn't reach his eyes. He gave her a hug and walked away.

Frankie looked down at her sister's grave. 'Sleep now, Jo.'

'Frankie?' Her father's voice came from over her shoulder. She turned to look at him. He flicked his eyes towards David's retreating figure, shoulders hunched, head bowed. 'You going to let Abbott take that away from you too?'

Frankie looked at David, then back at her old man, her eyes filled with tears. 'It's for the best, Dad.'

'Is it shite! Give it a few days before you make decisions you'll regret for the rest of your life, eh?' David was yards from his vehicle. 'Fuck's sake, the lone ranger is about to ride off into the sunset and you're going to let him? You won't find anyone better. Just as well you've got your running shoes on, Tonto. If you get a shift on, you might just make it.'

Acknowledgements

I'd like to thank my brilliant editor, fiction publisher Sam Eades, publishing director Leodora Darlington, project editor Anshuman Yadav and everyone at Orion Fiction who worked to make *Her Sister's Killer* the book you're holding in your hands or listening to. A full list of Orion personnel can be found on the credits page. I can't leave out my copy editor, Anne O'Brien, who has done a fantastic job as always. I must also mention audio narrator Colleen Prendergast. She's been on this journey with me for a very long time, but I only met and spent time with her recently. She's as lovely as she sounds! When you lose a publicist in the run-up to the publication of a book critics are describing as your best yet, it's a big deal. In stepped Sophie Calder (Calder Publicity), a real pro: motivated, unflappable and well-connected. I couldn't believe her work ethic and what she managed to achieve from a standing start. Thank you, Sophie. The man in my writing life is my friend and agent Oli Munson (A.M. Heath). If Oli hadn't recognised a smidgeon of talent – believe me when I say that's all it was – my career as a crime writer might never have taken off. I'd also like to thank William Welch who generously bid to have his name in one of my titles in aid of Young Lives vs Cancer, a charity that helps children, young people and families to find the strength to face whatever cancer throws at them. It's a great cause, so thank you, William. As ever, I must thank my family at home and away for their love and support, and Mo – partner, collaborator and consultant – for the endless hours she spends on her own while I make stuff up. You are the best. Love you, always.

Credits

Mari Hannah and Orion Fiction would like to thank everyone at Orion who worked on the publication of *Her Sister's Killer*.

Editor
Sam Eades
Leodora Darlington

Copy editor
Anne O'Brien

Proofreader
Claire Dean

Editorial Management
Anshuman Yadav
Jane Hughes
Charlie Panayiotou
Lucy Bilton
Patrice Nelson

Audio
Paul Stark
Louise Richardson
Georgina Cutler

Inventory
Jo Jacobs
Dan Stevens

Contracts
Dan Herron
Ellie Bowker
Oliver Chacón

Design
Charlotte Abrams-Simpson
Nick Shah
Deborah Francois
Helen Ewing

Finance
Nick Gibson
Jasdip Nandra
Sue Baker
Tom Costello

Production
Ruth Sharvell
Katie Horrocks

Marketing
Lucy Cameron

Publicity
Sian Baldwin

Sales
Catherine Worsley
Dave Murphy
Victoria Laws
Esther Waters
Group Sales teams across
Digital, Field, International
and Non-Trade

Operations
Group Sales Operations team

Rights
Rebecca Folland
Tara Hiatt
Ben Fowler
Alice Cottrell
Ruth Blakemore
Marie Henckel